THE AUTHOR

ALTHOUGH HER ancestral roots are in the province of Quebec, Gabrielle Roy was born and educated in Manitoba. For a number of years she taught school there, first in a small prairie village and later at the Institut Collegial Provencher at St. Boniface. Along with her literary interests went a talent for acting. Twice she took part in plays which won the French trophy at the Dominion Drama Festival, and in 1939 she went abroad to study drama in London and Paris. In 1947 she married, and is now living in Quebec City.

During all this time she wrote, beginning with articles for newspapers and periodicals. In 1945 she published her first novel, *Bonheur d'Occasion*, which was to become two years later a dramatic success in its English version—*The Tin Flute*. Among the awards which Miss Roy received for *The Tin Flute* are a medal from the French Academy, a prize from the French-Canadian Academy, the *Prix Fémina* in France, and the Governor-General's Award for Fiction, as well as a membership in the Royal Society of Canada.

Gabrielle Roy's second full-length book was *Where Nests the Water Hen*. Since its appearance in 1951 she has published *The Cashier* in 1955, *Street of Riches* in 1957, *The Hidden Mountain* in 1962, *The Road Past Altamont* in 1966 and *Windflower* in 1970.

Gabrielle Roy

THE

Introduction : Hugo McPherson

TIN

General Editor : Malcolm Ross

FLUTE

Translated from the French by Hannah Josephson

New Canadian Library No. 5

McCLELLAND AND STEWART LIMITED

The following dedication appeared in the original edition:

TO
MÉLINA ROY

0-7710-9105-2

Introduction © 1969 McClelland and Stewart Limited

The Canadian Publishers
McClelland and Stewart Limited
25 Hollinger Road, Toronto

PRINTED AND BOUND IN CANADA

INTRODUCTION

I REMEMBER a year in that exciting decade that followed the Second World War when people kept asking each other: "Have you read *The Tin Flute*? It's Canada's most devastating novel"; or, "Who *is* Gabrielle Roy? She must have lived through a lot to write a book like that." In those years, I think, many of us felt that something extraordinary was happening in Canadian writing. With such figures as Ethel Wilson, Morley Callaghan, and Hugh MacLennan, our literature was coming of age. But even in this upsurge of literary activity, Miss Roy set a number of new records. For a first novel, *The Tin Flute* was phenomenally successful. In addition, it hurdled the language barrier that keeps so many French- and English-Canadians at a polite mispronouncing distance; and then it soared over the 49th parallel into the paddock of an American book club. In France, it was awarded the *Prix Fémina* for fiction in 1947. And in Canada it gained its author a fellowship in the Royal Society.

But whatever the value of these tokens of popularity, the book had a more important success: it was good art. Popular entertainers like Upton Sinclair or Kathleen Winsor come and go: Gabrielle Roy gives us something of durable value. Even in this first statement (in which intensity of vision must compensate for minor weaknesses in technique) we recognize an artist of importance. Miss Roy sees in the problems of a particular age and locale an image of the timeless human enigma; the people of her Montreal slum illustrate piercingly what it means to be human. Yet despite her uncompromising awareness of the pain and imperfection of life, she is no pessimist; to an age that has fallen on the thorns of various "isms" (including egotism, the ism of pride), she brings a profound tolerance and compassion. She is committed not to any exclusive patriotism, intellectual humanism or religiosity, but to a deep love of mankind.

Gabrielle Roy, then, is an artist of real stature. Nevertheless, we cannot doubt that the most immediate reason for the success of *The Tin Flute* was its startling documentary quality. Even in an age enthralled by the *exposé* it had a stinging authority: for the Québequois it arraigned the monster of big-city poverty with an accuracy that caught the last syllable of the market-vendor's cry and the tragic rhetoric of the Saint-Henri bum; to the English-Canadian it spoke brutally of a city which he had known only through the genteel drawing-rooms of his Westmount relatives or occasional night-club sprees on Canada's "Big White Way"; and to the American and British audience it revealed a situation which, however unpalatable at home, could be enjoyed vicariously when spiced with *un zeste du Canada*. To a reader in search of both entertainment and instruction, a novel about the wretchedness of a Quebec (or Peruvian) suburb is bound to be more interesting than a novel about the facts of his own backyard squalor.

But for the many who have been haunted by *The Tin Flute*— who have read it as parable rather than *exposé*—the book is impressive for a deeper reason. What it gives us is an image of modern life that has all the clarity of nightmare, or of an apocalyptic landscape by El Greco. We are caught in this phantasmagoric world of railroad crossings and soot and factory whistles, and made to scrutinize its every detail and to admit the *truth* of the picture. It is an image which comfortable citizens (like those of Westmount, looking out across the "picturesque" lights of the lower town) have never really *seen*; an image which makes the terrors of world war look like a happy release. In Canada's army the untouchables of Saint-Henri will at least feel that they have a purpose and a place.

The focus of the story is the Lacasse family (the name means "box" or "locker"). They typify the poor, the failures, the "also-rans," who populate Saint-Henri. Their chief characteristic is that all of them are thwarted—trapped; and each of them has his own world of dreams and hopes. Florentine, the most promising member of this family, is a pretty, semiliterate little thing who has risen to the pinnacle of a red-and-gold dime store, where she works as a waitress. But she rejects with her whole spirit the background of pain and privation that has produced her. Reacting instinctively against the young men who belong to Saint-Henri, she falls in love with Jean Lévesque (Mr. "Bishop"), a ruthless young orphan who has set his eyes unwaveringly upon the mountain heights of Westmount. Florentine is seduced, in spirit and in fact, by this young egotist. Then, when she realizes that her fairy prince merely despises her, she marries his shy friend, Emmanuel Létourneau ("a starling"). Emmanuel's name will legitimize her child and protect her reputation. Ironically, she does not recognize (and is probably incapable of recognizing) that his brand of love, devoid of all ulterior motives, is the only possession that really matters. Perhaps her only excuse for accepting his devotion is that she feels an all-too-human antipathy to the kind of destitution that her experience has taught her to dread. It is here—in the central situation of the novel—that Miss Roy's irony reaches its deepest level. Young opportunists like Lévesque are anything but admirable, yet their victims—yearning young people like Florentine—are often equally ignoble; and neither opportunist nor victim is really in control of his destiny. We must forbear judging them, then. The facts of poverty and pain drive men to cruelty and selfishness, but riches are not necessarily a remedy, for wealth can be hideous too. Neither condition is quite bearable unless it is somehow warmed by compassion and love. And the tragedy of poverty is that it often blinds its victims to all motives but acquisition.

The other members of the Lacasse family round out this vision of the human condition. The father, Azarius, has always dreamed of grandiose successes for his family; in this childish game of protecting his *amour propre* he wastes both time and opportunities; but he does love his family genuinely. It is the fact of this love that enables Rose-Anna to accept all of his failures; she has confidence in the sincerity of his motives. But when Azarius joins the army and thereby provides his family with what seems a "fortune," his wife feels the act as a betrayal; his enlistment is an "escape" from the love-pain nexus that belonging to others involves. Money will not recompense Rose-Anna for the spiritual loss. In the same way, little Yvonne dreams of being a nun, but her mother senses that this wish is in some sense an abdication of the problems that life presents. Even little Daniel—happy in the atmosphere of a hospital where he is dying of leukemia—"escapes" the ordeal of life almost before he has begun to live it. But can we judge this innocent, who asks no more of life than the joy of a tin flute? If we do, we ally ourselves with those who think that economic paupers must be spiritual paupers as well.

The central perception of the book, then, and its chief irony, is Gabrielle Roy's understanding of the nature of poverty. On the one hand, Saint-Henri produces ambitious young materialists like Lévesque (the orphan who has no real roots in the "family" of his community), and the perpetually green Boisvert, who abandons his fellows for a world of prices and account books. These young men will not be poor in fact, but they may well end as spiritual paupers. On the other hand, Saint-Henri produces the trapped Lacasse family and such saving spirits as Emmanuel. All of these long for a world of light and warmth—a world in which they "belong." The narrowness of their situation often makes their dreams frivolous (as with Florentine), or impractical (as with Azarius), or pathetic (as with little Daniel); but the dream, however tawdry, has it peculiar nobility. The economic paupers may be, in reality, rich in spirit, however misguided their dreams. Can we say, indeed, that the Lacasse family is more pitiable than the millions who live in a waking dream of *things*?

As if in answer to this question, we see Rose-Anna, a truly great figure. She is the universal *mater dolorosa* who stands, finally, as a true image of poverty and boundless wealth. It is she, the undemanding, infinitely loving mother of the Lacasse brood who represents the "poverty of spirit" that will inherit the earth. And what is Rose-Anna's secret? It is not, certainly, a conscious formula; it is simply a question of unpremeditated giving. As the mother of twelve children, she knows that she can never give enough, either in material protection or in emotional assurance. Her family will move beyond her arms, beyond her power to protect them from life's bruises; but her care will be unending. She is, in existentialist terms, totally *engagé*—absolutely committed to a way of life in which compassion and love are the fundamental values.

Yet if Rose-Anna's fortitude and love rise before us as an ideal —if this is beatitude—the novel as a whole offers no easy cure for the pains of the human condition. One solution might be a return to an earlier, better age. Several figures in the story recall with nostalgia the happy days before the atmosphere of the big city began to close in. But there can be no return to Eden. Rose-Anna realizes this when her return to the idyllic sugar-maple grove of her childhood reveals that she, like her mother, has become old and careworn. Even Emmanuel, whose vision approaches close to that of Rose-Anna, finds no solution to the enigma of the human situation. He goes off to war in sad perplexity, alternately believing and doubting that there is *any* means of ameliorating the lot of his brethren in Saint-Henri. But one must go on, and, as the novel ends, Emmanuel sees from the train windows a desolate city: "Low on the horizon, a bank of heavy clouds foretold a storm." Emmanuel may give his life for mankind, but will this help?

The structure of *The Tin Flute* falls somewhat short of the distinction of its statement. Rather than attempting formal innovation, Gabrielle Roy chose to rely on a well-tried pattern which she could employ with assurance. Thus the narrative is developed by episodes, each adapted to a single chapter, with passages of analysis or description at appropriate points. Except for brief scenes of recollection, the time scheme is chronological, and the narrator is the omniscient observer of traditional fiction. Now all of this is perfectly proper and acceptable. Indeed, young novelists may be well advised to begin by adapting conventional forms to their needs. But so implacable is the thrust of the dark tide of Miss Roy's story that the reader occasionally becomes uneasy; he senses in the polite pattern of the "well made" novel a certain inorganic stiffness which conflicts with the sweep of the action. It is as though a powerful river, which should find *its own* channel, has been diverted into a series of canal locks.

The novel is saved from becoming static, however, by three distinguished gifts which Miss Roy brings to its creation: she recreates brilliantly the data of the senses; she has a faultless ear for the nuances of spoken language; and she is so acutely sensitive to the objects that surround her that many of her images gain something of the weight of symbols.

The first of these gifts—Miss Roy's ability to convey in words the very temperature and pulse of sensory experience—immediately draws us out of ourselves and into the atmosphere of Saint-Henri. The people of this community are not thinkers, detached from their experience, but sentient beings, wholly involved in the travail of living. And we come to know them by sharing their ordeals: we are assailed by the smells of cheap perfume and cheap food in Florentine's dime store, and by the noise, the jostling, and the steady *brouhaha* of talk; we feel the chronic ache of Rose-Anna's back as she bends over her sewing machine, cowering away from drafts, or pausing stoically as a passing train sets the house trembling and reverberating. And when we venture out— as we must at every hour—we give ourselves up to the fierceness of wind and snow, or to the thick atmosphere of soot, foghorns, slaughterhouse smells, and the wails of sirens and children. And all of this conveys, with an intensity that stuns mere thought, an awareness that the prime stuff of life is not ideas but sensation, and that for millions who live in places like Saint-Henri this experience is an almost constant outrage of the senses.

Miss Roy's second gift, heightening and completing the first, is her flair for capturing with an uncanny fidelity the accent and idiom of French Canada (whether rural *patois* or Montreal *argot*). Unhappily, the reader of the English translation must take this gift largely on trust, for the market-place French of Quebec is no more to be translated than such familiar English as: "I'm feelin' kinda droopy"; or, "Yer loaded, aintcha, ya lush!" If the translator attempts a formal transcription, all of the relaxed simplicity and the comic overtones of the idiom disappear. On the other hand, if the translator attempts to substitute the nearest equivalent in English slang, much of the flavor of both speaker and setting is lost. We must be prepared, then, to believe that certain awkward expressions are not Miss Roy's blunders but the inevitable defeats of translation.

A prime example of this problem is the translation of profanity which, in French, often employs religious expressions. *Mon dieu!* we know, is such a commonplace of French idiom that it merely means "good heavens!" or perhaps "ye gods!" But when Azarius, at the moment of the family's most desperate need, tells Rose-Anna that he has not bothered to apply for a job, how shall we translate her response—*Doux Jésus, non! . . . Azarius?* Certainly the literal meaning—"Sweet Jesus, no!"—suggests the crudity of the barrack-room. Rose-Anna's cry is prayerful and agonized; it means "Dear Lord," or "Gentle Saviour."

Very often, however, the French comes through beautifully by undergoing a sea-change. Gabrielle Roy's title, for example, has no English equivalent. *Bonheur d'occasion* suggests, at best, the rather feeble "chance happiness"; but it also implies "grab-bag" happiness, "bargain" happiness, and "false" happiness. The translator, bowing to the impossibility of any literal translation of this expression, has chosen an image from the novel which sums up exquisitely the mingled joy and pathos of the story. The tin flute—symbol of little Daniel's hopes and disappointments—distills in a single image the whole substance of the life of the Lacasse family. It is a life of frightening difficulty, whose music comes from an instrument of tin, procured only when the player is past the point of playing. But *love* is at the heart of this symbol; it is love that gives the tin flute its meaning and value.

Finally—and this is the gift that sets Gabrielle Roy apart from the majority of popular writers—we have a perceptive use of pattern which constantly deepens and broadens the significance of the specific events of the novel. Miss Roy is not a symbolist, and we do not expect of her the kind of patterning that we find in a Conrad, Woolf, or Joyce. She is a "novelist" in the worthy tradition of artists who depict *la comédie humaine*, or its tragedy. Her interest is always in the specific event, and its *meaning*, as applied to individual character or to the character of society. Her use of pattern, then, never takes us beyond the world of factual events, but makes these events luminous and moving. It is as though she looks at experience so intently that she pierces *through* its tangled surface to reveal its deeper relevance.

Thus, for example, the nightmarish, smog-covered life of Saint-Henri stands out menacingly between the dreamed-of heights of Westmount (with its fresh air, security, private gardens, and steel fences) and the childhood "Eden" on the banks of the Lachine Canal, with the droll Pitou calling in tragic innocence : "Wait for me. I'm coming too." But Saint-Henri is the bitter present; Westmount and the canal landscape are an unrealized future and past. In the same way, the novel develops a "make-up" or "mask" theme to contrast the terrible insufficiency of such youngsters as Florentine and Eugène with the tawdry materialism that is their symbol of "success." Florentine is swept away by the "different" clothes that Jean Lévesque wears, and when he unexpectedly takes her to a fashionable restaurant she feels it "a great consolation" that she has brought her lipstick. Even Rose-Anna, taking her children to visit their grandmother, must stay up all night to make them presentable; but Rose-Anna, at least, knows that the painful truth shines through the mask, and with her mother's resigned gesture of helplessness, she rubs her fingers abstractedly against the edge of the chair.

The Tin Flute is a work which speaks powerfully to the family of man, not in any theoretical jargon, but dramatically—through the experience of living people. It does not warn us against the economic hells that our society spawns; it simply presents them to us in all their painful destitution and degradation. It suggests, moreover, no solution to the eternal problem of life, unless Love is a solution. In two later essays in spiritual autobiography (*Where Nests the Water Hen*, and *Street of Riches*) Miss Roy treats the same theme in pastoral settings, timelessly beyond the era of the big city. But her statement is the same; and since it is a view which many of us no longer learn from the preacher or the teacher, we may well consider its expression in fiction. For Gabrielle Roy does not bridle at facts or shy away from difficulties. She is an artist who prompts us to examine the deepest reaches of our experience and to bear witness to its truth.

University of Toronto, HUGO McPHERSON
  May, 1958.

CHAPTER I

WHERE WAS the young man who had given her so many admiring glances yesterday? Florentine found herself watching out for him eagerly, although the memory of his bantering tone was still fresh in her mind. The noon-hour rush was in full swing.

The fever of the store communicated itself to her in a kind of irritation, mingled with a vague feeling that some day all this seething activity would come to a stop, and her purpose in life would become plain. It never occurred to her that she might meet her fate elsewhere than here, enveloped in the pungent aroma of caramel, between the tall mirrors pasted over with strips of paper announcing the day's menu, and to the crackling report of the cash register, a sound like the very expression of her frantic hopes. For her this place summed up the pinched, hurried, restless character of her whole life in Saint-Henri.

Her glance slipped past the five or six diners she was serving toward the front of the store—the restaurant was in the rear of the five-and-ten—and in the play of light on the nickeled panels, the glass and the tinware, her peevish smile attached itself aimlessly to sparkling objects here and there.

Her duties as waitress permitted her no leisure in which to dwell on the memory of what had happened yesterday, but in fleeting moments the face of the unknown youth came back to her again and again. Neither the clatter of the dishes, however, nor the shrill voices of the other waitresses as they called out their orders, could rouse her completely from her reverie, which from time to time sent little tremors over her face.

Suddenly she felt disconcerted, almost abashed. While she had been watching out for him among the crowd at the swinging doors of the store, the young stranger had seated himself at the counter and was calling her impatiently. She moved toward him, pouting. It was annoying to have him take her by surprise just as she was trying to remember his features and the tone of his voice.

"What's your name?" he snapped.

More than the question itself, his mocking, almost insolent manner put her back up.

"You'd like to know, wouldn't you?" she answered scornfully, but without finality, not as if she wanted to silence him. On the contrary, her tone invited a reply.

"Come now," he urged, with a smile. "My name's Jean. Jean Lévesque. And to start with, I know yours is Florentine. . . . It's Florentine here, Florentine there . . . Florentine's in a bad temper today; you can't get a smile out of her. You see I know your first name. I like it, too."

Then he changed his tone imperceptibly and gave her a rather stern look.

"But you're Mademoiselle who? Won't you tell me?" he insisted with feigned seriousness.

As he moved his face closer she could read all the impudence in his eyes. Today for the first time she noticed his firm wilful jaw, the insufferable mockery in his dark eyes, and she was furious with herself. What a fool she was to have bothered about a fellow like that! She drew herself up so sharply that her little amber necklace rattled.

"Next you'll be asking me where I live and what I'm doing tonight," she said. "I know your kind!"

"My kind! What kind?" he mocked, pretending to look over his shoulder to see if there were someone behind him.

"Oh, you!" she burst out in vexation.

And yet that common, almost vulgar touch placed the young man on her own level, and displeased her less than his usual language and behavior, which, she felt dimly, put a distance between them. The smile returned to her face, a petulant, provocative smile.

"Okay," she said. "What'll you have today?"

But he continued to stare at her impudently.

"I hadn't got around to asking you what you're doing tonight," he answered. "I wasn't in that much of a hurry. Usually it takes me at least three days more to get to that point. But as long as you give me a lead . . ."

He threw himself back in his revolving chair and spun around from side to side, his eyes narrowing as he examined her.

"Well, Florentine, what are you doing tonight?"

He saw at once that his question had upset her. She caught her lower lip in her teeth to keep it from trembling. Then with a businesslike air she pulled a paper napkin from the container, unfolded it, and spread it out in front of the young man.

She had a thin, delicate, almost childish face. As she struggled to get a grip on herself the small blue veins in her temples swelled and throbbed, and the skin of her cheeks, smooth, and fine-textured as silk, was drawn toward the almost transparent wings of her nose. Her mouth quivered from time to time. But Jean was particularly struck by the expression in her eyes. Under the high arch of her plucked and penciled eyebrows, her lowered lids concealed all but a glint of bronze, but he could see that the eyes were watchful, and yet extraordinarily eager. Then the eyelids fluttered open and the whole pupil became visible, full of a sudden iridescence. A mass of light brown hair fell over her shoulders.

In observing her thus intently the young man had no definite purpose in mind. She surprised him more than she attracted him. He had not planned his last words: "What are you doing tonight?" They had sprung to his lips without his being aware of it; he had tossed them out as one might test the depth of a pool with a pebble. However, the result encouraged him to go on. Would I be ashamed to go out with her? he wondered. And then the idea of restraining himself for such a reason, considering how little he cared for the girl, annoyed him and put him on his mettle. With his elbows on the counter and his eyes glued on Florentine, he waited patiently for her next move, as if they were playing a cruel game.

She stiffened under this brutal examination, and he saw her more clearly. Catching her reflection in the mirror against the wall, he was startled to see how thin she was. She had pulled the belt of her green uniform about her waist as far as it would go, but her clothes still hung loosely on her slender body. The young man had a sudden insight into the narrow life of such a girl afloat in the turbulent eddy of Saint-Henri. Like all the girls of her type, she had probably been scorched by the meager little fires of fictitious love in the pages of cheap novels.

His voice became sharp, incisive.

"Do you come from around here, from Saint-Henri?" he asked.

She twitched her shoulders, and gave him a rueful smile by way of response.

"Me too," he added with mocking condescension. "So we can be friends. No?"

He noticed that her hands were shaking, hands as fragile as those of a child; he saw her collarbones sticking out above the opening of her blouse.

After a moment she leaned sideways against the counter before him, trying to hide her uneasiness under a sulky air, but he no longer saw her as she was. He saw her in his mind's eye all primped up, ready to go out in the evening, her cheeks plastered with rouge to conceal her pallor, cheap jewelry rattling all over her skinny person, wearing a silly little hat, perhaps a veil, her eyes glittering with make-up, a flighty girl, bent on making herself attractive to him, Jean Lévesque. The thought went through him like a gust of wind.

"Then you'll come to the movies with me tonight?"

He was aware of her hesitation. If he had taken the trouble to state his invitation more politely, in all likelihood she would have agreed immediately. But that was how he wanted it: hard and straight, since he was inviting her in spite of himself, against his will.

"All right then. It's a date," he said. "Now bring me your famous special."

Whereupon he pulled a book out of the pocket of his overcoat, which was lying on the seat beside him, opened it, and immediately became absorbed.

A flush spread over Florentine's cheeks. She hated him for his power to disturb her deeply one moment and put her out of his mind the next, dropping her as if she did not interest him in the slightest degree. And yet it was he who had made all the advances in the last few days. She had not taken the first step. It was he who had aroused her from the torpor in which she had taken refuge from the disappointments of her daily life, it was he who had awakened her from the deep trance where suffering could not touch her, where she was alone with her undefined hopes. It was he who had given form to those hopes, now clear, sharp, tormenting as desire.

As she looked at him her heart contracted. She found him very attractive. To her he seemed the well-dressed young man, unlike the others she waited on at the store, dull salesmen or workmen with greasy sleeves and collars. He was a cut above the silly youths she ran across at the neighborhood cafés, juke-box joints where she and Pauline and Marguerite went dancing in the evening, or idled the hours away in a booth, nibbling chocolate and giggling at the boys as they came in. Yes, he was different from anyone she had ever met in the course of her timid, uneventful life. She liked the way his thick black hair bristled up from his forehead; at times she had to suppress an impulse to seize his wild thatch with both hands.

She had marked him out the first time he had come to the five-and-ten, and had schemed to wait on him. Now she longed both to run away from him and defy him at the same time, to prove that he meant nothing to her. Some fine day he'll try to make a date with me, she had said to herself with a strange sense of power in the hollow of her chest. And then she wondered: Will I take him up?

The other girls, Louise, Pauline, Marguerite, all except Eveline, who acted as manager, were always teasing each other about making dates with young men at the lunch hour. Pauline claimed that you ran no risk if the fellow called for you at home and took you to the movies. Then you had plenty of time to look him over and decide whether you wanted to continue seeing him. Louise had even become engaged to a young soldier she had first met at the restaurant. Ever since the war began the new recruits had shown considerable eagerness to form attachments before they went off to training camp. Friendships sprang up quickly and under altogether novel conditions, some of them ending in marriage.

Florentine dared not follow her thought through to the end. Even while reading, the young man wore a quizzical expression at the corners of his mouth that baffled her.

I'll show him, she thought, pursing her lips. I'll show him that I don't give a rap for him. But curiosity to see what he was reading overcame her momentary vexation. She leaned boldly over the open book. It was a trigonometry textbook. The queer shapes of the triangles and the polygons, the heavy black print of the equations, all of it totally incomprehensible to her, made her smile inwardly.

"No wonder you're so fresh," she said, "when you read stuff like that!"

And tripping over to the order phone she called out in a shrill, affected voice: "One thirty-cent special!"

Her piercing tone carried all over the restaurant, and Jean Lévesque felt the blood rush to his face. His eyes flamed darkly for a moment with resentment. Then pulling his book closer, he bent over it again, his face in his strong brown hands.

New customers were crowding around the counter in the usual noon-time rush: a few workmen from nearby factories, store clerks from Notre-Dame Street in white collars and felt hats, two Sisters of Mercy in gray cloaks, a taxi driver, and several housewives breaking up a shopping tour with a cup of hot coffee or a plate of fish and chips. The five waitresses were on the go constantly, colliding with each other as they darted about. Sometimes a spoon fell to the tiled floor with a hard, ringing sound. A girl would pick it up in passing, toss it into the sink with a grumble, and tear off with lowered head, leaning forward to gain speed. They were always in one another's way. Their brisk staccato steps, the rustle of their starched blouses, the click of the toaster when the toast popped out, the purr of the coffeepots on the electric plates, the buzzing of the kitchen phone, all these made a sustained clatter, a vibration as of summer, distilling vanilla flavors and sugary scents. One could hear too the stifled rumble of the malted-milk shakers, like the interminable murmur of flies caught in glue, then the tinkle of a coin on the counter, and the ring of the cash register from time to time, like a period. Although the swinging glass doors at the entrance to the store were covered with frost in fantastic patterns, here, in the rear, the heat was tropical.

Marguerite, a big fat girl whose naturally rosy cheeks seemed to be smarting from cold even in this hot-box, had charge of the ice-cream. She would lift the lid of the cooler, plunge the scoop into the cream and empty the contents into a large glass dish. Then she would squeeze a bit of whipped cream out of a pastry bag like toothpaste from a tube. Over this went a spoonful of marshmallow, caramel or some other syrup, the whole surmounted with half a maraschino cherry of an alluring red. In a twinkling the fifteen-cent sundae special, a favorite with the customers, appeared on the table, like a cool fountain on a burning summer day. Marguerite would pick up a coin, deposit it in the cash register, and return to create another sundae special. The procedure never varied, but Marguerite took as much care and innocent pleasure in building her masterpiece the tenth time as the first. Of peasant stock, she had only recently come to stay with relatives in the city, and she had not yet lost her illusions about the cheap glitter of the quarter. Nor was she surfeited with the wonders or the sugary smells of the restaurant. The animation, the flirtations going on about her continually, the atmosphere of pursuit and recoil, of halfhearted compliance, of temptation and daring, all this amused and delighted her, without troubling her deeply. "Florentine's boy-friend," as she designated Jean Lévesque, had made a great impression on her. And as Florentine went by, carrying a plate loaded with food, she could not help making her usual remark, with a hearty, kindly laugh :

"Your boy-friend's giving you the eye, eh?"

And licking her moist lips, which always seemed to taste of marshmallow, she added :

"I think he's smart, Florentine, and a good-looker, too. He'll come around soon."

Florentine gave her a smile of disdain. Marguerite was such a fool. To her life was a perpetual round of sundaes, at the end of which each one of the girls, without half trying, without lifting a little finger, would find herself engaged, married, in her wedding dress, with a little bouquet in her hand. As she approached Jean Lévesque, nevertheless, Florentine had the not unpleasant thought that the young man must really have shown her some special attention since a girl as dumb as Marguerite had noticed it and could tease her about it. But what a funny way to pay attention to a girl, she thought with a start, her face clouding over.

She placed the food in front of Jean Lévesque and waited for him to speak to her. But absorbed in his reading, he only murmured "Thank you," without raising his eyes; then, absent-mindedly, he took his fork and began to eat, while she lingered, irresolute, finding his silence even harder to bear than his odd way of talking. At least when he spoke to her she had the pleasure of a retort. She walked slowly back to the other end of the counter to watch the hot dogs on the grill. All of a sudden she felt unutterably weary and depressed. Her body drooped against the edge of the sink.

God, how tired she was of this job! Waiting on rough men who made insulting advances, or else others, like Jean Lévesque, who made sport of her. Waiting on people, always waiting on people! And forever smiling, when her feet felt as if she were walking on a bed of hot coals! Smiling when her aching legs were about to give way with exhaustion! Smiling no matter how enraged and miserable she might be!

In repose her face took on a look of stupefaction. For the moment, despite her heavy make-up, the image of the old woman she would become was superimposed on her childish features. By the set of her lips one could foresee the wrinkles into which the fine modeling of her cheeks would dissolve. All youth, confidence, vivacity seemed to have fled from her listless, shrunken eyes, leaving a vacuum. But it was not only the mature woman that appeared portentously in Florentine's face; even more shocking were the marks of inherited debility and deep poverty that she bore. These seemed to rise from the depths of her somber pupils and spread like a veil over the naked, unmasked face.

All this passed in less than a minute. Abruptly Florentine straightened up, and the smile returned of itself to her rouged lips, as if it responded not to her will, but to some powerful reflex, the natural ally of her challenge to life. Of all the confused thoughts that had run through her mind, she retained only one, a conviction as clear and sharp as her congealed smile, that she must immediately stake everything she still had to offer, all her physical charm, on one wild chance of happiness. As she leaned over the counter to pick up some dirty dishes, she caught a glimpse of Jean Lévesque's profile, and it came to her with the force of a staggering blow, that whether she wished it or not, she could no longer be indifferent to him. She had never been so ready to hate him. Save for his name, which she had just learned, she knew nothing about him. Louise, who was a little better informed, said that he was employed at a foundry as an electrical machinist. From Louise too she had heard that Jean never went out with girls, an item that had intrigued her. It was a pleasing thought.

She glanced down the length of the counter. Out of the corner of her eye she could see a row of faces bent over plates, mouths open, jaws chewing, greasy lips—a sight that usually infuriated her—and then, at the end of the table, the square shoulders of her young man in his well-cut brown suit. One of his hands cupped his face; his brown skin was drawn tight over his cheeks; his teeth were clenched. Fine lines spread fanwise from his chin to his temples. Young as he appeared, light furrows were already drawn on his stubborn brow. And his eyes, whether skimming over nearby objects or studying his book, were hard and brilliant.

Florentine stole up on him and observed him minutely through half-closed lids. His suit was made of English cloth, unlike the stuff to be found in the neighborhood stores. It seemed to her that his clothing indicated a special character, an almost privileged kind of existence. Not that the youth dressed with studied elegance; on the contrary, he affected a certain carelessness. His tie was knotted loosely, his hands still bore slight traces of grease, he wore no hat in any weather, and his hair was thick and unmanageable from exposure to sun and rain and heavy frost. But it was just this negligence in small details that lent importance to the expensive things he wore : the wrist watch whose dial flashed with every gesture, the heavy silk scarf draped about his neck, the fine leather gloves sticking out of his pocket. Florentine had the feeling that if she leaned over him she would catch the very essence of the big city, with its well-dressed, well-fed, contented people on their rounds of pleasure. She visualized St. Catherine Street in Montreal, the windows of the big department stores, the fashionable crowd on Saturday evening, the florists' displays, the revolving doors of the restaurants, their tables almost flush with the street behind glittering plate glass, the brightly lit theater lobbies, with their long passages beyond the cashier's cage leading up between walls of mirrors, past polished rails and potted plants, up, up toward the screen where the most beautiful pictures in the world are shown : all that she most longed for, admired, envied, swam before her eyes. Surely this boy knew how to have a good time on Saturday night! As for her, when did she ever have a good time? On rare occasions, to be sure, she had gone out with young men, but only to a cheap movie in the neighborhood, or to some run-down dance hall on the outskirts of town. In return for such paltry entertainment they always tried to get their money's worth in kisses, and thus she could not even enjoy the movie because she would be so busy holding them off. Her few trips over to the west side of the city with some other girls had not proved enjoyable. On the contrary, she had been angry and ashamed to be seen in a group of chattering females. Every passing couple had caught her eye and increased her resentment. The city was made for couples, not for four or five silly girls with their arms interlaced, strolling up St. Catherine Street, stopping at every shopwindow to admire things they would never own.

But the city beckoned to her now through Jean Lévesque. Because of this stranger how brilliant were the lights, how gay the crowd! Even the spring no longer seemed so far away; the stunted trees of Saint-Henri seemed about to turn green! But for the extreme constraint she felt in his presence, she would have cried out: "Let's be friends; we are made for each other!" And again she felt an absurd impulse to bury her hands in his tousled hair. Never before had she met anyone who bore so many visible marks of success. He might be nothing but a machinist at this moment, but she was confident that he would be prosperous in the future, a future with which a strong instinct urged her to ally herself.

She came to, from far away, and asked him in the tough accent she assumed for the customers:

"Well, do you want dessert?"

Jean raised his head, squared his broad shoulders and gave her a glance of mingled impatience and mischief.

"No. But you . . . you haven't told me yet if I'm to be the lucky guy tonight. You've had ten minutes to think it over; what have you decided? Are you coming to the movies with me, yes or no?"

He saw Florentine's green pupils light up with impotent rage, but quickly she lowered her eyes. When she replied, her voice was both angry and mournful, yet with a conciliatory undertone.

"Why should I go to the movies with you? I don't know you! How should I know who you are?"

He chuckled. It was obvious that she was fishing for information about him.

"Come now," he said. "You'll find that out gradually, if you've a mind to."

Dismayed less by his evasion than by his detachment, Florentine thought to herself in some shame: He wants me to do all the talking. Maybe he only wants to make fun of me. And she herself broke into a forced laugh.

But his attention had turned from her. He seemed to be listening to sounds out in the street. A moment later Florentine heard the distant beating of drums. A crowd was gathering in front of the store windows. Salesgirls who were unoccupied hurried to the street side of their counters. Although Canada had declared war against Germany six months before, military parades were still a novelty in the Saint-Henri quarter.

A platoon filed past the five-and-ten. Florentine leaned forward to see with breathless, almost childish interest, as the soldiers swung by, lusty fellows, stalwart in their heavy khaki coats, their arms stiff under a light powdering of snow. She whirled around to look at Jean, as if to have him witness the girlish delight in her face, but his expression was so hostile, so scornful, that she shrugged her shoulders and left him, eager not to miss anything of the show going on in the street. The latest recruits were moving into her line of vision; they were in civilian clothes, some in light suits, others wearing shabby fall coats, torn and patched, pierced by the bitter wind. She knew by sight some of these young men marching behind the soldiers. Like her own brother, like her father, they had long been on relief. And suddenly, mingled with her consciousness of the exciting and inscrutable elements of the military pageant, she had a vague intuition that desperate poverty had found its final solution in war. As in a dream she recalled the depression years when she alone of her entire family had been able to bring any money home. And even before that, when her mother had gone out to work by the day. A vivid picture of Rose-Anna passed before her eyes, making her wretched as usual. For a moment she saw these men marching by in their tattermalion rags through the eyes of her mother. But her mind could not long retain an idea with dreary associations. Such as it was, the parade was a distraction, a break in the monotony of her long hours at the store. Her eyes wide, her cheeks flushed under the rouge, she turned again to Jean Lévesque, and remarked coolly, almost light-heartedly :

"It's crazy, don't you think?"

Far from smiling at her sally, as she had hoped, he eyed her with such animosity that she felt a flicker of joy, almost of vengeance, as she thought: "Why, he's a crazy fool too!" And it gave her a spark of satisfaction to have judged him so severely in her mind.

He meanwhile was rubbing his hand over his face as if to wipe out unpleasant thoughts, or perhaps simply to hide a sardonic smile, and then, catching the girl's eye, he pressed her once more :

"What's your name? Tell me your name."

"Florentine Lacasse," she answered drily, already sobered after her little victory, and angry because she could not wriggle out of his clutches.

"Florentine Lacasse," he murmured, as he felt for change in his trouser pocket. "Very well, Florentine Lacasse, until you find a soldier boy to suit your taste, you can always meet me tonight in front of the Cartier Theater. Eight o'clock, if that's all right with you," he added, almost in jest.

Florentine made no move. Disappointed though she was, the temptation was great. She thought it over. This was not the kind of date she had hoped for. However, they were showing *Bitter Sweet* at the Cartier. Yesterday Marguerite had told her the story; it was thrilling. Florentine felt more and more comforted as she remembered her new hat and the perfume she had just bought, and thought of what a handsome couple they would make, she and Jean, since they were both about the same height. People would look at them twice as they walked down the street. She went so far as to imagine the gossip that would be spread on her account. The idea of being a subject for gossip tickled her. What did she care what stupid people thought! She pictured herself after the movie in a smart restaurant, alone with her young man in a booth, while soft music was wafted to them from the automatic phonograph. There she would be sure of her power and her charm. There she would make this insolent boy eat out of her hand. She would lead him on to offer one invitation after another. A dreamy, artless smile began to play about her mouth just as Jean rose and threw a half-dollar on the table.

"Keep the change," he said coldly. "And use it to eat some solid food. You're much too skinny."

A nasty retort rose to her lips. She was deeply hurt, more by her secret subjection to him than anything else, and would have thrown the coin back at him, but that Jean was already slipping into his overcoat.

"You hate me, don't you?" he murmured. "You hate it here, you hate everything," he continued relentlessly, as if he could see clear through to the very core of her, a waste land where nothing grew but bitterness and dissent.

Then off he went with quick strides, his shoulders swinging with determination and nervous energy. It was unnecessary for him to elbow his way through the crowd; a path opened at his approach. As she watched him leave, Florentine had almost a presentiment that she would never see him again if she did not keep the appointment. She had a blind conviction that this stranger knew her, instinctively, better than she knew herself. He came to her darting lightning, and in an instant she had discerned a thousand aspects of her life that had hitherto been obscure. Now that he had gone she seemed to be sinking back again into ignorance of her own thoughts. A deep uneasiness took possession of her. I won't go, I won't go, he'll see if I go, she said to herself, digging her nails into her palms. But just then she caught Eveline's watchful eye, and repressed a giggle. Marguerite pushed past her, carrying a sundae, and whispered:

"It wouldn't get me down if he made eyes at me, that guy. He's just my type!"

And Florentine's anger subsided, making way for the agreeable sensation of being envied. Never in her life had any object, or friendship, or experience acquired value for her save through the eyes of others.

CHAPTER II

ALL AFTERNOON at the foundry, although he was working on a difficult repair job that required all his attention, Jean's mind went round and round in the same groove. How could I be so idiotic! How could I be such a damn fool! I don't want to start an affair with Florentine. When kids like that stick, they stick like leeches. I don't want ever to see her again. What got into me to make me ask her out?

He had expected to be able to break off the flirtation whenever he wished, since he had scarcely committed himself. On the few occasions in the past when he had attempted a conquest, he had always stopped halfway, either because the chase seemed too easy, or because he was unwilling to give it the time. Consumed by ambition, he was straining every nerve to rise in the world, and only one thing seemed really important to him : the profitable use of his time. Up to now he had devoted all of his spare time to study, doggedly, relentlessly, without being conscious of any sacrifice or regret.

But at the end of the day, as he was walking home to his furnished room in St. Ambroise Street, he became irritated because he could not drive the thought of Florentine from his mind.

She's just like all the rest, he reflected. She wants to be entertained, make a man spend his money, take up his time. That's all she wants. It's not me; any Tom, Dick or Harry would do. But then he recalled her thin body, her childish mouth, her tormented eyes. No; she's a bit different from other girls. Maybe she does interest me a little.

And then suddenly he burst out laughing as he walked along. The street was already dark. He had just seen himself as Florentine must see him : a dangerous fellow, rather a scamp, but attractive, like all really dangerous people. That's how she had probably sized him up. In that same moment of illumination he recognized also all the contradictions within himself, the wide difference between the real Jean Lévesque and the personality he had created for the eyes of the world. This last was a wily chap who shocked simple people with his boasting and his supposed debauchery, but a man to be admired nevertheless. The real Jean Lévesque was another person entirely. He was obstinate, reserved, a hard worker above all. This was the character he preferred at bottom, this pragmatic individual, no silly dreamer, who loved work, not for itself, but for the ambitions it nourished, for the success to which it would lead him, a youth who had dedicated himself to work almost in a spirit of revenge on the world.

As he thought of the way he closeted himself night after night in his tiny room, and pored over his correspondence course, his self-satisfaction became intense. No obstacle could dishearten him. If his knowledge proved inadequate to the tasks he had set for himself, he would add to it. Anyway, who ever learned anything from teachers? He was his own teacher, a harsh and inflexible taskmaster. He had complete control over himself. As for the rest, by which he meant the outward aspects of success: money, public esteem, they could wait a while. For he already knew the intoxication of true success when, cut off from the world in his cubicle, he set his jaw over a tough problem in algebra or geometry and stormed: I'll show them! Some day they'll see how far I can go. In a few years he would have his engineer's diploma. And then those who were too stupid to recognize his worth now would be dazzled by his accomplishments. They would see what stuff Jean Lévesque was made of. And he himself, later on, when he looked back on this present period, would know that it contained in embryo all the elements of his triumph, and that it was not, in spite of appearances, mean and barren.

Reaching home, he was about to sit down at his worktable out of old habit when the recollection of his appointment with Florentine began to torment him again.

"Bah!" he said. "I won't go, that's all," and he opened his books and set out his notepaper. But his thoughts wandered rebelliously, and at the prospect of getting less done than usual he was so vexed that he shoved his papers aside in disgust.

One night's entertainment in a week usually provided him enough relaxation. It satisfied his need for diversion and by contrast gave his more studious evenings greater value. Once a week, on Saturday preferably, he walked over to St. Catherine Street alone, went to a movie at the Palace or the Princess, and then had a late supper at a good restaurant on the west side of town. Returning home to the foggy streets of Saint-Henri, he would whistle as he strode along, feeling refreshed and happy, as if he had received confirmation of his secret ambitions. At such moments he would congratulate himself that he was alone and free, entirely free, without parents or friends who might have deflected him from the path he had marked out for himself. This weekly excursion corroborated his faith in his own great future, and for this reason it was absolutely necessary to him. Just as he felt that he must wear the very best clothes to maintain his own self-respect, so he needed to mingle with the crowd occasionally. Contact with the common herd bore out his conviction that he possessed something rare and precious in his refusal to give up the least particle of his difference from the mass of men. But there was another element in his nature that gave him some anxiety: an intense curiosity about people, a curiosity akin to pity. Pity or scorn, he could not have said which, but he suspected that his desire for pre-eminence fed itself on a certain compassion toward human beings totally unlike himself.

Pity or scorn? he wondered, returning to the thought of Florentine. Who was she? How did she live? There were many things he would have liked to know about her, but without sacrificing any of his precious time, and above all without relinquishing any of his personality to her demands. Ever since he had first caught sight of her in the five-and-ten, her image had appeared before him at the most unexpected moments, sometimes at the foundry, among the dancing flames in the open-hearth furnace, and sometimes here in his room when the wind bombarded the windows, as it did this evening, in furious gusts. At length he had become so obsessed with her that he had seen only one way to be rid of her: to be deliberately hard and cynical, making her hate and fear him, forcing her to leave him alone so that he need not make the effort himself. And yet, after one or two trials of this kind, he had returned to the restaurant once more. He had seen Florentine again, and today he had allowed himself to make a date with her. Was it pity? Was he really interested in the girl? Or had he asked her to meet him simply to commit some irreparable act that would effectually separate them? For she should have refused so abrupt and clumsy an invitation. Had he counted on her refusing?

Again he pictured her pale face, the clouded look in her eyes, and he wondered: Could she have taken me seriously? Will she be reckless enough to keep the engagement?

His curiosity, as he well knew, was completely unbridled. It had become a passion with him to satisfy his curiosity, the only impulse he did not try to master, probably because it seemed to be the basis of all self-cultivation. Curiosity ran unchecked through him, like the wind outside through the deserted streets, along the canal, around the little wooden houses, everywhere, as far as the mountain.

Jean turned to his work once more, but after setting down an equation or two he found his pen tracing the name of Florentine.

Then, hesitantly, he added the word "Lacasse," and almost immediately crossed it out angrily. Florentine was a youthful name, joyous, spring-like, but her last name had a common turn, an air of poverty that ruined all the charm of the first. She herself was like her name no doubt, half common, half gracious springtime, a short springtime, quickly faded.

These idle thoughts, so unnatural to him, ended by exasperating him. He rose and went to the window, opening it wide to the wind and snow. Sticking his head out, he breathed deeply of the night air.

The wind roared down the empty street, and the snow on its heels rose fine and sparkling, now leaping into the air, now sweeping against the thresholds of the houses, now rising again in grotesque capers. The wind was a circus master brandishing a whip, and the snow a mad, graceful dancer, pirouetting or sinking to the ground as he commanded. As the wind subsided for a moment Jean could see only the long streamers of a white scarf on the doorstep below, barely quivering. But again the whip cracked, and with a great bound the dancer rose to unfurl her misty veil as high as the lampposts. She rose higher and higher, above the roof tops, and her plaintive, weary wail broke against the barred shutters of the houses.

"Florentine . . . Florentine Lacasse . . . half slut, half song; half springtime, half poverty . . ." murmured the young man. Through staring at the snow beneath him, he imagined it had taken on human form, the very form of Florentine, weary unto death, but unable to stop spinning, spending herself. She danced on in the night, the prisoner of her own gyrations. Girls like Florentine, he thought, dash to and fro like that, running blindly to their own destruction.

Seeking distraction from his thoughts, he turned around and began to examine his room, as if a brief survey would restore all his fortitude, all his certainty in his way of life, all his pride in the choice he had made. Hanging from the low damp ceiling was an electric wire, fastened by a cord directly over his worktable. The raw light of the bulb fell harshly over open books, slips of paper black with notes, and a pile of thick volumes. In one corner of the room there was an electric plate, on which a coffeepot stood boiling, dripping blackish foam with an angry hiss. The bed had not been made; more books lay on the pillow, while others were thrown pell-mell among clothes on an old plush-covered armchair. No shelves, closet, or dresser; there was no place in the room where things could be arranged neatly. It looked as if it were always moving day. But this was just what Jean wanted. He took pains to preserve the transitory character of his life in order to be reminded that he was not made for poverty or reconciled to it. It had always been necessary for him to have both beautiful and ugly things about him to strengthen his resolve. The room had the same effect on him as his solitary walks in the fashionable quarter of Montreal. It roused him, it stimulated him as an immediate obstacle to be overcome. As a rule, whenever he entered the room, he immediately felt his ambitions and his passion for study bubble up within him. All other desires left him. But this evening his narrow cell failed to cast the usual spell. The walls pressed in on him; he felt caged, uncertain of himself. His mind revolved round the single question : Would Florentine keep the appointment?

He realized at last that he would not be able to exorcise her image until he had satisfied his curiosity. With a shrug he decided that there were plenty of other experiences as rewarding as study. Gratifying his curiosity had always appeased him, even enriched him in some strange manner.

He dressed and went out quickly.

The street was absolutely silent. There is nothing more peaceful than St. Ambroise Street on a winter night. From time to time a figure slips by, as if drawn to the feeble glimmer of a store front. A door opens, a square of light appears on the snow-covered street, and a voice rings out in the distance. The passerby is swallowed up, the door bangs shut, and only the spirit of the night reigns in the deserted street between the pale glow of lighted windows on one side and the dark walls bordering the canal on the other.

At one time the suburb had ended here; the last houses of Saint-Henri looked out on open fields, a limpid, bucolic air clinging to their eaves and tiny gardens. Of the good old days nothing is left now on St. Ambroise Street but two or three great trees that still thrust their roots down under the cement sidewalk. Mills, grain elevators, warehouses have sprung up in solid blocks in front of the wooden houses, robbing them of the breezes from the country, stifling them slowly. The houses are still there with their wrought-iron balconies and quiet façades. Sometimes music penetrates the closed shutters, breaking the silence like a voice from another era. They are lost islands to which the winds bear messages from all the continents, for the night is never too cold to carry over alien scents from the warehouses : smells of ground corn, cereals, rancid oil, molasses, peanuts, wheat dust and resinous pine.

Jean had chosen this remote, little-known street because the rent was low, and because the deep rumble of the quarter, the whistle blowing at the end of day, and the throbbing silence of the night spurred him on to work.

In the spring, to be sure, the nights ceased to be quiet. As soon as the channel was free of ice the sirens blew from sunset to dawn, echoing from the bottom of St. Ambroise Street over the entire suburb, and even as far as Mont-Royal when the wind blew that way.

The house where Jean lived was opposite the drawbridge at the corner of St. Augustin Street. Flatboats passed before his door, tankers reeking of oil or gasoline, lumber barges, coalers, all hailing him with three powerful blasts on their sirens—a salute in passing and a cry for liberty, for the open sea they would reach some day when they had left the cities behind and dipped their keels into the waters of the Great Lakes.

But the house lay not only in the path of the freight boats. It was also on the railway line, at the crossroads, so to speak, of the East-West railroads and the shipping lanes of the city. It was on the road to the ocean, the Great Lakes and the prairies.

To the left of the house the rails gleamed through the night, and directly across the street red and green signal lights twinkled gaily. At night the house was bathed in coal dust, and shook to the reverberation of wheels, the frenzied gallop of locomotives, bracing itself to meet the long-drawn-out steam whistles, the clipped puff of tugboats, the sustained drone of propellers, threaded through with the spasmodic tinkle of the danger signal. Waking in the night in the middle of all the uproar, Jean often had the sensation of being on board a steamer or a pullman car in motion; he had closed his eyes and fallen asleep under the illusion of being in flight, in constant flight.

From the street the narrow façade of the house had a comical look, slightly askew, as if to break the shocks to which it was subjected. Its side walls, spread out in a V, gave the effect of a blunt-nosed boat trying to push its prow through the thunder and darkness in which it was immersed.

Jean leaned against the doorframe for a moment. He liked this house better than anything else in Saint-Henri. He and the house were two old allies who never admitted defeat.

A puff of wind caught him off balance. Swept forward, buffeted about, he went off down the street clinging to the walls of the buildings. At the corner of St. Ferdinand Street the sob of a guitar filtered through a leaky shopwindow. Peering through the clouded pane past the cardboard window display, he saw the bright, ruddy face of Ma Philibert, the proprietor. She sat perched on a high stool behind the counter, stroking a black cat whose tail swept the worn and polished wood. Several other faces quivered in a thick warm steam rising from wet clothes flung over the stove-guard. Jean could not see who was playing the guitar, but he could just descry the instrument and the hand plucking the strings. In the background there was another musician, who was beating the backs of two spoons together in imitation of castanets. The boys, thought Jean, were up to their old tricks: having a good time at small expense.

In the rear of the shop there were two or three strangers whose faces were blurred. Occasionally a guest was invited to these evening gatherings, a new hand at the cotton mill, or a boy on the dole, whom Ma Philibert welcomed as warmly as her regular customers. For a long time now her shop had been the refuge of a noisy, shifty bunch of youths, who were penniless for the most part.

Jean remembered the time when he too had worked as a spinner in the cotton mill, when he too had frequented the joint every evening except on payday. For even in those days a tradition had been established: on Saturday evenings they all went down in a band to the picture-show on Notre-Dame Street, while the rest of the week was devoted to the card games, the music, and other inexpensive diversions to be found at Emma Philibert's. "Fat Emma!" they called her. The gentlest, the most maternal influence in his life had come from this big-hearted woman, thought Jean. He could hear her ranting at some beggar who asked for credit, which she always granted. "You damn fool, you'll never have a red cent!" she would say. Then, groaning as she got off her stool, she would add in a conspiratorial whisper: "I'll bet you need some tobacco too to poison your lungs and blacken your teeth. Here, take some. You'll pay me some day, I guess, in a month of Sundays." And aloud, "Beat it!" she would cry. "You can't put one over on me! You'll get nothing from Emma Philibert!"

Jean was on the point of going in. An evening here might change the drift of his thoughts, above all would prove to him that he had spent his time profitably in the last few years, since he was so far ahead of his old comrades. Ma Philibert would cluck over him, squeeze his arm, feel the cloth of his suit, go into ecstasies about how well he was looking. Whenever she saw her old beggars prospering, rigged out from head to foot in new clothes, she was as delighted as a mother superior when she hears of the success of a pupil for whom she had predicted great things. She had seen all sorts pass through her shop since she had bought this soft-drink stand to help her husband out during the depression. She had seen kids who were downhearted, kids wild to make good, strong ones, weak ones, disappointed ones, rebels, boys who had been kicked around or browbeaten, some blabber-mouths, some tight lipped—she had seen the whole generation between two wars. If anyone in the quarter were to write his impressions of the period, it ought to be Ma Philibert, thought Jean. How many yarns she must have heard! How many smutty stories she must have listened to! And yet, he mused, a fat mamma like that probably sees nothing, understands nothing, and thinks everything is just as it should be!

His conceit nevertheless prompted him to reveal himself to her and the gang in all his newly acquired importance. He played with the notion of astounding these simple people by his superior judgment and his air of authority, as he had in the old days. But at the same time he recalled the futility of all such discussions, as well as the solitude they had created around him. With a shrug he went on his way toward Notre-Dame Street. No, tonight nothing could distract his mind from the thin girl with the burning eyes, whom he saw standing behind the counter at the five-and-ten like a question mark.

The clock on the church stood at a quarter to eight when he reached the center of the suburb.

He stopped in the middle of Saint-Henri Place, a vast expanse furrowed by railway tracks and trolley-car lines, and imbedded with posts and safety barriers striped black and white. Between the steeples and domes the clearing was exposed to the assault of howling locomotives, the peal of bells, the grating screech of trolley cars and the steady hum of traffic from Notre-Dame Street and St. Jacques Street.

The railroad warning bell rang. Its thin, sustained, nerve-racking clang pierced the air around the signal booth. In the distance, through the whistling storm, Jean thought he heard the thunder of drums. Almost every night now this new note of gloom was added to all the torment of the suburb, the beat of drums or the tramp of hobnailed boots from Notre-Dame Street or occasionally from the barracks at Westmount, when the wind blew from the mountain.

Then all these sounds were drowned out.

A long shudder shook the quarter.

At Atwater Street, at Rose-de-Lima Street, at Convent Street, and now at Saint-Henri Place the railroad barriers fell. Here at the crossroads of two main thoroughfares, eight black and white arms tipped with red lanterns joined to halt traffic.

At these four intersections, morning, noon and night, pedestrians stood straining at the leash, and solid blocks of cars idled fretfully. Often there was a raucous tooting of horns, as if Saint-Henri had suddenly given tongue to its exasperation at the roaring trains that cut it in two hour after hour.

The train went by. An acrid smell of smoke filled the streets, and a cloud of soot hovered between the sky and the roofs of the buildings. As the soot fell toward the ground, the church steeple emerged without a base, like a spectral arrow in the clouds. The clock appeared next, its illuminated face breaking through puffs of steam. Little by little the whole church stood out, a tall edifice in the Jesuit style. In the center of the garden a Sacred Heart opened arms wide to receive the last particles of soot. The other parish buildings came into view, rearing themselves in their tranquillity and enduring strength, school, church, convent, a venerable pile with deep roots in the heart of the city and throughout the whole St. Lawrence Valley as well. Beyond it serried ranks of low houses stretched out on either side toward the slums, at the upper end toward Workman Street and St. Antoine Street, and at the lower toward the Lachine Canal, where the people of Saint-Henri toil at making mattresses, spinning thread, tending bobbins and driving looms, however the earth may shake and whistles blow, and ships, propellers and rails sing of the open road.

Not without joy, Jean thought that he himself was like a ship or a train gathering speed as it passed through the suburb, in preparation for headlong flight beyond the city limits. Living in Saint-Henri for a while caused him no grief; it was merely a period of preparation, of waiting.

He reached the viaduct at Notre-Dame Street, almost directly above the little red-brick station. At first glance its rustic appearance, its little tower and narrow wooden platforms remind one of retired shopkeepers and their wives on a holiday trip, or of country folk coming to town in their Sunday clothes. But beyond it a broad opening in the buildings frames the town of Westmount in all its stuffy English comfort, spread out over the mountain. Thus the little station invites the mind to journeys of another kind, journeys without end. Here wealth and poverty stare each other in the face, Westmount from above, Saint-Henri at its feet. Between them rise the belfries.

The young man's glance wandered over the tower of Saint-Thomas Aquinas, the colonnaded turret of the convent, the spire of Saint-Henri, and rose directly to the mountainside. He liked to stop at this point during the day and look at the cold gateways, the red and gray stone mansions so sharply delineated up there. At night he could see their lights twinkling in the distance, like signs on his road. In moments like these his ambitions and the wrongs he had suffered awoke and beset him; his heart ached with the old anguish. Before the mountain that dominated him he swelled with hatred and a sense of power.

From St. Antoine Street once more came the tread of marching feet, which had become the invisible weft of life in Saint-Henri. Jean thought of the war with furtive delight. Was it not the great event that would bring all his talents into play? How much skill that had not been utilized up to now would be called upon in this national emergency? In a flash he saw the war as his own personal opportunity, his chance for a rapid rise. He saw himself in a world of constantly changing values, afloat in a raging sea of men, in which he would be carried to the top of the highest wave. He beat his strong brown fists on the stone parapet. What was he doing here? What was there in common between him and a girl called Florentine Lacasse?

Wishing to belittle her, he tried to recall her vulgar intonation, her awkward gestures. And on the spot a captivating plan suggested itself to him: he would spy on Florentine without being seen by her. After all, he could allow himself the pleasure of making sure that she was caught in his toils.

He crossed the street, slipped into a store entrance, and waited, his hands in his pockets. Five minutes passed. He began to smile. If she didn't turn up that would end it all. If she were not so foolhardy as to come to him he would let her alone. He gave himself five minutes more respite, and later he was often to wonder what had kept him there in the shelter of the building, watchful, nervous, and yet anxious to have it all over with. Gradually his curiosity became more acute; his vanity was touched. Why didn't she come? Didn't she care for him at all? Up to now, the girls he had pursued had come over three-quarters of the way to meet him. Was Florentine making fun of him? He had a vague sense of disillusionment, as if he suspected that he might be less attractive physically, less fascinating than he had believed.

He moved forward a step, peering through the shadows. Then quickly he shrank back.

A thin figure had come in sight near Convent Street.

He recognized her immediately. Doubled over to breast the wind, clutching her hat with her hand, she was tripping along as fast as her legs could carry her.

And then from the depths of his being, from a part of him he hardly knew, a strange feeling arose, not mere curiosity or vanity, but a gentler emotion that warmed him in some inexplicable manner and filled him with an almost adolescent emotion.

He was sorry for her. A particle of pity had pierced his hard shell. He was troubled, he was deeply moved to see her flying to meet him through the wind and storm. He had a momentary impulse to run to her, to help her fight the wind and climb the hill, to shield her from the snow that whirled about her. And yet he shrank farther back into the darkest corner of the recess and watched her as she drew near. Why had she come? Why was she so reckless, so foolish? Could she believe that she was running to meet happiness, all alone in the wild night?

And a blind rage that she could be won so easily stifled all compassion in him.

Perhaps she will not stop, he said to himself. And he waited to see if she would pass on in the wind, disappearing like a mirage. With the little pity that was left in him he prayed that she would flee.

But as soon as she reached the movie theater, the girl slowed down. She stood waiting, then wandered over to examine the posters of coming attractions, took a few steps in the opposite direction, and returned to stand under the crude glare of the lights. He saw her looking first right, then left, challenging the darkness.

That's that, he said to himself, I'm through with Florentine. She's no different from the rest of them. Now I can go.

Florentine was stamping her feet and beating her hands together to restore the circulation, and her dark coat slipped open to reveal her thin knees. Then again she stood frozen in front of the posters.

What do I mean by saying I'm through? the young man wondered irritably. What is it that I have to finish? I felt for her a few minutes ago; what was it? Am I really through?

A group of girls passed the doorway where Jean stood, a shade among the shadows. A few steps from the movie theater, one of them hailed Florentine.

"Are you waiting for someone?"

Jean did not hear the answer, but he saw Florentine hesitate a moment, looking quickly about her. Apparently her friends were suggesting that she come along with them to see the movie. Once more she scanned the horizon, and then followed them into the lobby. Then only Jean drew a breath of relief. His arms relaxed and his fists gradually became unclenched.

Am I through? If she had not come, would I have tried to see her again? No, I'm sure. But then, I wonder . . . In any case, he thought, I'm rid of her. A smile came to his lips, and he whistled as he set out on his way again.

A certain doubt remained in his mind, however, and a moment later he realized that he was not completely satisfied. Did she come to meet me or her friends? he wondered. If she came to meet her friends I am no further ahead. He foresaw that he might waste two or three nights more because of a girl he did not understand, whose character and motives he had not been able to unravel, for he would continue to ask himself all sorts of questions about her when he should be studying. At bottom, perhaps, he needed to believe that she did not despise him, or else he could not drop her. "But I should worry!" he exclaimed aloud, at the end of his patience.

Both the desire and the energy to go back to work had left him. Overcome by lassitude, he longed to mingle with men and hear them talk. Their contradictions and their spirit of resignation might restore his sense of superiority again. As he was walking along, he saw on his right the white brick façade of a cheap restaurant, the Two Records. He placed his hand on the knob. The music of a phonograph sifted through the door. He shook the snow from his feet and went in.

CHAPTER III

THE TWO RECORDS, like most establishments of its kind in the quarter, was not really a restaurant, but a neighborhood hangout where you could buy soft drinks and sandwiches, ice cream, cigarettes and chewing-gum. It took its name, however, from the sale of merchandise totally unconnected with the restaurant business, namely, phonograph records. In Saint-Henri there was always a demand for recordings of French and American popular songs that were already out of date in Montreal proper. As you came in the door you could see records attached to the wall and hanging from a long wire stretched across the room. Another wire over the counter carried a display of newspapers, weeklies, and illustrated magazines. Patrons could be served in the booths at the far end of the room, where the ceiling was low and the lights dim, but most clients of the Two Records preferred to eat their hot dogs or sandwiches at the counter, where they could gossip with Sam Latour, the proprietor.

On those rare occasions when Sam went to the trouble of serving a customer who had chosen to sit down in one of the booths, he was not churlish about it, but he seemed greatly surprised that anyone should require him to walk the length of the restaurant a couple of times, especially when he was in the middle of a conversation. If a patron was bent on keeping aloof, it was customary for him to stop at the counter, give his order, and carry it off wherever he wished to sit.

Sam Latour was not grouchy or pompous, but like most French Canadians he disliked waiting on table, which calls for a deference quite foreign to their nature. It mortified him no less to abandon a lively discussion and retire to the kitchen to heat up a cup of coffee or a bowl of soup. You might have thought he had set himself up in business for the sole purpose of being able to jabber in comfort. His original intention in buying the place, to be sure, had been to develop it into a large restaurant. But gradually he had become reconciled to the idea of a modest place, because even though business was slow and the profits negligible, he was satisfied to be his own master. A stout jovial fellow, with round cheeks and a ready laugh, he liked nothing better than an argument about politics and war. As Jean Lévesque appeared at the door, bringing a draft of cold air with him into the restaurant, Sam was spouting his views to an audience of four or five men lounging against the counter.

There was a moment of silence, and then the talk was resumed, on a lower tone. The Two Records was near the railroad station and taxi stand, and only a stone's throw from the Cartier Theater, in fact at the most frequented spot in Saint-Henri. A newcomer aroused much less curiosity here than in the little hot-dog stand in St. Ambroise Street. In bad weather, however, practically the same group gathered of an evening in the warmth of the fat-bellied stove: a cab-driver, free for a few minutes between trains, a ticket agent, a watchman who had just been relieved at the signal tower, a trackman from a gang working overtime. Once in a while an usher from the theater nearby, in a blue uniform trimmed with red braid, a railroad porter or a dispatcher would rush in for a quick drink. A few men who were out of work spent the whole evening there.

The subject generally discussed was the war, and particularly conscription, which was supposed to be imminent. Stories about the fifth column and a network of secret police were on everyone's mind, and aroused considerable mistrust of strangers. The men in the shop therefore stopped talking to glance at the young man who had just come in, then, doubtless reassured by his appearance, went back to their argument. Their voices rose quickly and soon reached the usual high pitch.

Sam Latour looked inquiringly at Jean, served him a soft drink at one of the booths in back, and immediately returned to his usual post behind the counter, picking up where he had left off.

"The Imaginot Line! What good is an Imaginot Line? If you block me in front and block me on one side, but leave a gap for me to get through on the other side, what good will your Imaginot Line do me? If that's all France has to fall back on, she's cooked, I tell you."

But the man to whom he was speaking seemed unshaken.

"Don't you fear, Latour," he said. "France is prepared. France has the Maginot Line. And even if there was no Maginot Line France still has enough friends all over the world to come to her rescue. No country in the world has more friends than France. While the totalitarian countries are alone because of all the atrocities they've committed. They say: 'We're better than you are and we're going to take you over. We're the master race.' Look at them, they have no friends, those countries."

The speaker was a well-built fellow, wearing the badge of a taxi driver. He might have been near forty, but his fresh complexion, his flashing teeth, the enthusiasm in his eyes under the visor of his cap, and his strong, wiry hands indicated that he was approaching middle age with his strength unimpaired, perhaps with all the fire of his youth. He spoke in a clear melodious voice, and he often used high-flown words like "totalitarian," distorting them perhaps because the sense eluded him somewhat. But it was evident that he enjoyed hearing their rich sound.

"France," he continued, and the word came from his lips with an almost lover-like intonation, "France can't be beaten. First of all, as long as the Maginot Line holds——"

"Listen, Lacasse," interrupted Sam Latour, back at the very subject that interested him most, "suppose I'm at war with you, big boy. Good. I'm behind my counter. Okay. You can't attack me head on, but what's to stop you from coming around the end and stabbing me in the back? That is the way it happens in war," said he, going through all the motions of a surprise attack, then leaping backward and pointing to the breach, "that's strategy. No, I can't see how the Imaginot Line is going to stop the Germans. Maybe France made a big mistake in going to war."

"France had no choice," said Azarius Lacasse in a more conciliatory tone.

"No, she didn't have much choice, with England poking her in the behind," retorted a young man in overalls, who had kept out of the argument thus far.

The mention of England immediately livened up the dispute.

"Wait a minute," said Azarius. "There's no use getting bitter about England. I haven't much love for England, but I have what you might call respect for England. You can't deny that we've been just as well off under the rule of England as we would have been on our own. You mustn't blame everything on England. And to tell the truth, England had no more choice than France in the Munich affair. You saw how little Chamberlain accomplished with his umbrella——"

Everyone burst into laughter, which was cut short by a caustic voice from the rear of the restaurant.

"According to what you say, then, we didn't go to war to help the English!"

"I don't say that we didn't come in for that too," answered

Azarius. "But our main reason was to stop Germany. Why did Germany fall on poor defenseless Poland like a wild beast? Why did Germany swallow up Austria and Czechia—Czechiaslavia? There's more to this war than England's interests. We must think of humanity——"

A short, underslung man, with a weasel face, advanced toward the counter.

"By George," he said, "we're fighting to save democracy again!"

A renewed outburst of laughter greeted this sally.

"Yes, democracy," put in Sam Latour, "they've been singing us the same old tune since the last war. What the devil does it mean anyway?"

"By George, I'll tell you," replied the weasel-faced man. "It means the bread line, it means taking charity, it means unemployment—a third of the population on relief and a lot of poor suckers cleaning the snow off the streets for thirteen cents an hour four or five days in the spring. That's democracy for you!"

"It's also the right to say what's on your mind," Azarius added.

"Sure!" Sam Latour blurted out, his ruddy face gleaming with derision, his round belly shaking with laughter under the white apron. "Sure, that's a great help!" He was on the point of adding: "when you're starving to death," but restrained himself, remembering the worst years of the depression, when Azarius Lacasse had suffered as much hardship as anyone he knew.

As his kindly instincts got the better of his desire to crack a joke, he was willing to change the subject. But Azarius, showing no signs of embarrassment, went on serenely:

"I maintain that this war is being fought for justice and to punish the guilty."

A guileless smile, mirroring the ideas behind these words, came to his lips, and revealed him for what he was. He had not only remained young physically, but he had clung to a childlike, ineradicable belief in the right. It was then that Jean, leaning out of his booth to get a glimpse of him, caught the resemblance he was looking for. Florentine's father, obviously. Jean's lip curled with scorn for these common people. This good-natured sap, for example, thought he had the right to express a personal opinion on a world-wide upheaval whose underlying principles he could never understand. They were all like pygmies in the jungle who come on a piece of complicated machinery, and try to figure it out while holding it upside down. Whether they burned with hatred for England or whether they tended to be submissive, they were all equally far from the truth.

A murmur of disapproval had risen in the group around the counter. Meeting only hostile or mocking glances about him, the cabby looked for support elsewhere, and catching sight of Jean Lévesque in the booth in the rear, he called out:

"Hey there, young man, what do you say? Don't you agree that our boys ought to go and fight? Ah, if I were only twenty again!"

Jean smiled contemptuously, as if to himself, in a way that made his face look hard. "Here's what I say!"

He thrust his head forward, then in a calm, biting voice, clipping his words, he declared:

"They tell us that Germany wants to destroy us. But the German people want peace as much as we do. They're no worse than we are. Yet right now they're falling for the same line that's handed to us. They're told that we want to keep them shut up in a country too small for them, that we want to prevent them from getting living space. On both sides there are people who swallow all that hokum. Maybe it's the Germans who are wrong. How can we tell? But as for me, I have no desire to kill a guy who never did me any harm. How can he refuse to obey his leaders? I have nothing against the poor fellow. Why should I go and shove a bayonet through him? He wants to live too. He values his life as much as I do mine."

Jean's insolence, his air of detachment, caught the men by surprise. The idea he had expressed was foreign to them, and left them quite unmoved. The people in the quarter had become used to all manner of reactions to the subject of the war—indignation, self-interest, violent opposition, rebellion, fear. But since none of them had experienced war at first hand, the idea of universal compassion on which the young man based his argument, was new to them. His supercilious air added to the unfavorable impression he had made. The men therefore laughed and nudged Azarius to show that they stood by him. But he only remarked in an unfriendly tone of voice:

"Pacifist, eh?"

"No," said Lévesque calmly. He was amused to note that these men, who carried the fear of conscription about with them like the germ of a contagious disease, could attach so much scorn to the word "pacifist." Some of them, he knew, would rather run off to the big woods than submit to military training. They preferred to be called slackers rather than pacifists.

"No," he repeated, "pacifists are heroes. They are willing to sacrifice their own best interests for an idea. How many pacifists do you know? To me most men seem like profiteers. Have you any idea how many men have made a good thing out of this war, even though we've only been in it six months? Starting with those who found a job in the army. A dollar and thirty cents a day isn't a pile of money, but it's enough to get plenty of boys in line. Then take the fellows in the munitions plants. Don't you think they're making money out of the war? All up and down the ladder, everybody's after the jack. We're all profiteers, but if you'd rather not hurt the war effort, let's say we're all good patriots."

He was trying to arouse consternation in his auditors just as Azarius Lacasse enjoyed spreading good feeling about him.

"But our patriotism," Jean went on, "consists in offering larger profits to those who stay behind than to those who get their heads blown off at the front. Wait another year, and you'll see some fine goings-on here. You'll hear some sweet sermons and some fine speeches. And you know how far that'll carry us."

Azarius pulled on his driving gloves, eyeing the young man as he did so with dignity.

"One of these days," said he, "when I have the time, I'll take you up on this, young man, if I run into you again. In the meantime don't forget that there are concentration camps for saboteurs."

"And what about your freedom of speech?" interposed Sam Latour with a snort.

Azarius nodded. His unruffled smile indicated that he was not without a sense of humor.

"Yes, of course. Well, time is passing," he said, ignoring Lévesque pointedly, "the next train'll be in soon."

The conversation around the counter took on a more intimate tone.

"Are things going better with you?" asked Sam.

"Not so bad. It could be worse," answered Lacasse. "My daughter is still working—you know, across the street, at the ten-cent store."

"Oh yes, Florentine, the oldest girl. That must be quite a help, eh?"

Jean caught the name out of the air. He leaned over his table and began to study the cabby's face intently. There was a mixture of dislike and curiosity in his feeling for the man. An idealist, a ne'er-do-well, a dreamer, Jean suspected, who gave his family no sense of security.

"Yes," Azarius went on, "ever since Florentine's been getting steady wages, it's been a great lift."

His head came up with a jerk and he flushed.

"But it isn't fair to make a girl give all her earnings to support her folks," he said. "I don't like it, Latour; I don't like it, and I mean to put a stop to it. If only the building trade would pick up——"

"Yes, I know. I just can't see you cruising around in a cab."

"No, it gets you down," the chauffeur blurted out. "I'd get out in a minute if I could, I give you my word. It's a dog's life."

He sagged against the counter for a moment as if all the bounce had gone out of him, as if some voice within him had charged him with failure.

In his unsteady tone, in the look of uncertainty that came over his face, Jean now found the likeness to Florentine completed. Like Florentine, the cab-driver was maladjusted; he despised the work he was obliged to do. As long as he could juggle big words, and set himself up as the champion of noble causes, all was well, but the moment he came in contact with realities, he lost his footing. The secret torment these two suffered put an insuperable barrier between them and other human beings, and of the two, thought Jean, it was not the father who was most likely to be doomed, but the girl. He saw her again in his mind's eye running through the storm, and he sensed the turmoil in her heart.

He reached the door almost at the same time as Azarius. Pushing ahead of the other man, he braced himself and stepped out into the wild night.

Florentine's pallid, strained face still harassed him, and he was vexed more than ever by unsatisfied curiosity. It was obvious that she hated her job, hated every moment of her life of servitude, and yet she gave almost everything she earned to her family. The girl was consumed with loathing for her daily tasks, but still she was devoted to her parents. What a strange girl!

He struck off at random into one of the dark alleys opening into Notre-Dame Street. As he came within the feeble glimmer of the street lamps, he could see "For Rent" signs tacked to the walls of the houses on either side.

The annual upheaval—moving day—among the restless people of Saint-Henri, was already foreshadowed.

Spring was on the way.

It seemed to him that the "For Rent" sign should be attached not only to the houses. It should be worn by the men and women of the quarter too. Their hands were for rent. Their empty days were for rent. Their strength was for rent, and above all their ideas, which could so easily be tampered with, which could be made to go in any direction by a shift in the winds of doctrine. Their slumbering energy, unspent for so many years, was ready for any chance use, their hopes were ready, like these houses, for strange tenants. They were thawing out, the mildew was dropping away from them. They were ready to heed the call that was ringing out across all frontiers.

They were ready for war.

And me, what am I ready for? he wondered, for at certain

moments he still felt that he was not entirely sure of the path he should take. Two conflicting impulses of almost equal strength sometimes struggled for mastery in him, pulling him in opposite directions. At any rate he could weigh the alternative, and imagine what would happen if he were to give way to his more generous instincts. This had appealed to him strongly at times. But there was hardly a doubt in his mind now that he had acted wisely in choosing the other course. He would take his stand and drive toward his goal.

CHAPTER IV

WHILE JEAN LÉVESQUE roamed about the town, wishing he had a friend to whom he could un- burden himself, Emmanuel Létourneau, the only person in the world he really esteemed, was on his way to Ma Philibert's restaurant.

He reached the dimly lit door, stumbled over a step buried in the snow, and with a long "br-r-r" was blown into the little shop.

"Look who's here! Manuel!" cried Emma Philibert.

"Look who's there! Ma Philibert!" cried the young man, mimicking her. He ran to meet her behind the counter, where she had ducked down to retrieve a slipper she had dropped in her haste to get off the stool.

"Ma Philibert," he declared, "you're just as big and fat and round as ever." He pinched her chin. "And just as beautiful as ever."

"Crazy boy!" she tossed back, laughing with delight. But sur- prise made her breath come in gasps, and she smoothed her hair archly.

Then, as she noted his uniform, she turned serious.

"Emmanuel! Then it's true that you're in the army!"

Seated at one of the few tables in the shop, three youths looked on at the scene, one restlessly, like a puppy eager to join the fun, another in a sulky mood, and the third with an air of indolent boredom.

"Pitou, Boisvert, and Alphonse; Alphonse is here too," said Emmanuel, turning to each in turn and lifting his hand in greet- ing.

He stood in the middle of the room, a tall, thin, rather awkward young man, his face pinched with the cold, but glowing with candor and friendliness. He seemed a trifle embarrassed by the silence with which his greeting had been received.

"Well, how's everything, boys?" he began.

"Okay," said Boisvert. "First rate. But you're in my light." Then he grumbled, "Shut the door properly, will you? You probably didn't notice that it was cold out. It's twenty below zero tonight, no less. Is it as warm as all that where you come from?"

"Just about," said Emmanuel, abashed.

Pitou perched himself on the counter, his legs dangling, and his guitar in his lap. He was still shy, and he alternately stared and grinned at Emmanuel. Alphonse kept aloof, but condescended to give the newcomer a world-weary smile. It's hard meeting old friends again, even after a short time, thought Emmanuel Létourneau. And he debated whether to sit down or buy a pack of cigarettes and go away.

These three had been his boyhood playmates, to the horror of his mother, who wanted him to keep better company. Later he had had the advantage of going to the Jesuit college, while they were already out looking for work at the age of thirteen or fourteen. But before graduation he had rashly left school in a gesture of rebellion against his father, and had found a job as a spinner in the cotton mill on St. Ambroise Street. Within a short time he had become a foreman at the mill, a stroke of luck that had given him great prestige in the eyes of his jobless friends during the depression years. The only thing they still had in common was the memory of their school days together. All the children in Saint-Henri attended the same primary school, at least for a time, without class distinctions. Shopkeepers' sons, ragged brats from the streets along the canal, the pale and sickly children of the families on relief, all sat side by side on the benches of the parochial school. So far as Emmanuel was concerned, the glimpse of poverty he had had as a little boy plagued him still. For this reason he had never completely lost sight of the lads he had been fond of at that period: Boisvert, a shrewd, slippery boy, so famished that he spent more time stealing apples and nuts from his comrades' pockets than studying his lessons; Alphonse, as reserved and bitter then as now; and Pitou, who used to tear his breeches and dreaded going home because he was sure to get a beating. Pitou, who once stayed home from school for three weeks because his mother owned no thread with which to mend his breeches. Pitou, who returned to school one day in the pants of his older brother, at long last dead of tuberculosis!

These boys, he found, expressed the real attitude of his generation. It could be summed up by internal torment, outward raillery, and enforced indolence. When he had made up his mind to quit his job and enlist in the army, all these memories of his childhood had come back to him and played a part in his decision.

Only a few months earlier he had stopped by at Emma's after work, and treated the boys to a coke and a pack of cigarettes. And yet on entering the restaurant tonight he had sensed a feeling of constraint on their part. Then he understood; it was his uniform that prejudiced their minds against him. The moment he set foot in Saint-Henri he had felt a certain uneasiness, even silent disapproval, in the people he passed in the street.

Ma Philibert, however, was no less delighted to see him than before. All agog with surprise and joy, she made him turn around, and examined him from head to foot.

"Now then, sit down, Manuel," she gushed. "It's not been the same here since you went away. Sit down. You look well, but you're pretty skinny, you know. Do they give you enough to eat in the army?"

"Sure," said Emmanuel, smiling, "we get plenty to eat."

The smile gave his face an expression of great sweetness. He had tawny eyes, high cheekbones, and held his head tilted to one side, as if his neck were too fragile to support the weight. Digging in his pocket, he came up with a lighter and a package of cigarettes, which he handed around before helping himself. The stove glowed red in the middle of the floor, and Ma Philibert's face was framed as usual between jars of peppermint sticks and pink candies ranged on the counter. The little bell over the door tinkled with every breath of wind. Boisvert, as was his wont, took out his pocketknife and began paring his nails. No, nothing had really changed here. It was only he, Emmanuel, who had a different outlook on life. He stretched his legs out to the warmth of the stove with a sigh of contentment.

"You always were a good pal," said Pitou.

He puffed thriftily at his cigarette, watching it disappear with comic terror.

"You always have cigarettes to lend a guy," he went on. "Not like Boisvert. He'd rather sneak out for a smoke all by himself than give us a puff. You're a real pal."

He had moved to his usual place on top of the soda cooler. Balancing himself on the red cover, he gripped his guitar between his legs and seized Emmanuel's overseas cap, which he tipped over one eye.

"You brat," said Boisvert. "All you can do is bum cigarettes. Do you ever give any away?"

Pitou shrugged his shoulders and smirked, then, dropping to the floor on his thin legs, he peered into the mirror on the showcase and tried Emmanuel's cap on over his red curls in different ways, admiring his own reflection.

Rocking back on his heels, he suddenly asked:

"How long have you been in the army, Manuel? Four months? How do you like it? Can a guy get along in the army?"

"It's not too bad," said Emmanuel.

No one spoke. Alphonse stirred, and as always when that long, gawky body showed a little animation, everyone turned to look at him. He was leaning back in his chair, his hands clasped behind his neck and his feet resting on the stove screen.

"Why did you enlist, Manuel?" he asked, in his slow way. "You had a good job. It was nice clean work. You didn't need to go into the army to earn a living."

"No," said Emmanuel.

And he added, laughing, "I can't say I did."

"Then it's true that you gave up your job to go into the army?" cried Ma Philibert. "I couldn't believe it. Why did you do it, Manuel?"

"There's a war on, you know," said Emmanuel.

"Yes, I know, but all that's so far away. What has that to do with us?"

"So what!" said Pitou. "We can't let everybody get beaten up like the Poles."

"The Poles, the Poles!" Ma Philibert exploded. "They're not our kind of people!"

"The world isn't made up of two kinds of people," Emmanuel muttered, but he seemed wrapped in his own thoughts and had not yet come around to answering their questions.

"Don't you try to tell me," said Emma, "that Poles and Ukrainians are as good as we are. They beat their wives! They live on garlic!"

As she became more excited she began tapping the counter with her pudgy fingers. Seeing this, the cat stuck out his pink nose in the belief that she wanted to stroke him. She scratched him behind the ears, her large bust heaving.

"Do you want me to tell you something?" she concluded stormily. "You've been listening to their fine talkers! They're always on the lookout for boys like you. I'm sure they got you drunk to make you sign up!"

Emmanuel smiled, but the smile grazed his features without becoming fixed anywhere. Even here, he mused, one found indifference to universal suffering, an indifference based not on personal interest or self-love, but on the instinct to survive, to survive somehow in the midst of poverty, blind and deaf to the misery of others.

"But Ma Philibert," he said, trying to soothe her, "if your neighbor's house was burning, you'd go and help him, wouldn't you?"

"The devil I would."

Boisvert snorted. "Ugh! We have our share of burning houses right here. And plenty of troubles of our own. You don't have to go so far away to find 'em."

"I know," said Emmanuel. "I didn't enlist to save Poland either, believe me."

"Then why did you?" demanded Boisvert, nonplussed.

He was a puny little fellow, with sharp, restless eyes, and dun-colored hair standing out on either side of his head in two long stiff brushes. While he was speaking he went on paring his nails; when he paused he pointed the blade of his knife at the others. Then he frowned and began biting the cuticle of his thumbnail. He chewed furiously for a moment, his eyes round and suffering above his bruised hand, and finally spat out bits of dead skin.

Through the blue cigarette smoke Emmanuel contemplated him steadily.

"Has it never occurred to you," he asked, "that sometimes a man helps himself when he helps others?"

"The hell he does," replied Boisvert. "These days it's every man for himself."

He nibbled away at a particularly tough cuticle, then he snapped his knife shut, and walked toward the middle of the room, his lip curling.

"I'm going to tell you a thing or two, Manuel. For the last fifteen or twenty years society's never given a damn about us. We were told to make the best of it and shift for ourselves. Then one fine day society falls on our necks. They need us all of a sudden. 'Come and protect us,' they cry. 'Come and protect us!'"

He stopped in front of Emmanuel, a sturdy figure despite his short legs, a lock of hair falling over his eyes.

"You've had lucky breaks," he said. "If you want to play the hero that's your business. But what have the rest of us got out of society? Look at me, look at Alphonse. What has society given us? Nothing. And if that's not enough for you, take a look at Pitou. How old is Pitou? Eighteen. Well, he hasn't earned a day's pay in his life. It's nearly five years since he was kicked out of school, and he's been looking for work ever since. Do you call that justice? For five years he's been running around in circles, not learning a thing but how to play the guitar! Our friend Pitou smokes like a man, eats like a man, spits like a man, but he hasn't earned a damn cent in his whole life. Do you think that's right? I think it's disgusting."

To all of this Pitou kept nodding his round woolly head. From time to time he plucked a string of his guitar, which gave forth a melancholy cry. He was extremely impressionable, and Boisvert's dramatic presentation of his sad case struck home. On another occasion he would have stuck his tongue out at Boisvert, but since he was being held up as an object of compassion he rushed to support his friend.

"He's right," said he. "I haven't had a day's work since I quit school. I'm too old to sell newspapers and they won't have me in the factories. Nobody wants me, nowhere."

"That's just what I said!" exclaimed Boisvert. "It all comes back to what I've always said. Society never gave us a thing. Not a thing."

"You ought to be ashamed of yourself!" screamed Ma Philibert at this juncture. "Saying a thing like that when I provide the wood to keep you warm every night."

"That's not what we were talking about," retorted Boisvert. "We're talking about society in general."

"When I was young," Emma grumbled, "we didn't expect to have things handed to us. We were told that we had to give something ourselves."

"That's when you were young," the boy cut in impatiently. "It's not the same nowadays. As I was saying, society never gave us a thing."

"Wait a minute, wait a minute," murmured Alphonse lazily. "That's not quite true. Society's given us something. Yes, it's the truth, society's given us something. And do you know what that is?"

He sat very still, his eyes half closed, his lips barely moving, so that his voice seemed to be coming from someone hidden behind him.

"Well, I'll tell you. Society has given us temptations!"

"Crazy, crazy!" cried Ma Philibert hysterically.

"No, he's not crazy," Emmanuel interposed gently. "What were you going to say, Phonse?"

There was no answer for a moment, but they could hear Alphonse chuckling under his breath. When he went on his voice rose from the shadows as if the shadows themselves had become vocal.

"Have any of you guys ever walked on St. Catherine Street without a cent in your pocket and looked at all the stuff in the shop-windows? I guess so. Well, I have too. And I've seen some fine things, boys, as fine as you can see anywhere. I can hardly describe all the fine things I've seen while tramping up and down St. Catherine Street! Packards, Buicks, racing cars, sport cars. I've seen mannequins in beautiful evening dresses, and others without a stitch on. What can't you find on St. Catherine Street? Bedroom suites, with a doll in a silk nightie on the bed. Sporting-goods stores, with golf-sticks, tennis rackets, skis, fishing-poles. If any one has the leisure to play around with such things, it's us, eh? But the only fun we get out of it all is to look. And the grub! Have you ever passed one of those restaurants where they roast chickens in the window when your belly was flapping against your ribs? But that's not all, my friends. Society spreads everything out before us, all the finest things in the world. But don't get the idea that that's all. Ah no! They urge us to buy too. You'd think they were scared we weren't tempted enough. They're on our necks day and night to buy all this fancy stuff. Turn on the radio, and what do you hear? A bigwig from the loan company who wants to lend you five hundred bucks! Boy, you could buy a secondhand Buick with five hundred bucks! Or a fellow begs you to let him clean your old rags. You're stupid not to wear the latest styles. You're a fool not to have a frigidaire in your kitchen. Look at the paper. Buy all the products in the ads; the papers are full of them. Buy cigarettes, buy Holland gin, buy headache pills, buy fur coats! No one should be without these things! In this era of progress every man has the right to have a good time."

He rose and emerged into the light, a tall thin boy with narrow hips, red swollen eyelids, and large ears standing out from his head.

"That's what society gives us, temptations. From beginning to end that's all we get. The whole bloody circus is set up to tempt us. And that's how society, the dirty slut, gets a grip on us. Don't get any ideas into your heads, boys. Sooner or later we all fall for it. It requires no great temptation either to make us give up our wretched little lives. I know a guy who enlisted, do you know why?"

Putting his hand in his pocket he drew out a toothpick and stuck it in his teeth.

"To get a winter coat. He was tired of buying his clothes from the old-clothes men in Craig Street, wearing rags that stank of sweat and onions. One day he got the idea that he wanted a coat with brass buttons. And how he shines up those brass buttons nowadays, how he polishes 'em! They cost a pretty penny, eh?"

He glared at Emmanuel.

"D'you want me to tell you another? D'you want me to tell you another story?"

Emmanuel smiled. He knew that it was just as difficult to stop Alphonse when he was well started as to draw him out of his silence at other times.

"Go to it," he said. "There's something in what you say. You're off the track at times, but you're funny."

"Sure I'm funny," agreed Alphonse with a scowl. "I'm funny to look at, funny to listen to. And some day I'll be a funny stiff."

He opened his eyes wide—a rare occurrence—and his whole face became transformed. Strangely enough, the one interesting feature of that uninviting countenance was his deep-set eyes, which were a beautiful dark violet, and at moments almost velvety.

"Don't you worry, all those who are still good for anything will enlist eventually," he continued grimly. "It won't be long now. I know another fellow who went into the army in order to get married. He had it all figured out. Ten days' furlough and a small allotment for madame while he sails away to have his head blown off to pay for the wedding. He'd been going around with the same girl for five years, walking in the park and standing in doorways. No place for them to sit down."

Pitou burst into a raucous laugh. He pointed at Léon Boisvert.

"Just like you and Eveline," he mocked.

Boisvert's normally pale face turned crimson. Any allusion to his relations with Eveline, which had been going on for several years, drove him frantic. He reached over to seize Pitou by the collar, but Alphonse stuck out his leg and they both tumbled to the floor.

"Let Pitou laugh," he said. "Even he thinks it's a joke when people like us want to get married. There's nothing funnier than a marriage of beggars, of people on relief."

He shook with silent laughter.

"That always reminds me of the midgets in the circus who were married. Neither of them was bigger than that," and he indicated the seat of a chair. "When you looked at them you just couldn't believe they could be in love. Sometimes I wonder if we aren't in a circus too. They give us something to eat, just enough to keep body and soul together—like throwing peanuts to animals in the zoo. They let us marry so there'll be more midgets, they take care of us if we want to go into the army, they let us watch everything that goes on. But sometimes we get tired of being outside looking in. We hide in our holes, keep our mouths shut, and take what they give us. Then they say we're hardhearted."

He stretched out once more in his chair.

"Hardhearted rascals," he drawled. "That's what we are."

Through half-opened lids he shot a look at Emmanuel, who was studying him quietly.

"You forget one thing," said the soldier, breaking the silence at last. "You forget the biggest temptation of all."

"Well, what d'you know?" mumbled Alphonse. "Is that so?"

"The temptation that comes to circus animals and even to

midgets," continued Emmanuel. "The temptation to break the bars of their cages and get out into the stream of life. A temptation you've forgotten, old man, the temptation to fight."

"Fight?" cried Boisvert, bridling. "Fight for what?"

"Fight," Emmanuel went on steadily, "because it's your only chance to become a man again. Good God, don't you see that that's why we must fight?" His voice rose with excitement. "Because Boisvert's going sour with nothing to do but twiddle his thumbs. Because you, Alphonse, have such crazy ideas that one of these days you're going to jump into the canal. Because Pitou will end up as badly as the rest of you if this goes on. Because so far as being down and out is concerned, you're not the only ones in the same scrape. You're only three among thousands, millions of men, the masses, as some people call them, the midgets, as Alphonse says. Because nearly everybody's in the same fix. Once they break out of the circus no one can stop them. Can't you see that the boys who go to war this time are going to ask for more than a tin medal?"

Alphonse raised his lids languidly, let his eyes rest briefly on Emmanuel, then broke into a snicker.

"Sure, but what do you think they're going to get? The same old patriotic rot, just as before, with the millionaires on top and the unemployed down below, quarreling among themselves."

"No," said Emmanuel, "they're going to get a chance to live!"

"Live in a shellhole with bullets popping all around them," snarled Alphonse.

"Oh, shut up," barked Boisvert, coming to life. "You're barking up the wrong tree. There's only one chance for us. And that is," addressing Emmanuel, "if enough guys like you decide to enlist. Then there'll be room for the rest of us. What we need is room. There are too many people in the world."

He pushed his unruly locks back and stared at them arrogantly.

"Go on, Manuel," cried Pitou. "What you say is true. I'm listening anyway. Go on."

Emmanuel took the cue. "Well," he said, speaking directly to the little redhead, "you see, Pitou, it's money that keeps us all behind bars in the circus. It's the guys with plenty of cash who decide if you're to get work or not, depending on whether it pays them, or whether they don't give a damn. But this war is going to destroy the cursed power of money. Every day you hear someone wailing that no country can keep on spending at this terrific rate. I don't know how many millions go into ships that are sunk and planes that burn up and tanks that are knocked out in three days. When money goes for destruction it destroys itself. Well, so much the better! Because money is not wealth. Wealth is work, it's the hands and brains of people like us, the great mass of people. That's the only wealth that'll be left after the war. And that's the kind of wealth that will permit everybody to live in a just world.

"People like us," he continued more mildly, "have always given everything they had for war. We'll give it this time too. But not for nothing, this time. Not to go back to the same old circus. Some day we must settle accounts——"

Then, as if his mind had run into an obstacle, as if he knew that he could not put his thought into words, he stopped and grinned, leaving his sentence incomplete.

Alphonse grasped the reason for his stopping short. "Of course," he said, "there are plenty of people who are willing to believe that. But——"

He dropped his eyes and fell silent. Then, perceiving that Emmanuel was preparing to leave, he hoisted himself painfully to his feet.

"Wait for me," he said stiffly. "I'm going your way." He sighed as he looked around for his coat. "That's all poppycock. It's not much help to a chap who'd like to lay his hands on a dollar or a pint. A little money and a bottle of scotch are a lot better for a man's state of mind."

Emmanuel leaned across the counter to say goodbye to Ma Philibert, who had dozed off on her stool, her elbow crooked, her double chin cupped in her palm.

Then he flung out of the door, with Alphonse at his heels. Behind them the voice of Pitou was already lifted in song. He sang of rolling plains, of deer roaming the woods, of fawns with great innocent eyes, and elk coming down to drink among the reeds at nightfall, he sang of magnificent horizons where no man is seen. And as he sang he accompanied the words with an occasional chord on the guitar : Dling . . . dling . . . dlong.

The plaintive melody followed the two men for a few minutes, then was lost in the howl of the wind.

The storm came lashing at them like a cat-o'-nine-tails. Alphonse, his teeth chattering, took Emmanuel's arm and clung to him for warmth.

"If you're not in a hurry, come with me," he said. And then he added, without transition, "Pitou's a lucky devil; he has his music. Boisvert speaks up in public, but then he goes back to his private affairs. He rails at society, but at bottom all he wants is a safe little berth. He's a cautious fellow."

He hastened his pace to keep with Emmanuel.

"But you and me, we're thinkers. We use our brains. Of course it doesn't do much good to think . . ."

The sentence broke off with a hollow laugh.

"There are three ways to stop oneself from thinking," he continued after a moment. "The first is to go for a ride in a rowboat, all alone. The second is to drink a bottle of scotch. But that's not easy for beggars like me. Maybe there's a third——"

"What is that?" asked Emmanuel.

"I'll tell you some other time," said Alphonse. "No use rousing my hopes till I'm sure."

They turned into St. Ambroise Street and walked in the direction of the grain elevators. At times they could see clearly before them, only to fight their way through blinding clouds of snow the next instant.

After a moment Alphonse came out with it.

"Have you any cash on you?"

"Don't beat around the bush," said Emmanuel. "How much do you want?"

"One buck," said the other resentfully. "I never borrow more than one buck at a time. Otherwise I'd get into debt, don't you see?"

Emmanuel unbuttoned his overcoat to draw out his wallet.

"No hurry," mumbled Alphonse.

His breath was coming in gasps, yet he kept pushing Emmanuel along to make him walk faster.

They turned into a dark alley. Here Alphonse slowed down, as he looked for a particular house number. At last he stopped altogether. On the second floor of a drab building, occupied at the street level by a laundry, a reddish light was burning. Alphonse squeezed Emmanuel's arm. He was no longer cold. He had even unbuttoned his wretched overcoat, and stood there mopping his brow, his clothes plastered to his thin frame by the force of the wind.

"Everything's okay," said he. "Charlotte hasn't moved yet."

Then Emmanuel understood. He hesitated a moment, then thrust a bill into his friend's hand, and left without a word.

Reaching Notre-Dame Street, he continued walking aimlessly. A longing for love had taken possession of him. He tried to recall various girls he had taken to the movies or met at parties in the old days. Their names came back to him readily enough, but he could not remember a single feature of their faces. Claire, Aline, Yolande . . . he turned the names over in his mind, trying to prod his memory. But none of them stirred his heart.

They were all like phantoms from another life, the irresponsible life of a young man about town, which he had put behind him forever when he went into the army. He had never really been in love. Several times he had been momentarily attracted by a pretty face, but something always kept him from committing himself.

The farther he walked, the more he realized that he was hungry for affection. What was he seeking? Friendship? Or something in himself that friendship would bring out? Whichever it was, he felt so lonely and on edge that he would have been glad to talk to anyone in the street. Some of his buddies in the army had told him that this need for companionship became more compelling and more painful with each furlough. With all his capacity for affection unused, he felt the hollowness that precedes a great love.

Suddenly he thought he recognized Jean Lévesque walking ahead. He quickened his pace. They had been inseparable companions at high school. And since then, despite differences of opinion, and although they met only rarely, their strange friendship had survived, perhaps because the very clash of their temperaments created a mutual attraction.

The man he was following entered a tavern after a few minutes. Emmanuel followed suit, and found Jean about to sit down at a table in the rear.

"Well, well," said Lévesque. "I was just thinking about you. Have you come back to get recruits in Saint-Henri?" he joked, with a smile in which his habitual cynicism was tempered by affection.

"Yes, I've come after you," replied Emmanuel in the same spirit.

For a moment they said nothing, then Jean, holding his head in his hands, murmured:

"We two differ on one very important point. You think that it's the soldiers who change the world and lead the people, whereas I believe that it's the fellows who stay home and make money out of the war."

Emmanuel made a gesture of annoyance. He had no desire to go once more over the reasons for his decision to enlist. All he felt was an emptiness, a vibrant disquietude. By explaining his motives at such great length to the boys at Ma Philibert's, he had only succeeded in setting free his natural yearning for happiness and love, and yet he could find no assurance that these would come to him.

"Two beers," he said to the waiter. And turning to Lévesque, he burst out gloomily: "I've been home about three hours, and I'm bored to death already."

"And how about Fernande, Huguette, Claire, Yolande?" Jean listed them playfully.

Wincing as the shaft struck home, Emmanuel averted his head. Then he asked:

"Have you ever met a really nice girl, Jean?"

"There aren't any," said Lévesque.

He took a draught of beer as soon as the waiter placed the glass before him, and then put it down with a look of sudden recognition. The image of Florentine had passed before his eyes, Florentine running toward him through the gale.

"Ah!" exclaimed Emmanuel, who had caught his expression. "You were thinking of someone! Tell me who."

Lévesque lit a cigarette, and broke the match into tiny pieces, throwing them one after another into the ash tray. He was on the point of mentioning Florentine's name. His forehead wore a slight frown, but he smiled broadly, showing his strong, even teeth, which always made him look as if he were taking a big bite out of life.

"I was thinking of a girl at the five-and-ten," he said. "A waitress. Too skinny, perhaps, but damned attractive. A waist no bigger than that," he added, with a descriptive gesture, "and a body full of the devil, like a drowning cat."

Emmanuel turned away. For some unknown reason his heart contracted suddenly, as he remembered a waitress he had once seen at a station restaurant, a pale, delicate, harassed girl. In order not to lose any tips, or more likely because her job depended on it, she gave everyone the same sad, weary smile, which was fixed on her face like a grimace. It's a hard life, thought Emmanuel. And as he leaned toward Jean, he envied his friend's fine carriage, his air of detachment and cynicism, which was so fascinating to the girls.

"Have you fallen for her?" he asked.

Jean threw himself back in his chair, exploding with laughter.

"Look here, don't be a fool. Of course not. You know me. You know the sort of girls I like. No, no," he protested with a vehemence that surprised himself, "I know her name, that's all. I mentioned her for fun, just for a laugh."

"Oh, for a laugh," echoed Emmanuel in a peculiar tone of voice. "What's her name?"

Jean hesitated a second.

"How long are you going to be in Saint-Henri?"

"A week."

"All right. Come to lunch some day next week at the five-and-ten. You'll see her there."

Then he pushed the ash tray aside and slipped his head down against the back of his chair.

"Let's talk about something more interesting," he said. "Let's talk about the war. If I run across a job in a war plant that pays more than the one I've got, I may try for it. I'll see. But I'm not afraid of being drafted, since I'm a highly skilled machinist . . ."

And as he went on to describe his plans he diverted himself by drawing figures on the table.

CHAPTER V

THE LACASSE CHILDREN lay sleeping on the two sofa-beds and studio couches in the dining-room. At the other end of the connecting room Rose-Anna was stretched out on her own bed, where she dozed off from time to time. Waking with a start, she would look at the clock on the night table, and her thoughts turned not to the little ones asleep under her watchful eye, but to the other members of the family who were still out. Why had Florentine rushed away in such a hurry after supper? And without telling where she was going? And where did Eugène spend his evenings? And Azarius, what was he up to? Poor man, he would never learn. He was working, to be sure; he was bringing his pay home, little as it was. Anyway, they were almost making ends meet. But day after day Azarius spoke of great plans, of giving up his job as cab-driver and trying something else. As if he were free to choose, when there were so many mouths to feed, and new expenses kept cropping up every hour of the day! As if he were free to say that one type of work suited him and another didn't! All his life Azarius had shown a tendency to give up a sure thing for a gamble. Poor Azarius!

She lay there in the dark, her eyes closed and her hands folded on her breast, while all her present anxieties and her memories of past misfortune preyed on her heart. But more haunting than any definite knowledge of trouble to come was her fear of the unknown. Life had never seemed so threatening to her before, and yet she did not know what it was she feared. Some vague calamity, she felt, was hovering over them in the little house in Beaudoin Street.

A man's footfall was heard at the door. Rose-Anna roused herself to learn the worst, or to set her mind at rest, whichever might be in store for her. She dropped her hands to her side and sat up, straining to see through the darkness.

"It is you, Azarius?" she asked in a whisper.

All she heard was a man clearing his throat behind the hall curtain, and the regular breathing of the children in the other room, where the night light burned.

Somewhat giddy, as she often found herself after a few minutes' rest, she staggered toward the hallway. Lifting the faded curtain, she saw her eldest son, Eugène.

She sighed with relief. "Ah, you scared me. I thought it was your father; I thought he was afraid to show himself because of bad news."

The wind swept through the house with a great moan, rattling a tin pan hanging behind the kitchen door. Rose-Anna wiped the sweat from her forehead.

"I must have been dreaming," she said apologetically. "I thought your father came to me with bad news. You think of so many things when you're alone, especially when there's a storm blowing outdoors," she confessed. It had been long since she had admitted any such weakness to her big son with the low brow and the furtive glance.

And as she looked at him, it struck her suddenly that he was practically a grown man. They were almost strangers to each other now; Eugène came home only to eat and sleep, and she received nothing from him but clothes that needed mending. An instinct to draw him closer to her prevailed over all her other anxieties. A kind of panic struck her as she thought: We've been growing farther and farther apart all these years since he was a boy. And I haven't noticed it till now. He has troubles of his own, troubles I know nothing about.

"I must have been dreaming," she repeated. "And I can't remember whether it was about you or your father. If it was your father," she admitted, "I'm sure it means he's going to lose his job."

This drew Eugène out of his suspiciously strange silence, which hung about him like ill-concealed guilt.

"That's clear enough," he said drily. "He sure will lose his job if he doesn't stop chewing the rag at the restaurant across the street instead of attending to his business. The boss is fed up. All the more because Father's always telling everybody what's what."

They stood huddled in the hallway, whispering because of the sleeping children. There was no other place in the house where they could have any privacy. And it had been so all their lives. No confidences could be made until the dead of night, when the house became still. It was several years, Rose-Anna recalled, since Eugène had last crept to her at night. The last time was when he had stolen a bicycle. This time she wanted to forestall the confession he seemed about to make. His brow was overcast, his eyes shifty.

"Listen," she said, assuming that he was downcast because he had no job, "your father told me this morning that he means to get a cab of his own. He thinks he can make more that way. And give you a job too."

At this point Eugène almost spoke out. But he could not bring himself to do it just because of his mother's optimism. How absurd! She ought to know better than to catch at straws this way.

"That's only a dodge, Mother," he said. "Where would he get the money? He's got us in a stew often enough to go easy for a while. He was on relief; he should have stayed there."

"Relief . . ." sighed Rose-Anna. "No, anything but that, Eugène."

"Yes," he repeated after her, "anything but that."

He wandered into the dining-room, and sat down on a chair piled high with children's clothes, crumpling a little dress spread over the back. Stockings hung from a makeshift clothesline stretched across the room near the stovepipe. He looked about him with a feeling of revulsion that came over him every time he entered the house. Then his mouth relaxed in a smile. Running his fingers through his hair, he deliberated for a moment. At last he stood up, his heart pounding with joy. He was free at last! When he spoke, however, his voice was gentle, rather timid.

"Listen, Mother, I have something to tell you. I didn't mean to talk to you about Father. He can do whatever he wants. But I——"

Rose-Anna, however, clung to her original idea. She began picking things up and putting them in order, for her mind always worked better when she was doing something.

"But if your father could give you work, Eugène——"

"It's too late to go into that now," he said dully. "Mamma, you might as well know right away——"

His eyes met Rose-Anna's questioning glance, then wandered off into space.

By the light of the flickering candle Rose-Anna could see how pale he was. And then she realized that what he was about to say was very serious. Her heart cold with dread, she came toward him, and smelled the alcohol on his breath.

"What is it, Eugène?"

She waited for an answer. Eugène looked away, then suddenly he flared up and announced:

"Well, I just enlisted, Mother!"

"You enlisted!"

Rose-Anna tottered. Everything whirled around her; the portraits of her parents and the pictures of the saints on the wall, the knick-knacks on the dresser, the faces of the children and the snowflakes driving against the street lamp outside the window. And yet in the midst of it all she could see the figure of Eugène as a little boy going off to school.

"Is that true?" she murmured incredulously.

Her voice shook. She could not form the words that were exploding in her head. The dizziness passed. She recovered quickly and nerved herself for battle. It was not the first time she had come to Eugène's rescue. She remembered all his boyish misdeeds, his petty thefts, his lies, and she remembered too all the trouble she had taken to cover him up; and yet all that seemed as nothing compared to what she felt capable of doing now to save him. Besides, now that the first alarm was over, she could not quite believe that he was really in danger.

"See here, Eugène," she said, "you've been drinking. You don't know what you're saying. You ought to be ashamed to give me a turn like that."

"I'm not trying to frighten you, Mamma. I tell you I've just enlisted in the army."

She leaned forward, her eyes gleaming with determination.

"In that case, you must get out of it. It's not too late to get out of it. You're too young. You're not yet eighteen. I want you to tell them that you didn't know what you were doing, that we need you. I'll go myself if you wish. I'll go and explain——"

He stemmed the flood of protest with three words.

"I signed up." And then, forgetting to whisper, he cried: "And I'm glad of it!"

"Glad!"

"Yes, glad."

"Glad, glad!" All Rose-Anna could do was repeat the word, turning it over in her mind, trying to understand it. "So you're glad! Is there any sense in your saying that to me?"

She went on folding the children's clothes, smoothing them out absent-mindedly, to keep her hands busy. Then she raised her head.

"Was it because I didn't give you enough pocket money?" she asked humbly. "You know I would have given you more for cigarettes and other expenses if it didn't come from Florentine. It's not fair to her, when she brings almost all her pay home."

"She can keep her money," he blustered. "I'm going to make as much as she does now."

"All the same," said Rose-Anna, "I gave you all I could."

The boy finally lost patience with her.

"That's not it. But listen to me, Mother. I'm sick and tired of begging for a measly dime or a quarter. I'm fed up with looking for a job all over town. The army's the right place for a fellow like me. I have no trade, no education. I'll be better off there."

"Good Lord," sighed Rose-Anna.

And yet she had always felt that one day Eugène would become disgusted with doing nothing. She had also suspected that his impulsive character would lead him into disaster. But that he would enlist, no, that she had not foreseen.

"I had no idea you took it so much to heart," she said. "You're still so young. You would have found a good job in the long run. Look at your father; he went for years without doing anything."

"I know, and that's what I don't want to do."

"Not so loud!" Rose-Anna implored. "You'll wake the children."

Little Daniel was groaning in his sleep. She went to his narrow iron bed and drew the covers over him.

Simple as it was, this touch broke Eugène down. He followed his mother, caught hold of her apron strings, and began to play with them as he had when a very little boy. It came to him that this would be the first time in his life he'd be able to give her anything.

"Listen, Ma," he whispered coaxingly. "This'll be a great help to you. As long as I'm in the army you'll get twenty dollars a month."

His voice was charged with emotion, with a kind of wonder. Like his father, he had a remarkable gift for dramatizing a situation and finding some reason to congratulate himself for what he had done. Like his father, too, he never could distinguish between self-interest and generosity. At this moment he was almost convinced that he had acted for purely altruistic reasons. He was so pleased with himself that the tears sprang to his eyes.

"Twenty bucks a month, Mamma! It's a stroke of luck for you, eh, Ma?"

Rose-Anna turned toward him slowly, as if reluctant to see what was before her. Light from the street lamp fell on the spot where she stood. Her face seemed drawn, with dark hollows where the eyes should have been. Wisps of hair fell over her cheeks and her lips moved without sound. She seemed old, ready to cave in.

"Yes, I see," she said from a great way off, "I see why you enlisted, my poor child!"

She raised her hands but did not touch him, continuing plaintively, but in a chastened, spiritless voice, stripped of all rancor:

"You shouldn't have done it, Eugène. We could have got along without that."

And yet she spoke with courage, bowing her head meekly to known evils, evils that had become as familiar as night and day, and therefore less to be feared than other more terrible things hidden in the mists of the future.

A sob escaped her. She pulled at her apron. And then suddenly all her torments and misery for lack of money, her terror and her desperate need for money, revealed themselves in a wail of protest:

"Twenty dollars a month!" she quavered through her tears. "Won't that be wonderful? Think of it, twenty dollars a month!"

A greenish light fell on the tears streaming down her cheeks, and on her clasped hands, which seemed to be pushing the money away.

She saw Eugène shake his head, as he always did when he was crossed, and disappear into the kitchen. She heard him take down the cot bed that was stored behind the door during the day, and set it up between the table and the sink.

Drying her eyes, she went back to her bed and flung herself down again in all her clothes. She had still to wait for Florentine and Azarius, then bolt all the doors and make sure that everyone was asleep before she herself could turn in for the night.

At the foot of the bed, a darker shadow marked the place where an Ecce Homo hung framed on the wall. Beside it there was a lithograph of Our Lady of Sorrows offering her bleeding heart to a pale ray of light from between the window curtains.

Rose-Anna tried to remember the words of a prayer she used to say every night, but her mind was on other things. In place of the statuette of a saint she had visualized since childhood when at her devotions, she saw a fat roll of dollar bills. The roll burst apart, and the bills flew off into the air, whirling and falling through the night, driven by the wind. Dollar bills. The wind in the night . . .

CHAPTER VI

THE SALESGIRLS were beginning to leave the five-and-ten-cent store. Night had fallen. Most of them came out in groups, buttoning their coats and putting on their hats as they slipped out through the main door. When they reached the sidewalk they stopped short, dazed for a moment by the stinging wind, then arm in arm they scampered off toward Saint-Henri Place, laughing and shrieking. Others crossed the street with lowered heads and hove to at the streetcar stop, stamping their feet on the hard-packed snow. As soon as one group was swallowed up by the side streets or settled down to wait at the safety zones, a fresh batch of girls streamed through the swinging doors to repeat the process. Trolley cars already filled to bursting came down St. Jacques and Notre-Dame Streets and took on a crowd of passengers at the corners.

Jean Lévesque stood lurking in a store entrance, shuffling his feet against the cold stone. The swelling tide flowed past him, a tide of weary people in a hurry to get home. They came in crowds from every part of the suburb toward Saint-Henri Place, where they divided and went off in different directions. Masons covered with lime, carpenters with their toolboxes, workmen carrying lunch pails, spinners, girls from the cigarette factory, puddlers, steelworkers, watchmen, foremen, salespeople, shopkeepers; the six o'clock crowd included not only employees from the neighborhood but also workers from Ville-Saint-Pierre, Lachine, Saint-

Joseph, Saint-Cunégonde and as far away as Hochelaga, some of whom lived on the other side of town and traveled vast distances in the streetcar before reaching home.

At frequent intervals a bell clanged harshly up Notre-Dame Street, and a trolley car swayed by. Through the misted windows Jean could see arms raised to straps, newspapers opened up, bent backs, a heap of weary bodies. And sometimes a face would stand out from the others, with a sad, beaten look that seemed to express the mood of the whole crowd, a look that remained with him for a long time.

Nevertheless he kept his eye on the store exit most of the time. With growing vexation he wondered if he could have missed her somehow. But just as he was about to give up, the swinging door was pushed open by a small bare hand, and Florentine appeared, alone, as he had hoped.

He tugged at his scarf with a gesture that would have struck him as ridiculous, had he been in the mood for self-analysis, and hurried to catch up with her.

"Hello, Florentine!"

He hoped their meeting would seem quite accidental, but she was not deceived for a moment.

"Ah, so it's you," she sneered. "You hang around here all the time, don't you?"

Jean refused to be put out of countenance.

"I wanted to explain about last night, Florentine——"

"You needn't go to the trouble of making excuses," she interrupted him.

She took a grip on her handbag. Her straight little nose quivered with her rapid breathing; her nostrils were blue with cold.

"Who d'you take me for? Did you think I took you seriously? Did you really think I intended to meet you? Not me, you may be sure."

"Is that right?"

He took her arm gently and smiled deep into her eyes.

"So, Florentine, you meant to keep me waiting in the cold! I never expected that of you! Why, we were made to understand each other, you and I."

He pressed her arm; she must have felt that her defenses were weakening, for with a brusque movement she tried to shake him off.

"Anyway, I don't care to see you again," she said.

"You wouldn't be hard on a lonely fellow like me, would you, Florentine?" he said reproachfully. "Come and have dinner with me in town, will you?"

Under the veil her eyes sparkled with indignation, and yet, deep down, a glint of defiance met the challenge in his bold glance.

"That beats everything!" she exclaimed.

Exasperated by his impudence, she bit her lip with her sharp white teeth. And yet his proposal had a very different effect on her too; it worked on her and began to arouse her vanity. Besides, it was very cold; she was shivering so violently that her faculties were dulled.

"I'm not dressed to go to town," she said plaintively.

Thus she betrayed herself.

Seeing that she was almost won over, he piloted her toward a trolley-car stop.

"Don't worry, Florentine. You're all right just as you are. A little rouge and powder won't make any difference."

A streetcar came lumbering up. She turned to him suddenly with a look of distress.

"I'd really rather not go tonight," she said candidly.

But the crowd was piling into the streetcar; she was caught in a surging mass and propelled to a seat inside.

She was thinking: Maybe I didn't wait long enough last night. Maybe he did come to meet me. Hanging from a strap in front of her, Jean was studying her face. She met his glance; it was as if she saw herself in a mirror, and her hands went up to set her hat at the proper angle. She had of course hoped to go out with Jean some day, but she had always pictured herself as dressed in her best clothes. Her heart ached when she thought of her pretty new frock, which was cut to show off her little round breasts and her tiny waist, with a slight flare at the hips, a very becoming flare. With a pang she passed in review all her costume jewelry, from among which she could have chosen a pin for her hair, bangles for her arms, perhaps a brooch to wear on her blouse. What a shame!

And now a panic came over her as she thought of something else. Had she brought her lipstick with her? With shaking hands she opened her cheap handbag and began to search frantically among all her belongings. She ran her fingers over a comb, a box of rouge, some small change. Hastily she moved all sorts of things from the bottom of the bag over to one side. Her mouth was set in a grim line, and her eyes wandered restlessly, unable to fix themselves on anything. At last her hands fell on the cherished case; she clutched it joyfully. What a relief, heavens, what a relief! With a little encouragement she would have taken it out and painted her lips immediately, but a meaningful glance from Jean restrained her.

It was a great consolation to know that she had her lipstick. After a while, when Jean turned his eyes elsewhere, she would use it. It lay in her hand at the bottom of her bag, ready to be pulled out instantly. There was no great hurry; she could wait. She gave him a set smile and crossed her legs, which pulled her dress up over her knees. Then, to her horror, she saw a run in her stocking. She was mortified. What was the point of going out in her shabbiest dress and with a run in her stockings besides! In her dresser at home she had an elegant pair of chiffon silk stockings. Maybe she'd been foolish to buy them—they had cost her two dollars—but they were very fine gauge and exactly the color of her skin.

Jean was swaying back and forth over her with every jolt of the car. A mocking smile played over his face.

"If you pull down your skirt and don't cross your legs no one will see the run in your stocking," he murmured, bending over to whisper in her ear.

Florentine choked with indignation. She tried to think of something crushing to say, but her brain was muddled. The moist warmth of the car, the stale air, the constant clatter made her head reel. When she was with Jean, nothing ever turned out the way she had planned. It was infuriating.

Nevertheless, she stopped tormenting herself and sat quietly, not answering a word, her head rocking from side to side with the motion of the car, her lids drooping over her weary eyes. She felt clammy and numb for the rest of the trip. A cold blast struck at her when they got off the streetcar and ran for the bus. The gentle drone and the real warmth of the bus as it rolled along was somewhat better. But to Florentine everything seemed a bit hazy, the cold, the heat, the voices about her, the wind, her own doubts and despair, until they entered a small restaurant, where dazzling white tablecloths and glittering crystal danced before her eyes. Then the evening became dreamlike, and she walked bravely into the dream to play her part. And yet it required a painful effort to attain the high level of the dream.

"Oh," she exclaimed, recovering her animation instantly, "I've never been here before. It's swell!"

Her shabby wool dress and the run in her stocking were forgotten; she was enormously flattered. Turning to Jean, she gave him a look of rapture.

A waiter in a black suit and white shirt-front bowed low before them and led them to a table decorated with flowers. She assumed that they were of paper, but to her surprise they had the fragrance and texture of real flowers. The waiter held the chair for her, and Florentine sat down, taking off her coat awkwardly, with her elbows high in the air. Then a menu was placed in her hands, and Jean was asking her in a courteous tone that did not seem to belong to him:

"Will you have a cocktail, Florentine, a Manhattan?"

She had never heard the name before, and suspected that Jean was putting on airs. Averting her eyes, she nodded her assent.

"And after that?"

She clutched the bill of fare in her hands bleached with dishwater. The long list of strange words, which she deciphered letter by letter, moving her lips in an effort to pronounce them, filled her with dread. Her heart began to thump. But by taking her time, and studying the whole menu, she at last found a word that seemed familiar. Sure of not going wrong on this, she declared:

"I see they have roast lamb. I'll take that."

"Oh no, Florentine, you must start out with a soup. Leave it to me, I'll order for you."

In order to seem knowing, she murmured:

"All right then, I'll take the consommé."

She was playing with the menu now, pretending to make up her mind. Jean could only see the upper part of her face, and, standing out against the white pasteboard, her nails, from which pieces of lacquer were chipped off. There was almost no polish left on her little finger, and this bare little nail, contrasted with the carmine on her next finger, fascinated him. He could not tear his eyes away. And long after, in thinking of Florentine, he was to remember that pathetic little nail, grooved and spotted with flecks of white, the nail of an anemic.

For her the magic was only beginning, but for him a feeling of pity killed all desire. I could never harm her, he was thinking. I could never bring myself to harm her.

"Won't you have some hors d'oeuvres?" he suggested.

The next moment, to his great embarrassment, he saw Florentine rummaging in her bag and bringing out all her cosmetics. Between the cutlery and the glasses she had already set out her lipstick, her compact, and even a comb.

"Not here," he muttered, looking around to see if they were being observed by any of their neighbors. "There."

He pointed to a heavy drapery over which LADIES stood out in subdued lights.

"Oh, I see."

With a defiant grin, as if she found Jean's embarrassment totally misplaced, she returned her belongings to her bag and marched off toward the rear of the restaurant.

When he saw her coming back he was even more vexed that he had let her out of his sight. She had applied her make-up liberally; her lips were thick with rouge, and her approach was heralded by a perfume so explosive and vulgar that on every side the patrons looked up and smiled.

Why did I bring her here? he wondered, gripping the edge of the table. I suppose I wanted to see her as she really was and get over any illusions about her. He watched her as she walked toward him, so thin in her tight dress. Did I bring her here to see her eat her fill for once? Or was I hoping to dazzle her so that I could seduce her more easily, and thus make her more wretched than before?

He rose as she reached the table. This mark of gallantry baffled her, and she looked at him with a timid smile.

The cocktail was waiting for her. Her eye was caught by the cherry, which she took out of the glass and placed on the edge of the plate. Then tipping back her head, she swallowed the cocktail at one gulp. She was at once taken by a coughing fit.

Her cheeks burned. And she began to talk. She talked volubly, her elbows on the table, her eyes now dreamy, now bright with happiness. One course followed another, hors d'œuvres, soup, filet of sole, rib-roast, salad, French pastry. And still she talked. At times she stopped to peck at her plate like a bird. She tasted of everything and said that it was all good, but in reality she was too excited to notice any flavor in the food. What intoxicated her most was her own reflection in the mirror behind Jean. She leaned forward frequently to admire her shining eyes, her transparent complexion, her blurred features, and finding herself so desirable, she wanted to convey her sense of triumph to Jean. It needed little more for her to fall in love with a man in whose company she made such a pretty picture.

Toward the end of the meal she began to call him Jean, as if they were old friends. She did not notice that he was scarcely listening to her; she never suspected that he might be bored, although he gave her an occasional hard look. She was really talking to herself, to the burning eyes that offered her so much encouragement, so much approval, so much dizzy joy from the depths of the mirror.

Later on in the evening, after they had got off the bus and decided to go the rest of the way by foot, she grew calmer, almost reticent. The temperature had risen sharply, as often happens at the end of February. It was really a mild evening, although the snow still fell, powdering their clothes, their hair, their eyelashes. Huge flakes sailed through the air, and as Florentine passed under a street lamp she could see their myriad forms. Some were like stars, others reminded her of the monstrance on the altar. It seemed to her that never in her life had she seen such large or beautiful snowflakes. She dared not say anything more, and sometimes a tormenting thought came to her: Had she really made a good impression? Jean seemed so preoccupied that she could not tell.

They had reached the viaduct at Notre-Dame Street, opposite the Saint-Henri station, when Jean stopped and looked up at the mountain, where the lights at this distance twinkled like a handful of stars.

"Have you ever been up on the mountain?" he asked.

Her smile was a bit ironical, a bit constrained. What an odd person he was! She could not make him out. Then her thoughts flew back to the restaurant, where she had had a moment of real happiness, and she too stopped to dream, leaning over the parapet. She too looked up at the mountain; her eyes shining through the snow, blinking at the falling flakes, she too looked up at the mountain, but what she saw was the mirror in the restaurant and her own face, her own soft lips, her own fluffy hair, all reflected as if in a dark sheet of water.

Jean was studying her meanwhile over his shoulder. She left him quite cold now. He had no desire even to kiss her. And he felt that this was a good thing. Since he no longer was driven by overpowering passion, he could disclose his worldly ambitions to her, and intimate what a great distance there was between them.

He put his hand on her wrist and began to laugh.

"You may not think so, my girl," he said, "but I expect to get my foot on the first rung of the ladder pretty soon, and then goodbye to Saint-Henri for me."

A strange misgiving came over her, and she remained pensive, her hands clasped on the parapet. A passing locomotive enveloped them in a cloud of steam. For a moment she felt lost in a boundless fog. Then she calmed herself. Why should she be uneasy? Everything would work out all right. She knew all she had to know for the time being. When Jean had taken her arm as they left the restaurant, she had known a moment of panic. Where will he lead me now? she had wondered. The notion of having to fight him off made her bristle all over. But when she realized that he was taking her straight home, she had recovered her poise. A thought became rooted in her mind, bringing her great comfort. He does not hate me, she said to herself. He wants to be my boyfriend.

She stood beside him, smiling mysteriously, and revelled in the words: my boy-friend. Certain that this odd young man loved her and respected her, she had the courage to hold her own emotions in check. I'm not madly in love with him, she reasoned with herself. I can't say I really love him. His big words and his wild ideas get on my nerves. But I must admit he's not like the other fellows in Saint-Henri. In fact, although she did not know what made him different from other men, it was his very nonconformity that raised him in her esteem.

Slowly they resumed their walk, each following a train of thought so diametrically opposed to the other's that never again would they understand each other.

Jean: *I'll never see her again. Oh, maybe once or twice, not to have it on my conscience, but I must end it soon.*

And she: *I must arrange to invite him to the house.* She was more and more eager to encourage the respectful attitude he had taken tonight. It was all the more necessary as their relations had begun in an extremely unconventional way. *I must invite him to the house. But how can I? It's so small and ugly. And there are so many children underfoot.*

And Jean again: *She's really too pathetic in her shabby little dress. Why don't I drop her right away?*

At Beaudoin Street she stopped in front of an ugly run-down wooden house. On the right a low damp opening led to a small enclosed court where light from the windows fell on bits of refuse and junk. There were about twenty such houses on the street, cut through here and there by similar passages to yards within. At the end of the street a steep embankment led up to the railroad tracks.

"Do you live here or in back?"

"Here."

Florentine pointed to the house nearest the street light, a gloomy building with the paint peeling off. In the harsh glare of the arc lamp, her cheeks looked sunken, her lips bold under the heavy layer of rouge.

"Don't stand there," Jean said.

He pushed her into the shadows. And the shadows were kind to her. They rubbed out all trace of make-up, they made her seem fragile and childlike, they clothed her in mystery and turned her into something remote and dear and sweet. He studied this new face for a moment, holding his breath, and then without warning he took her in his arms. He embraced the shadow of Florentine, the pale mystery of her smile, her weakness, her credulity, the dark recesses of her eyes. His lips caressed her cheeks and sought the warm curve of her mouth. The wind whirled about them, and the snow fell on their faces, melting and running down between their lips.

Florentine sank into his arms. She was so light she might have been a bundle of clothes, an inert thing, soft and damp. Jean tightened his embrace until he could feel her thin-fleshed shoulders under the light coat. His hand ran up her arm. Then gently he repelled the shadowy figure all powdered with snow and smelling of winter and frost.

She remained standing where he had pushed her, her eyes closed. Jean leaned forward and pressed his lips to each eyelid, then quickly turned on his heel and went off down the street.

And Florentine, her heart uplifted, her head in a whirl, was aware of only one thing: *He kissed my eyes.* She could remember other kisses, but never before had she felt lips caressing her eyelids. The schemes she had laid earlier in the evening, her resentment and vexation, all had vanished, leaving her on fire, her hands stretched out toward Jean's retreating figure.

Groping blindly, she reached the door of her house. In the dining-room a tiny thread of light came through the window from the street lamp, and by this she began to undress immediately, moving as quietly as possible in order not to wake up the household, but conscious of the wild drumming in her ears, and fearful above all of breaking the spell. *He kissed my eyes.*

From the depths of the connecting room, however, where the mass of a large bed loomed in the darkness, a voice arose in the night, the voice of one weary of trying to sleep.

"Is that you, Florentine? You're late."

"It's not late," murmured Florentine.

Seated on the edge of the studio couch, she was taking off her stockings, only half conscious of what she was doing. She was floating on top of a huge wave, her heart missing a beat as she rolled with it drunkenly.

"Your father hasn't come home yet. I wonder what he's up to," continued the plaintive voice. "I'm very much afraid he may have lost his job. Anyway he didn't get his pay yesterday. And Eugène——" she added with a sigh, "Eugène enlisted in the army, Florentine. Oh dear, what's to become of us?"

Florentine was still riding the wave. When it tossed her very high, she felt she could hardly breath. From now on these tiresome problems could not touch her. Would she ever feel the old heartache as she listened to these midnight confidences, whispered through the silence heavy with the breathing of sleeping children? She was cradled on a wave of joy, a long, smooth-flowing wave. And when she sank in the troughs, surrendering herself, she was like a wing, a feather, a bit of fluff borne along ever more swiftly.

"I don't know what's to become of us, Florentine."

He kissed my cheeks, my eyes, and his lips were so soft!

"If your father loses his job again, we'll have to get along on what you can give us, my poor Florentine. We can't go back on relief."

There was a long, painful silence, broken only by gusts of wind rattling the windows.

Again Rose-Anna raised her voice to speak, but now it was to herself she spoke in the solitude of her bed. Near as Florentine was, she gave up all hope of reaching out to her for sympathy. Florentine was perhaps too weary to talk, or too sleepy to pay attention. Rose-Anna made excuses for the girl, and yet she had to speak aloud. She could not lie there alone in the darkness without speaking, without disburdening her heart.

"The landlord's given us notice to move on the first of May," she said.

And her mind was so troubled that even if no one had been near she would have spoken aloud. "What will become of us if your father can't find another job now that we must move? Rents are getting higher and higher, and now——" She hesitated on the brink of still another confession. And then she dropped it into the unfathomable darkness, the blind, deaf, pitiless darkness: "When there were only ten of us it was hard enough to get along, but soon we'll be eleven——"

Florentine came to with a start. Gone was her wave of joy. She suppressed it grimly.

Her throat dry, she gasped:

"You're expecting again?" Her tone was almost indignant.

For some time past she had been eyeing her mother on the sly, but Rose-Anna's figure had been deformed by so much childbearing that it was hard to tell whether she was growing larger. At times Florentine had suspected the truth, but she would dismiss the idea, thinking: It can't be that. Mother's over forty!

"Toward the end of May," said Rose-Anna.

The admission seemed painful, but she regained command of herself quickly. She asked: "Will you be sorry to have another little sister, Florentine?"

"Good gracious, Mother, don't you think there are enough of us?"

The blunt question escaped her. Florentine regretted it promptly, she would have taken it back if she could, but it hung in the air in the silence of the room, it spoke louder than the wind moaning at the panes. The darkness seemed to repeat it over and over again.

Rose-Anna turned over on her pillow. It was damp with sweat. "Not so loud, you'll wake the children," she begged. Then after a pause, she whispered: "What do you want, Florentine? We can't do as we like in this world; we do the best we can."

That's not so, thought Florentine. I'm going to do as I like. I won't be miserably poor like Mother.

The wave of joy swept her up again, carrying her high, high in the air, singing in her ears, its soft melody running on and on through the night. She put on her nightdress and slipped into bed beside her sister, Yvonne. The little girl's eyes were closed, but her mouth was quivering. At thirteen, Yvonne was already engaged in a lonely struggle to find the key to human mysteries.

Florentine moved her icy feet against those of the little girl, then, heavy-eyed, she murmured:

"Wait and see, Mother. Don't worry, we'll manage somehow. We've gone through worse troubles."

And she fell asleep almost immediately, dropping off to one last intoxicating memory: *He kissed my eyes.*

Yvonne lay panting beside her, motionless but wide awake. Her eyes stared up at the ceiling, and her hands were pressed against her chest to push back a weight that threatened to stifle her.

CHAPTER VII

A S SHE WATCHED him puff away at his cigarette, sitting calmly beside the kitchen stove, yesterday's paper open on his lap, Rose-Anna felt very bitter.

From the heavy sweater buttoned loosely over his deep chest, the column of his neck rose white and smooth, like that of a young man. His complexion was fresh, with hardly a wrinkle. She resented his having remained young and blooming, while she showed so many signs of fatigue and hard wear.

He was only two years younger than she, a difference in age that had seemed unimportant when they were married. Now he looked about ten years younger. With a feeling of despair Rose-Anna began to poke at the fire. As she took the lid off the stove her lips quivered over the glowing embers.

The flame leaped up with a sharp crackle. Azarius raised his head. He caught a whiff of dried wood-shavings—a small supply was stacked in front of the oven door—and of toast, which he liked best of all. He gave a sigh of well-being as he thought of other cold mornings when he sat waiting for a fare at the taxi-stand. This was more than Rose-Anna could bear.

"Why in heaven's name did you have to give up your job? This is no time to look for trouble. Florentine is sticking to her job!"

So began their day. A pale sun shone through the kitchen window. So their days had begun so many times before. Rose-Anna, hearing the sound of her own voice, wondered whether she were not repeating the phrases of old quarrels. But Eugène's little cot-bed, leaning against the wall, reminded her that her eldest son had gone, that she was growing old and that Azarius had not changed a whit.

"You're right in my way too," she said. "How do you expect me to get breakfast? You might push your chair back at least."

His smile had a tinge of surprise; he was not accustomed to reproaches any more than he was aware of wrong-doing.

"Give me a little time," said he. "I have good prospects. Can't a man think about his affairs?"

"A fine way of thinking about your affairs, sitting by the fire!"

"Now look here, Mother, I might as well sit here as anywhere else. I might as well be seated while I make my plans."

"Make plans!" she said in a withering tone, and the sound of her slippers on the floor stopped abruptly.

"Make plans! Can't you do anything else? All your life you've been making plans. And where did it get you? You're no further ahead. You think making plans helps poor people like us?"

A dull pain took her by surprise; she stopped talking, and pressed her hand to her bulging waist.

"Go lie down again, Mother; I'll do your chores today."

His swagger was gone. He had not lost his sense of being misunderstood, nor his underlying self-confidence, nor his easy optimism. But he had lost his bounce. He wanted to be forgiven. It would have been hard to find even a remote resemblance in this contrite figure, huddled by the stove, to the spellbinder of the Two Records. He was always thus in the bosom of his family, as if his home were a bed of thorns where it did him no good to pluck out one because they multiplied so fast. Even the intonation of his voice was different from the one he used outside to speak his mind, to express his daring and generous views. At home his tone was conciliatory, apologetic.

"Well, if you must know the truth, my good woman," he sighed, "I got the sack. But it's just as well. I would have given it up anyway. How could I give my attention to my own affairs when I was tied up in that outfit from morning till night?"

Rose-Anna turned her face away quickly. She had had time to cool down, but it was just as well for him not to know it too soon. As she busied herself with setting the kitchen table, she recalled a remark of old Madame Lacasse: "You'll never hear a hard word from Azarius. And for that you can forgive him many faults, my child."

It was true, mused Rose-Anna. Azarius had never spoken a word to her in anger.

"All right, let's forget it. Try to make yourself useful at any rate," she said without rancor.

She sat down to her breakfast in a corner by the stove. In this way she managed to eat only a crust of bread and set aside a larger portion for the children without making her self-sacrifice known. Then she began to sway back and forth as if she were in a rocker, an old habit, even when she sat in a straight chair. Any movement seemed to help her think.

"Listen," she said, "it might be a good idea for me to look around for a house as long as you're here to watch the children."

She was not asking for advice, for as soon as she had spoken, her decision struck her as reasonable and proper.

"We must have a place to live," she added, "however badly off we are."

A bit of saliva ran down the corners of her mouth. She licked it up with her tongue and rose from her chair, a round little woman with a fine head, courageous brown eyes, and lines that came and went between her brows.

Over her housedress she threw on her old black coat, now greenish in color; she took her hat from the dining-room buffet, and picked up a worn brown handbag that Florentine had cast off. As her eldest daughter waked up at that moment, she brought her her shoes and stockings and told her to hurry, for it was after eight-thirty.

Florentine, emerging from sleep, looked about her with a slight frown, then, becoming aware of the tumultuos joy that dwelt within her, she bounded to the edge of the bed.

"Quick, you're late," said Rose-Anna.

She passed through the kichen on the run, as if she had to catch a train, pushing aside the little ones who clung to her skirt crying: "Bring me a chocolate bunny, Mamma! Bring me a flute, Mamma!"

They were all old enough to go to school except little Gisèle, but Rose-Anna had been keeping them at home for several weeks, Lucille because she had no overshoes and Albert because he had a bad cold. As for little Daniel, he had been wasting away for two months now, without any outward signs of serious illness. Philippe, who had reached the age of fifteen, obstinately refused to go back to school. Rose-Anna had caught him smoking his father's cigarette butts and reading detective stories.

When she reached the sidewalk Rose-Anna turned around to look at them huddled in the doorway, little Daniel half-dressed, because his shirt and breeches had not dried enough during the night to be put on. Only Yvonne was not there. Awaking at dawn, the little girl always washed under the cold-water tap in the kitchen, dressed quickly, slipped a crust of bread into her school bag, then, noiselessly as a shadow, flitted away to early morning mass before going to the convent. She took communion every morning. In good weather and bad she was always the first to leave the house. When they tried to keep her at home on very cold days, she would fly into the most terrible rage, an extra-ordinary sight in such a self-effacing little girl, usually so gentle. One day when Rose-Anna had used force to keep her from going out, she had burst into tears, sobbing that if she missed one mass she would be deserting Our Lord in his torments. Rose-Anna had understood the simple story: in Yvonne's classroom at the convent there was a heart pierced with thorns, and every little girl who went to mass had the right to pull one out as she came to school. With tears streaming down her white face Yvonne had said: "Oh Mamma, there are so many wicked people who put thorns in the heart of Jesus every day. Let me go to mass."

The mother had never again opposed the child. But in the evenings, weary though she was after the long day's work, she had made a good warm coat for Yvonne out of some old material, with a double interlining. And from then on, when Yvonne ran off into the chilly dawn, she had the consolation of knowing that the little girl was warmly dressed.

Rose-Anna looked back at the children from the sidewalk. They were surprised to see her go, because she practically never went out. Daniel cried out in his weak treble: "A flute, Mamma, don't forget!" Gisèle had begun to cry, but Azarius stopped this by lifting her in his arms and making her wave her hand. Rose-Anna's anger dissolved. As she went off, she resolved to buy something, perhaps not the flute Daniel had been begging for for so long, but possibly four little chocolate bunnies, as a foretaste of Easter. She walked gingerly through the soft snow, stopping sometimes to catch her breath or lean against a wall.

The sun had grown warmer since the beginning of March, and the snow had turned to slush in places.

She crept along slowly and wearily. Her confidence was beginning to weaken; her courage was oozing away. Already her hopes seemed futile. The cloudless sky and the softness of the air did not move her. She foresaw the coming of spring by other signs. The spring was in a measure her enemy. What had it meant for her? During all her married life two events were always associated with the spring: she was almost always pregnant, and in that condition she was obliged to look for a new place to live. Every spring they moved.

The first few years they had always looked for a better place. It had irked Azarius, and her too, to live in such small quarters. As soon as the winter was over they began to long for something cleaner, lighter, and larger, too, as the family had increased. Azarius especially had extremely romantic notions. He would speak of having a house with a little garden where he could plant cabbages and carrots. And she, being a country girl at heart, would brim over with joy at the prospect of seeing vegetables grow under her windows. But this had never come about; she had never seen anything but factory chimneys and other ramshackle houses from her windows.

Later, when Florentine and Eugène were old enough to go to school, they reached the point where they never moved of their own volition, but because they were behind in their rent and must find something less expensive. From year to year they looked for cheaper and cheaper lodgings, while rents went up and habitable dwellings became more and more scarce.

In the old days when she went out to look for a house, she had very clear ideas of what she wanted. She wanted a veranda, a yard for the children to play in, a sitting-room. And Azarius used to encourage her. "Get the best place you can, Rose-Anna. Take the very best." But for a long time now her activities had been limited to finding a home, no matter what kind. Walls, a floor, a ceiling, some sort of shelter.

A bitter thought came to her: the larger their family had grown, the smaller and darker their home.

Azarius had been one of the first to be affected by the depression, for he was a carpenter by trade. Too proud to take any old job, he had looked for work only in trades allied to his own. At length he had lost hope, and applied for public relief.

Those were dark times, thought Rose-Anna. The rent allowance had been almost nothing. The landlords laughed when they were offered ten dollars a month rent for a four-room house. So Azarius always agreed to pay the difference of a few dollars. An incurable optimist, he would say: "I'm sure to make a little money somehow; we'll get along." But in the end he had found nothing to do, or the money had gone to stop up other holes. He could not keep his promises, and once again a furious landlord would put them out in the spring.

The sun poured down on the street. Long slender icicles hung from the eaves, shining like crystal. Some fell off with a crackling sound and broke into slivers at Rose-Anna's feet. She moved slowly among the pieces, looking for something to hold on to, in terror of falling. Then her feet encountered the soft slush again, and she plodded through it laboriously, but no longer afraid that she might slip.

How she had loved the spring once upon a time! There had been two happy spring seasons in her life. The one in which she had met Azarius, who even then was so lighthearted that old Madame Laplante, her mother, had prophesied: "I don't think he'll ever amount to much. He's much too inclined to look on the bright side of things." Then the spring when Florentine had been born, her first child. All the sweetness of those two springs came back to her, so clearly that at times she thought she could even smell the fragrance of the budding leaves. She remembered pushing Florentine's go-cart on a sunny day, while the neighbors shook their heads over the laces and ribbons and said: "You're going to a lot of trouble; when you have your tenth you won't bother about all that."

Rose-Anna tried very hard to walk more quickly. People were sweeping or shoveling the snow away from their doors. Several of them recognized her as she passed, and greeted her cordially: "Hello, Madame Lacasse! Are you house-hunting?"

Others seemed to be enjoying the prospect of warm weather, and said dreamily: "This time it's the real thing, eh? Spring is here!"

"Yes," answered Rose-Anna, "but we'd better not depend on it."

"Oh, of course we'll still have frost, but it's good as long as it lasts."

"Yes," she agreed, forcing a smile. "In the meantime we can save on fuel."

She went on her way, pursuing the thread of her own thoughts. It was not that lodgings were hard to find. Wherever she looked Rose-Anna saw "For Rent" signs. Once a year the whole quarter seemed infected with a wanderlust that could be gratified in no other way than by a universal migration on moving day. At that time two houses out of five bore the same dirty signs: "For Rent, for Rent, for Rent."

Rose-Anna met several other women on the same errand walking along slowly, studying the signs. Many families were already looking for new lodgings; in a few weeks there would be hundreds of them. Rose-Anna cautioned herself to hurry, in order to avoid the great April rush. And yet she could not bring herself to enter any of the houses. She would approach a door, glance inside the vestibule, and then walk on. Either the run-down condition of the house would dishearten her, or else it would seem clean and well kept, and she would say to herself that it wasn't worth while asking the price; it would probably be too dear for them.

Nevertheless she forced herself to enter one brick house on St. Ferdinand Street. When she came out she felt giddy and faint. The smell of baby clothes drying over the stove and the sight of the lavatory, without a window, opening on the kitchen, had been so revolting that she thought she would be sick. And they wanted sixteen dollars a month for that hole! She had noticed that none of the rooms were light except those giving on the street. The others looked out on an enclosed court. Sixteen dollars a month, she mused. Out of the question. We could never manage it.

And yet she began patiently to reckon everything out again. Rose-Anna carried in her head the exact figure of their tiny income, which was made up largely of Florentine's wages. She also knew by heart the total sum of their absolutely necessary expenses. She could have said, almost to the penny: "I need so and so much to carry me through this month." And she would surely have added at once: "To make ends meet." Even in her most secret thoughts she used this ambitious phrase that represented success, for she had a strong instinct, like all poor people, to mistrust figures. She refused to bow before their immutable character.

Absorbed in her own interior struggle, she passed several houses that were to let without seeing them. Her gait became more brisk as she thought of how to cut certain expenditures, but with all her scheming the total always exceeded their resources. It was at this point that Rose-Anna, prisoner of her cares, her torments, her figures, but still an imaginative woman, escaped from reality in spite of all her troubles. Simple, childish ideas came to her. She pictured some rich uncle she had never known, who would die and leave her a great fortune; she fancied herself finding a pocketbook crammed with bills which she would naturally return to its owner, thereby earning a large reward. This obsession became so vivid that she began to scan the pavement with a feverish eye. Then she became ashamed of her fantastic notions, and went to the opposite extreme, becoming extremely practical.

Whatever the dream, Rose-Anna always returned quickly to her calculations.

She turned into Saint-Henri Place so absorbed in her arithmetic that she plunged across, ignoring the streetcars, the railroad warning bell and the harsh smoke that weighed on her eyelids. When a truck grazed her, she was more startled than terrified. In her eyes was the look of an absent-minded bookkeeper whose attention is distracted from his accounts for only a moment.

On reaching the sidewalk, she went over her sums from the beginning. And it was then, for the first time since Eugène had enlisted, that she remembered the twenty dollars a month of which he had spoken. Compressing her lips, she turned the idea down firmly. But a little later, with a gasp of shame, she realized that those twenty dollars had already been swallowed up; she had spent them in her imagination to the last penny.

As if to confound her, suddenly she saw a recruiting poster on the wall of a store, representing a soldier with fixed bayonet. His eyes were shining and his mouth was open in a rallying cry. In the sky over his head, great black letters were printed: "Let's go, fellows! Our country needs us!"

Rose-Anna was overcome with emotion. The young man looked

like her Eugène. The mouth, the eyes were the same! Spelling out the words, she thought they read : "Let's go, fellows! Our mothers need us!" She clasped her hands over her coat. Eugène seemed to be standing there in sight of the whole quarter, uttering a cry of anguish that trumpeted their poverty to the four corners of the world.

Her steps uncertain now, her heart sinking, she walked toward the slums behind the Saint-Henri station.

A few minutes' walk brought her to Workman Street, so appropriately named. Work, man, she thought, wear yourself out, suffer, live in filth and ugliness.

Rose-Anna picked her way past the gray-brick tenements, a solid block of houses with identical windows and doors at regular intervals.

A swarm of ragged children were playing on the sidewalks in the midst of refuse. Thin, sad-looking women appeared at evil-smelling doorways, blinking at the sunlight that lay among the garbage cans. Others with listless faces sat at the windows, giving suck to their babies. Everywhere there were windowpanes stuffed with rags or sealed with oiled paper. Everywhere there were shrill voices, the wailing of infants, or cries of pain coming from behind tight-closed shutters.

All the houses—wrongly called houses, for it was impossible to distinguish one from another save by the number over the door, a pathetic attempt at individuality—all the houses in the block, not two or three out of five, but *all* of them were to let.

Every spring this frightful street emptied itself; every spring it filled up again.

Borne on the wind, the sickly sweet smell of tobacco-curing at the cigarette factories near by assailed her nostrils. But pervasive as this was, the air also reeked with the acrid smell of white lead and linseed oil, a foul stench that made its way in through the mouth as well as the nose. It lay thick on her tongue and parched her throat.

No, Rose-Anna said to herself, Florentine would never consent to come here. . . . Retracing her steps, she walked over toward Convent Street, and found herself on a quiet little avenue, flanked with middle-class dwellings. There were lace curtains hanging at the windows; the blinds were drawn halfway; there were copper name plates at the doors, and here and there, on the window sills, were healthy potted plants that had more air and space, thought Rose-Anna, than the children she had seen a few minutes before on St. Ferdinand Street. She knew full well that this quiet little oasis was not for them. Besides, none of the houses were for rent. But she breathed more freely here, and began to take heart. Her visit to Workman Street had after all comforted her. It had given her some satisfaction to feel that they were not yet reduced to the lowest depths of poverty.

On her right stood the church of Saint-Thomas Aquinas. Her fatigue was so great, her need to sit down and think things over so imperative that she went in and collapsed on the first bench in the rear of the nave.

At first her thoughts wandered incoherently, without direction or purpose. Then her strength returned.

She said to herself: I must pray, I'm in church. Sliding forward to the edge of the bench, she knelt down and began to say her beads.

But even as she whispered the *Aves* her mind went off at a tangent. She continued to move her lips, but in reality she had begun to address a silent colloquy to no statue or relic or presence.

"It's not fair to my children," she was saying. "Eugène never had a chance; it's not fair to him or Florentine either. At her age, I was not asked to support my parents." And she added: "Hear me, O Lord!"

Only rarely did she pray directly to God; ordinarily she preferred to ask the intercession of the saints, who were more familiar to her through pictures and statues. Of God himself she could form no picture, and for years she had not even attempted it, for try as she might, all that came to her was a vision of cotton-wool clouds, with a dove flying over them. But at this moment she addressed herself to the white-bearded old man of her childhood, the one who is God the Father in the group of the Holy Trinity. Her needs seemed too urgent to be entrusted to intermediaries.

She said all sorts of things without trying to arrange them in order, but with a natural tendency to justify herself and to disarm Divine Providence. "I have done my duty, Our Father, I have had eleven children. I have eight living and three who died very young, perhaps because I was already worn out when I had them. Will the new baby be as sickly at the last three, O Lord?"

Suddenly she remembered that God knew her whole life and that it was not necessary to go into all the details. But she also thought: Perhaps He's forgotten. So many people call on Him in their hour of need. And so the only flaw in her faith came from this frank supposition that God was as distraught and as harassed as she was, and could only give half an ear to the prayers of human beings.

She took her time when she came to material problems, for it seemed to her that a certain address was perhaps as necessary in prayer as in any other petition. All this was instinctive, and more or less buried in her subconscious. It would have embarrassed her to ask for anything for herself, but for her family she was not afraid to set forth just what she wanted. This was where she drew the line between spiritual and temporal benefits.

A picture of Yvonne flashed through her mind. She stopped praying with a sudden pang. Perhaps she was one of those people the child meant when she said that they drove thorns into the heart of the Savior?

But thinking it over, she quickly rejected the idea. At bottom her intuition told her that God was gentle and at one with her. Her whole life set her apart from the unhealthy piety of little Yvonne. She felt relieved. Her prayer was less an attempt to throw off her burdens than a humble way of diverting the responsibility for them toward Him who had imposed them on her.

With firm tread she walked to the font, sprinkled herself, and then went out, taking her first breath of spring air with a kind of innocent surprise.

As soon as she reached the porch of the church she felt her spirits rising. It was still early in the season. Since Azarius was not working she could if need be spend the whole day and other days as well looking for a suitable house. Her energy came back together with her old habit of making the best of the slightest advantages that offered.

The street was filled with sunlight. She saw it flooding the house she hoped to find. Timidly at first, she could not have said how, she began to imagine a little room with windows on the south, where she could place her sewing machine. Then the sunlight reached the dining-room, it crept toward the kitchen, and entered there, falling on geraniums in earthenware pots. It made the kettles glisten, it blazed on a white tablecloth, it shone on a little girl in a highchair.

Rose-Anna shook her head. The corners of her mouth rose in a melancholy smile. What she had just imagined was the home she had lived in as a bride; the child was Florentine; the sunlight was of her twentieth year.

All clouded with visions her eyes returned to the quiet street in front of the church. She went down the steps. Then she walked on rapidly, clutching her poor old handbag to her side bravely, almost defiantly.

CHAPTER VIII

F LORENTINE WAS WAITING on Emmanuel and Jean Lévesque, her sharp regular teeth flashing in a bright smile.

Every chair at the counter was occupied, and behind the row of people gulping down their food others stood, waiting to slip into a gap in the ranks. Housewives, determined to grab the first vacant place, gripped their packages and kept twitching their heads from right to left. A few women had deposited their purchases on the floor and were standing guard behind diners who seemed about to finish their meal. Men in working clothes stood in the background away from the pungent fumes, with a look of resignation on their faces, with the grave, anxious demeanor they assume when they present their cards to the timekeeper at the factory gate, or when they enter a crowded taproom.

As soon as one patron got up, another took his seat; in a trice his place was set with a glass of water and a paper napkin; a green blouse leaned toward him, then went off in a crackle of starched cotton; the waitress shouted an order into the kitchen telephone; the dumb-waiter creaked and a plate of steaming food appeared at the edge of a trap door.

The cash register rang almost constantly. Customers urged the waitresses to hurry or tried to catch their eye by snapping their fingers.

Florentine nevertheless refused to be hurried. The midday rush left her unperturbed. For her the bustle and noise subsided as she waited for Jean to arrive, and when he did come, she wove her thoughts around him. Leaning sideways against the counter, she was carrying on a conversation with the two young men. Sometimes a great clatter of dishes prevented her from catching what they said; she would bend over farther, watching their lips out of the corner of her eye; then straighten up slowly with an arch look. Underneath the paper rose stuck in her hair, her trained ear quivered to every sound that required her attention; the impact of a spoon on the counter, a foot shuffling on the tiled floor, the waspish remarks of a fat woman calling to her. Florentine would shrug her shoulders, wrinkle her nose, then bestow another smile on Jean and Emmanuel.

This morning her face had unusual animation. There was a kind of glow about her, so that for once her make-up seemed natural, and set off the brilliance of her eyes. Her face was so expressive that Jean could see exactly what was passing through her mind. He knew that she was thinking of their kiss in the storm, and as it came back to her she became even more vivacious. At times her shining eyes met his with an eloquent appeal. Then in order to keep Jean guessing, she would try her wiles on Emmanuel; she would address the young soldier very amiably, even boldly, as if her relationship with Jean were sufficient to give her certain rights over his friends. Moreover she was too eager for admiration not to encourage Emmanuel's spontaneous homage, although she intended merely to attract Jean more by seeming attractive to Emmanuel.

Her eyes darted from one to the other, her smile hung suspended between them. Warming to the game, Emmanuel began to tease her.

"Haven't I met you before, Mademoiselle Florentine?"

"That may be," she laughed, tossing her head, "the sidewalks of Saint-Henri are narrow and lots of people go by."

"Haven't we spoken before?"

"Maybe. But anyway I don't remember."

Then she began to question him rapidly in her turn. He gave her off-hand answers, more interested in the play of her features and the interest she showed in him than in her words themselves, which rang out above the clatter of the dishes with an occasional falsetto.

"How long have you been in the army?" she asked, while she rubbed her nails against her uniform, examined them critically in the light, and polished them again. She struck a pose of benevolent interest.

"Six months," said he.

Whenever he spoke to her, he leaned over his plate to make sure that she heard him, then drew back again in a rocking motion that made him self-conscious.

"D'you like it?"

"Oh, it's all right."

"I suppose the drill and everything is a bore after a while, eh?" Emmanuel indulged in a smile.

"Do you expect to go overseas soon? I hear some of the boys have sailed."

There was no secret passion for adventure, no curiosity or admiration in her question, but he misjudged the light in her shining green eyes and suddenly felt that she was attracted by the unknown as much as he.

"I hope so," he said. "I want to go overseas very much."

"You'll see plenty of trouble over there, I bet."

Then she began to smile.

"What's your name, by the way?"

"Oh," exclaimed Emmanuel, "you've forgotten already!"

She was completely unconcerned, seemed to be trying to remember, then murmured:

"Oh yes, Létourneau."

She glanced at Jean. And her eyes said: You see, he likes me too. There are others, but I like you best. Only I want you to know that you're not the only man in the world. But I like you best. Her eyes softened, she fluttered her lids and tried to sweep him off his feet with a glance. She wanted to remind him of their great moment, a moment full of wind and cold and snow, when they were alone together in the storm. The snow whirled before her eyes. Then she composed herself and spoke again to Emmanuel.

"It must be nice to get away on leave. How long did you say your furlough was?"

"Only a few days."

"Ah, only a few days. They go fast, don't they?"

"Yes," he murmured.

Intrigued by the gleam in her eye and the spasmodic movement of her hands which were never still, he wondered if she were not offering him an opportunity to meet her again. The blood rose to his cheeks. He was so conscious of his shyness that he could think of nothing to say. Vexed with himself, he began to crumble a piece of bread.

"How's the chicken?" Florentine asked, mischievously.

Jean answered for his friend in a hard, biting voice. "You there," he asked, "do you go out often? Have you many sweethearts?"

The smile stuck to Florentine's lips, but her blue-veined hands turned white as she clenched them tightly. Why this slap in the face? Hadn't she been nice to him? And nice to Emmanuel too out of regard for him? She'd gone out of her way to be pleasant, letting other customers wait while she took care of them! How she hated him at that moment! As much as she had hated him the first day she ever saw him, with his mocking brown eyes, his wicked, unfathomable brown eyes! And the cold, flinty lines of his mouth! And yet how she loved those eyes and that mouth! And how entrancing to remember that that arrogant mouth had touched her eyelids! She was entranced and bewildered and humiliated all at once. Would she never be able to make him suffer as he made her suffer? She must not risk losing him. And yet she couldn't take that sort of thing without a murmur.

"That's my business," she said lamely, with a pitiful smile, a pale ghost of a smile. Her thin chest was heaving under the cotton uniform, and all the life had gone out of her face; her eyes were riveted to a scratch on the counter, which she scraped with her nail; her feet tapped the floor. She was lost, lost in an old nightmare that was always ready to pounce on her when she was unhappy.

"Of course you won't tell us," continued Jean relentlessly, "about the boy-friends you meet after hours, will you? Would we have a chance, Emmanuel or me, I wonder?"

She looked him straight in the eye. "That's a stupid question," she said.

She busied herself with the sauce bottles, the salt and pepper shakers, lifting them up and putting them down and wiping them with her dishcloth. An icy hand seemed to encircle her bare neck, and she was so chagrined not to be able to find words with which to snap back at him that she turned her head away. In the old days she had known just how to parry such thrusts. What had come over her? It was silly not to have an answer on the tip of her tongue.

"Pay no attention to him, Mademoiselle Florentine," said Emmanuel. "He's just trying to make you angry. He doesn't mean a thing."

"I am sort of angry," she answered, but she was somewhat mollified by the suggestion that Jean was trying to tease her. "I'm pretty mad. It wouldn't take much more to get me hopping mad. And then I'd tell you where you get off at!"

"Get off at!" Jean repeated, shaken with laughter.

"Yes, get off at. I talk as I please," she retorted. "I don't talk fancy."

"Pay no attention to him," said Emmanuel again.

He stretched his hand out across the counter.

"No," she said, "of course I won't pay any attention to him. Of course not," she repeated, overcome with embarrassment and trying to speak more correctly. "But still you're——"

She gave Emmanuel a lukewarm smile of appreciation.

"But still your manners are better than his."

"What do you think of that!" sneered Jean.

She stiffened.

"Now would you mind telling me what you'll have for dessert? I haven't got all day!" She looked off into space and recited in a monotone: "Apricot pie, raisin pie, apple pie, banana custard. And lemon pie," she went on, shaking her curls impatiently. "Make up your mind."

She turned on her heel and flounced off, her long silky hair catching glints of the nickel and copper in her passage.

"Ask her to go out with you," Jean whispered in Emmanuel's ear.

"Don't be a fool," said Emmanuel.

The mirror showed their heads against a background of pink lingerie. Their eyes met there, Emmanuel's blue ones filled with doubt.

"She'll put me in my place," he said.

But he did not quite refuse to lend himself to the game. Emboldened by Jean's self-complacency, he considered making her a pretty speech, saying something gentle and courtly that would win her regard. His face in the mirror showed no confidence, but a will to be gay, to have a little fling.

"No, she won't!" said Jean.

He was on the point of telling how he had made Florentine's acquaintance. It was on the tip of his tongue to say: "It's easy. You've no idea how easy." Then he gave it up. In the depths of his confused nature curiosity began again to prompt him. If only he could remove the last bit of confidence he still had in human beings, the last bit of friendship he felt and inspired, he would have cut the last bonds that tied him to his fellows. He would be alone in a state of voluptuous disenchantment, in which his ego could blossom freely.

"Ask her," he insisted.

"I don't know if I should," said Emmanuel sadly.

At the other end of the passage Florentine had bent down to pick up a stack of dirty dishes. The veins in her arms stood out on her delicate skin. A look of dejection had spread over her face, settling into old lines around her eyes and forehead, and at the corners of her mouth. Banished for a moment by her forced smile, it returned again to haunt her eyes.

"I don't know," said Emmanuel.

And to himself he thought: Let her alone. I wish everybody would let her alone. She once had a happy smile, I'm sure. May she have it again! May her eyes look untroubled as she goes through life. I wish everybody would let her alone, by God!

"Ask her," urged Jean. "And if she refuses you, I'll ask her next. Hey, Florentine!" he called.

She waved her hand in a gesture that might have indicated anger or impatience or resignation. As she approached them she picked up other plates and when at last she reached them she was carrying a pile of dirty dishes as high as her chin. A damp strand of hair was plastered to her cheek.

"What do you want now?"

"Emmanuel has something to ask you," began Jean.

She put down the plates, and shook her hair away from her face, giving him an inviting look. But her inflection was derisive, not too encouraging.

"Well, let him ask me," she said.

Let her alone! Let her be natural and lose that hungry, defensive manner, thought Emmanuel. I'd like to see her happy for a little while. I'd like to dance with her too. She's graceful and thin. I'll bet she dances well.

"Do you like to dance, Mademoiselle Florentine?"

"Is that what you wanted to ask me?"

Her face darkened, but there was a spark of curiosity in her eyes. Breathing hard, she looked at him guardedly, yet excited as she always was by the least mark of attention from a man.

"So that's what you had on your mind."

Let her alone, he thought. We ought to go away and let her alone.

Then aloud: "I'm sure you like to dance."

In spite of herself, her hips began to sway as if in time to jazz in the distance. But all she could think of was dancing in the arms of Jean. She had never danced with him. Some day she would dance with him. Maybe Jean had primed Emmanuel to ask her what she liked to do. But then again it might be a trap.

She looked at Jean through her lashes.

"It depends on who I dance with," she said.

Emmanuel was embarrassed more by Jean's ironical attitude than by the girl's apparent agitation. Carried away by excessive timidity, he blurted out a question he had never planned to ask, and which he regretted as soon as it passed his lips:

"Are you free tomorrow evening, Mademoiselle Florentine?"

"What for?"

Her delicate nostrils quivered. And suddenly she perceived how very domineering Jean was. He was showing her how tough he could be, but she too could be tough and unbending. She pointed a finger at Jean and said harshly:

"He told you to ask me that, didn't he?"

Her lips were set in a scowl. She'd show Jean Lévesque that she didn't give a rap for him! Why shouldn't she too pretend that their kiss in the storm was only a joke, and that she had forgotten all about it? But suppose he left her and never came back? What good would it do her to get even with him?

"Oh, you're both crazy!" she said bitterly. "I never met such a pair of lunatics!"

Her lips still bore faint traces of a smile, but her eyes flashed with anger and pain. She glared at Jean, her mouth working.

"No," she said. "I wouldn't go if you invited me to the Normandie Roof, so there."

"Look here, not really," said Jean.

"I mean no. No to both of you, no, no, no."

Her voice rose. A couple of young men at the counter laughed and egged her on.

"That's it, Mademoiselle Florentine," said one, "hand it to them."

"No," she continued, raising her voice shrilly. "Who do you take me for?" She bit her lip. "Some people don't think we're good enough for them. And they're not so far away. I could name them."

Marguerite passed at this moment, dragging a huge can of marshmallow across the floor, and interposed:

"Now, now, don't be so mad. You're making a fool of yourself. "You're making a fool of yourself," she repeated, but she threw a reproachful glance at Emmanuel and Jean.

"I'll be angry if I please," said Florentine. "I'm funny, am I? Don't you think I mind having people make fun of me? Some folks will do anything for a joke!"

"I didn't mean it as a joke," said Emmanuel.

"No? Then why did you start it all? I'm not here for fun!"

"That's it! Let him have it!" guffawed a young workman.

"Bet your life I'll let him have it!"

"There's nothing to get angry about," Emmanuel tried to explain.

"No, nothing to get angry about!" she answered ironically. "That's what you think!"

As a matter of fact she was not addressing him at all. Her burning eyes clung to Jean's face. He had lowered his lids and was smiling coldly, as if he were beyond her reach, beyond all attack. With a lazy flick of the finger he spilled his cigarette ashes on the floor. He's mine, he's mine, she was thinking, terrified of losing him, and yet she was so resentful of his power over her heart that she lashed out in all directions with heavy sarcasm.

"We're here to wait on you. All right!" she continued. "But not to listen to your stupid remarks! We don't have to stand for that!"

Her cheeks were shining, and she kept tossing her head to shake her hair loose from her face. At last she pushed her long curls back with one hand, and arching her neck, gave Emmanuel an expectant smile in which there were still traces of defiance.

"Get angry, I don't care," she said. "All right, get angry, I don't care."

"Ah, but it's you who are angry," said Emmanuel gently.

Lifting her arms, she patted the ringlets at her temples.

"Me angry? Not a bit! Not the least little bit!"

"I wouldn't want you to be angry," said Emmanuel.

"But I tell you I'm not angry!"

"Because if you're not angry," said Emmanuel, "I'd like to see you again."

He was thinking of the party his parents planned to give him before he went away. In a rash mood, without consulting his mother, he decided to invite Florentine. Why not? She must have a party dress, something for a special occasion. And she's so pretty. It gave him pleasure to imagine the consideration he would show her, little attentions that might efface the unfortunate impression of their first meeting. It pleased him too to plan how he would introduce Florentine to his friends: 'This is Mademoiselle Florentine," he would say. And perhaps he would add: "This is my girl-friend." Why not? If the girl by chance should commit some little blunders, he would not be offended. The prospect of the party, which had bored him earlier, seemed to take on unexpected interest now that he thought of inviting Florentine. He even foresaw that he would probably take her home after the party.

Moistening his lips, he leaned over his plate and gave her a warm, straightforward smile.

"Do you know what would give me great pleasure, Mademoiselle Florentine?"

"No, I don't."

"Very great pleasure——"

"I haven't the slightest idea."

"My mother is giving a party tomorrow night." He touched Jean's sleeve. "And we were wondering, my friend and I, if you would care to come."

"At your house?" she said in astonishment.

"Will you say yes?" asked Emmanuel.

A smile of satisfaction passed over her lips. She averted her head.

"Just a minute," she said. "I don't know—I don't . . ."

But already she saw herself in her new black silk dress, in her best stockings and her patent-leather pumps. At last Jean would see her well dressed, not in her old rags. "So that's what you had on your minds, you two," she murmured. And she prolonged the delicious moment of hesitation, a moment in which she could still pretend to be haughty and refuse the invitation.

"Will you come?" asked Emmanuel.

"I haven't said I would yet. I've got to think it over."

"Say yes," he begged. "Say yes without thinking it over."

"I'll be all alone. I don't know anybody at your house."

She not only enjoyed keeping him on tenterhooks, but she had a notion Jean would admire her more for it. Then it occurred to her that Emmanuel might grow tired of asking her, and on the spot she made up her mind.

"All right, I'll come," she said. And she added rather sulkily: "It's very nice of you to think of me. Thank you."

He burst out laughing for joy.

"Shall I come and get you?"

She reflected, disturbed by Jean's silence.

"This Saturday I work late," she said. "It's for Saturday, isn't it?"

"That's right. Tomorrow's Saturday."

She was waiting for Jean to speak, to give her some assurance or encouragement. But as he rose and tied his scarf without a word, she stammered:

"No, I'll come. I . . . yes, all right, I'll come by myself."

"Don't forget now," Emmanuel cried.

He smiled at her, his head tilted over his shoulder, his arms hanging awkwardly at his side.

"Be sure you don't change your mind."

Leaning forward, she devoured Jean with her eyes, driven by the old fear that she would never see him again. Sometimes she felt that his heart was as cold as the night when they had found warmth in each other's arms. He was the pitiless wind, he was the killing frost that blasts the tender hopes of spring. They had found each other in the storm. But the cold and the storm would come to an end. He had come into her life like a tornado, leveling everything in its path. Perhaps he had come into her life only to point up the squalor and ugliness about her, once the cyclone had passed. Thus, today as never before she had observed the beaten look on the faces of the customers seated before her. Never before had she felt so much like them and so resentful of the likeness! Never before had the smell of hot grease and vanilla been so revolting to her! And now Jean was taking himself off as if his work were done, as if he had nothing more to do here . . . But still for her he represented the desire for escape she had suppressed for so long. She must follow him to the end, forever. She would never let him get away from her!

"Oh no," she said, in response to Emmanuel, but with her green eyes directed at Jean, who stood there with a calculating look on his face. "Oh no, I never change my mind. Never. When I say yes, I mean yes."

And long after the two men had threaded their way out into the street, Florentine wrestled with herself, employing a thousand subterfuges to overcome her better judgment. No, she would never stop trying to make Jean love her. Anyway it would be idiotic to give up the game just when she had a chance to see him again, to show herself radiant and proud, to dazzle him so that he would be blinded to everything but her. Already she was picturing how she would conduct herself and what she would say, building up the role she would play at the party. She fancied herself surrounded by young men, the light focused on her in the middle of the room. Jean would be sure to single her out, when all the other young men flocked around. She loved to indulge in these idle reveries, in which she occupied the foreground and everything else was vague. For all the other figures in her daydream rose up like shadows around her, Florentine. They had no faces; one by one they took her by the waist and whirled her off in a dance; she floated in the air with these shadows, but she alone held the spotlight, her hair streaming over her shoulders; she was clothed in light.

The Létourneaus' house on Sir Georges-Etienne Cartier Place must be quite grand, she was thinking. Of all that Emmanuel had said to her she remembered only a few words : "Give me a ring when you're free tomorrow night. I'll come and get you. We live on Sir Georges-Etienne Cartier Place." She was deeply impressed as she repeated the address, visualizing a living-room with modern furniture and shaded lights, guests with polished manners, and cordial hosts serving refreshments. Her heart began to melt, not because Emmanuel and his friends in her heated imagination were thronging more and more eagerly about her, but at the thought that she, Florentine, had by her own efforts come to merit such homage.

Her hands were deep in dishwater, but she hummed as she worked, for she was no longer Florentine the waitress, irked and mortified by her menial job. Customers might bawl her out or make passes at her, but they could not touch her; she had the power to rise above the petty annoyances of these dreary days. She was Florentine, a person she hardly knew herself, a girl she esteemed highly, whose soul had been released the night she ran to meet Jean in the storm—oh how right she had been in every move!—she was Florentine, intoxicated with the shadows she had brought forth, all of them the victims of her charm, like butterflies around a lamp; she was Florentine, and she doted on herself.

Gone was her fatigue. She was so wrapped in her thoughts that when she saw her mother entering the store at a little past one, she was shocked, almost stupefied. Her mother! Rose-Anna shuffled along, blinking at the shiny brass fixtures and nickel panels. As she caught sight of her own reflection in the mirror, she faltered and hurried to stuff her threadbare gloves out of sight.

CHAPTER IX

FLORENTINE WAS STRUCK dumb. Her first reaction to the sight of Rose-Anna was to heave a sigh of relief that she had not turned up sooner, when Jean and Emmanuel had been at the restaurant. But the next moment she reproached herself for this. Leaning far over the counter, she greeted Rose-Anna with forced gaiety.

"See who's here!" she cried. "My mother!"

This was not the first time Rose-Anna had dropped in to say hello to Florentine when passing the store, but for many months she had left the house so seldom that this visit was totally unexpected.

Florentine looked at her mother in wonder. As often happens to members of a family who see each other every day, she had been blind to the changes that had come over her mother's face. There were wrinkles at the corners of her eyes that Florentine had never seen, there were lines of fatigue she had never even dimly perceived, and yet at one glance the girl beheld all the suffering, all the courage in that face. So after a long absence or some violent emotional experience, one sees in a flash what the years have done to a remembered image.

For a long time she had not seen her mother anywhere but at home, bent over the stove, or mending, and for the most part in the dim light of early morning or evening. Rose-Anna had only to appear in the bright glare of the store, dressed in her street clothes, she had only to emerge from the twilit obscurity in which she had buried herself so many years for Florentine to see her as she really was. Her pathetic smile, that gave the effect of trying to escape notice or at least of diverting it from herself, made Florentine heartsick. Up to then she had helped her mother out of a sense of fair play. She was proud to do her part, but to tell the truth she was far from meek about it and sometimes she felt as if she were being imposed upon. Now for the first time in her life she knew a moment of pure joy at the thought that she had not been ungenerous to her family. But that was not enough. She was filled with a sudden desire to be good to her mother today, to be gentler and more attentive and more generous than she had ever been, to mark the day with some special act of kindness, the memory of which would be sweet no matter what happened. And in the same breath she understood why this strange wish had come to her: it was that her mother's life appeared to be like a long dreary voyage under leaden skies that she, Florentine, would never make. It was as if today they were in a sense saying farewell. Perhaps this very moment marked the point of separation. In any case Florentine foresaw an inevitable parting of the ways. The threat of separation is needed to make some people aware of their own feelings: thus Florentine realized only now that she loved her mother.

"Mamma," she said in a transport, "come and sit down!"

A little breathless, Rose-Anna sat down on one of the revolving chairs.

"I thought I'd stop in as long as I was passing by," she explained. "Your father is home, as you know. Out of a job!"

It was just like her mother, thought Florentine, to speak of their private troubles without a moment's delay. Once she was out of the house she looked about her with a shy smile that seemed to be seeking warmth from the youthful faces about her, but however she strove to be gay, the language of tribulation came to her lips as soon as she opened her mouth. Those were her words of greeting. And perhaps those were the ones most likely to touch a member of her family, for what held them all together if not their common troubles? Over a period of ten or twenty years, could not their family life be summed up by the troubles they had shared?

She continued, but in a lower voice, as if she were abashed to speak of such things in strange surroundings:

"And so I went out early to look for a house, Florentine."

She had said all this in the morning. Florentine frowned, and hated herself as she felt her good resolution weakening. Then she rebounded to her gentler mood.

"You were right to stop in," she said. "It just happens that we have chicken at forty cents today. I'm going to treat you."

"But Florentine, I only wanted a cup of coffee to perk me up a little."

And her lips seemed to be muttering with terror: "Forty cents, how expensive!" Knowing the price of food so well, knowing how to prepare filling meals at small cost, she had always felt a peasant's reluctance to go to a restaurant and pay for food that she could have cooked—she could not help estimating the difference—for so much less money. But all her life too, she had had a suppressed desire to indulge herself just once in the extravagance.

"Oh well," she said, her stern self-control breaking down with fatigue, "a little piece of pie, Florentine, if you insist, or a couple of doughnuts. I might try that."

"No, no," cried Florentine.

In contrast with her mother's dread of spending money she suddenly recalled Jean's lordly gesture when he gave her a tip. That may have been what she admired most in him, his careless way of tossing a coin on the counter, his look of indifference as it fell from his hands. She and her family on the other hand hated to let money out of their sight even to pay for what they needed. They followed it in their minds, clinging to it as it left them, as if it were part of them, as if it were torn from their flesh. When Rose-Anna was low in her spirits, her children often heard her for no apparent reason bemoaning the fact that she had not got her money's worth out of a tiny expenditure made long ago.

Florentine lifted her chin, nettled by her own thoughts, which seemed to set Jean so much above the rest of them.

"No, no," she repeated impatiently. "You're going to eat a big meal, Mother. You don't visit your daughter for dinner often enough!"

"That's true," said Rose-Anna, rising to Florentine's high spirits. "It's the first time, I think. But just give me a cup of coffee. Really, Florentine, that's all I want."

Her eyes dogged the waitresses as they bustled about, dazed by their youth and energy. She glanced furtively at Florentine, because here amid the shining mirrors and the bright colors her daughter seemed to have climbed high above her family, and for a moment she felt as much diffidence as pride. In a confused way she felt too that it was unwise to badger Florentine with their domestic problems, that it was cruel to cast a cloud over her youth, and she made up her mind to assume a happier expression, however awkwardly it sat upon her face.

Smiling, but ill at ease, she said: "I mustn't form the habit of going out, or you'll have me on your hands more often than you like. It's nice and warm here. And it smells so good. And you look quite fetching yourself, I assure you!"

These simple words were like balm to Florentine's heart.

"I'm going to order the chicken for you, you'll see how good it is," she cried.

She wiped the table where her mother sat, brought her a napkin, a glass of water, offering her all those little attentions that she paid to strangers day after day without any pleasure, but which today filled her with real joy. It seemed to her that it was the first time she had gone through the motions of cleaning the table and setting a place, and a song rang through her head as she moved to and fro, making the work effortless.

"You have a fine job. This is a good place," commented Rose-Anna, misunderstanding the reason for Florentine's good cheer.

"That's what you think!" cried the girl, with a quick shrug of the shoulders.

Then she burst out laughing.

"I've had good tips today, I must admit," she confided.

A picture of Jean and Emmanuel came to her mind. Unable to perceive that their liberality indicated that her position in regard to them was almost like a servant's, she nodded her head complacently, recalling with delight the large coins each of them had left for her.

"I always get more tips than any of the other girls, you know," she said.

Then she brought Rose-Anna a full plate, and, since the rush hour was over, took a few minutes off to watch her mother eat.

"Is it good? D'you like it?" she asked repeatedly.

"First-rate," said Rose-Anna.

But again and again some deep-seated conviction that spoiled the slightest extravagance for her would make her add:

"But it's too dear, you know. Forty cents! I don't think it's worth all of that. You must admit it's quite dear!"

When she finished the chicken, Florentine cut her a piece of pie.

"Oh, I can't," said Rose-Anna. "I've eaten too much as it is."

"It's all included in the price," insisted Florentine. "It doesn't cost extra."

"All right then, I'll try it," said Rose-Anna. "But I'm not hungry any more."

"Taste it all the same," said Florentine. "Is it good? Not as good as yours, is it?"

"Much better," said Rose-Anna.

Then Florentine, seeing her mother relaxed, almost happy, felt a deep, overwhelming compulsion to add to the happiness she had conferred. She slipped her hand into her blouse and brought out two crisp new bills, which she had been saving for some new stockings. And as her fingers touched the stiff paper, she saw in her mind's eye the sheer silk stockings she might have bought, and a sigh escaped her.

"Here," she said, "take this. Take it, Mother."

"But you've already given me your money for the week," objected Rose-Anna, slow to understand.

Florentine smiled and said:

"This is extra. Take it."

And she thought to herself: I'm good to Mamma. I'll be repaid for this; it will be counted in my favor. She still felt a twinge of regret for the loss of her silk stockings, but this only gave her renewed assurance that she would be happy presently. She pictured the party next evening and in her incredibly childish way supposed that by reason of this single generous act she would cut an even more brilliant figure there, that she would receive deep and touching confirmation of Jean's regard for her.

A flush had spread over Rose-Anna's cheeks.

Brushing the crumbs from her coat, she mumbled, "I didn't come here for that, Florentine. I didn't come here to ask for money. I know that you don't have much left over from your pay."

Yet she took the two bills, put them in her change purse, and the change purse in her handbag for greater safety. Carefully folded, hidden away, they seemed already to have embarked on their mysterious career, their battle against so many wants.

"To tell the truth," confessed Rose-Anna, "I happen to need it right now."

"Oh!" exclaimed Florentine, losing some of her pleasure at these words, "and you wouldn't have told me!"

She saw her mother's piteous, beaten look, full of gratitude and admiration. She saw her mother rise painfully and leave, skirting the counters and stopping here and there to touch an object or feel a piece of material.

Her mother! Rose-Anna seemed very old to her. She moved slowly and her tight coat made her stomach bulge out. With two extra dollars hidden deep in her bag, the bag held close to her side, she was less sure of herself than before. Pots and pans, bolts of material, all the things she had long denied herself the privilege of looking at, fascinated her. Countless yearnings swelled within her, but she went steadily on her way, the money that had given rise to them buried in her pocketbook. Certainly she was poorer now than when she had entered the store.

As she watched this silent drama, all Florentine's joy was turned to bitterness. The rapture she had felt in being generous and un-selfish gave way to a sense of aching frustration. It had been a total loss, completely useless. It was a drop of water in the desert of their lives.

At the other end of the store, Rose-Anna had stopped at the toy counter, and picked up a little tin flute. As a salesgirl approached, however, she put it down hastily, and Florentine knew that Daniel's desire for the flute would never be any closer to realiza-tion than this. Her mother's good intention was quickly sup-pressed. Likewise between her desire to help Rose-Anna and the peace of mind her mother would probably never have, nothing would be left but the aching memory of a good intention. If she alone could escape from their narrow life, that would be a great achievement, but even for her it was very hard. She would have been happy to take her family with her and raise them also to a position of ease and comfort, but she knew that it was useless to think of it.

She forced herself to smile at her mother, who seemed to be asking her advice: "Should I buy the flute, the pretty little toy flute, or should I buy stockings, underwear, food? Which is more important? A flute like a ray of sunshine for a sick child, a happy flute to make sounds of joy, or food on the table? Tell me which is more important, Florentine?"

Florentine brought herself to smile once more as Rose-Anna, deciding at length to leave the store, waved goodbye, but by that time she was ready to rip all her good intentions to shreds, like a useless rag.

CHAPTER X

THE LÉTOURNEAU APARTMENT, on the first floor of a tall brick building, was all lit up. From every window lights shone across the snow in the quiet square. Florentine stopped at the foot of the steps and listened with beating heart to the festive sounds, muffled by the wet snow. She was not so much shy as deeply vexed at the idea of coming alone to the house of people she did not know. Until the store closed, she had kept hoping that Jean would call for her; she had counted on it in fact. She was all prepared for the evening this time, with her silk dress on under her uniform and her patent-leather shoes brought from home in a paper bag. At nine o'clock she had left by herself, in such an angry frame of mind that all the way, as her steps led her in spite of herself toward Sir Georges-Etienne Cartier Place, she could not decide whether to go to the Létourneaus' or not. In either case she was resolved to show Jean Lévesque how little he meant to her. She blew hot and cold, and whichever choice she was inclined to make seemed at the time to convey the full weight of her displeasure.

Underneath, however, and she knew it, she had made up her mind not to miss the party, for Jean would probably come later on, and she must not lose this chance of seeing him again. After all she was wearing her prettiest dress, a dress Jean had never seen, and it would really be a pity to go home now, when her heart under the silk dress was pattering away in step with the party, the people, the dance music, in a soft, silken, ceaseless rustle.

There were people dancing up there, for shadows passed back and forth. In the light streaming from the windows the snow could be seen dancing too, each separate flake gyrating like a moth around a lamppost. The graceful white forms flung themselves against the panes and died there, glued to the brightness within.

Florentine ran up the steps and rang the bell quickly, before she lost her courage. Emmanuel opened the door almost immediately. He was in uniform, just as she had seen him the first time. She hung back as he stood there on the threshold, peering out into the darkness. When he recognized her his face lit up.

"Oh, Mademoiselle Florentine, you've come!"

She seemed so uncertain, so intangible, so much like an optical illusion induced by the play of light and shade on the doorstep, that he hesitated a moment before offering her his hand. Then he drew her inside. The warm house was full of cigarette smoke and appetizing smells from the kitchen. He gave her a broad smile, as if it gave him real pleasure to see the ardent, stubborn little face he remembered so well. The snow was melting on her cheeks.

"You've come," he said joyfully.

He took her gloves and handbag while she opened her coat and shook the snow off her narrow fur collar.

"Come to Mamma's room," he said.

Leaning over her, as he led her through the hall, he continued: "May I . . . May I call you Florentine?"

"If you wish," she said, half pouting, half smiling. "I don't care."

"And will you call me Emmanuel?"

"If you wish. I don't care."

Pricking up her ears, she listened to the clatter of voices from the parlor.

"Are there many people?" she asked uneasily.

"You're used to many people," he replied. "At the ten-cent store you see them from morning till night. You're not afraid of people, are you?"

"It's not the same thing," she said.

"No?"

"Of course not. At the ten-cent store I wait on plenty of people. I get tired of waiting on so many people. I'm fed up with it. But people at a party . . . I don't know how to say what I mean."

She stopped short with a frown, wondering why she was going into all this for Emmanuel's benefit. The warmth of the house had affected her no doubt, and perhaps for a moment she had thought she was talking to Jean across time and space. Yes, that was it. When she was with Emmanuel she really talked to Jean, a Jean who had grown attentive and listened to her eagerly, trying to understand her.

"I've no idea why I tell you things like this," she said archly, giving him a light tap on the hand with her glove.

It occurred to her that there would be no harm in being pleasant to Emmanuel. It made no difference how she behaved toward him, for he had no power to make her heart contract with terror or burst with joy. She need not watch her step with him, since he did not inspire her with love. Therefore she could divulge to him all the confidences she had been preparing for Jean's ear. With him she could let herself go in unguarded little gestures of affection, such as she would never dare try with Jean, for fear of giving herself away. She might even let Emmanuel kiss her, if he went about it the right way, in order to remember Jean's kisses better and to stem the torrent within her that Jean must never suspect.

Emmanuel drew aside to let her pass into his mother's bedroom, which was decorated with lavender draperies, bedspreads, dressing-table skirt, and table runners, all in the same heavy silky material.

"If you need powder," he said, "you'll find some on the dressing-table."

"I have my own things," she said, almost indignantly. "I have my own powder."

Going directly to the dressing-table, she avoided touching anything, but looked curiously at the array of jars and bottles in the lamplight. Then she took her comb out of her bag and began to smooth out her windblown curls. It amused her to see her reflection at various angles in the triple mirror. As she raised her arms to her head her dress was pulled up above her knees, revealing a white slip edged with torn lace.

Thinking his presence might embarrass her, Emmanuel murmured :

"I'll go and ask Mamma to introduce you to everyone."

"No," she said fearfully. "Stay with me. You must introduce me."

He slipped his arm through hers, drew her to him, and gave her a long look, without trying to kiss her. Realizing that he had been a bit forward to presume on such a slight acquaintance, he was still amazed to find that she had accepted his invitation. He feared that his parents might not give her a cordial welcome. But his apprehension that she might be out of her element in his parents' home only made her more sympathetic, more touching. He enjoyed her blind trust in him; she was a surprising creature.

"Don't fear," he said, "I won't let you be bored."

"Oh, so far as that's concerned," she answered with a shrug, "I don't expect to be bored, but I don't want you to leave me alone."

As she spoke she was listening to the murmur from the parlor and trying to distinguish Jean's voice. The effort alone made the blood rush to her cheeks. A mist came over her eyes, but she clung to Emmanuel's arm, giving him a coquettish glance. Above all, she wanted Emmanuel to appear to be in love with her, enough at least to annoy Jean. She wanted to be adored tonight; she wanted to be the belle of the ball.

Hand in hand they entered the parlor, which communicated with the next room by a pair of French doors, now open. About twenty guests were seated on folding chairs, rented for the occasion. Lined up against the walls, they looked as if they were gathered together to see a play rather than to entertain one another. The rug had been taken up and the larger pieces of furniture pushed into a corner. In another corner stood the radio and from time to time all eyes were fixed on it. Eager to start dancing again, the young people were tapping the floor impatiently.

In front of each group, Emmanuel murmured: "Mademoiselle Lacasse."

Then quickly he named four or five of the guests. And each time Florentine smiled stiffly, her nose in the air, and said:

"I'm sure I'll never remember all these names." And she whispered very low to Emmanuel: "You told me there weren't many people."

When they reached the kitchen door she found herself confronting the young man's parents: Mme Létourneau, a round little woman with a sweet doll-like face and goggle eyes, magnified by powerful glasses, and M. Létourneau, whose plump figure, sleek mustaches, and civil smile—polite rather than friendly—bore a strong resemblance to a portrait hanging on the wall, which must have been that of his father. He sat with one elbow resting on the arm of his chair, his hand either cupping his chin or twirling his mustaches, and seemed to be sitting in judgment on all the young people assembled under his roof, and through them, on the extravagant character of the age, which he regarded with indulgent scorn. As a dealer in religious objects, ornaments and church wines, he had by long association with provincial prelates and priests acquired a slow, unctuous way of speaking, and benign, deliberate, sweeping gestures, as if with each movement of the arms he were lifting some heavy, precious material. It was said of him that in order to tempt the young priests who came to his shop he would put on one of his dazzling chasubles or a lace surplice and parade up and down in front of the prospective customer, turning and twisting to bring out the beauty of the fabric in the subdued light among the statues, the plaster figures of Christ, and the jeweled clusters of beads that gave the place the air of a sacristy.

Outside of business hours he associated almost exclusively with people of Traditionalist views, and occupied a post of honor in several religious and patriotic societies. His reverence for the past made him reject at once anything that seemed tainted with modern ideas or foreign elements. And yet he tolerated parties at his house, and received young people of whose language, manners and levity he disapproved. There was an element of curiosity in this, as well as a certain worldliness.

For some years now the relations between Emmanuel and his father had been correct and polite, but cold. As for Mme Létourneau, timid, loving soul, she had so long tried to reconcile the two men that she had become like a mirror, reflecting in caricature the vivacity of her son and the pompous dignity of her husband. She would switch abruptly from the most childish effusiveness, for Emmanuel's sake, to unbending severity, as if to express the respect and devotion she felt for M. Létourneau and to take his part against all opposition.

Emmanuel next presented Florentine to his sister Marie, a gentle, serious girl, to a little brother of high-school age, who resembled him strikingly, and to a great-aunt whose hands moved constantly in the folds of her black dress as if she were saying her beads.

Florentine had never felt so out of place, so lost and disconsolate. She knew now that Jean was not one of the guests, and rating them a dull lot at first glance, she doubted that he would come. She would have liked to snatch her coat and run away. Mme Létourneau went to some trouble to put her at her ease. She chattered away in a cooing voice, with only the barest hint of reserve.

"Emmanuel has been talking about you ever since yesterday," she said. Then, touching the girl's hair, she asked: "Are these lovely curls natural?"

"Yes," said Florentine.

M. Létourneau then questioned her with all the appearance of paternal interest, and Florentine observed with some annoyance that he was leading her to confess what she would never have admitted normally. Despite his courteous smile and air of affability, it was as if he were proving beyond question that she was out of place in that house.

Quick to seize certain shades of the voice and to interpret them, she was deeply wounded by his assumptions. If I were in love with Emmanuel, she thought, I wouldn't let him stand between us. And the certainty that she could make Emmanuel risk all for her gave her a flicker of pleasure.

The young man was talking with several people grouped in the window embrasure, which was decorated with a large potted fern. In an effort to regain her composure Florentine had taken out her compact to powder her nose. Catching M. Létourneau's scornful eye, she continued until she was done, without flinching.

Suddenly her glance met Emmanuel's, an absent glance wandering in a vacuum. It struck her that he was as lonely as she was, in his own home and among his own people, as if he were surprised to find himself here, as if he were waiting for someone, and had been waiting for a long time. As his wistful eyes met hers, he came to himself, and his face lit up. Jean never looked at me that way, she thought, as if he had known me for a long time. Jean always looks at me as if he were trying to place me all over again, as if he didn't recognize me, she mourned.

What general conversation there was sounded labored and artificial. The guests from the city, to distinguish them from the young men of Saint-Henri, did most of the talking. A young medical student, one of Emmanuel's high-school friends, dazzled everyone with his choice vocabulary and elegant diction. Near him was another student with a thoughtful air, who intrigued the young ladies even more. They nudged each other and whispered:

"Who is he?"

"A painter," claimed one.

"A writer," said another.

No one seemed to know for certain. The girls sat whispering together in one corner, their handbags on their knees, while the men formed separate groups, talking among themselves. A few of them had taken refuge in the hall and on the stairs where they laughed and told each other jokes like boys out of school.

Florentine kept her eye on the door. Late as it was she still hoped that the bell would ring and Jean would appear in the doorway, his black hair powdered with snow. The picture was never far from her mind. She prayed for this, she longed to see his lips parted in a half-smile, a smile that might go out to her when he found her there.

At last Emmanuel turned on the radio. A savage blast of music, with saxophones blaring, filled the room. The girls began to flutter in excitement, patting their hair, setting their dresses straight, pulling out their compacts to make sure that they were ready to dance. Their legs began to twitch expectantly. Emmanuel stood before Florentine. He took her hands and drew her to him.

"Our dance," said he. "Can you jitterbug?"

He laughed. His habitual awkwardness fell away when he was emotionally stirred. He became ebullient; he held his head straight, and he smiled broadly, abandoning himself to the happiness of the moment.

From the very first step Florentine followed Emmanuel in perfect harmony. Despite her rebellious and willful nature, she was remarkably pliant in the hands of a dancing partner. Yielding her whole loose-jointed body to the rhythm, she gave herself to the music with almost primitive passion.

"Is that some new Negro dance?" asked M. Létourneau. "Where did Emmanuel learn it?"

"They dance well together," murmured Mme Létourneau. "You'd hardly believe this was the first time." Then leaning toward her husband, she said pleadingly: "We don't give enough parties, my dear. We don't know young people."

Emmanuel held Florentine around the waist, then let her go at arms' length. For a while they moved abreast, their bodies stiff, their legs shaking below the knee, as if animated by a life of their own. Then raising her hand, Emmanuel had her pivot around in a whirl that made her skirt, her necklace and her bracelets float in the air; then again he clasped her around the waist. They next broke into a jerky step, face to face, breath to breath, each seeing his prancing reflection in the other's eyes. Florentine's hair flew free, swinging from shoulder to shoulder and falling over her face when she pirouetted.

"Where did Emmanuel meet that girl? Lacasse . . . Do you know her?" asked M. Létourneau.

"Don't you remember the cleaning woman who used to come to work for us many years ago?" whispered Mme Létourneau.

"Her daughter?"

"Yes. You'd never guess. She looks rather smart."

"Does Emmanuel know where she comes from?"

"He must. Anyway, that wouldn't discourage him."

"The fool," muttered M. Létourneau, twirling his mustaches. "That boy will never learn to stick to his own class."

"I could dance with you all night, Florentine, do you know?" Emmanuel was saying. "I could dance with you all my life."

For she was as light as a bird, a tireless bird, without a care in her smooth little head.

"Me too," she said, "I love to dance."

"I'll never dance this dance with anyone but you," he added. "And d'you know what else? I'll never let you get away."

She bent her head back, and flaunted her smile at him. What she liked even better than dancing was to be the center of attraction in a gathering. The guests had fallen silent all about them, asking:

"Who is that girl?"

And with a shudder she could imagine the answer:

"Oh, a little waitress from the five-and-ten."

Very well, she'd show them that she knew how to captivate Emmanuel, and not only Emmanuel. If she wanted to she could captivate all the young men! She'd show them what kind of girl she was! As the speed of the dance increased her heart swelled with defiance, and the blood rushed to her cheeks. Two little lamps seemed to have been lit in her eyes—two little lamps that flickered like a spark of fire in her pupils. With her coral necklace dancing at her throat like a feathery chain, her arms like a chain about Emmanuel, her silk dress rustling around her, and her high heels tapping the bare floor, she was dancing her life away, burning herself up, and others would catch fire from her.

Emmanuel's infatuation with her, his evident excitement, were the proof of all that, his fixed smile and his pallor were proof enough that she had a rare power over men. Ah, how wonderful it was to have power over men! It canceled off so many humiliations that had secretly cut her to the heart. It gave her a new outlook, new confidence. It was almost a guarantee that Jean too could not help loving her, perverse though he was.

Panting, her teeth gleaming through half-open lips, she dreamed about Jean, and yet it gave her joy to feel Emmanuel's heart pounding through his thick woolen tunic. With a caressing gesture she laid her cheek against his, and then through the thin silk drawn tight over her trim bosom she felt the devil's own tattoo, so loud and so close that she could no longer tell whether it was her own heart or Emmanuel's that was leaping about in such frenzy.

The music stopped. Emmanuel saw that Florentine's brooch had come loose.

"Your pin . . . your pin . . . is open," he stammered. "You . . . you'll drop it."

He tried clumsily to fasten the brooch into the material at the opening of the blouse.

Florentine stiffened and drew back, then clasped the pin herself. She was trembling a little.

When she raised her eyes again, she found Emmanuel's burning eyes on her.

"Dearest," he whispered very low, hardly breathing.

The radio had begun to play a waltz. He seized her almost roughly.

Slow music was less to Florentine's taste. Emmanuel held her too close, crushing her fingers in his moist hand. At every step they collided with other couples. The room seemed much smaller now that all the young people were on the floor. Blocked everywhere, they either marked time or moved in a solid mass from side to side. The room was lit by a branched chandelier with seven luridly tinted bulbs, but the shadows of the dancers on the walls seemed to make everything dim.

Florentine was not moving fast enough to stop thinking. Slow music was such a bore! She still laughed at Emmanuel's remarks, but without hearing a word. She was only aware of a sense of foreboding. Jean had failed to come expressly, because he meant to avoid her. He had decided never to see her again. And what was the use of having someone else fall in love with her when the man she yearned for had left her?

Her arms and legs ached. If she had been dancing a fast step, whirling round and round without stopping, she would not have felt so tired. But weariness lay on her limbs like a heavy, heavy weight, as if her life were a ball and chain that she dragged about with her with no prospect of release, of future happiness.

Emmanuel held her tight in order not to be separated from her. He was hot, and his heavy woolen uniform was rough against Florentine's bare arm. Raising her head to look him full in the face, she suddenly detested him. "Dearest," he had said. What right had he to call her "dearest"? It wasn't he whose endearments she craved. She wanted none of his tenderness, for to her mind it only made Jean's indifference even more obvious. She remembered the turmoil that Jean aroused in her, all the desires that had lain dormant in her, that might have remained dormant forever if not awakened by his kiss. Should she mourn for the dull peace of the days before she met him? Should she continue loving the man who had opened her eyes? Or hate him? She did not know, she did not know!

A little later she came to her senses with a start. It was very hot in the parlor; the house had central heating. The flowers on the piano looked wilted. She stared about her in bewilderment, catching a phrase out of the air: "The French-Canadian race, the family . . ." M. Létourneau was discoursing on his favorite topic.

Another group, around Emmanuel, was discussing the war. She heard scraps of a hot argument. "Poland was attacked . . . the democracies . . ." She closed her eyes. When she opened them again she was startled to find the cold, smiling eyes of M. Létourneau fastened on her. This man seemed to see her for what she was, a waitress, the butt of coarse jokes, a girl born for menial work and destined to be a slavey all her life. The moment he looked at her she felt as if she were being relegated permanently to the scullery; she could feel the greasy dishwater on her hands and smell the roasting hot dogs.

"Have you been going out with Emmanuel a long time?" asked a girl seated near Florentine.

The voice tried to be matter-of-fact, but without success.

Florentine was taken aback. It would have given her pleasure to annoy the girl, who seemed uneasy. To hurt someone would have been a relief. But she contented herself with an even greater pout.

"He's not my steady anyway," she said.

"And who is your steady?" continued the girl, her eyes woe-begone. "You love him," she chanced, trying to be conciliatory.

She was a dainty little thing, but clearly in some distress. Her eyes followed Emmanuel with a hopeless look.

"My steady!" exclaimed Florentine, and she flushed with anger. My steady, she was thinking. I haven't any steady. I'm nineteen years old and I have no boy-friend to take me to the movies on Saturday night or go with me to a party. I'm nineteen years old, and I'm all alone.

She heard the girl beside her speaking again.

"Where did you buy your dress?" she was asking.

Her intention was doubtless innocent, but Florentine thought she could detect a note of snobbery in the question. And while she sat there pondering her reply she had a sudden vision of her mother cutting out the dress one winter evening. The black silk lay spread over the dining-room table as Rose-Anna stood poised to make the first cut with the scissors, and the wind whistled against the frosty windowpanes. How beautiful the material had seemed that night, and how well she remembered the first fitting, when she had tried the dress on before the sleeves were sewn in, peering into the mirror over the buffet and then mounting a chair so that she could see it all, first the blouse and then the skirt!

"I don't remember where I bought it," she muttered.

And it was as if she had denied all Rose-Anna's work those long nights. The joy of owning a pretty dress was gone. Now she knew that it was very dowdy. She would never again put it on without hearing the cry of the scissors in the expensive material, without seeing it half finished, basted together with white thread, a dress that had cost her mother suffering, hours of labor under a poor light. Her dissatisfaction with the dress made her feel that it was in some way responsible for the evening's misfortune and in a moment of rancor she vowed never to wear it again.

"A penny for your thoughts!"

While she sat there dreaming, her head propped in her hand, Emmanuel had come up quietly and placed his hands over her eyes.

"Who is it?" he asked, laughing.

"Oh," she said, pushing him away impatiently, "it's not hard to guess," but she laughed as she gave him her hand.

The joy had gone out of her dancing. Her pumps were too tight and too stiff; her feet hurt. She felt as if her whole weight rested on her high heels, which slowly dug into her flesh. But no one must know how exhausted and unhappy she was. She laughed a little louder than before, and by sheer force of will—she had learned how to do it—made her eyes sparkle more brightly. They must think that she was having a fine time; no one was to know that she was tired and heartsick. If she put up a good enough pretence of high spirits, perhaps she would end by enjoying the party. Her lips moved.

"What are you saying?" asked Emmanuel.

"I said I'm having a swell time."

"Are you glad you came?"

"Sure I am."

"You're not too tired?"

She raised her eyebrows.

"I never get tired," she declared.

"Do you go to many parties?"

"Pretty often . . . whenever they come up."

"I should have met you long ago, Florentine. We've lost so much time."

"I won't run away," she teased.

A shadow passed over Emmanuel's face.

"No, you won't run away," he murmured, "but I must leave soon."

The great sweetness of his tone, a strange sensation for her, hovered in the air.

"Why did you enlist?" she asked. "Your parents don't seem to take it too well."

"Nobody takes it well," he answered in a voice of indescribable loneliness, as if looking to her for comfort.

But she was not interested in the subject. She swung her shoulders and abandoned herself to the music with a new access of energy.

As it was Lent, the refreshments were served a little after midnight. Marie Létourneau, assisted by her mother and Emmanuel, gave everyone a printed paper napkin, a glass of soda water and a paper plate containing a sort of picnic supper of thin sandwiches, a couple of olives, a stalk of celery and a little cold salad. Marie Létourneau seemed like a rather dispirited girl. She had taken little part in the festivities except to oversee the arrangements.

After supper the dancing was resumed, and so it went till the night ended. Couples were still spinning round when Mme Létourneau disappeared for a while. She returned gloved and hatted to go out.

"It's Sunday," she said. "We might as well go to mass before we break up."

The guests from the city, the medical student and his mysterious friend, had left several hours before; the Saint-Henri people who still remained fell in with her proposal.

CHAPTER XI

THEY PUT ON their wraps and went out into the mild dawn, walking two by two under the dripping trees. The tall trunks of the maples were already beginning to stand out in the twilight square. The snow was melting into deep muddy pools. Only the houses still lay in darkness. From basement to roof the windows were black holes in the cold brick fronts. Over the tops of the houses a strip of watery blue cut across the otherwise dark vault of the sky. The stars were fading.

The young people crossed the square in a body, casting a vague shadow on the snow when they reached the first lamppost. They had all turned silent, except for one playful couple who now and then burst into shrill peals of laughter. But even their laughter ceased when for a moment they disappeared in the shade of a tree.

In Notre-Dame Street a few lights were already visible, flickering behind windowpanes slapped by sudden gusts of wind. The air was rather warm but oppressive, as if in forecast of a spring shower. To lungs full of cigarette smoke, however, the morning seemed delightfully fresh.

Emmanuel drew in great breaths of air. He wondered at the mildness of the dawn, and even more at the quiet mood that had come over him. Walking beside Florentine, holding her arm to keep her from slipping in the wet snow, he felt relaxed and calm as he had never been. Would this girl become his friend, or something more? He had a suspicion that he was falling in love, even though his emotions were vague and blurred.

The solid mass of Saint-Zotique Church loomed up before them out of a white mist, as if a cloud of incense were rising from the portal. Other shadowy figures were converging on the church. Emmanuel and Florentine entered in the wake of several old women who always came to early mass.

The warmth inside enveloped Florentine. After a rapid genuflection she sat down, exhausted, scarcely able to keep her eyes open. But not even her fatigue could blunt the edge of her suffering. Unlike Emmanuel, who had felt himself miraculously transformed by the magic of the night and full of bright hope for the new day, Florentine was aware only of the magnitude of her disappointment.

Emmanuel . . . Why had he kneeled down beside her, as if he were her fiancé? Fiancé—the word aroused in her an inexpressible longing to see Jean again. It was he who should be kneeling beside her, not Emmanuel. Emmanuel was a stranger to her, she was not even curious about him. The tender regard he had shown her only made her bitter now. His attentions were worthless to her. A little more and she would frankly loathe them, she would spurn them as dangerous, something that might separate her even further from Jean.

Why isn't Jean here beside me? she kept thinking. Another image came to her weary brain, rousing her from her torpor. She remembered the day Jean had invited her out for the first time, and recalled his saying that it would be up to her to become acquainted with him gradually. And again she saw him squaring his shoulders as he left her that day.

She realized that this picture was graven on her mind, unchangeable, crystallized forever.

A panic came over her. Hysterically she tried to alter the picture, to summon up some other image from her memory. Impossible. She could see only his back, as if he were a man who had passed her on the street without a glance to right or left.

Then with a gasp she understood love: the torment at the sight of the loved one, the greater torment when he was absent, torment without end. She whispered to herself: "If I had the chance I would make him love me," hoping secretly to afflict Jean with her own passion rather than be cured of it herself. For what she meant by this was: "I should like him to suffer as I suffer because of him."

At her side Emmanuel was praying. His lips were moving but the rest of his features expressed a calm joy and repose. Florentine slipped down to the prie-dieu beside him and she too began to pray. But her prayer was almost a command, almost a challenge: "I must see him again. Holy Mary, let me see him again, I want so much to see him again."

Then she grew calmer, and by ever so many feminine wiles sought to bring the Virgin over to her side. "I will make a novena," she vowed, "if I meet him this very day." The futility of pledging herself without any hope for success lay on her heart like a cold hand. She added: "And the first Friday of every month for nine months. But only if I meet him today. Otherwise it doesn't count."

She prayed with all her soul, yet her eyes remained hard, her mouth motionless.

At the elevation she met Emmanuel's glance as she bowed. For a fleeting moment, she dreamed of imploring the Virgin to root out the love that was eating at her heart. But as she rested her brow against the edge of the chair in front of her, the vision of

Jean's retreating back came to her again. And she clasped her sorrow close, clinging to it like a drowning man to a spar.

She was prepared to do many other things, whatever the cost, to gain the intercession of the Virgin. She would go to mass every morning. She would even—and this was a great sacrifice!—give up going to the movies for six months, perhaps more. What wouldn't she do? She would go as a penitent to the Oratory on the mountain, climbing the steps on her knees like a crippled beggar seeking a miraculous cure! Her eyes unflinching, she stared at the lighted tapers, never suspecting for a moment that her yearning for Jean's kisses might compromise her appeal to the pale forms visible in the shadow of the apse.

"I'll begin my novena this very day if I see him, Holy Virgin." And that was her prayer until she found herself in the street again.

"Dear child, you're all worn out," said Emmanuel. "Let's take a taxi."

A cab was just slowing up at the curb as the little group of worshippers filed out of church.

The Lacasse house was only five minutes away by foot. But Florentine was so full of spleen that she was not unwilling to have Emmanuel pay for extravagances. He'll never be able to do enough for me, she thought, imagining her mother's astonishment when she drove up in a taxi. She gave a nod of assent, and accentuated the chattering of her teeth to win his sympathy.

The sun was rising, round, sulphur-colored. A soft snow, threatening to turn into rain, had begun to fall. Touched by her evident exhaustion, Emmanuel wrapped her fur collar about her throat and helped her toward the taxi, protecting her as best he could.

She smiled and curled up on the seat like a cat.

"You seem so cold!" said Emmanuel, covering her legs with his coattails.

She shivered again, simply for the pleasure of being pampered, although a warm current of air came up from the heater. The radio sputtered a sentimental ballad through screeching static. The atmosphere of the church had already been erased from her mind. Why worry? If she were patient enough, she'd get what she wanted in the long run. And in the meantime, why not accept Emmanuel's kindness? The young man could not understand by what association of ideas she came to her question when she asked:

"Didn't you invite your friend Lévesque, the man who came to the store with you the other day, to the party? Why didn't he come?"

She was looking calmly out the window at the houses rushing by, her hand resting on Emmanuel's knee.

He looked vexed.

"Oh, let's forget about Lévesque," he said, drawing closer to her.

She dropped her handbag, bent over to pick it up, and continued with false gaiety:

"Oh well, I was just wondering why he didn't come. It seemed odd. I thought you were great friends. Where does he come from?"

"Yes," said Emmanuel simply. "We were once friends, and we still see each other now and then. He's had a hard life, you know. Nowadays he seems to have a grudge against all his old cronies, as if they were responsible for his troubles. . . . But let's talk about ourselves, Florentine. We haven't much time left."

Again she pushed him away, not rudely, but pretending that she was too warm now, and laughing as if he had said something funny.

"He strikes me as a curious fellow," she went on, with a look of distaste. "Where does he live?"

"He has a little room at the corner of St. Ambroise and St. Augustin Streets. He likes to live alone. He spends most of his time studying and doesn't care much about girls. And yet most girls think he's quite attractive."

He stressed the last word, and glanced at her to see her reaction.

Florentine opened her eyes wide and looked him straight in the eye. With one hand on her heart, she forced a laugh.

"Not me, at any rate," she exclaimed acidly, "I think he's . . ." And she looked for a word that would soothe her own wounded feelings and perhaps reach Jean through Emmanuel. "Oh well, I don't think he's attractive," she continued. "I don't think he's attractive at all."

The vehemence with which she spoke made Emmanuel smile.

"So much the better," said he, "so much the better for me, I mean. I owe Jean a good deal, I feel friendly toward him in spite of everything, but if you were my sister I wouldn't want you to go out with him."

"Why not?"

He answered simply and directly:

"Because he'd make you unhappy."

"Oh," said she, as if she were both amused and incredulous.

"But there's another reason," he said, seizing her hand.

"What's that?"

"You're not my sister, fortunately, and you mean a great deal to me."

She laughed.

"As much as that?"

"A great deal."

The taxi stopped in front of her house. He got out, paid the driver, and helped her out. She had begun to shiver with cold again, involuntarily this time. The deserted, ugly street was all the more depressing under leaden skies. They were the only living beings, the only touch of color in the gray passageway between the sad houses. Emmanuel glanced around in embarrassment, then proposed timidly:

"A kiss, Florentine?"

She seemed to wake with a start from a troubled dream, and looked at him wearily, uncertain what to do. In the course of the evening he had been the only man who had not tried to get her off in a dark corner for a little necking. She had expected him to want to kiss her. But now, when Jean was in her thoughts, gnawing at her heart . . . She made a face and turned her head away, so that his mouth only grazed her cheek. Intoxicated by this slight caress, he immediately wanted more.

"Not like that, Florentine. Better than that."

He seized her so roughly that she lost her balance. Flushed and trembling he struggled to find her lips.

A door slammed somewhere. Quickly he released her, but gripped her by the wrists.

"I won't see you again before I leave, Florentine. I must go this evening. But from now on, you're my girl-friend, aren't you?"

She gave no answer. I have time to think it over, she mused. I don't have to decide right away.

But as soon as he left her she wiped her mouth. She watched him as he walked away, noticing that he carried his head tipped to one side, slightly askew, and she didn't know whether to laugh or cry.

CHAPTER XII

THE WINTER was coming to an end in overcast skies and sudden squalls. Early that afternoon, a bank of clouds settled on the south slope of the mountain and the wind swept down on Saint-Henri in the valley.

Toward eight o'clock in the evening the powderworks exploded. Loose shutters banged; from the roofs of the houses came the sound of tin being ripped off; windowpanes rattled under a fusillade of musketry; trees writhed and cracked in agony; and the snow went on falling, sifting under doors and through the joints of windows, seeking shelter everywhere from the fury of the wind.

Neither sky nor earth could be seen. The buildings were only darker masses in the darkness, pierced here and there by the feeble glimmer of a lantern. It was as if some hand were fumbling in the storm, trying desperately to bring forth light; but the street lamp went out immediately, the bulb flickered and died. On Notre-Dame Street the brightest electric signs barely illuminated the pavement; from the sidewalk opposite the movie theater, one saw only a vague red glow, like the distant gleam of a burning house.

Driven by the wind, Azarius emerged from the shadows, passed quickly through the dim halo of a lamppost, and hurried toward the Two Records, doubled up against the blast. The white front of the restaurant blended with the whirling snow. Three steps away it was indistinguishable, but with the certainty of old habit, Azarius found the doorknob.

The restaurant was almost empty. At ease near the roaring stove, Sam Latour sat smoking a cigar, blowing smoke rings and contentedly watching them rise toward the ceiling. Behind the counter, his wife, a sprightly brunette, was looking through a magazine, her elbows propped up on the ledge, one palm against her cheek. There was only one other customer, sitting stooped over a newspaper with his back to the door.

"Ah, here's our spellbinder!" cried Latour good-naturedly. "Was it the storm that brought you? Nita was just saying that we wouldn't see a dog tonight."

"Uh-huh, not many out tonight," said Azarius laconically.

Leaning against the counter, he unbuttoned his overcoat and asked for a coke. He seemed reluctant to start the ball rolling, although it was not his custom to remain silent very long. He stood there, wiping the neck of the bottle on his sleeve, his cheeks flaming red from the cold, his eyes wandering restlessly about the room. His brow was smooth, but his whole expression was bewildered and unhappy.

"In fact," said Anita Latour, picking up the nickel that Azarius had placed on the counter, "Sam was just saying that not many people would be out tonight."

This affectionate couple had the habit of upholding each other even in the most commonplace statements. Whatever remark one dropped, the other repeated, prefacing it with the tactful comment:

"Sam was saying . . ." or "Nita was saying . . ." And having made this acknowledgment they thanked each other with a smile.

"And that's just what I thought when I saw the storm coming," continued Anita. "Sam will be alone all evening, I said to myself. That's why I came."

Sam's laughter had a ring of mischief.

"Did you ever see anything like her, Lacasse? There's no one like Nita. She's so good it hurts."

Azarius took a swig from his bottle and wiped his mouth with the back of his hand. He seemed perplexed. For a picture of Rose-Anna had come to his mind, not as she was today, but as she had once been : gay, with soft velvety eyes and a voice full of warmth. Then the image faded, and he saw Rose-Anna bent over in the lamplight this evening, mending children's clothes. He saw her rise to move closer to the lamp, holding the dark material a few inches from her eyes to sew a few stitches.

He had tried to help her; he had offered to thread her needle. He had asked her humbly to tell him what he could do for her and she had not answered a word. Then, for the first time in his life, he had raised his voice to her :

"By God, it's enough to drive a man to drink, do you hear?"

And even to that she had not replied. Then he had slowly put on his coat, hoping that at the last moment she would try to hold him back. He could bear her reproaches, but not her silence.

The atmosphere of the house had become intolerable.

"I'm going to take a turn outdoors, Mother, as long as you feel that way."

Nothing.

When he reached the street, his feet had led him instinctively to the Two Records. And now, in the comforting heat of the restaurant, he began to relax. Here he was in his element; if he spoke someone would listen to him. Sam would contradict him, but he would listen to him all the same.

"How are things going?" inquired Anita.

Azarius started. A ghostly smile flitted over his lips.

"Not too bad, considering everything, thank you."

"You gave up the cab?" said Sam. "Your boy Eugène told me so the other day. Oh yes, he's in the army now, isn't he? How do you feel about it?"

"So far as I'm concerned, it's quite all right. Eugène did well. He's young and strong. I wish I were in his shoes."

"Yeah?"

"Yeah. I'd do it in a minute."

"Uh-huh . . . The Russians got off to a bad start with the Finns, I see. But aside from that, there's not much news. Neither side seems anxious to get going. The French are playing cards in their fortress and the Germans the same, seems to me."

He rubbed his hand over his chin and sighed: "Looks to me like a phony war."

Azarius sighed in his turn.

"Yes, a phony war!"

Then, raising his head, he added: "It doesn't pay to run a cab. That's why I gave it up. Six or seven dollars a week, that's all I made out of it. There's a limit to everything, you know. A man can't sweat blood for nothing because he's out of luck." Little by little he was warming up; his voice was growing more assured. "With their damn relief," he continued, "they've pushed wages down so low it doesn't make any sense. They think because a man's out of a job for four or five years he'll take anything. But a man's only human, by God!"

Then, as if he suddenly heard the hollow echo of his own words, he sagged against the counter.

"I might just as well not work, and go back on relief," he said.

Sam had risen and was pacing back and forth.

"Yes, but don't forget that they're going to stop all that. There won't be any more relief. They're going to put a stop to it." He clasped his large hands behind his back. "And it's about time it stopped. If anything put this country on the rocks, it's that. Take me, for example. I pay taxes. Well, part of my profits went to support guys who weren't doing a thing."

"All we wanted was work," interposed Azarius stormily.

"Sure, and that's what's wrong. You and many others would have been glad to hold down a job and draw a salary, that goes without saying. But instead, you had nothing to do, and the rest of us, whoever made a bit of cash, paid for it. We paid through the nose to keep you doing nothing. Here in Canada it came to the point where two-thirds of the population supported the other third in idleness."

"And yet there was plenty of work to be done," interrupted Azarius. "Houses were still needed."

Sam Latour began to laugh, and tugged at his collar, which was too tight for his thick neck, with the impatience of a ploughhorse at his halter.

"All right! Have it your way, we needed houses and roads and bridges. And grade crossings too. We could have used one here in Saint-Henri. It's got so bad that the cars and buses are held up five to ten minutes every time a train passes. Sometimes cars are lined up for half a mile on each side of the track."

At last he succeeded in loosening his necktie and started off again, more at ease.

"There was never any lack of work to be done. Nor men either.

I've seen fifty men fighting for one job. I wonder then what *was* lacking."

"Money," said Azarius.

"Yes, money," thundered Sam. "There was never enough for old age insurance, never enough for the schools or for orphans, never enough to give everybody a job. But look here, there's money enough for war. They've got money for that!"

"There's always enough money for war, that's a fact," replied Azarius.

Tipping the bottle up, he swallowed the rest of his drink, then bent his head once more and stared at the floor as he murmured:

"Maybe a bit of it'll come our way."

"Very possibly," said Sam, sitting down again.

There was a short silence cut by the crackling of the fire in the big stove, then Azarius spoke up.

"I've been thinking that business would improve in my line. I heard they were planning to build airplane hangars at Saint-Hubert."

"So what?"

"Oh, some other guys got the job. There's only half enough work to go around. Still, things are looking up."

"But not so fast, eh?"

"No, not so fast."

The little man at the other end of the room, a stranger to both Azarius and Sam Latour, broke in at this point.

"Business is improving," he said, "but mainly in war industries. That's a good line to be in nowadays. If I were beginning over again, that's what I'd do. But I'm a builder by trade, a mason. And d'you know how long it is since I worked at my trade? I'm not speaking of plugging little holes in a wall, jobs that don't pay my expenses. D'you know how long I haven't held a steady job?"

From the depths of a booth, where he sat with his hands flat on the table, he spoke quietly, a pathetic and somehow comical figure with a nervous tic that screwed up the right side of his face.

"Well, I'll tell you. It's eight years since I worked at my own trade. Eight years," he continued in a monotone, without raising his voice. "But I've done many other things. For example I worked as gardener over at the convent, I worked as a paper hanger, and once, during an epidemic, I earned a living as an exterminator, killing bedbugs and cleaning the lice out of mattresses."

Unconscious of the droll effect of his sing-song voice and his wistful air, he babbled on:

"And that's not all. If you want to see a man who's tried everything, look at me. I'm the man for you. After the bedbug job was finished, I got an idea, a good one. You may laugh, because to look at me you wouldn't think I was the type to go from door to door. All the same I set myself up as a salesman. There's nothing I didn't try to sell : insurance policies—everybody starts with that, you think you're cleverer than you really are—then vanilla flavoring, green tea, Christmas cards, scrubbing brushes, trusses, horse remedies, everything under the sun! I would say . . ."

He rose suddenly to recite his sales patter. Buttonholing Sam Latour, who looked enormous beside such a wisp of a man, he raised his voice and piped :

"So you don't care for any baking powder today, mamzell! But maybe your mother, that good-looking lady back there, would be interested in this new brand. This new baking powder will make your cake rise four times higher than the old kinds. No? Very well, you, sir, what do you say to trying my corn remedy? All right, so you have no corns, but maybe you have heartburn? Try this bottle and see if you're not cured in three days. You have no heartburn? Then how about this scrubbing brush? I'll be around again next year . . ."

He made a little gesture of farewell, half-discouraged, half-comic, and then went back to his chair.

"There's nothing I haven't tried," he confessed grimly, not addressing anyone in particular, but as if he were searching his own soul. "I've worked at everything except my own trade. They say you have to specialize these days to find work. Well, let me tell you, a trade doesn't mean a thing any more. A man spends half his life learning a trade and the rest of his life forgetting it. No, the good old days in the trades are finished. Today you have to do odd jobs to get by."

The atmosphere had become more cheerful during the little man's demonstration; now it turned gloomy again.

During a silence heavy with thought, Azarius studied the stranger whose life story was so similar to his own.

"You're right," he said. "Me, I'm a carpenter by trade. Yes, a carpenter, sir," he repeated as the little man looked at him with some interest. "When the building trade hit bottom I had the idea of making furniture for a living. Small things, you know, footstools, smoking stands, things like that. At first they sold rather well. But one day I realized that it wasn't worth the time I was putting into it. It's like dressmaking. My wife is a first-class dressmaker. When we were first married she used to make a dress for two dollars, and she had all the work she could do. Now no one will give her even that much. You can buy a dress ready-made for a dollar and a half. A dollar and a half for a silk dress! Can you imagine the wages they pay in the factories to be able to sell a dress for a dollar and a half?"

"Right you are," said the mason. "It's the same all over. We're losing our skill. We're forgetting our trades. Everything's done by machine. And yet——"

His small gray eyes under the thick black tufts of his eyebrows blinked with excitement. It was as though some strange refulgence had appeared before those myopic eyeballs.

"And yet, is there any finer occupation on earth than building? Take masonry, now. Setting up a new wall, straight as a die, how about it, there?" he said, with a shy smile at Azarius.

"Yes, sir," replied Azarius in the same tone of exaltation, uplifted by memories of the happy past. The approval for which he hungered had by some miracle come to him this evening, soothing his wounded feelings.

He took a step toward the mason, who might have worked beside him in days gone by, and lifted up for all to see his carpenter's hands, hands that had loved to handle wood, his broad nostrils quivering as if they had caught a whiff of new lumber.

"To be perched on a scaffold," he cried, "between earth and sky, with hammering in your ears from morning till night! Watching the wall rise smooth and firm as a rock from the foundations; and then one day seeing a house all finished on a street where there were only empty lots and weeds before, that's the life!"

"Yes, it's good work," said the mason.

"Good work," repeated Azarius.

After a moment, Anita signaled to her husband.

"Say there, Sam, wasn't there someone in here this morning looking for a man to drive his truck? Who is it? D'you remember?"

"Yes, you're right, it was Lachance, I think. Hormidas Lachance. You might go and see him, Lacasse."

Azarius' face grew sombre.

"Lachance," he snapped, resenting this attempt to change the subject. "That bird! His name fits him to a T. Yes, I know him. He's one of those who expected men to work for almost nothing a few years ago. He made it his business to take people who were on relief; he got them for practically nothing. Then when the men quit, he'd squeal on them so they'd be thrown off relief."

"Why don't you try him, anyway?" pleaded Anita. "He might be in a better mood now."

"I'll see," said Azarius with unusual sharpness.

He took off his cap, then pulled it down over his head again. Then, looking at the clock on the wall, he whistled between his teeth.

"Good God, the time goes fast. Well, I must be on my way.

Goodnight, and thank you all the same for the suggestion, madame. Goodnight, Latour."

At the door he turned around, and stared at the mason, who had gone back to his reading, once more the mild little man who might have been mistaken for a retired clerk completely satisfied with his life.

"And to you too, goodnight there!" cried Azarius.

Then he opened the door quickly and plunged out into the storm.

Unlike his usual placid self, he marched along briskly, mumbling angrily. At one point he felt angry with the mason for reminding him of his youth. In his bitter mood the poor old man seemed like the personification of his own failure. He was also angry with Sam Latour for bringing up the subject of Lachance, which put him in the embarrassing position of having to make a decision. And he knew how loath he was to make a decision all by himself. Like all wavering characters, he only pretended to struggle against his own inertia, which he knew to be insuperable. And perhaps he really felt more angry with himself than anyone else, for having thought back on the old days with longing. He had lived so long in a sluggish state, free of self-questioning and riding along on the vaguest hopes! And now he must prod himself once more, devise reasons for his actions in order to be at peace with himself again. He strode on, his head sunk between his shoulders. The storm was abating, exhausted by its own violence. A few stars were beginning to appear between the breaks in the clouds.

When he reached Beaudoin Street, Azarius began to hurry. As soon as he realized that he was near home his anxiety at having left Rose-Anna alone with the sick children had revived. He ran to his own door and rushed in as if he expected that some calamity had befallen his family.

"Rose-Anna, are you there?" he cried. "Do you need me?"

She was in the kitchen, sorting out the children's clothes, putting those that were not too soiled to one side, and soaking the rest in the sink. Her startled glance skimmed her husband's face, then she turned away without answering.

"Can't you wait till tomorrow to wash?" he said. "You're killing yourself, Mother."

He had these sudden illuminations about Rose-Anna's health very often when he himself was disheartened.

"It must be done," she replied coldly. "You know very well that the children have no change of clothes."

Azarius sat down at the table and began to untie his boots. As he took one off he dropped it with a clump to the floor.

"I just saw Sam," he said after a moment. "He gave me to understand that Lachance is looking for a man to run his truck."

Knowing how Rose-Anna had detested Lachance, he hoped to wring a violent protest from her, while touching her at the same time by his good will.

But she turned to him stiffly, her eyes bitter.

"Well, what are you waiting for?"

"Mother!" he exclaimed. "D'you forget what he did to us? D'you forget that he was the one who had us thrown off relief?"

From the dining-room a fretful voice called: "Mamma!"

"What's wrong with him?" asked Azarius, struck by the child's querulous tone. "It's Daniel again. Is he no better?"

"I don't know what's the matter with him," said Rose-Anna. "He had a nose-bleed a while ago. We ought to take him to the doctor."

She took a glass of water to the little boy. Azarius heard her telling him to go to sleep. A few minutes later he looked up to see her studying him from the doorway, and he shrank from her steady gaze.

"Listen, Azarius," she said implacably, in a new tone for her, "this is no time to be proud. Not when the children need underclothes, and maybe medicine. Sweet Jesus, no! Go and see him in spite of everything, Azarius."

"You don't really think I should, Mother!"

The wind moaned against the windowpane.

"I'll go tomorrow morning, early," he continued. "But I have the feeling it's a waste of time, Rose-Anna. Something better may turn up, and once I'm stuck with Lachance, I'll miss out on it. But if you insist, I'll go tomorrow. Early tomorrow morning."

"No, Azarius, if he's in a hurry, Lachance will find someone between now and tomorrow morning. And I know you! Tomorrow you'll change your mind. Go right away."

"Right away! What's the rush? It can wait."

He watched as she tore her apron off and quickly smoothed her hair with her hands.

"I'll go myself," she said.

"Now Rose-Anna, don't be foolish! A night like tonight!"

She disappeared into the next room. He decided that she was just testing him, that she had gone to fetch her sewing from the dining-room and that she would come back in a little while. She would sit down beside him in the kitchen, where it was warmer, and they would talk it all over more calmly. He took off his other boot and sat there silently, one elbow resting on the table, his eyes dreamy. Perhaps I'll go tomorrow, he was thinking, but first I'll drop in at the contractor's, at Holliday's. But anyway, I must think it over.

And suddenly Rose-Anna stood before him in her street clothes, calmly tieing the inside belt of her coat. He rose instinctively to bar her passage.

"You're not going out on a night like this. I'll go, I tell you."

"No, let me go, Azarius."

Their eyes met. Hers had the stern, energetic look of the days when she went out to do housework, and took in sewing, toiling from morning till night to keep the wolf from the door. Azarius bowed his head.

"It's better for me to go," she explained in her calmest voice. "Lachance will be ashamed when he sees me coming, don't you see? I'll call him to account for all the trouble he gave us. I'll explain everything. I'll make him give you a job, don't you worry."

"Tomorrow will be time enough," Azarius began again.

But Rose-Anna had put her hand on the doorknob. She said :

"Fill the wash-kettle and put it on the stove, if you want to help me. I'll finish my washing when I come back."

The rest of what she said was lost in the wind.

He saw her careening on the threshold as a gust caught her off balance, then the door slammed shut. And he heard nothing more but the sound of water dripping from the tap.

He groped toward his chair and sat down, his arms loose at his sides, his eyes fixed dully on the pile of dirty clothes hanging over the sink. His health had not declined during the years of unemployment and odd jobs. He still had the thick hair of a young man, a ready smile, color in his cheeks, good carriage. He could speak well; he knew how to reason things out; he knew how to make a good impression when he looked for work, and at bottom he was not lazy. What then had happened to him?

Suddenly he buried his face in his hands.

What had happened to him?

His whole life passed before him, some of the events clear and precise, others blurred, hazy. He saw himself first as a carpenter, building cottages in the suburbs. In those days Rose-Anna used to prepare a lunch for him to take to work with him. And at noon, sitting on a high joist, his legs swinging in the air, he would open his lunch box and always find something good to eat, some pleasant surprise. It might be a big red apple whose seeds he would spit out into the street, a meat pie wrapped in several layers of waxed paper to keep warm, a bunch of green grapes, or a couple of buckwheat cakes, of which he never had enough. Those meals up in the air on a bright summer day, with the sun warm on his neck, were an important part of his life. He could not understand why so many insignificant details were so fresh in his memory, such as the rap of the hammer, the taste of the nails on his lips, the grating sound of a door newly hung as it was opened and closed for the first time, and the flavor of those lunches of long ago.

And then the break came. Azarius felt that he must retrace his steps to that very moment of his life in order to understand what had happened to him. For from then on one image after another sped by like an accelerated motion-picture film.

He was no longer a carpenter, and he saw himself dimly at other jobs for which he was ill suited. He perceived a man who must have been himself and yet was not himself. This man was at the wheel of a delivery wagon; he would jump down and carry milk bottles from door to door. But it was not long before the man tired of the monotonous routine; he looked for something more interesting. Later he engaged in many different occupations : the milkman became an iceman; the iceman gave way to a store salesman; the salesman disappeared in turn. Then there were only odd jobs, a day's work here and there, at a dollar, thirty cents, even ten cents a day . . . And then nothing. The man was sitting down near the kitchen stove and stretching himself lazily : "I think they'll give us enough to live on, Mother, while I'm waiting . . . Until the building trades recover."

Azarius was surprised at the sound of his own voice. He had spoken aloud without knowing it. For a while he hearkened to the moan of the wind, and wondered whether he had dozed off.

Then the idler that he was now tried to renew his acquaintance with the first man, who still suffered from his downfall and would not admit it. In those days he had become quite a talker, a man of pronounced opinions in the coffeepots and neighbourhood bars he frequented. It was then that he had begun to boast of all the convents, churches and rectories he had built, and of others he would build shortly, to hear him talk. To tell the truth he had never built anything but suburban cottages for newlyweds, but by dint of speaking of churches, rectories and convents he succeeded in persuading himself that he had constructed hundreds of them. At that period he firmly believed that he was about to hit on some great money-making scheme. For this reason he had not hesitated to squander the two hundred dollars Rose-Anna received at the death of her father in the purchase of tools for the manufacture of occasional furniture. He was convinced that he had a fine business up to the last, when he woke up to find his shop full of furniture that could not be sold and huge bills at the lumber yard.

But far from cooling him off, this reverse had only incited him to take even greater risks. He raised a hundred dollars from Tom, Dick and Harry, and invested it all in a foundry and repair shop, in partnership with a fellow he barely knew. The little shop on

St. Jacques Street bore the name of Lacasse and Tremblay for exactly two weeks. Then the partner decamped, leaving Lacasse to face their creditors without a cent, and new names appeared on the shopwindow.

And yet Azarius had never lost his self-confidence. He always refused the little jobs that friends, through the intercession of Rose-Anna, tried to find for him, declaring that he was not made for such petty chores. In the quarter he had gained a reputation as a ne'er-do-well who would rather let his wife go out as a charwoman than do an honest day's work himself. And yet this was not true; every time he saw Rose-Anna leave the house to wash clothes for some other family, he had reviled himself. And yet he had never said anything to stop her. He would show them all that he was able to support his family properly. Give him time! And at the first opportunity he had launched into what Rose-Anna called his "fiascos."

He had pushed his credit as far as it would go with his brothers-in-law to try his luck in the sweepstakes. That time he had nearly had a run-in with the police. He had tried again, and failed, and tried once more.

Suddenly he stumbled to his feet, his head reeling. In spite of everything he was no more stupid than most men. Why was it that he failed in everything? Probably because luck was against him. But some day his luck would change and his great venture, one of his great ventures, would make up for all the scorn and shame he had suffered.

He looked about the wretched room goggle-eyed, as if waking from a bad dream. Rose-Anna has lost faith in me too, he said to himself. She never had faith in me. No one believes in me. He was afraid to wake up completely and see himself as she had seen him for twenty years, as he really was, perhaps.

And all at once he longed to escape from it all. His passion to escape was so intense that his mind teemed with the most absurd plans. He imagined himself making up a bundle and running away before his wife returned. He would hop a freight, he would go to work in the mines. Or else he would very simply walk up St. Jacques Street toward the city limits, toward the country, and there he would take the highway, following his nose until fortune beckoned at last. He was made for a life of adventure. He would walk along through snow and rain, in sunlight and starlight, all his worldly goods in a kerchief tied to a stick, and somewhere, sometime, at some fork in the road, he would find what he had been seeking ever since birth. He yearned for escape so desperately that he felt as if he were strangling. He wished that he had no wife, no children, no roof over his head. He wanted to be a hobo, lying in the hay under the stars, his face wet with dew. He longed for the dawn that would find him a free man, without ties, without cares, without love.

And then his eyes fell on the sink. The rusty tin basin had filled up from the dripping faucet; a thin stream was running over on the floor. Azarius rolled his sleeves up to his elbows and plunged his hands into the water.

A clock struck the hour.

Like an automaton, with stiff, clumsy movements, Azarius rubbed away at a little black apron, so worn and threadbare that the material fell to pieces in his hands.

CHAPTER XIII

THE WHIR of the sewing machine broke in upon the silence; when it stopped one could hear the kettle humming on the stove. Rose-Anna leaned over to examine her seam, her lips pursed, then her foot came down on the pedal and the machine took up its plaintive chant again.

The lamplight fell on mother and daughter. Every time she raised her head, Rose-Anna saw Florentine curled up on the sofa, holding a magazine with a yellow cover. The girl would read a few lines, and then look up with a blank stare, her brows puckered, her teeth grinding away steadily at a piece of chewing gum. She was only too evidently bored and fretful, but Rose-Anna was so pleased to have her daughter with her that she disregarded this.

The little ones were sleeping. Rose-Anna had put them to sleep in her own bed at an early hour in order to have the dining-room free until she finished her sewing. The room looked restful and tidy with the cretonne-covered daybeds ranged against the walls. Rose-Anna liked to see it this way; it gave her a feeling of repose. But she hurried through her work because Azarius would be home soon. Thanks to the steps she had taken, Azarius had gone back to work, and even seemed quite content with his job. What more did she need? As long as the family was assured of survival her heart was at peace.

For two weeks now she had been rising very early, in order to prepare Azarius's breakfast. He often protested that he could make himself a cup of coffee without any trouble; he would beg her to stay in bed, but in a voice so halfhearted, so hopeful that she was not deceived. She knew that Azarius felt more cheerful when he heard her slippers shuffling across the kitchen floor while he shaved. There was no question but that he liked to come into a room with the fire crackling in the stove to take the chill out of the air, and the steam from the kettle misting the windows. She was sure that his toast had a better taste when she served it to him all buttered, and his coffee had more flavor when she poured it for him, while holding back the full sleeve of her kimono. The glances they exchanged then were eloquent. Rose-Anna asked for no other recompense. And besides, no mark of respect seemed too great for the man of the house when he went out to work, especially now that his hours were very long. She would go to the door and hold it open for him, then shrinking from the cold, she would say goodbye without too overt a display of affection, but with dignity and courage. She herself would close the door after him, and return to sit in his chair, indulging herself in a few moments of idleness, her hands clasped on the table.

This evening too she was idle at times. Despite all the mending she wanted to finish, her hands occasionally lay still, and her mind began to wander. In the lamplight her face showed lines of fatigue drawn by her unending toil from early morning till late at night, but her mouth was calm and relaxed. And in order to justify a sudden access of hope, which experience had taught her to consider a weak reed at best, Rose-Anna began to list the causes of her contentment. In the first place, Eugène had paid them a short visit; he had only dropped in, so to speak, on a twenty-four-hour pass. Yet she had been reassured by his look of good health. Little Daniel was still very pale and weak, but it seemed to her that he took a little more interest in his play. And for Rose-Anna, a child who played, however strangely and gravely, was a healthy child. Thus she never noticed that the little boy was far too serious for his age. She was rather amused to see him writing or pretending to read all day long, whenever she happened to look at him. And finally (wasn't this her greatest source of joy?) Florentine remained at home almost every evening now, and although they had little to say to each other, each wrapped in her own thoughts, it was consoling to know that the girl was there. She's fretting about something, thought Rose-Anna. But she'll get over it and I'll have my lively girl back again. I wonder what can have depressed her so much. Is she in love? Rose-Anna tried to recall what Florentine mumbled in her sleep; she tried to remember where the girl had gone out recently. But she tended to be forgetful of that sort of thing, and she reassured herself quickly.

She sat bemused at the machine, her eyes unseeing. Then, ashamed of shirking her many duties, she pressed her foot quickly to the pedal. The sewing machine whirred again its monotonous chant, accompanied by the whistling teakettle in the kitchen. The wind blew softly at the windows, no longer the sharp, raucous blast of winter, but a gentle spring breeze that shook the last patches of snow from the trees and rubbed the wet branches against one another.

"Your father should be home soon," said Rose-Anna. "It's almost eight o'clock."

Occasionally she made a commonplace remark like this for her own pleasure. Her words dropped into the silence without a ripple. She did not continue, but returned to her train of thought, now and then heaving a little sigh that plucked at the bib of her apron.

For there was, alas, a dark cloud on the otherwise tranquil horizon, a problem she returned to with dread. They had not yet found decent lodgings, and moving day was almost upon them. Azarius kept repeating that there was no hurry, that they ought to wait until they had some money to put down as a deposit for the first month's rent. In that way, he claimed, they could get a better place. Perhaps he was right. She asked nothing better than to believe him. And yet the memory of former disappointments warned her that in practical matters she could trust no one but herself.

Perhaps her greatest affliction came from the fact that in making important decisions she had no one in her family to lean on but Florentine. Rose-Anna felt that she was not naturally a leader, being rather of a yielding disposition and probably, in spite of all her efforts, inclined to be dreamy.

And yet she had been obliged to take the helm, and the result had often been to cut her off from her husband and children. All her attempts to better their condition, which she had made in fear and trembling, had left her uneasy rather than proud, for she had the impression that by proving Azarius in the wrong she had only widened the cleavage between them.

More and more she noticed in her children their father's tendency to live in the clouds, to shun practical matters. In what dream world did they take refuge, a world closed to her despite her lively imagination? Little Yvonne, in her religious exaltation, was the first to detach herself from her family. Even when she was in the room, bent over her schoolbooks, Rose-Anna felt that the child was remote and elusive. In some obscure way, Yvonne's escape from reality caused Rose-Anna more misgivings than that of the others. Fortunately there was Florentine, who was so different from the rest, so sensible!

As she continued sewing, Rose-Anna stole a quick glance at the girl. She was no more effusive with her children than with her husband. Her expressions of affection as a rule went no further than commonplaces or tender glances. Anything more demonstrative would have embarrassed her. This evening, however, her heart overflowed with love as she realized that Florentine was the only one of her children who lived on her own plane, fully conscious of their daily cares. In the warmth of her feeling she was willing to submit to Florentine's judgment in all things. As often in the past, she had the thought that Florentine would be their salvation. The girl had so much assurance and resourcefulness. Florentine will do this . . . She'll settle that; it will be up to her to decide since she helps us so much, thought Rose-Anna, and her lips began to move as if to speak. This soundless movement of the lips helped her to carry on her interior monologues. Then perceiving the gap between her secret thoughts and her usual turn of speech, she made ready to broach an altogether different subject.

"Your father will be paid tonight," she said. "Let's hope he comes home right away and doesn't spend it all first!"

Then she was ashamed to have voiced such a suspicion.

"No, I shouldn't have said that," she corrected herself quickly. "Your father never spends money on himself, we must grant that. But there might be an accident; he might be robbed."

But as she thought it over, even that seemed silly. She tried again:

"You're sure his supper is warm? He'll be hungry when he comes home."

And it was as if she were saying: He will come in with his day's work done, with his dignity restored, with the sweat on his brow, all the things I loved in him, but he will come in too with his ravenous appetite, his fatigue, his wounded vanity, and I will not fail him in what he expects of me any more than he fails me now. I will take as my due whatever he brings: whether it's merely his tired body or some delightful surprise.

"Azarius!" she said aloud, carried away by her reverie.

"Who are you talking to?" asked Florentine, without looking up.

She was bored to death in the quiet room. More than bored, she was filled with hatred of their poverty-stricken home, which was like a cage from which none of them could escape. For three weeks, ever since the day he came to the ten-cent store with Emmanuel, she had not seen Jean. He had vanished with the last great winter storm. Oh the misery, the indignity of waiting for him day after day, without daring to breathe a word about him to anyone. She had made some indirect inquiries about him, however, only to learn that the man without whom life had become impossible for her went on breathing, sleeping, going about his affairs without a care in the world. And then anger grew up beside her love, twining about her love like brambles in a thicket of flowers, killing them one by one, strangling them in a thorny embrace.

Life would be unbearable if she lost all she had hoped for. A bitter thought, so galling that she wanted to lament her lot aloud. But who would hear her cries of woe? Everyone in the house lived in a world of his own. No two of them desired the same thing, penned together though they were, close enough to touch one another. No two of them were bound in the same direction: each went on his way privately: Rose-Anna figuring out how to make ends meet—how could she think of anything else when she had the problem of feeding them?—Azarius toward his mirage of some big deal, stumbling over every obstacle in the road. And if she herself, all hemmed in by cruel thorns as she was, if she were to find something worth while, would she not cling to it stubbornly and refuse to give it up?

She was drowning in boredom, sinking deeper with every tick of the clock. And just as the smouldering fire in the stove leaped up with each puff of wind in the chimney, so the fever in her heart was fanned by the slightest sound from outside, the sound of a man's step on the glazed snow, a voice in the street.

How tedious it was to remain at home on her Saturday night off! If only she could smoke a cigarette, it would calm her nerves and help pass the time, but she dared not because of her mother.

She had hidden a package of cigarettes under a cushion, however, and after much hesitation, she nerved herself to dig it out and put a cigarette to her mouth. Before lighting up she said:

"Do you mind, Mother?"

Rose-Anna was somewhat shocked when Florentine crossed her legs, lit her cigarette, and blew a puff of smoke toward the ceiling. With her thin little figure and her devil-may-care pose she looked like a boy. I mustn't always be scolding her, thought Rose-Anna, in order to hide her own timidity from herself. She coughed and said doubtfully:

"You think it's good for you? All right, if you like it, Florentine."

And she returned to her sewing without another word. In all the years that they had lived together there had never been enough time for her to stop her work and become acquainted with her family. The wheel of the sewing machine turned again; it turned between Florentine's boredom and Rose-Anna's fitful reverie; it turned as the earth turned, heedless of what went on from one pole to the other. And the house seemed to be caught up in the inexorable movement of the wheel, seemed to be filled with the sound of toil, too deafening for speech or mutual understanding. The hours slipped by as it went round, as voices were stilled and a thousand things remained unsaid while it hummed on indefatigably.

Sometimes the spell was broken by something unforeseen, by a word or a complaint. This evening, it was the arrival of Azarius.

Toward eight o'clock they heard him slam the kitchen door with unusual force. He came in whistling, tossed his cap on a nail, and dropped his lunch box with a bang. They could not tell whether he was the bearer of good or bad news until he appeared in the dining-room doorway, his face streaked with dirt. He was clearly glad to be home, but his eyes had a sparkle that implied something more.

"It's an ill wind that blows no one any good, Rose-Anna!" he said.

She looked up at him, not knowing whether to smile or take alarm. Impressed by the deep feeling in his voice and yet intent on finishing her seam, she took a moment to bite off a thread before answering:

"What is it, Azarius?"

He stood leaning against the door-jamb, his teeth flashing. His hair hung in damp strands over his forehead, flattened out where his cap had been pulled tight, leaving a deep line. He looked young and gay, as if he had counted up his assets and found himself the possessor of riches he had never suspected.

Rose-Anna stared at him in silence for a few seconds; she could hear her heart thumping. There were moments when Azarius had the power to carry her back to the days of her youth.

"What's the news, you sweet fool? You have news? Tell us."

Her bosom resting on the sewing machine, she kept her eye on her husband, but her look was a shade less severe than usual, and her lips still bore vestiges of the smile with which she always said "sweet fool," a fond, teasing epithet of their courting days.

Azarius exploded into laughter.

"Ah, you're curious, aren't you now?"

Since he seldom had any great treats to offer his family, he loved to gild his little surprises, lend them the character of a great event, and prolong the period of expectation as much as possible. He loved to see Rose-Anna smile. But his greatest pleasure came from bringing her something out of the blue, something she never expected in the wide world! For Azarius, earning a livelihood for his family was not enough; something more was needed to make the heart leap with joy. If he wanted to confer happiness he looked for it elsewhere than in ordinary things. After several weeks of unemployment his wages seemed more than enough for their basic needs, and he yearned to indulge in some extravagance, as if to compensate for the work he did against his will.

He postured before his wife.

"Get the children ready!" he said.

"Get the children ready? What are you up to?"

"I tell you to get the children ready," he roared. "We're going away tomorrow. We're going to visit your family. We're going to take a holiday tomorrow. The whole day. We're going tomorrow, my love."

Pale with emotion, she waved her hand to stop him, her heart swelling with delight and wonder.

"Is this a joke?" she asked at last.

"I assure you it's no joke. I have the truck. We'll start off tomorrow, early in the morning, at dawn. We're going to the country. Aha," he said, as if proud of having guessed what would bring her the most happiness, "you've been pining to go out there and see your relatives for a long time, eh? Well, now we'll do it. We'll go tomorrow morning. You want to see your mother, your brothers and all the rest of them. And do you know, Rose-Anna, the sap is running, the sap is running, Rose-Anna!"

She was listening to his voice in a transport. He had never known how to relieve her pain nor calm her fears, but five, six, perhaps ten times in her life, in moments of illumination, he had lifted her to the skies! Because of him she had been cold and hungry, because of him she had lived in wretched hovels, felt the constant dread of the morrow; but because of him too she had heard the birds at dawn—"Can you hear the blackbird on the roof, my love?" he would say on awakening—because of him she still realized that the seasons changed and sometimes the spring came again. Because of him, something of her youth, some rapture, a hunger perhaps, had remained in her to mock at the passage of the years.

Could Azarius be unaware of the emotion he had aroused in her, that extraordinary man? Once again he had found his way to her buried desires, hidden away as if in terror of themselves. "The sap . . ." The two words had hardly reached her ear when she was off on her own private dream. So it was happiness of which she had had a presentiment when Azarius came home, and it had upset her almost as much as some misfortune because she had lost the habit of being happy. She could hardly breathe for joy. Come now, she must be more sensible and not lose control of herself. And yet she saw herself there already, in the home of her childhood, walking through the sugar bush over melting snow toward the sugar house, and by some miracle she was walking along with the stride of a young girl, breaking branches in her passage . . . An instinct warned her not to venture into this dream too soon, but it was no use. Had she not already set foot in the scented forest of her youth? Who could pull her back now? For the turn in the road leading to the farm had come into view, she was there, she had thrown off twenty years of her life as she hurried toward the sugar maples. And she discovered her joy in the past as if it were something that had died in her, unaware of the fact that it was a living part of her at all times. Now she saw the sugar bush gleaming in the sun! With eyes closed or open, it mattered not: everything had become visible, crystal clear. She could have said: "This old tree has been giving sap steadily for six years, that one much less, and that one over there has run for only a few days every spring." But she could not have told what moved her most: the ground under the trees splattered with sunlight where the snow had melted and left the brown earth bare and flecked with rotting leaves, or the damp trunks of the trees themselves, with the drops of moisture glittering like morning dew, or the broad avenue through the wood, vast and airy, the sky showing through the leafless branches.

The joys of her childhood unrolled before her in an endless film. At the feet of the tallest trees she could still see patches of snow, but every day the sun rose higher in the sky, striking deeper between the maples where busy figures were running to and fro; her uncle Alfred was driving the team, carting wood for the huge fire in the sugar house; the children in red, yellow or green woolen caps were skipping about like rabbits; and Pato the dog was following them through the clearing and into the woods, the hills echoing with his yelps. Everything was bright and in sharp focus. She could see the tin sap buckets at the base of the maples; as the overflowing pails were carried away she could hear a dull clink when they hit against some object, and she heard too a faint murmur, fainter than a rustle, softer than the whisper of a spring rain on new leaves. It was the sound of a thousand drops falling one by one from the bleeding wounds of the maples, the first drops hitting the bottom of the buckets with a deep note; others running into a bucket three-quarters full with a subdued purl; some hurried, some slow and interrupted; all mingling in a rippling cascade of sound coming from every point of the maple grove. Rose-Anna could hear the crackling of the great fire in the sugar house; she could see the pale yellow sap in the arch bubbling up, she could taste the syrup, she could smell it; the whole forest came to life in her mind.

Then the picture changed. She was in her parents' house, with her brothers and sisters-in-law, surrounded by their children, some of whom she had never seen, since they were always having babies. She was talking with her old mother, who was seated in a rocking chair in a corner of the kitchen. Although she was never demonstrative, old Mme Laplante would have a warm welcome for her daughter whom she had not seen for so many years. The old woman would say a few cheering words, and the moment would come for a few intimate confidences. The whole house would hum with the distant murmur of the sugar bush. There would be a great tub of snow on the kitchen table; they would pour the syrup into the snow, and it would harden immediately into a block the colour of honey. Rose-Anna trembled. She could see her younger children regaling themselves with the snow candy, and dipping their bread into the hot syrup for the first time in their lives. She came back from a long and wonderful journey, and as her eyes fell on the piece of sewing in her hand a sigh escaped her.

"Seven years!" she whispered.

"Yes," he answered, as if he knew what she meant, "it's seven years since you saw your mother."

But what she meant was seven years of fighting off the desire to see them. Seven years! How long can I go on struggling?

She leaned forward and said timidly :

"Have you thought of the expense, Father?"

"Yes, Mother, it's all settled. The truck costs me nothing."

"Lachance will let you have it?"

Azarius's face turned a darker brown.

"He'd better! I do enough for him. But I've another idea. I'm going to bring back thirty or forty gallons of maple syrup to pay for the trip. I have orders for even more."

"Orders?"

For a moment she suspected that Azarius was hatching another one of his great schemes. As a rule his enthusiasms were based on pure conjecture. If the risk were large and unlikely to succeed, it made him even happier, even more intoxicated. But Rose-Anna had been robbed of joy for too long a time not to give in right away. Perhaps she had already yielded, and was only continuing to raise objections to punish herself for her prompt assent.

"And the children, Father?" she murmured.

"What do you mean? Of course we'll take them. They ought to see it for once."

"They have nothing to wear," she said. "This doesn't give me much time to get them ready."

She had her pride. She could bear poverty bravely as long as her relatives were not there to witness it. No, she would never consent to go home with her children in rags. They were supposed to be in comfortable circumstances; and the fact that her people did not know exactly how poor they were was a kind of consolation to Rose-Anna.

"Will you have time to patch up a few things for them before tomorrow morning, Mother?"

Rose-Anna did not answer at once. She was brooding over the fact that poverty is like a pain, dormant and not unbearable as long as you don't move about too much. You grow used to it, you end up by paying no attention to it. But once you presume to bring it out in the daylight, it becomes terrifying, you see it at last in all its squalor and you shrink from exposing it to the sun.

"I'm not sure," she said. "The children have practically nothing to put on their backs."

"Take it easy!" answered Azarius. "I'll give you a hand."

He was rubbing his palms with pleasure, for he saw only the flight from his cares, while Rose-Anna, wherever she might go, always carried her burdens with her. He went over to Florentine, who had been following the discussion with an air of slight hostility, and bent over to give her hair a playful tug.

"You too, my lass. You'll see how the hicks'll play up to you!"

Florentine shrank back with a frown; the corners of her mouth fell.

"No, I'm not going," she said, "but you go, the rest of you. I'll take care of the house."

Azarius saw a look of determination come into her eyes. He was nonplussed. The girl was his pride and joy, not only because of her good looks; he also believed that she was level-headed. On his way home in the truck, he had been thinking that he would love to show Florentine to his Laplante relatives. Beyond the lighted strip of road on which his eyes were fixed sleepily he had had a vision of his daughter in her new spring hat, her straight slender legs scurrying through the dust in the glare of the powerful headlights. Usually it was a picture of Rose-Anna that accompanied him on his trips home at night, when he would let his hands grip the wheel loosely and hum a song to keep him from dozing off. Twelve hours at a stretch on the road! At such times many faces appeared before him, as he wearily put the miles behind him. But tonight he had seen Florentine fleeing from the huge tires of the truck. Florentine, so lithe and slender that his heart always skipped a beat when he thought of her! Florentine in her holiday clothes, running breathlessly on the dark highway! And then to rid himself of a vague sense of guilt he had promised himself to be kinder to Florentine. After that his thoughts had taken a calmer and more pleasant turn. Florentine . . . He never failed to notice the trinkets, the silly little hats and the silk stockings she acquired, and although these were bought out of her own wages, most of which went to keep up the house, he had always felt as if he were being liberal toward her when she came home after a shopping expedition. He considered himself a good father because she managed to dress smartly. She at least did not advertise their poverty. Like him, she knew that their bad luck was a passing thing. He was grateful to her for sharing his faith that better days would come. It was in this mood that he had arrived home, proud of the great treat he had planned for both Florentine and Rose-Anna, looking forward to the fine impression his daughter would make on his wife's relatives. Basically he was depending on Florentine to offset their peasant-like mistrust of him. Florentine would be a feather in his cap. He had not expected her to walk out on his fine scheme.

"But Flo-flo," he said, trying to jolly her along, "aren't you tempted to come along to see the sugaring? And maybe find a handsome beau too?"

"D'you think I care about those things?" said she, lighting another cigarette.

Strangely enough, his vision of Florentine running madly down the road came again to his mind. His face grew somber. Anita Latour, who was in a position to know everything going on in the neighborhood, had intimated to him that Florentine might have a sweetheart.

"Is it because you have a boy-friend?" he asked.

But he had always been afraid to get to the bottom of things, and he did not press her when Florentine broke away from him.

"Let me alone," she said. "I just don't want to go, that's all."

Azarius stood there awkwardly for a minute, his hands grappling the air. Then he covered up his disappointment by a complete change of front.

"All right, that's that. Florentine will stay at home. The rest of us can leave without worrying. Now what's on your mind, Mother? Don't you want to get some new clothes? We mustn't miss a chance like this, after all."

"A chance like this . . ." she repeated.

She met his glowing eyes, from which the traces of disappointment were already fading. Her last fears set at rest by a glance at Florentine's unruffled face, she joined wholeheartedly in the scheme.

"No," she said, "you're right, we mustn't miss it. If we put it off we'll end by never doing it." Feeling the need to explain herself further, she added: "It's better to make up our minds quickly, and not wait."

What she dared not betray too openly was that she had been won over to Azarius's madness. For once she would go along with him in his madness, she who had always pleaded for the sensible thing. Now she was going the way he had always wanted to go, and not only that, she was taking the lead and passing him. She would wander through the scented woods of her youth, she would hear the silvery ripple, the voice of springtime, which had called to her in vain all these years of drudgery, she would go with her children toward the happiness for which they all hungered, she would lead them into the forbidden kingdom and would open the gates for them herself. They had thought she was a crabbed old woman, unwilling to see anyone merry; it was time she corrected that impression.

"Listen," she said, and the quiver in her voice showed that she had decided on something quite contrary to her principles, "the stores aren't closed yet; it's Saturday. If you hurry you'll have time to buy me a few things. Listen," she said, and her voice became so grave that you could hear the appeal of outings that had been put off eternally, of desires that had been pent up forever tearing at her heart, "listen, you must buy——"

She paused for a long time at that dreadful word, her bogey. She heard it as if in a dream, doubting that it was she who had spoken it.

"You must buy——"

They were all panting, even Florentine, who wondered on what the poor woman's choice would fall. And they could see her hesitating as a thousand things suggested themselves to her. Therefore it was all the more astonishing when she quickly reeled off a long list of articles.

"You must buy," she said, "two yards of blue serge, three pairs of cotton stockings, a shirt for Philippe if you see one, no, four pairs of stockings and a pair of shoes for Daniel. Don't get the size wrong, he wears a seven."

She stopped to reconsider, and then made a digression:

"But he's not the one who really needs them most. He probably won't be well enough to go back to school this year. Perhaps I can manage some other way. Shoes are so dear. Albert's are worn through."

Her face was torn with indecision. She wanted to be fair to all the children. Like many other mothers in Saint-Henri, she felt no urgency about sending them to school when they were ready for the first grade. Hence she kept the younger ones at home, if they lacked warm clothing, with no great scruple, while all her efforts were bent toward getting the older children to attend their classes regularly. This seeming favoritism had often made the little ones cry, Daniel particularly, as the most frequent victim. It occurred to her now that because of his illness the child had been deprived of new shoes for a very long time. She therefore clung to her original idea and put her customary prudence aside. If she made one of them happy, the others must be made happy too. But it was so hard to divide up happiness and see to it that there was enough to go around.

"Size seven," she whispered, pressing her hands to her throbbing temples. "Well, as I said, serge, stockings, shoes, a shirt——"

At this point Albert, who was supposed to be asleep, begged:

"Can I have a tie?"

"Oh dear," murmured Rose-Anna, "if you see a fairly cheap tie, Father——"

"And me," squeaked little Lucille, "you've been promising me a dress for a long time, Mamma."

Their entreaties waked Daniel. Not knowing what it was all about except that the time had come to make his wishes known, he stammered from the depths of his misery:

"Is it Christmas?"

And they all laughed, with a catch in their throats.

Rose-Anna quickly saw that she would be overwhelmed by the torrent she had unloosed, and in sudden fear began to scold:

"Go back to sleep, all of you, or you won't go tomorrow."

"Where are we going tomorrow?"

The children hung halfway out of the big bed and listened with rapture to Albert, who told them the whole story.

"Quiet! I think we're going to grandma's to see the sugaring."

From the smallest one up, they were all in such transports, they had flown so far away from the house, the dark shadows everywhere, they were in such a fairyland that it seemed only natural for Azarius to ask:

"And you, Mother? You really ought to have a new dress."

She gave him a wry smile, as if she took a more indulgent view of his improvident character, since she too had taken flight. All her love went into the glance she gave him. Yes, she wished with all her heart to hold on to the moment of ecstasy, but no finery for her. What did she need? Nothing. The important thing, the thing that would clothe her regally, was to have her children well dressed. She would be judged by her children.

"Can you see me in silks and satins?" she said jestingly. "I'd be a fine sight!"

She joined in his laughter, for the time to laugh had not yet gone by, the time to look at each other with new eyes and follow the same adventurous road. But then she became grave again.

"Be sure you get what I said," she warned, "and above all don't let them foist any trash on you. And don't pay any fancy prices either!"

Azarius pulled out a notebook and wet his pencil on his tongue.

"Well, if I'm to remember everything, I'd better make a list. You said a shirt, two yards of blue serge, shoes——"

But Rose-Anna, at the idea that her plans, still in the dream stage, might suddenly materialize and be translated into terms of money, hesitated and beat a retreat.

"No, better let the serge go. Unless you see something very good and very cheap. D'you think you'd know?"

Thus at the last minute she burdened Azarius with her fears.

And neither of them, standing together for a moment in the circle of lamplight over the sewing machine, neither of them noticed that Florentine was slipping into her coat and hat.

Rose-Anna read the list over; she put a figure beside each item; then she added it all up and stopped in horror at the total. Yet she was determined to cross out nothing. For if you measure out and water down your happiness, the time comes when it ceases to act as a tonic. No, she thought, if you want to be happy you must let yourself go, you must take a full dose.

Suddenly the door of the kitchen was opened from the inside. A cold draft swirled around her legs. Rose-Anna looked up in surprise.

"Who went out? Florentine! Where is she going at such an hour?"

A cloud passed over her face. Then her fever to complete their plans rose again, and she held out the list to Azarius with a trembling hand, unable to look him straight in the eye. Peering into the future, weighing the cost of each moment of happiness, and aware in every fiber that happiness makes trouble that much harder to bear, she said:

"Go quickly now, before I change my mind. It seems as if we want to have our cake and eat it too, my dear, but God in Heaven, we don't have cake every day. We might as well have a taste of it when we can."

The children went back to sleep in their mother's big bed. They would not be disturbed for the rest of the night, because all night long the drone of the sewing machine would go on, accompanying Rose-Anna at her work, whirring through the quiet house like a promise to be fulfilled.

Her shoulders sagging, her back stooped, her eyelids heavy, Rose-Anna was sewing for the holiday, not daring even to sing lest her joy take fright and run away.

CHAPTER XIV

THE WINDOWS of the Montreal Metal Works on St. Jacques Street seemed to be on fire. In the soft, clear night air, the clang of hammers and the creaking of winches rose above the general pandemonium and spread over the quiet neighborhood.

Although Florentine hovered at a certain distance from the foundry, her figure was brightly lit up as she passed within range of the windows. She was afraid to approach too close because an armed guard was posted at a sentry box near the door. Coming to a stop on the other side of the street, she tried to peer into the ground floor. Through the sooty panes she could make out vague shadows which became distinctly outlined only when they moved about in front of the leaping flames to draw a piece of white-hot metal from the gaping furnace. She ventured a few steps in one direction, then in the other, clinging to the walls of the houses, fearful of attracting the attention of the guard. After a while she saw a man come out of the door, his lunch box under his arm and his cap pulled down over his eyes. She went up to him and mumbled almost unintelligibly, as if the whole atmosphere of the place had terrified her.

"Is this where Monsieur Lévesque works?"

And she was even more frightened when she heard herself mention Jean's last name.

The man peered at her from under the visor of his cap.

"Lévesque? The machinist? Yes, madame . . . mademoiselle. He must be in the machine shop."

Then, after a moment :

"Would you like me to call him? If it's something urgent——"

Florentine stopped him with a quick shake of the head.

"No, I'll wait."

Then she blushed as she nerved herself to ask :

"Will he be much longer?"

The man shrugged.

"I don't know. We've got more work than we can do these days."

And touching his hand to his cap, he went away.

After a while a group of workmen came out, presumably apprentice molders and polishers new to the job, for Florentine heard them complaining bitterly about their working conditions.

Their voices faded away down St. Jacques Street. Then Florentine saw another figure at the door of the foundry. By his broad shoulders and slim waist she knew it to be Jean. Her heart beat madly, her brow grew moist, but she waited until he stepped out on the sidewalk before slipping out of the shadows to intercept him.

She stood before him without a word, smiling shyly, her bosom heaving.

"What are you doing here?" he asked.

He gave her a sharp look, and the lines between his eyebrows deepened.

She began to trot along beside him.

"It's so long since we've seen each other," she said, "and I happened to be passing by tonight——"

As he gave her no encouragement, she broke off her explanations, realizing that he would take no stock in them in any case. Studying his profile eagerly, she saw how hard the line of his jaw was, although it quivered involuntarily with fatigue now and then.

After a moment, Jean rubbed his hand over his forehead and slowed down a bit. Then he began to speak, almost in a daze:

"That's right, it's been quite some time since I've seen you. We're working overtime these days. This week I worked eighteen hours two days running. A man can't tell if he's alive or if he's been turned into a machine."

He shook himself and continued, talking into space:

"And now they've dumped four new apprentices on me. Fellows who don't know a blamed thing. I have to show them everything. And how they grumble! Nothing suits them. 'What have you got to kick about?' I asked them tonight. 'Before you came here you were making fifteen or twenty cents an hour. And now you make thirty an hour and forty for overtime. If you keep at it you'll have a nice little nest egg when you're on your uppers.' "

He stopped, gasping for breath, so worn out that he found it hard to make himself clear. Then he suppressed a yawn:

"Yeah, it's a funny life! Either you don't make a red cent and you have all the time in the world, or else you get double the money and you don't have a moment to spend a penny of it."

"Is it that bad?" she said, just to attract his attention, for she knew quite well that he was not talking to her, but to himself.

He glanced at her furtively and continued his monologue:

"I'm section foreman now."

And without having her particularly in mind, he asked:

"Did you know?" and expected no answer.

What value could her dumb admiration have for him tonight?

She was just a nuisance. Formerly, when he was still unsure of himself, it would have been somewhat pleasant. The devil take it, but he was tired! He could scarcely collect his thoughts. And yet his mind was bubbling over with ideas. They came to him so thick and fast that he was all on edge. Yes, section foreman! A good beginning! For even though he had to give up studying in the evening, at least it was not at the sacrifice of his promotion.

"Yes," he went on aloud, "nowadays a man is rated according to his ability and not by some slip of paper. I'm not afraid of anyone. It takes a war to bring the best men forward."

Disconcerted by all this, Florentine looked at him uneasily. As they passed under a street light, she noticed that the skin around his eyes was drawn, as if he had not slept in a long time.

"You're all done up, aren't you, Jean?" she said.

She was trying to be sympathetic, but as she reached out to take his arm he moved on ahead, and her hand remained in the air.

"What brought you here anyway? I thought you and Emmanuel were such great friends. Wouldn't you like to be a war bride? With a ten-day honeymoon, a nice little soldier boy, and a pension from the government?"

His laughter stung her. Then after a few moments, without seeing her, shunning her, as she felt, he added:

"You'd be better off with a guy like me, wouldn't you? A guy with a head on his shoulders?"

She did not answer. His eyes fell on her shadow, tripping along beside his. And a slight sense of pity, not to speak of a twinge of jealousy, drove him to pursue the attack:

"You were playing up to Emmanuel all right, a few weeks ago at the store."

"I don't hate Manuel," she answered, choking. "But he doesn't mean anything to me."

She stumbled as she tried to keep up with him, and her chin quivered.

"Why have you come here anyway?" he insisted.

Her humble little smile was lost on him, for he was looking straight ahead, but it was reflected in the girl's awkward reply:

"Someone told me you were working late, so I thought I'd wait for you. You know it's three weeks since I saw you last. You didn't come to the Létourneau party either, though you said you would."

She tried to project her thought in a clumsy gesture. Moistening her lips, she burst out:

"I thought you might be angry at me."

He faltered in his stride. Then she humbled herself to a point she had never thought possible, her voice full of pleading:

"Maybe I hurt your feelings, without knowing it?"

He shook his head vehemently.

"No," he said, "but I'm not your boy-friend."

He was walking so fast that she found herself running to catch up with him. But her shadow doggedly kept pace with his.

She was disgusted with herself for not having found a more plausible explanation for being there. But it was very difficult to explain so impulsive an act. And yet she did not regret it, although a voice within her warned: *He doesn't care about you. You don't mean a thing to him.* She refused to heed the warning. She must follow out the line of conduct she had planned when she left the house. Again she tried to lead him to make some concession:

"Even if you're not my real boy-friend, we needn't be on bad terms."

So much naïveté and persistence combined made him smile, a smile so cruel that Florentine broke down. What pride remained to her was touched at last. She bit her lips; her nostrils dilated.

"Oh well," she said, "don't be frightened. I won't chase after you. You'll see."

Sobs began to choke her voice as she added:

"You started it."

He seized her by the arm.

"All right," he said. "We'll have a bite of supper together, as long as you're here."

Now he was hard put to it to keep up with her, for she was setting a stiff pace, walking with her head thrust forward, her teeth biting into her lip. Again and again she tried to release her arm, but there was a mist before her eyes, and she could barely see where she was going.

They reached a restaurant ablaze with lights, and went in; it was very new, and still smelled of paint and lumber. Jean led Florentine to a booth and helped her off with her coat. She offered no resistance, she spoke no word, although her lips continued to tremble. And at this Jean felt a change of heart.

Under the garish lights Florentine no longer seemed a clinging vine, a shadow he could not brush off when he wanted to be alone, but a vibrant, appealing girl. Her brown sweater fitted her snugly, showing her tiny pointed breasts. She wore no jewelry to-night, and almost no rouge. For once she faced him without coquetry, with her guard down, fearful, submissive. Stripped of all artifice, the poor girl reminded him of the saddest years of his life, long ago. He was vexed to find his heart melting, because for three weeks he had done his best to forget her. Besides, when he discovered that Emmanuel was attracted by her, he had resolved never to see her again. Emmanuel's coming offered a happy solution of all his doubts, permitting him to leave the field open to his best friend while retaining the illusion of his own indifference. As a matter of fact, the night of the party at the Létourneaus', he had passed the house several times before he could bring himself to go away. Bah, he was not such a bad fellow as one might suppose, since he had pushed Florentine into the arms of a man who was really capable of loving her. But he had not foreseen that he might meet her again. Neither at the five-and-ten, which he avoided studiously, nor by chance. Certainly not in a deserted street, at night. He contemplated the girl with mingled feelings, thinking: So much the worse for her; whatever happens is her own fault.

Meanwhile Florentine had grasped the change in his face. She put her hand on the table, offering it to him. Already she was devising a new plan of attack. She was in no position to pass up the slightest advantage. Her hand continued moving across the table until he took it in his own.

"Aren't you afraid, Florentine?"

Afraid? Yes, she was afraid, insanely afraid that Jean might turn away from her, but observing that he was troubled—and perhaps less skillful than she at hiding it—hope welled up in her.

"Afraid of what?"

She smiled uncertainly, as one does in dreams when one has the sense of being led by a strange hand; and she shook her head with a graceful movement that rippled her hair over her shoulders.

"Afraid of a fellow like me," he specified.

His lids were heavy, but his shining eyes took her all in. And yet as he studied her closely he came to the conclusion that the more he wanted her, the fewer illusions he had about her, and the less he loved her perhaps.

Lost in silence, Florentine was thinking of what Emmanuel had said: "Because he'd make you unhappy." This was really important, and ought to make her stop and reconsider. But not now, she thought. Not now, just when she was beginning to breathe easily after so much pain and grief! Besides, what had she to fear from Jean? If he were the wild fellow he pretended to be, wouldn't he have tried to take advantage of her before this? But instead of that he had taken her home after their evening out; he had only kissed her gently. In spite of himself, whether he wished it or not, he would be her boy-friend, her only boy-friend, her steady! They would go to the movies together every Saturday night, perhaps even twice a week. What fine prospects lay before her, if only she were game enough to forget her pride for the moment! Later on she would learn how to have her own way.

Her hand trembled in his. And suddenly she lifted it to his mouth, pressing her palm as hard as she could against his lips.

At that moment a waiter appeared at the entrance of the booth. Jean made a move to push away her hand, but she held it to his lips with an impudent grin. She was no longer afraid to be seen on the most intimate terms with Jean. A show of affection in a public place was very flattering to her vanity, and besides, she was so carried away by passion that everything else seemed remote. Close as she believed she was to Jean, she was already on the brink of unimaginable solitude. Her passion was blinding her to reality, propelling her in a strange direction, and only much later would she be appalled by her loneliness, her self-delusion.

They ate little, Jean examining her steadily, sometimes giving her a faint smile, Florentine lifting her fork to her mouth only to let it fall the next instant.

When the dessert came, he moved over to sit beside her. He encircled her wrist with his fingers as if he were measuring it; his thumb pressed against her swelling veins. For a moment he stared at her bruised wrist as if hypnotized, then his fingers inched their way up the inside of her arm until they reached the elbow, where his hand stiffened on her tender skin. To Florentine the hand seemed to be burning her. Her lids grew heavy; she dropped her head against his shoulder, brushing her hair against his cheek. And then a mist closed down around her completely. She was somewhere in time, in space, perhaps in another world; her life up to that moment seemed infinitely far away; it amounted to no more than a few trivial events, a few pale memories that went spinning off toward oblivion.

"Let's go," he said suddenly.

She gathered up her coat and hat like an automaton, her eyes clouded. Once outside, where the wind had turned sharper, she grew a little more calm.

"I only came to meet you to find out if you were angry at me," she murmured, leaning against him.

She looked at him as if she were a little drunk and pulled at his coat sleeve. To touch his clothes, and breathe in the smell of hot sand, molten metal, cold cast-iron they still gave out, kindled her emotions anew.

"I also wanted to invite you to come to see me tomorrow. Sunday," she added dreamily.

In spite of all, she realized the importance of going through with her plan, which was to induce Jean to visit her on Sunday. While her parents were away, they would have the house to themselves, to kiss each other as often as they wished. It was a bold scheme. Knowing instinctively that the situation would whet his appetite, she nevertheless felt quite sure that he would respect her innocence if she showed that she trusted him. She scarcely admitted to herself that her plan was so well formed in her own mind, and yet she gloated over it.

"Will you come?" she urged.

He answered with a vague pressure of the arm. In silence they came out on Sir Georges-Etienne Cartier Place. Between the elms and maples, stiff with cold, shadowy figures were passing two by two. The benches were empty. There was enough of a nip in the March air to keep the lovers strolling constantly, with only a furtive stop in patches of darkness now and then.

Jean began looking for a dark patch out of the corner of his eye. Spying a huge tree that threw a broad mass of shade, he led Florentine into the black arabesques cast by the branches.

Florentine closed her eyes and lifted her lips. But at that moment he was struck by the fragility of the face so near him, and whispered almost in horror:

"How thin you are!"

He dropped his arms and recoiled. When she opened her eyes he stood a few feet away, with his hands in his pockets. She threw herself at him then, she left the shadow of the tree to fling her arms about his neck, wild with fear that her plans had failed and that Jean might escape her still. Almost sobbing, she burst into a wail, her words so disjointed they sounded like a nervous giggle:

"I love you so, Jean. I know it doesn't make sense; it's not my fault, but I love you so!"

His arms hanging at his sides, he stood staring over her head, over the roof tops across the square at the pale crescent of the rising moon. His eyes were hard and dry; at times he made a grimace of exasperation. The whole scene was extremely embarrassing. He had not anticipated this.

"Why the devil do you want me to come to your house tomorrow?" he asked.

Without raising her eyes, she gave a little nod to indicate that she had set her heart on it. Her pointed chin dug into his chest with every movement she made. After a while he felt her grow still. Guessing that he would agree to come to her house in order to get out of his present ridiculous fix, she was already congratulating herself on her tearful outburst. He took her by the chin and forced her to look him in the face; then without malice, almost gently, but knowing well that this was to be the last time he would ever be patient with her:

"I am not your boy-friend. You mustn't get ideas in your head just because I played up to you at the store once. I'm telling you, marriage is not for me."

He was watching to see if she would balk at this; he had almost come to hope for it. But she only pressed her thin arms more tightly around his neck. She stood on tiptoe to lay her cheek against his chin, mingling her breath with his, trying to smile through her tumbled curls. Fearful that a passerby might come upon them thus, he had a cowardly impulse to end it all as soon as possible, and promised evasively :

"All right, if I don't have to work all day tomorrow I'll come to see you."

Then with a possessive, shameless gesture she took him by the arm and walked on through the night by his side, smiling to herself.

CHAPTER XV

TO THE CHILDREN, the country was only a crazy-quilt, with patches of grayish snow interspersed with plots of bare earth and an occasional tall brown tree standing alone, but Rose-Anna and Azarius often gave each other meaningful glances, smiling as their thoughts took the same course.

"Do you remember this?" one would say.

"Yes, it hasn't changed," the other would reply.

Trifles that plunged them into blissful recollection.

Sitting next to the door, Rose-Anna inhaled the pure air with delight. As soon as they left Victoria Bridge, she had lowered the window to take a deep breath.

"What good air!" she had said, her nostrils dilated.

They were speeding along now on the main highway. Although she had spent the whole night sewing, Rose-Anna showed few signs of fatigue. Her eyes were a bit heavy, but the lines about her mouth were without strain.

One by one she recognized the villages of the Richelieu Valley, and something like the high spirits of her girlhood prompted the comments that only Azarius understood.

Then suddenly she stopped talking. With a great leap of her heart she hailed the foaming river at the base of Fort Chambly. From that time on she began to watch out for every turn in the road, each curve that brought them within view of the Richelieu. Not that hills or streams in themselves had any great attraction for her. She barely noticed them and often did not remember them except in so far as they were linked with her own life. Thus she was almost indifferent to the St. Lawrence; but she knew every twist of the Richelieu, having lived beside it all through her childhood; and knowing it so well, she did not hesitate to tell her children:

"It's the most beautiful river in the country." Just as when she described a countryside, she would always qualify it by saying: "It's not as beautiful as the stretch of land at home, along the river bank." The standards of comparison she drew from her memory were purely arbitrary, but she knew how to communicate her enthusiasm so well that no one ever doubted her.

As soon as the Richelieu appeared on their left, she sat up straighter. Her hands gripping the window, she leaned out of the cab, and as they jolted through each village, she called out the name aloud: Saint-Hilaire, Saint-Mathias, Saint-Charles.

The banks of the river began to slope more gently, and spread farther apart. The stream flowed along so quietly in the fullness of its strength that one would hardly guess the depth of its dark waters under a thin layer of ice.

At times Azarius would turn around and yell to the children, who were seated on blankets in the back of the truck, shouting above the roar of the motor:

"Look at this, you Lacasse kids! Your mother and I used to come here in a rowboat long ago!"

And then little Daniel, whom they had placed on the seat between them lest he be too cold, would open his eyes still bright with fever. "Where is the river?" he would pipe feebly. He was too little to see out of the windows of the truck, and as far as he knew the Richelieu might have been the strip of blue sky he could see through the windshield, occasionally etched with a fretwork of black twigs and branches.

"What is a rowboat?" he once asked gravely, making such a great effort to understand that he was almost in a sweat.

From time to time he tried to stand up on the seat in order to see more of the countryside and place all the things his parents were talking about. But in his mind the Richelieu was always to be a bit of sky over his head, sky of a blue he had never seen before, banded with soft white clouds that might be rowboats.

Back to earth for a moment, Rose-Anna covered him up to his neck, for he seemed to be shivering as he huddled against her.

Then her own village came into view at the end of an avenue of trees.

"Saint-Denis!" shouted Azarius.

And Rose-Anna's eyes suddenly were wet with excitement. Her mind shot ahead of the turn in the road, the hill at the end of the village. But at last the landscape opened up to reveal her father's house. The gabled roof came into view among the maples, then the railed porch, with the shriveled remnants of a cucumber vine climbing over it. Swaying toward Azarius, Rose-Anna shuddered with as much physical pain as emotion, murmuring:

"Ah, here we are! It hasn't changed much!"

Her joy had lasted until then and was to last a bit longer, for the door of the house burst open and her brothers and her sister-in-law appeared on the step, their hearty welcome buzzing in her ears: "Well, well! Look who's here! This is great! Guests from Montreal!"

But as she was getting out of the truck, her feet wobbly and her head spinning with the country air, trying to smooth out her old coat, a coarse joke from her brother Ernest cast the first shadow on her happiness.

"By Jove, if it isn't Rose-Anna!" he said, giving her a searching glance. "I'll be damned if you're not going to raise a brood of fifteen, like your mother!"

Rose-Anna shrank from this dubious welcome. She had drawn her corset as tight as she could in the hope that her pregnancy would pass unnoticed, not out of false shame, but because she had always come to visit her relatives in that state, and also because she had wanted this day to be one of relaxation, of refound youth, perhaps of illusion. Yet she forced a smile and tried to take it lightly.

"Well, that's a family for you, Ernest. What do you expect?"

But she knew now how fragile a thing her happiness was, and how easily it could be shattered.

A ruder blow came from her sister-in-law, Réséda. As she helped Rose-Anna take off the children's outer clothes, young Mme Laplante cried:

"But how pale they are, Rose-Anna! Are you sure you give them enough to eat?"

At this Rose-Anna became very angry. Of course Réséda said that in spite, because her children were always so badly clothed. They were really dressed like ragamuffins, with their coarse woolen socks and their sloppy breeches hanging down to their ankles. Rose-Anna called little Gisèle to her to smooth out the curl in her hair, and to pull her skirt up over her knees in the current fashion. But as she was hastily tidying up her children she caught sight of Daniel and Réséda's eldest, a chubby, pink-cheeked boy. She stifled a cry. The little peasant had fallen on his city cousin like a healthy puppy and wanted to roll on the floor with him. The sickly child had no stomach for a fight. He was obviously hoping to be let alone.

Rose-Anna stuck up for her boy: "Yours is older than mine, too."

"No, no," protested the young woman. "They were born the same year, and you know it."

"No," maintained Rose-Anna stoutly. "There's six months' difference between them."

And then came long explanations to determine the exact date of birth of the two boys.

"It's Albert who's the same age as yours," insisted Rose-Anna.

"Stuff and nonsense," said Réséda sharply. "You know very well that they were both born in the summer."

She was walking about the room as she spoke, trying to pacify her youngest baby, who was wailing to be fed and plucking at her bodice with surprisingly strong hands. And she said emphatically:

"You can't convince me. I know very well that they were born the same month."

The two mothers glared at each other defiantly for a moment, the country woman's eyes full of insolent pride. Rose-Anna lowered hers. Her anger subsided. Timidly, fearfully, she looked around at her children, wondering if she had ever seen them as they really were until now, with their thin little faces and their skinny limbs.

Réséda's next youngest was crawling toward her on short fat legs, with plump knees, and suddenly, beyond the baby, she saw a row of spindly shanks. Her children were seated in a row against the wall, and all she could see of them was their legs, their long, bony, scrawny legs.

The final wound was to come from her mother. Dinner was served in two shifts, an exhausting operation in which she had helped her sister-in-law as much as possible, and Rose-Anna at last found herself alone with old Mme Laplante. She had yearned for this moment when Réséda would be busy with her baby and the men would gather around the stove talking business, so that she could have a few moments of privacy with her mother. But the first words from the old woman were fatalistic:

"Poor Rose-Anna, I suspected that you were having a hard time. I knew it. Life is no easier for you than for others. You see, my girl, things never work out the way we want them to. Years ago you thought you knew more than I . . ."

Her voice was shrill, but without emotion or rancor. Old Mme Laplante stubbornly denied all hope. It was not that she had never shown any spirit of charity. On the contrary it pleased her to think that she was going to meet her Creator, full of good works, and with all her sins remitted. She might almost be said to picture herself entering Heaven like a prudent traveler, who all her life had done the sort of thing to assure herself a comfortable sojourn there. According to her own expression, she had "gone through Purgatory on earth." She was not without certain merits. But in all her acts the comforting gleam of hope had been wanting. Thus she had sacrificed herself to her duty, as she saw it, with so little warmth that it took on its most repulsive aspect.

She was one of those who love to listen to tales of woe. If she heard of someone's good fortune she would smile mistrustfully. Nothing surprised her so much as a face glowing with happiness. She did not believe in happiness; she had never believed in it. If someone had come to her and said that all was going well, she would have frowned and declared with conviction: "It can't be so, you should not be so happy. You can't put anything over on me!" In addition she had such a great desire to be right all the time that she seemed almost to rejoice when her direst prophecies were borne out.

At the other end of the kitchen the men were in the midst of a discussion that soon rose to a lively pitch. Rose-Anna had drawn her chair close up to her mother's rocker. It made her feel awkward and uneasy to sit twiddling her thumbs. Of a sudden she felt rather ashamed to be coming to her mother, not as a married woman with the strength that responsibilities are supposed to confer, but as a child in need of help and light. The old woman's admonitions, delivered in a preachy tone as cold as her white, angular face, made their way to Rose-Anna's ears, but gave her heart no comfort.

What had she expected to find? She did not know any more, for the longer she talked with her mother, the less distinct grew the picture she had conceived of her at a distance. The old woman was just as she had always been, and Rose-Anna wondered how she could have been so mistaken. There was no use hoping for any sympathy from that source.

Mme Laplante had raised fifteen children. She had risen in the middle of the night to care for them in illness; she had taught them their prayers; she had taught them their catechism; she had spun and woven and sewed for them with her own hands; she had set food before them; but she had never bent over them with a look of affection in her steely gray eyes. She had never taken them on her knee after they outgrew their swaddling clothes. She had never kissed them—if that dry peck could be called a kiss—except after a long absence, or on New Year's Day, and even then with a certain solemnity, as she repeated the usual compliments of the season.

She had held fifteen little heads to her breast; she had had fifteen tots hanging to her skirts; she had had an affectionate, a devoted husband, but all her life she had spoken of the cross she had to bear, of her trials and burdens. All her life she had spoken of Christian resignation and human suffering.

On his deathbed, old man Laplante had muttered:

"At last you will be delivered of one of your crosses, my poor wife!"

"How is your Azarius getting along?"

Rose-Anna started, and came back to the present. Then she leaned again toward her mother, for she knew that the old woman in her phlegmatic way was trying to find out how things stood with the Lacasse family. She had always said: "*Your* Azarius, *your* family, *your* Florentine, *your* children, *your* life." For Azarius, a city fellow, she had shown even less regard than for her other sons-in-law, who were all country folk. When Rose-Anna was married, she had declared: "You may think you'll have no cares now that you're going to play the lady in the big city, but mark well what I say: trouble finds us out. You'll have plenty. But you've made your choice. Let's hope you won't repent it."

This was the only good wish her mother had ever offered her, Rose-Anna recalled.

"Azarius," she said, emerging from her reverie, "Oh yes, he's working now. He's much more cheerful. Then Eugène has enlisted, as I told you before; he doesn't look bad in his uniform. It makes him seem a bit older. We manage to get along. Florentine has steady work ..."

She fingered the rosary of domestic incidents, choosing instinctively only those that would make the old woman see her in a happy light; she played up all these reasons for happiness, magnifying them so much that she seemed almost to be bragging.

The old woman fluttered her eyes. At every opportunity she said:

"Indeed! So much the better, so much the better if things are going as you say!"

But her yellowed hands kept rubbing the edge of her chair, which was quite worn at one spot by the constant friction, as if to underline her doubt that such things could be.

Rose-Anna went on defending her husband in the same sharp tone she had used long ago when her mother had tried to run him down.

"He's doing better now," she said. "If one thing doesn't work out, he tries another. He doesn't let much time go by without doing anything. He only took this job on the truck as a stopgap. Building will start up again because of the war, and he expects to go back to his trade soon."

She was surprised to find herself using the same terms as Azarius, even speaking with the same fervor of his trade. But at other times her words rang false in her own ears, and she wondered if it could really be her own voice saying such things.

Through the window overlooking the farm she could see the children skipping toward the sugar house, under the supervision of Uncle Octave. Little Daniel was stumbling through the snow, far behind the others. She stopped talking; her eyes wandered uneasily until she saw Yvonne come back to help her little brother. Then the voice of Azarius reached her with a dreamlike quality, because the circumstances were so different from those in which she usually heard him speaking. He was saying to his young brother-in-law:

"Listen here, if you think you're going to have plenty of maple syrup, just pass it on to me. I'll sell it for you on a small commission basis. It will be easy to dispose of it on my run."

He was putting on airs as he leaned back in his chair, with his feet propped up against the door of the stove. His suit, which had been carefully pressed the night before, was still passable, and permitted him to lord it over his brothers-in-law in their short sleeves, with their cravats untied and their suspenders dangling. Rose-Anna was disturbed to note that they seemed to be considering his plan seriously. As soon as events took a more favorable turn Azarius grew bold and hatched up some new scheme, about which he generally knew nothing. For this reason Rose-Anna half-dreaded any good fortune that befell them. She longed to put Azarius on his guard, and her brothers too. Philippe's behavior also was something she had not bargained for. To her great annoyance, she saw him hanging about with the grown men, swearing like a trooper, and rolling one cigarette after another while his grandmother looked on with a wry face. But instead of reproving him, Rose-Anna stole an embarrassed glance at her mother and went on describing their life in a monotone.

"Yvonne is at the head of her class; the Sisters are very pleased with her. And Philippe's going to get a job soon. It seems they're taking young boys like him in the munitions factories. So all together we'll manage pretty well."

From time to time she sat up high in her chair to watch the children outside; she saw them enter the sugar bush, a little mass of bright colors separating and walking in single file among the trees. And she was so sorry not to have gone with them that the tears rose to her eyes. She had not dared to go after her mother, rebuking her as if she were still a child, had declared: "In your condition, I hope you're not thinking of rambling about the woods!"

Rambling about the woods! Rose-Anna repeated to herself, broken-hearted. But sitting at home like this was not at all how she had pictured her outing. Probably she could no longer see herself as others saw her, and betrayed by her desire, she had dreamed the impossible. She was so fearful of discovering how absurd her dream was that she tried not to think of it, saying to herself: I knew I wouldn't go. I knew I wouldn't go to the maple grove.

But she paused a long time at the sight of the last red scarf fluttering among the branches. Through the window nothing moved over the fields deep in melting snow. Then she shook herself and returned to her mother, trying to remember other cheerful things to recount, but as she listed them, her voice grew more and more faint. She realized that some detail always had to be withheld, lest her mother break in with: "Yes, I thought so!"

When old Mme Laplante sent someone down to the cellar for a large piece of salt pork, some fresh eggs, cream and preserves, and had them all wrapped up for her to take home, Rose-Anna was touched by her mother's generosity. Knowing that the old lady disliked being thanked, she dared not say a word in acknowledgment. And that saddened her more than anything. She watched her mother rise painfully and add a homemade bread to the box of provisions, scolding and rearranging the packages in better order. She always gives us a lot of things when we come, thought Rose-Anna. She doesn't believe a word I told her. Poor old woman, she wants to help us in her way. She's peevish because she can't do more for us. Hasn't she always been openhanded? I know she wouldn't let us go hungry if she knew we lacked anything. All our lives, whenever we needed her, she gave us food and clothes and good advice. Rose-Anna's mouth puckered. And she asked herself: But is that all that a mother ought to give her children?

And suddenly Rose-Anna sank back in her chair, her face drawn. Will I have any more than that to give Florentine when she's a married woman if she needs me as I need someone today? she wondered. Suddenly she put a new interpretation on her mother's severity. Wasn't it her terrible regret at not knowing how to protect her children from suffering that had made her so stern?

And because she no longer felt certain that she could help her own daughter, now or in the future, because she had a suspicion that Florentine would not want her help and because she understood how difficult it was to aid her children in their secret troubles, Rose-Anna shook her head and relapsed into silence. Unconsciously, but as if the habit were already an old one, she rubbed her fingers against the edge of the chair in the same futile gesture as her mother's.

CHAPTER XVI

A T HOME in Beaudoin Street, nothing could be heard but the steam rattling the lid of the teakettle and, at intervals, the tap of Florentine's heels on the linoleum floor.

An indefinable melancholy pervaded the dining-room, a heavy, unwonted silence, as if the rearrangement of a few articles of furniture had subtly altered the relationship between the house and the people who lived there.

For Jean's coming the girl had dusted and waxed and swept everything; she had put away all the clothes, all the battered toys, all the children's things that might betray how cramped their quarters were. She had pulled the chairs away from the wall and grouped them around the dining-room table, thereby exposing lighter spots on the worn wallpaper. Stripping the buffet of all the odds and ends that had been accumulating there for a long time, she had covered it with a stiff embroidered runner, on which she had placed an earthenware vase with a few dreary paper flowers. On the wall above the vase hung a sacred picture, a cheap litho-graph depicting the Infant Jesus in a bit of scarlet drapery, with his arms around a Madonna in a dark blue robe. At this very moment Jean was staring at the picture gloomily.

Florentine was acting the busy little housewife, a role with which she hoped to impress the young man. She had not allowed herself to doubt for an instant that he would come, and from time to time she had gone to the window to watch out for him, draw-ing the curtain aside and letting it drop slowly from her fingers. As a footstep sounded on the sidewalk, slowing up before the house, she had known instantly that it was he, even before the bell rang. And she had drawn a deep breath of satisfaction.

Now that he was here, she was using all her little wiles to thwart her guest rather than to please him. Bright-colored beads hung about her neck and arms, bobbing up and down in a nervous tremor, and over her black silk dress she wore a little rubberized apron that rustled with every movement of her hips.

She was never still; at one moment she approached him to ask if he were bored; then like an attentive hostess she brought him a cushion or a magazine, or a photograph album with snapshots of herself; leaning over his shoulder she described where they had been taken; a moment later she was in the kitchen, humming a little song over the stove.

Jean was exasperated by all this fuss. She was obviously treating him as if their betrothal were tacitly understood, as if she trusted him fully. Thus she left him alone for a time while she made some fudge, but she kept up her conversation with him from the kitchen in a civil, rather offhand way. Her whole attitude reflected prudence and reserve. She avoided touching his hand, and when he asked her to sit down, she picked a chair across the room. Then she affected an air of preoccupation, playing with her bracelets and turning her eyes away as soon as she felt his glance on her. They were both ill at ease.

Florentine's little ruses at length brought a smile to the young man's face. Clever girl, he thought. If I hadn't seen you in another mood, I'd think you were frankness itself. But her restlessness got on his nerves. She was so artful at eluding him that at last he grew quite vexed. As soon as he made a move toward her she would shrink and pretend she had something to do in the kitchen. She could hardly have shown greater decorum if they were surrounded by all her family.

The footsteps of a man strolling by outside suddenly vibrated through the house. The echo died away; and Jean could measure their solitude by the utter silence that followed.

He looked about him with chagrin. Through the door of the kitchen he could see Florentine buttering a pan. He could hear the rustle of her apron and the ring of the aluminum against the table; the boiling sugar sizzled as it came in contact with the cold metal. These various sounds seemed to come to him from a great distance; domesticity rubbed him the wrong way and aroused all his instincts of self-preservation. Once more he stared at the Madonna and the Infant Jesus over the buffet. And he understood at last why the picture attracted and disturbed him. It evoked his whole past life, from his unhappy childhood through his troubled adolescence. As his memories flooded back into his mind, something awoke in him that he had thought long dead.

The first thing he remembered was the sacred picture hanging in the orphanage, and somehow related to this was a sensation of lying asleep while black-robed figures passed back and forth before his crib in the dormitory. The picture also reminded him of the cold chapel at dawn, and was linked in some mysterious way with the sound of his own voice in the choir.

The picture was associated with thousands of other memories, with the gray apron worn by the orphans, the thick drill apron that was the very color of their loveless days. He remembered tearing the gray material to shreds one day; even then he yearned to be different from others.

Then the picture shrank in size. It became a tiny souvenir that the Sisters slipped into his prayer book one day when a lady called for him at the orphanage. She was a taciturn, embittered woman, who had made a vow to adopt a child if her only daughter was restored to health. Thus he had served as a bargaining point in a trade with the saints, but the girl had died all the same, later on.

His mother—the woman had insisted that he call her by this name—had not been severe, but after the death of her child she had shut herself off from him, becoming so remote, so inaccessible, that Jean remembered being more lonely in her company than he had ever been at the orphanage.

Cruel words spoken at night, when they thought he was asleep, came back to him : "I'm not surprised. What can you expect from a foundling?" "No, his parents were known, you must recall that they were killed in an accident." "I guess you're right, but really I don't know where to take hold of him."

They never forgave him his slightest peccadillos.

Then Jean saw himself at high school, a moody boy, hard to handle, but with a quick, inquiring mind that puzzled his teachers. His foster-parents were not stingy about money, even though they gave him no affection. In those days he was well dressed, and with the liberal allowance he received he was able to make up for innumerable humiliations by jingling the coins in his pocket. At times he would offer money to his poorest schoolmates, more out of pride than kindness of heart, for he already knew that money bought respect and prestige.

Good fare made him shoot up quickly, and in a very few years he had reached his full height. He had strong muscles, broad shoulders, and a sharp eye; there was no trace of the puny orphan in the sturdy youth. Some mysterious strain had gained the ascendancy. The strength he felt stirring in him came from two strangers who had died soon after his birth. He would fain have torn their secret from the dead, for there were no links between him and the living. No tie remained but that curious, poignant attraction for a man and woman he had never known.

Meanwhile his character had undergone a transformation even more complete than his body. Overnight he shifted from apparent compliance to open rebellion. Mockery and sarcasm became his chosen weapons. There was a bite in everything he said, and he spared no one's feelings, often starting an argument simply for the pleasure of being contradictory.

With insatiable curiosity he had begun to devour all the books that fell into his hands. He would stop in the street to talk to men at work, in the belief that the common people shared his torments and his passion to learn and understand. One day he would regard them with love and pity, and dream of devoting himself to social reform; the next he would feel contempt for the masses, think of himself as a man apart, marked for a great destiny. And as time went on he grew more and more lonely. His shafts of wit often hit home, but they were followed by sulky moods or long silences that baffled his closest friends, and in the end alienated them too. At college he was noted for extreme arrogance. To give him a lesson in humility, his teachers had withheld all the prizes to which he was entitled at the end of the year. As he recalled this affront, Jean chuckled.

One night after a stormy argument, he had left his foster-parents' home for good. He remembered how he had packed up his clothes and stolen away through the deserted streets. By going away he had regained his mental balance. After that he had become a young man like so many others, looking for a job at a period when there was only one for every ten applicants. The fact that he owed his success to no one but himself filled him with pride. A furnished room somewhere, his first job as a puddler; another job, another room, the rest of his life up to now unreeled before his mind without a break. He had reached a relatively calm period, and like a shipwrecked sailor flung up on a desert island, looked at all the resources around him with a view to using them for his own ends. He had dedicated himself to years of struggles and poverty, at the end of which he would need only to stretch out his hand and gather in the fruits of his labor and his renunciation.

Jean rose to his feet in amazement, for he could not remember his point of departure. The silence weighed on him. The homely objects around him, all dedicated to basic human needs, rubbed him raw. He wanted to run away. Florentine was still in the kitchen, on tiptoe in front of the mirror over the sink, winding her curls around her finger. It irked him to be alone with her and yet he kept wondering how far he could go. In a fit of impatience he called her. She came immediately, holding out a dish of candy. Almost rudely, he snatched it from her hands, unable to tolerate a moment longer the restrictions she imposed on him.

"Why aren't your parents here?" he demanded. "Have they gone for the day?"

The girl's eyes were ingenuous.

"I'm not sure. But I guess they'll be back soon."

"You invited me here because you knew you'd be alone with me, didn't you?"

She took fright at the look in his eyes.

"No, no. They only spoke of going away this morning."

"Where have they gone?"

"I think they went to see the sugaring. Yes, that's it, papa spoke this morning of going to the sugaring. That's where they must be . . ."

The words stuck in her throat; she saw that he did not believe her. But in her anxiety to throw dust in his eyes, she went on with her tale.

"When Mamma saw what a fine day it was, you understand . . ."

Again she avoided his eyes, then suddenly made up her mind to seem very angry, very hurt by his suspicions.

"Oh, you think you know it all!" she cried.

He had seized her by the wrists and now he threw his arms about her as if he would crush her. He had come against his will, expecting to find her in the midst of her family. The prospect of a family party bored him to death, and yet he was determined to go through with it because he took pride in keeping his word, even when he had been unwise to give it. But no, as a matter of fact, he had come only because last night her tears had disarmed him, had aroused his pity. Stupid weakness on his part! The girl was more wily and tenacious than ever! She was smirking at him this very moment, trying to win him with all the blandishments that had caught his notice in the restaurant.

He was furious with himself for having given way to her the night before.

"Go get your hat and coat," he snapped. "We'll go to the movies."

But he still held her to him. He knew now what it was that Florentine's home reminded him of, the thing he had feared above all: the smell of poverty, the powerful smell of cheap, well-worn clothes, a smell he could recognize blindfolded. And he realized that Florentine herself stood for the kind of poverty against which his whole soul rebelled. At the same time he understood the attraction she had for him. She was his poverty, his solitude, his dreary childhood, his lonely youth; she was everything he had hated and denied; she was what lay at the root of his character, goading him relentlessly toward his fate.

It was his poverty and his melancholy that he held in his arms, his life as it might have been if he had not broken out of the mold. He rested his head on the girl's shoulder, and thinking of his great craving for love when he was a very little boy, he murmured, as if he had known her sometime in the past:

"Such a tiny waist! No bigger than my two hands."

He was remembering too that on occasion he had tried to bring solace to others as he went on his way through life. As a child, he had willingly given his candy away to less fortunate playmates. He was still capable of being generous, provided that it did not interfere with his own development along the lines he had chosen, if it left him untrammeled. How many friendships he had discarded, how many people he had forgotten, all because he could bear no claim upon him!

Florentine grew frightened at the grim look in his eyes, which turned wild as he glared at her. Her folly had at last become so plain that the outcome already seemed inevitable.

She tried to slip out of his hold, but as he made a move to clutch her, his fingers caught on her apron strap. It broke. And the torn apron, with its bib hanging, maddened him.

With a great effort of the will he managed to whisper:

"Go get your hat and coat . . ."

But he would not let her go, and over her shoulder he stared at the old leather sofa.

She fell on her back, her knees twisted, and one foot waving in in the air. Before she closed her eyes, she saw the Madonna and all the saints looking down on her. For a moment she tried to pull herself up again toward all those mourning, pleading faces. Jean might still be induced to let her go. Then she slid down all the way in the hollow where she slept every night beside her little sister Yvonne.

Outside, the bells rang for vespers over the Sunday quiet of the quarter.

CHAPTER XVII

JEAN LEVESQUE pounded the streets for hours that Sunday evening. He was enraged at himself, not so much because Florentine's tragic face haunted him, as because of the apprehension that he had forfeited his liberty. His head reared up as if to break the lock of Florentine's arms about his neck. From now on would he always feel tied to someone? Would he always be aware of an intruder, who made his former solitude a thousand times more desirable than he had ever imagined it to be? He was assailed by more definite anxieties as well. What attitude would Florentine take now, what would she expect of him? But to these he gave scant attention. His greatest torments came from the loss of his old self-sufficiency, that had left him free of all sense of duty to others. What had come over him? Up to now he had managed to limit his curiosity to cautious ventures, to halfhearted advances that involved no sharing of himself. In the back of his mind there had always been the fear that an affair with an inexperienced girl might have serious consequences. But why go back over all that, he thought, more in a mood of scorn at his own hesitations than at his conduct toward Florentine.

He crossed St. Jacques Street with rapid strides. The light of a street lamp struck him full in the face, then he was swallowed up again in the shadows of Beaudoin Street, which becomes darker and drearier as it approaches the Lachine Canal. He soon reached a somewhat brighter neighborhood at St. Emilie Street, with its tiny shops and ornate balconies, its identical bell towers at every street corner. As he passed under the arc lights, Jean could see rust-colored streams of water zigzagging down the house fronts. A gentle south wind had arisen at nightfall, and the snow was melting rapidly. You could almost hear it dissolving into rivulets of dirty water in the empty street. It ran off roofs and trees, here and everywhere, with the mournful drip of an all-night rain.

The need to justify himself preyed on his mind and, despite his bitterness and confusion, kept his thoughts running in the same channels. Had he really wanted to harm Florentine? He denied his guilt vehemently, almost aloud. No, no! Even today he had been inclined to spare her. It was precisely because he had disobeyed this inclination that he was so enraged at himself. In his heart he had wanted to remember her without contempt, he had hoped to think of her as a girl who had aroused some compassion, some sympathy in him at one time. When was that? He could not tell exactly. Perhaps it was an illusion?

Between Florentine and him there was no longer the thought of a stormy night to remind him that he had let her go when she tried to throw herself at him like a heedless, stupid child. From now until the end of time the creak of an old sofa, the squeal of a broken spring, a glint of light on a dented chandelier would always stand between them. Florentine's face might fade from his mind, her youthful charm might be blotted out, but he would never forget the frightful poverty that had been the scene of their moment of love. That was the supreme offense. It degraded him in his own eyes, it made him question his ambitions for the future. It might return to him at his moments of triumph, and all the more if he should be successful.

Jean hurried along, his hair flying in the breeze. It was impossible for him to ignore the fact that he was terribly upset, for there had been only one woman in his life before Florentine, a much older woman, who had made all the advances. He could not even remember her face. But Florentine! He recalled suddenly the humble way in which she tried to keep him from putting on his overcoat, as if she were afraid to be alone with her thoughts after he had gone. "Poor little fool!" he murmured, less touched by pity than by regret that it should have been he who caused her pain and disillusionment. For he knew now that only complete innocence had led her to compromise herself so foolishly. And in the light of his present knowledge, he understood why she had been so reckless. How basically timid and awkward she was! What childish hesitation she had revealed! But no, he did not want to go over it again. He would begin to feel remorse, or worse still, he would lose his sense of freedom.

When he reached Notre-Dame Street the clock on Saint-Henri Church stood at close to midnight. Guay Place was as silent as the grave when he crossed it, its ghostly trees throwing uneasy shadows on the pavement. In a sudden change of weather, the air was filled with a driving mist, like a spring rain.

It's the gift of imagination, thought Jean, that brings men to accept responsibility for their acts, imagination, nothing else. The more recent an event is, the easier it should be to forget it. Memories that date back to childhood leave a deeper imprint, but there must be some way to erase them too from the mind.

Jean's thoughts had gone beyond the point where the consciousness of wrong-doing paralyzes the mind, and holds it in suspense, as if from that moment forward life ought to take a new turn. He had passed that stage, and could no more stop to think about the consequences of what he had done than a tornado can pause to consider the destruction in its wake. Life would bring other adventures to make him forget this wretched incident of his youth. Each step he took carried him farther away from the state of confusion in which he had left Florentine. And the numb little voice saying: "Will I see you tomorrow, Jean?" only reached him now from a distance. When she had put the question to him, he had been aware of his own hesitation. Now the voice wandered through his consciousness without bearings, without meaning for him, without power to alter his purpose. For he was resolved not to be weak where Florentine was concerned, not to retrace his steps. Carried away by the importance of this idea, he exclaimed aloud: "Be done with the past! Leave all that behind!" And he knew that he was referring not only to incidents particularly wounding to his self-esteem, but to one whole act of his life on which tonight the curtain would fall. It had been prolonged because of a certain weakness of character he now deplored bitterly. It's about time I got away from all that, he said to himself. And what made him feel this even more strongly was the fact that the obstacle in his way took the form of a poor girl who had come not to bar his way but to attach herself to him timidly, tenaciously, without pride.

The thought that she really loved him and that only passion could have brought her to such a point of abandonment, occurred to him, but instead of placating him, it only embittered him. How could she have fallen in love with him when he had done everything possible to make her feel the distance between them? Under the circumstances her love seemed more like an insult.

He reached St. Antoine Street, which was shaking with the passage of a train farther down the line. After the dark streets through which he had passed, the bright lights from the shopwindows made him blink, but he walked on quickly, as if trying to shake off an obsession that had stalked him in the darkness and silence from which he had come. But what he wanted to escape from now was not so much the events of the evening as the exasperating conviction that Florentine loved him blindly, madly.

The mist turned to rain. Under the large, sparse drops the last vestiges of snow disappeared. Of the months of freezing cold nothing was left but a thin crust of ice that crumbled away beneath his feet. In a little while the pavement was washed clean by the slow, steady rain; it stretched out shining before him, reflecting a few lights and the tangles of bare branches.

Spring! What would it bring him? He felt that eagerness for the unknown, for renewal, that always comes with a change of season.

A woman's brisk footsteps on the sidewalk made him turn around, and seeing a solitary figure behind him, he recalled with annoyance the feeling of Florentine's arm on his. He remembered too how she had come running to meet him one stormy night, and in a flash of illumination he realized that she had run madly away from the poverty and uncertainty of her life to lay herself at his feet. To her he seemed dependable, no doubt, a successful man in the eyes of a poverty-stricken girl. Then remembering her shadow alongside his on the sidewalk near the foundry, he stamped his foot on the ground with rage. What the devil did he care about her gift? What difference did it make to him? The solitude in which he had chosen to live had never appeared more precious or more necessary to him.

Spring might melt other hearts, but not his. On the contrary, it hardened him, and made him spurn Florentine's claims upon him more violently than ever.

Spring was a season of paltry illusions. Soon there would be leaves screening the street lights; the people in the slums would bring their chairs out on the sidewalk in front of their houses; babies would be rocked to sleep on the pavement, breathing fresh air for the first time in their lives; children would make chalk marks on the street and play hopscotch; and whole families would assemble in the yards to talk or play cards in the feeble glimmer of light from the windows. What would they talk about, these needy folk whose days had the same monotonous pattern of toil? Here and there men would gather in an empty lot to pitch horseshoes. The nights would echo with the clank of iron, the shouts of children, and the murmur of thousands of happy voices mingling with the roar of locomotives and blasts of the siren.

As his scorn for the joys of the poor grew, Jean felt more and more easy in his mind. He pictured the end of April, when there would be a great exodus into the street. From all the houses, from damp cellars and mean garrets, from the tenements on Workman Street and the stone apartment houses on Sir Georges-Etienne Cartier Place, from dismal alleys near the canal, and tumble-down shacks on the railroad tracks, from quiet squares, here, there, and everywhere the crowd would emerge, and its deep-throated rumble would rise within the ring of factories and the mountain's flank to the distant stars. Only the stars would witness this incredible upsurge of joy.

In all the dark alleys, at all the dead-end streets, in the shade of all the trees there would be couples embracing each other. Two by two they would wander through the reek of tobacco and molasses and decaying fruit, the ground shaking under their feet; they would wander on, covered with soot, clinging pitifully to each other; and some spring night, if the wind should happen to blow gently and the air be filled with hope, they would go through the motions that guarantee mankind the perpetuation of its sorrows. Jean rejoiced that the passivity of most men permitted daring fellows like him to climb so easily. He looked at the dark mass of buildings, each of which cradled its own share of poverty and romance, and it seemed to him that the horrible springtime of the poor had completed his disillusionment with Florentine.

A door opened in the distance and a burst of jazz filled the street. A group of soldiers reeled out, accompanied by several bareheaded women who were shoving one another and laughing aloud. The youths were urging the women to come along with them. The women protested halfheartedly at first; then they all went off singing, and Jean, as he hurried on, found himself smiling. He was thinking of what he would escape by avoiding Florentine hereafter: the furtive meetings, the long aimless walks through the streets and the constant terror on both their parts of having to pay dear for their miserable little sin. A look of conceit appeared on his face. His conquest of Florentine had given him a taste for more difficult conquests. He thought of love as a luxury for which he was not yet prepared. But it'll come; it'll come, he said to himself, swinging along in a confident rhythm. From now on he would hold himself in reserve for the sort of triumphs that alone would satisfy his proud nature.

He had lost complete track of the time when he found himself at the corner of De Courcelle and St. Ambroise Streets. A sound of muffled thunder seemed to be coming from beneath his feet, and as he passed over a sewer vent he heard a crashing of waters. A whole network of subterranean pipes from all over the city met a broad conduit at this point. The rumble filled the street like the distant roar of a waterfall. As he carried this powerful voice away with him, a sound that was the first real expression of liberty in the quarter, the young man felt a sense of release. The strain was over, he was absolutely free.

He had made his way home by instinct, and was marching along smartly, his steps echoing along the deserted street. The grain elevators rose on his right, harsh, solid buildings. He looked at them with friendly feelings that dated from far back, and with new interest, too, as if he must obtain a confirmation of his high destiny from those imperious walls, those cement towers, the arrogant work of man.

Farther away the sky was darkened by the great mass of cotton mills that loomed up on both sides of the street and were connected by a bridge flung high above the sidewalk. Through the darkness Jean spied a couple approaching him slowly, hand in hand like children. A faint light from a window streaming with rain disclosed the pair as Marguerite L'Estienne, whom he had seen at the five-and-ten, and Alphonse Poirier. Jean smirked as he left them behind, not only because they looked ridiculous, but because he remembered that Alphonse had approached him only recently for a loan. As he hurried on past an empty lot, he began to understand something that had been at the back of his mind all evening long. It came to him now in the form of a definite resolution. Yes, he would leave Saint-Henri. It's time for me to get a change of scene, he said to himself, in order not to go into his less creditable motives. Everything in the quarter was disagreeable to him now, not only the memory of a forsaken girl, but even more the idea that he had spent a whole evening justifying himself. As if it were necessary to justify himself for anything! With his eye on the main chance, like all men of ambition in a great city, he saw that his departure would open up a new terrain to be exploited. It even seemed to him that he had only to leave in order to start a run of luck that would last his life through. Something was waiting for him in this war-torn world, something whose exact nature he could not foresee except that it would make up for the years he had been biding his time in Saint-Henri. At that moment he was exultant at the thought of facing the future with so much confidence and such a light heart, as if he had just thrown his ballast overboard. It was only later that he understood just what he had discarded that evening, just what had prevented him from using his powers to the full until then. Even though he did not yet know it, he was no longer weighed down by his sterile sense of pity. He had wiped out the picture of his early poverty and the memory of his recent past, and his frantic desire for action rushed in to fill the vacuum so quickly that he had no time for reflection.

He felt his way up the creaking stairs. The quiet of his room descended on him, but could not temper his haste to be up and doing. As he groped for the light he had a vision of Florentine as he had left her, her face even paler than usual, her eyes fixed on him with a frightful unspoken question. The idea that he was taking the most commonplace, perhaps the least dignified way out of his difficulties, passed through his mind, but he was beyond the point of self-criticism. On the contrary, his indignation, or what was left of it, was directed toward the girl who had tried the surest way to hold him.

As soon as he had turned on the light, he looked through the papers on his table and found an application form for a position with one of the largest munitions plants in the country. His pen flew over the paper with a scratchy sound, filling in all the blank spaces, even though his mind was on other things. With his experience as a mechanic, there was little doubt of his finding a job at good pay. If need be he would ask his present employer for a letter of recommendation. Before the week was out he would probably receive a satisfactory answer. And until then, no matter what happened, he must not give way.

Of what weaknesses did he still suspect himself capable? The letter to go with his application was soon finished; he slipped them both into an envelope, which he addressed and sealed.

Then he lay down on his bed in all his clothes. And at this a base thought popped into his mind, bringing him greater self-knowledge. After all, if I wanted to . . . again . . . before going away . . He rejected it forthwith, although gnashing his teeth in mortification, for he did not know how long his flesh would cry out in the lonely, dark days ahead for the poor girl with the slender hips. Florentine Lacasse!

CHAPTER XVIII

FOR FULLY AN HOUR Rose-Anna had been walking toward the mountain. With slow, plodding steps, the sweat rolling down into her eyes, she finally reached Cedar Avenue, but dared not tackle it immediately. Her way led up a steep hill skirting the face of the rock. A brilliant April sun was shining overhead, and here and there, in damp crevices in the stone, tufts of grass were already turning green.

As she stopped to catch her breath, Rose-Anna looked down over the city. On her left was an empty lot enclosed by a high iron fence, between whose palings the whole lower part of town could be seen, its countless belfries reaching toward the sky, where ribbons of smoke prolonged the gray cylinders of the factory chimneys. Grimy billboards cut across the blue horizon, and, struggling for space in this city of work and prayer, the roofs of the houses dropped down in graduated stages, becoming more and more closely serrated until they reached bottom at the river bank. In the background a light haze hung over the water.

The whole scene wavered before Rose-Anna's eyes. It never occurred to her to look for her own house in the distance, but with one quick glance she measured the height she must still climb before reaching the children's hospital at the top of Cedar Avenue.

Daniel had been taken there a short time after the trip to Saint-Denis.

One evening, as she was undressing him, Rose-Anna had discovered large purple blotches on his legs. The next day she put him in his little sled and pulled him over to the office of a young doctor in Convent Street for whom she had formerly scrubbed floors. The rest had happened so fast that she hardly remembered the order of events. The doctor had taken the child to the hospital immediately. Rose-Anna recalled only one thing clearly, that Daniel had not objected or cried. In his extreme weakness, he had surrendered his wasted little body to the kind stranger, and waved goodbye to his mother like a good boy.

Rose-Anna continued on her way.

Of Mount-Royal, which stretches out above Saint-Henri, she was familiar only with the Saint-Joseph Oratory and the cemetery where the people from down below laid their dead beside those who lived on the hill. And when the children of the slums fell ill, Rose-Anna observed to herself, they too came to live on the mountain, in the fresh air, free of smoke and soot and the hot breath of the factories that lay over the houses in the valley. This seemed a bad omen.

The splendor of the private houses, set back from the street in the midst of manicured lawns, amazed her. Several times she slowed down to stare, murmuring: "My goodness, how rich, how fine! How did they happen to bring Daniel here?"

She never dreamed of rejoicing that the child was in a place where the air was pure and wholesome. On the contrary, as she walked along she thought of the little fellow as lonely all by himself, and missing the rumble of the trains in the great silence up here. She remembered a game he used to play every day at home; she saw him placing the old kitchen chairs in a row and sitting down gravely on the first, pretending that he was on a train in motion. Sometimes when he was on board his imaginary train he would utter a feeble cry in imitation of a train whistle; he would shield his eyes as if blinded by the sun on the rails as they curved around through the quarter. The kitchen was not at all large, and Rose-Anna realized that she had often denied the child his pleasure, pushing the chairs away and sending him to play elsewhere.

Again she was so tired that she had to stop. She stood there panting, remembering all the misfortunes that had befallen them in the last few weeks. Her head swam with them, and when she opened her eyes to the bright sky again she wondered if it all could have been a bad dream. After resting for a moment, however, her heart stopped pounding, and she gradually recovered the strength to acknowledge and face her misfortunes.

Their trip to the country had been pure madness. Whenever they sought happiness it had always proved the surest way of bringing bad luck.

Everything was blurred in her mind: the accident a few miles from Saint-Denis; their return late at night to her mother's house; their arrival back in town on Monday evening. From Azarius's crestfallen manner it had not taken long for her to guess the truth. He had taken the truck without permission, and now that his bluff was called, he dreaded being fired, which was exactly what happened the following morning. But then, thought Rose-Anna, perhaps that was not the worst of their troubles. She suspected something still more ominous when a neighbor intimated to them that Florentine had entertained a young man during their absence, and that the young man had remained at the house until late Sunday night. Florentine's defiant air when questioned on the subject did nothing to relieve Rose-Anna's deep concern. And as if this were not enough to try her, there remained still the most pressing problem of all: Daniel's illness.

The doctor had spoken of red corpuscles and white corpuscles—she didn't know which were lacking—and of vitamin deficiencies. It had not been very clear to her, but she could see Daniel when the doctor examined him, the purple streaks all over his body, his limp arms, his swollen abdomen, and she felt ashamed.

Her other children seemed endangered now too. She remembered what she had been told at the clinic about a balanced diet to build up the bones and the teeth and make a child healthy. She smiled wryly. It had moreover been stressed that such a diet was within the reach of every budget. Had they not instructed her in her duty? Her eyes filled with anguish. Perhaps she was unequal to her task? She came to the conclusion that this was so, and for the first time in her life a mean, scheming look crept over her face.

Then rubbing her hand over her brow, she banished the thought, for she realized that if she were to solve her problems she must take them up one by one, with what strength she could muster. She shook her head and girded herself to climb the hill more quickly. It had been a long, hard trip—she had made it on foot because the shaking of the streetcar often made her feel sick—and now she was afraid that the visiting hours might be over before she reached the hospital.

The child sat propped up against the pillows in his bed. Toys were heaped up all over the blankets : a little tin flute such as he had always yearned to have, a teddy bear, a box of colored crayons and a drawing book. In one day he had received more toys than he had had in his entire life, and there were probably too many for him to enjoy them all, or else he was too serious for such things, for what engaged his attention was a pasteboard box containing block letters. He was arranging them with an air of the greatest concentration, and when he found himself making a mistake a shudder of pain passed over his tired little face.

As Rose-Anna entered the ward, she saw a young nurse, with magnificent clear blue eyes, look up at her with mingled surprise and pity. Under this frank glance she felt old, and unconsciously she covered her bloated belly with her shabby old handbag.

She approached the bed on tiptoe, partly because her heavy shoes creaked on the polished floor, and partly because she was overawed by the gleaming whiteness of the room. The light streamed in from many windows, making the whole scene very cheerful in spite of the bedridden patients.

Daniel smiled at her shyly, then immediately returned to his letters.

She wanted to help him, but his fretful little hand pushed her away.

"Let me do it all by myself," he said. "That's how the Brothers told us to do it in school."

He had only been to school a few weeks in all, and yet it had made a vivid but somewhat painful impression on his mind. There had been a few days last September in which he had been perfectly happy, when he had gone to school with his brand-new school bag on his back, holding Lucille's or Albert's hand. His lessons were not too hard for him then; he understood everything that he was told, and when he returned home it was his great delight to bring his primer to Azarius and show him what he had learned that day. Sometimes he would follow his mother all over the kitchen, reciting his abc's until the poor woman nearly went out of her wits. She would rebuke him gently, but it was enough to make him feel lonely and helpless.

In his struggle to hold on to this tenuous knowledge, he would wake up at night and go over scraps of his lessons like a monomaniac.

The next morning he would have a nose-bleed and headache. Then Rose-Anna would say: "He's too young to go to school anyway." And ignoring his tears she would keep him at home.

In the rainy season later on she kept him home again for several weeks because he had no rubbers. And when at last he returned to his little desk, he no longer understood the lessons quite so well; there were gaps in his memory, and when the teacher addressed him pointedly, he would be drenched with perspiration. It was not his fault, for he tried with all his might to do what was expected of him. Only after several days had gone by did he begin gradually to see a little light again.

Shortly after this a cold spell struck the town. There was always something to prevent him from going to school. Rose-Anna began to sew warm clothes for the children: first a coat for Yvonne, then a windbreaker for Albert. Daniel's turn came last. At length, however, Rose-Anna began to alter an old coat to fit him. Vexed at seeing her interrupt her sewing to attend to other chores, Daniel would follow her about as if possessed, pulling at her apron strings and pleading with her: "Finish my coat, Mamma, finish my coat."

It was dreadfully important that the coat be finished. At night she made some progress, but during the day it lay on the table, shapeless, without sleeves, held together with thick white basting thread. Daniel would try it on constantly, in spite of his mother's reproaches: "You'll pull out my stitches, you little busybody."

She could not understand his passion to return to school.

After several weeks went by, however, the coat had sleeves. And Daniel loved it dearly.

One morning before it was quite finished, he put it on secretly, collected his schoolbooks and tried to slip out without being seen. But Rose-Anna caught him at the door. She was not cross, she was merely sad, and she murmured querulously: "I can't go any faster. I have too much to do."

But that day she let her housekeeping go. She even left the dishes piled high in the sink while she sewed for long hours. In the evening, after the dining-room had been cleaned and the beds were made ready for the night, she went on sewing. Daniel fell asleep to the rumble of the sewing machine, and dreamed of his coat. Strangely enough he saw it in his dream with a beautiful fur collar, and when he opened his bright eyes in the morning, there it was, hanging over the back of a chair, trimmed with an old piece of black wolf that had been a wedding present of his mother's.

But he did not go to school that day. As she went to dress him Rose-Anna had felt his limbs and declared that he had a fever. For long weeks he lay stretched out on two chairs in the midst of all the household bustle with his coat beside him to console him.

When at last he returned to school after the holidays, it was all over. He was lost. The Brothers' words were incomprehensible to him. Between him and the lessons he was asked to do there was a stern face. The face was not ill-natured but it was displeased. And he tried ever so hard to do what the face wanted. But he could not. He sat grieving all by himself at the back of the classroom. He understood nothing, he knew nothing. The crayons and the pencil slipped from his hands and when he picked up a crayon again it was only to draw meaningless lines. He could not understand what was expected of him.

Rose-Anna saw the gleam of anguish in her son's eyes. All sorts of fears and obsessions were mirrored in that peaked little face.

"Don't bother about the letters," she said. "You'll wear your-self out for nothing."

But again the child repulsed her, and patiently, his eyes dilating, went on with his work. He was her child, to be sure, thought Rose-Anna, he would never abandon anything he had undertaken.

At least she could try to simplify the task he had set himself. But as she rose to help him, the box of blocks fell to the floor. In a panic, Daniel cried out:

"Jenny!"

Rose-Anna turned around in surprise. The nurse she had seen at her entrance was hurrying to his call. When he needs help now, thought Rose-Anna, he turns to her not to me.

Gathering up the blocks, the nurse put them within the child's reach; then, pulling the blankets over him, she asked him in English, as one grownup to another :

"All right now, Danny ?"

And Daniel smiled in his slow, shy way. Jenny with her blonde hair in the nurse's cap, Jenny with her clear blue eyes and dimpled smile, Jenny in her starched white uniform, Jenny with her unfailing patience helped him to cope with the stern face of his school days. In his pain and distress, right up to the end there would always be these two faces; sometimes one would prevail over the other, but he would never succeed in dissociating them, he would never be able to see only the face that represented peace.

Rose-Anna had an inkling of mysterious things going on, quite beyond her usual concerns. She was silent for a long moment.

But when the nurse went away, she leaned over the bed quickly. A horrible fear had come upon her that her child could not make his wants known. And all unawares another suspicion had crept into her mind and chilled her through and through.

"Can't she speak anything but English?" she asked with a shade of dislike in her tone. "When you need something, can you ask for it ?"

"Yes," said Daniel simply.

"Aren't there any other children who speak French here ?"

"Yes, the little baby over there."

Rose-Anna saw a tiny child standing up in his crib, gripping the bars with both fists.

"That one ?"

"Yes, he's my friend."

"But he's too young to talk yet. Haven't you anyone to talk to ?"

"Yes, Jenny."

"But does she understand you ?"

"She understands me."

He made a slight gesture of impatience. And his eyes sought Jenny's smile at the other end of the room. She was something quite wonderful and tender that had come into his life, and they always understood each other even if they did not speak the same language.

To recapture his attention Rose-Anna began to speak more cheerfully, and alluding to their trip to the country, she asked :

"You had fun, didn't you, when we went to the sugaring? Did you like the snow candy ?"

"Yes."

He was in fact trying to recall the nicest thing that had ever happened to him, but only in order to link it in some way with Jenny. He remembered his grandmother's farm, which he thought of as Saint-Denis; he remembered the blue sky through the windshield that might have been the Richelieu, a word he loved; and he said to himself that he should have brought some maple sugar from the country to give to Jenny. There was some confusion in his mind, for he had forgotten that he did not know Jenny at the time they made their trip to the country.

"And you call her by her first name?" Rose-Anna asked suddenly.

"Yes, Jenny," he said, his chest heaving. "Her name is Jenny."

Then he returned to his letters. A little while later his mother asked:

"Are you very fond of her?"

"Yes, I love Jenny."

"I hope you don't like her better than us?"

His weary glance showed a slight hesitation.

"No."

She was waiting for him to complain of something and ask to be taken back home. But he was very busy picking out his letters; and after a long silence it was she who broached the subject.

"Don't you want to hurry and get well, so you can go back to school like in the old days?"

Meeting his wistful look, she hastened to add:

"Maybe I'll have enough money to buy you a little cap to go with your nice new coat. That's what you want most, isn't it?"

"No."

And yet she thought that this time she had touched his sore point, for she remembered how he tried to be a little man as soon as he began to go to school. She drew her chair closer to the bed.

"What do you want most?"

The boy frowned. Perhaps he was precocious for his age, and had a vague notion that the poverty at home required him to be moderate in his demands; perhaps he was simply too tired to think. He took the time to glance around and smile at the baby who was holding its little fists out toward him, then with a shrug of his shoulders he said:

"Nothing."

There was another long silence, and when Rose-Anna spoke again, her voice had the sad, abstracted tone one uses instinctively when talking through bars or in a convent parlor.

"You have nice toys. Who gave them to you?"

"Jenny," said he with delight.

"Oh no, not Jenny. There are rich ladies who bring toys to sick little fellows, or other children who have more than they need."

"No, no, no. That's not so. Jenny gave them to me."

Rose-Anna was taken aback by his anger. Daniel's eyes were burning, and his mouth trembled in a way that perplexed and saddened her. Then, recalling that irritability and impatience were symptoms of his disease, according to what the doctor had said, she tried to calm him.

"Gisèle and Lucille miss you a lot," she said.

He nodded feebly to indicate that he heard her, but his lips scarcely changed expression. A few minutes later, however, he asked about Yvonne. But as his mother launched into long and somewhat involved explanations, he seemed to lose interest in the subject. His eyes wandered about the ward. Here, too, he was thinking, he was loved, and he felt comfortable with little playmates who never tried to involve him in tiring games. The children who were least sick sometimes played "hockey," a game that consisted of throwing the puck from bed to bed. The game had been invented by Jenny, and Daniel was always diverted by it. Even though he did not stir in his bed, Jenny called him goalie, and gave him points on her little blackboard.

Here he was in a world designed for children. There were no grown persons to trouble his sleep with their talk of disturbing things. There were no whispering voices around him at night; if he waked suddenly he heard no one speak of money, of the rent to be paid, of expenses, cruel words that used to plague him in the dark. He could lie at his ease here at last, for he had a bed that need not be closed up and put away every morning. For the first time in his life he had several things of his own. Above all he had never been in a room with so many windows and so much sunlight. This even made him forget his new coat, which Jenny had taken from him when he arrived at the hospital and put away with the new shoes he had got for the trip to Saint-Denis. He would never have permitted anyone but Jenny to take that coat away from him.

His breath came with an effort as he arranged his blocks to complete a word. When it was done, he crowed:

"See what I wrote . . ."

As Rose-Anna expected, the name Jenny was spelled out on the blanket.

"Can you write anything else?" she asked with a catch in her throat.

"Yes," he said kindly. "Now I'll write your name."

After a while he managed to bring together four letters spelling "Mamm——" and she tried to help him complete the word. But Daniel became very angry at this.

"Let me do it myself!" he cried. "Teacher doesn't like you to help."

His eyes were huge with terror; his mouth worked uncontrollably.

The nurse was at his bedside instantly.

"He's getting tired," she said in English. "Maybe tomorrow you can stay longer."

Rose-Anna screwed up her eyes as she grasped that she was being dismissed. With the docility of the humble she rose to her feet immediately, realizing that she was only a visitor, but she staggered a bit, for it was only now, after these few minutes of rest, that she felt twinges of pain all over her body. She took several plodding steps forward, her shoes creaking over the slippery floor. We live far away; it's different here, she was thinking. Then as she met Jenny's glance she bowed her head as if the young woman could read her secret thoughts.

She walked on and stopped, her reluctance to go increased by the difficulty of trying to remember a few words of English. She wanted to ask what treatment Daniel was receiving for his disease. As long as she must leave him in Jenny's hands she would have liked to describe the child's character so that the nurse might help him as much as possible. But the more she thought about it the harder it all seemed. She contented herself with a shy smile; then, turning around one last time, she saw Daniel's head sunk in the pillow.

At the foot of the bed there was a chart on which she could read: *Name: Daniel Lacasse. Age: Six Years.* But following this was the name of his disease, which she could not decipher.

"Leukemia," the doctor had told her, "a disease of apathy."

This had not alarmed her, because he had not thought fit to add that the disease was always fatal.

At the door, however, she was seized by a terrible presentiment. She turned around with a wild impulse to take the child in her arms and carry him home. An old mistrust of doctors and hospitals, which her mother had instilled into her as a girl, rose to her mind.

Jenny was tucking in his sheets, while Daniel, calmer now, was smiling. Rose-Anna waved goodbye awkwardly, like a child, her elbow at her side and her fingers at the level of her face. The baby, his pudgy hands still gripping the crib bars, was amused by her gesture. He burst into laughter, the saliva running down his chin.

Rose-Anna was swallowed up in the dark corridor. She tripped along uncertainly, worried about missing the exit in the dim light. A grim thought pursued her down the hall, ready to pounce on her like a wild beast. Daniel had everything he needed. He had never been so happy. She could not understand it, and yet she racked her brains to find some reason. But the only explanation that came to her stuck in her throat like poison. They've taken him away from me too, she thought. It's easy to take him away from me because he's so little. Her body stiffened as she walked down the staircase. The peace that had come to Daniel, the wonderful new peace, gave her no joy, but filled her with a sense of shame that she would never live down.

When she reached the porch, the glare of the sun struck her full in the face. Her hands groped blindly, fumbling in the sunlight as if they were looking for something. Never had she felt so poor.

And yet she opened her pocketbook to take out a streetcar ticket, for she was really too exhausted to walk home. Her eyes opened wide as she glimpsed a ten-dollar bill that had slipped into the torn lining of the bag. Then she remembered how she came by it; it was all she had been able to save, "to hide away" as she put it, out of the twenty dollars the government sent her when Eugène went away, a sum of money obtained at such great cost that she would not go into it any further for food or clothing or even to buy sweets for Daniel. With tragic resolution she was holding it in reserve for the time when they must move, and so she called it the rent money.

CHAPTER XIX

As ROSE-ANNA was getting off the streetcar on Notre-Dame Street, she saw a news bulletin hot off the press posted in front of the Two Records. A small knot of men and women had gathered to read it. From where she stood, she could see heavy black letters dancing on the yellow sheet above the heads and shoulders of the stricken group:

GERMANS INVADE NORWAY
BOMBS FALL ON OSLO

For a moment she held her breath, her eyes blank, her fingers pulling at the strap of her handbag. At first she could not grasp why this was such a paralyzing blow or how it touched her. Then, waking to the peril, her mind flew to Eugène. Some sixth sense told her instantly that her son's fate was linked with this news. She reread the words syllable by syllable, her lips moving silently. At the word "Norway" she stopped to reflect. Strange that such a distant country, which she could locate on the map only in the vaguest way, should have any bearing on their lives! Too bewildered to be rational, she forgot that Eugène's last letter stated explicitly that he was to remain at training camp for at least six months more. The words loomed up before her, full of imminent danger. And this woman, who ordinarily never read anything but her prayerbook, did a most unusual thing. She crossed the street quickly, rummaging in her pocketbook as she went, and as soon as she reached the opposite sidewalk held out three cents to the newspaper vendor. Leaning against a store window, she opened the sheet, the ink still damp from the press, and read a few lines, clutching her bag under her arm, as housewives emerging from the fruit store pushed and shoved at her. After a moment she folded the newspaper, her eyes burning with rage. She hated the Germans. She, who had never hated anyone in her life, hated the people of this strange country with an implacable hatred. She hated them not only because of the blow directed at her, but because of the pain they brought to other women like her.

Automatically she walked toward Beaudoin Street. In a flash of illumination she felt her kinship with all the women of distant countries, whether Poles, Norwegians, Czechs or Slovaks. They were women like her. Women of the common people. Working women. Women who for centuries had seen their husbands and children go off to war. One era passed and another came, but it was always thus: women in all ages had waved goodbye and wept to see their men march away. It seemed to her that she was plodding along this sunny afternoon, not alone, but in the ranks of thousands of other women, and that their sighs echoed in her ears, the weary sighs of the needy, of the working women of all ages. She was one of those who had nothing to defend but their husbands and their sons. She was one of those who never sang at the final leave-taking. She was one of those who looked on dry-eyed, cursing war in their hearts, as the men set out for battle.

And yet she hated the Germans more than she hated war. It was a feeling that troubled her, and she tried to shake it off, for she saw it suddenly as a possible reason for consenting to the sacrifice that was demanded of her. She tried to stop herself, to reject both hatred and pity. After all, this is Canada, she thought, as she hurried along; whatever happens over there may be important to them but it's not our fault. She tried desperately to cut herself off from the mournful cortège that accompanied her, but she could not move fast enough. A vast crowd had overtaken her, coming mysteriously out of the past, from every side, from near and far, new faces springing forth at every step, and all resembling her. And yet they had known greater sufferings than hers, these other women. Weeping for their blasted homes they came toward Rose-Anna with hands stretched out in prayer. For in every period women have known each other as sisters in time of mourning. Their arms were raised in entreaty as they uttered pleas for help. In Rose-Anna's simple heart a great battle was joined. She saw the despair of her sisters, she saw it clearly, without flinching, she looked it straight in the face and understood all its horror; then she put her own child's fate in the balance, and it outweighed everything else. Eugène seemed as forlorn and helpless as Daniel. It was the same thing; they both needed her. And when her protective instinct was aroused, she recovered all her strength, all her sense of direction. Nothing else mattered.

By leaving the streetcar a few blocks before the Beaudoin Street stop, she had intended to drop in at the five-and-ten-cent store to give Florentine news of Daniel, and buy some food for supper at the grocer's on Notre-Dame Street. All this was forgotten. She went directly home, her fists clenched, an intent look in her eyes, as if at her own threshold she expected to find some other pressing danger to be circumvented, beaten down, subdued, whatever the cost, or forestalled if she arrived in time.

At the first glimpse of her own house, however, she relaxed somewhat. With a sheepish smile, she realized how far her emotions had carried her; her thoughts had taken so many strange turns, she had had so many shocks and disappointments, such a sense of being lost and alone that the sight of her plain house seemed infinitely sweet.

She entered by the kitchen door, taking off her coat on the way. In the midst of her uneasiness she did not forget that it was late and that she must hurry to get supper ready. Blinded by the light outside she could at first discern only the familiar shapes of the furniture. She went into the dining-room to hang her coat and hat in the closet, then returned to the kitchen, tying an apron over her best dress, which she had no time to change for the moment. Rolling up her sleeves, she was heading for the stove when she saw Eugène seated at the table, smiling at her.

Her hands went fluttering out to him. Then, too moved to utter a word, she stood back and looked him over from head to foot. She was not unduly shocked to find him before her in the flesh, realizing that since she had hurried home with him on her mind, it was because she had divined in some way that he was there and needed her. And so when he stated his need later on, although it had no connection with his mother's fears, Rose-Anna was not surprised. She had reached a point where she would gladly have departed from her customary prudence in order to accede to the most unreasonable request of any of her children.

The little ones were playing out in the street. She was alone with Eugène, but fearing interruptions she led him quickly into the dining-room. Besides, she felt that she ought to put her best foot forward to entertain this guest, this handsome young man in uniform, whose cheeks were rosy with exercise, and who looked altogether unlike her picture of Eugène.

"How well you're looking!" she said, walking ahead of him toward the lightest part of the house and turning around at every step to admire him.

Despite herself, her voice rang with a certain pride to see him so erect and blooming. If she had searched her own mind, she would have been startled to discover that she could feel proud under such circumstances, as well as slightly embarrassed that her son had arrived at a moment when she was not prepared to receive him. The house was in disorder.

As soon as they sat down on the sofa, fear assailed her again. Eugène seemed worried about something. She took it for granted that he was AWOL.

"They wanted to send you overseas, I suppose!" she said bitterly.

And she pointed to the crumpled newspaper that she had thrown on the buffet.

The youth laughed. It was a hollow laugh, without sincerity, as if he were there under false pretences. He ran his hand over his thick curly hair.

"No, no! Now, Mother! You always get the wildest ideas in your head!"

They were both silent a moment, then Eugène began to tell her something about his life at camp, where he professed to be quite content. But in a little while he stopped, at a loss for the proper transition.

Rose-Anna continued to question him. How did they feed him in the army? Was he dreadfully bored? Had he made any friends? Eugène replied absently, smiling occasionally at her childish queries, and looking about him glumly. God, what a hole! He remembered how his mother used to set up his cot for him whenever he went to bed early, he remembered the warmed-over food she kept for him when he came home late from his ramblings around the quarter. He could see her white drawn face the day she went to the police station to speak in his defense; he had returned the stolen bicycle, but she had taken other steps to avoid a fine or further complaint. He could still see her faded little hat and her Sunday dress, which she had worn that day to make a good impression and arouse sympathy. How annoying all that was! If only he could remember an angry outburst or some act of injustice his mother had committed, it would have been easier to ask for what he wanted.

He felt that every passing minute worked against him. The problems, the worries, the sufferings of his mother would all fall on him again, ringing him round and undermining him if he let the house trap him once more. With all its childhood recollections, with poverty writ large over everything, staring out from every recess, the house really frightened him. Even the courage whose mysterious signs could be read on the grimy walls repelled him. How long he had wanted to flee from it all? He would never come back! He would go through the door and plunge headlong into a new life that tonight held promise of forgetfulness!

He stood up. The blood pounded at his temples, as a girl's face swam before his eyes. He took a few steps forward, then shifted his feet a few moments before he turned to his mother. His eyes had grown hard, and he was making such an effort to smile that his whole face twitched. Shielding his face with his hand, he spoke in the meek tone he always assumed for his mother.

"Did you receive twenty dollars, Mother, at the beginning of the month?"

She nodded.

"I managed to put away ten dollars," she confessed. "Your father's still out of work. He expects to find a job soon . . . but meanwhile I'm holding on to the ten dollars. At least we'll have that to put down on the first month's rent. I saw a house the other day that might do," she went on in a moment of confidence. "I have your ten dollars for a deposit if we decide to take it."

There was a shade of deference and gratitude in her voice as she said "your ten dollars," though for so long she had refused to count on the money.

"You understand," she added, "the first thing is to have a place to live. After that, of course, we'll get along as we can! Once we have a roof over our heads we have time to think about the rest."

She went into these details at some length, as if she were obliged to give him an accounting of what she meant to do with his contribution to the household, growing almost vehement as she cried: "I assure you I won't touch your money except as a last resort!"

He turned his head away, unable to bear listening to her. It was the same old story, the rent, their poverty, their basic needs. Would they never have anything else to talk about? Had he come home to get a bellyful of complaints once more? Outside people were hurrying by almost on the run, going toward the busier thoroughfares. And at this hour of the afternoon others were streaming into the motion-picture theaters. Girls were on the way to meet their boy-friends; the streets were gay with youth and music; all of this was waiting for him.

With an unsteady hand he pulled a cigarette case out of his pocket. It was stamped with his initials, and despite his troubled frame of mind he could not help admiring this marvelous new acquisition.

He took a drag, his glance fretful and stormy under his frowning brows. Then he threw the cigarette away and crushed it under his heel. Standing at the window with his back to her, he spoke quickly:

"I'm a little short right now, Mother. Can you slip me a few bucks? The train trip and a few extras, you know . . ."

His lean figure was outlined against the setting sun. Rose-Anna shuddered. Her heart went out to him immediately, just as it had when he was a little boy begging for a nickel. Then too he used to stand facing the window, watching the people in the street, his head averted.

"Sure," she said. "But aside from the ten dollars I only have a little change. I might be able to dig up fifty cents . . ."

Eugène's eyes blazed. He came to her directly.

"No, don't bother. Give me the tenner, I'll bring you back the change."

His demand struck panic to her heart. She had a terrible suspicion that Eugène meant to go off with all the money, weak as he was and ignorant of its value. She saw her close, frugal calculations swept away with a kind of despair. Then she controlled herself. God, how quick she was to jump to conclusions! Eugène would go to the corner store and bring back the change immediately.

She opened the buffet drawer where she kept her pocketbook, and drew out the crisp new bill.

"It's your money after all," she said. "If you hadn't enlisted, we wouldn't have it. But try not to spend it all, Eugène."

This time she caught his eye and held it, her hands extended as if in appeal.

"Don't you worry," he said peevishly. "I'll give it back to you with a little extra."

With the money in his pocket, he plucked up courage. Everything was going to be different henceforth. It would be his turn to take things in hand. His father had never had the slightest notion of how to take care of the family. Well, he, Eugène, would take the lead now.

"You know, Mother," he said, "our troubles are almost over. I might be promoted, and then you'll get more than twenty dollars a month, you'll see, Mother. You'll have enough to live on. You won't be counting the pennies all your life. We'll be there, the rest of us, to look after you."

As he contemplated these rosy plans he became more and more cheerful; the blood rose to his face and his eyes sparkled with pleasure. He leaned over and kissed his mother's cheek, murmuring slowly :

"What would you like to have? What would you like me to buy you? A dress? A hat?"

Her smile was pathetic as she saw where this was leading, but the years had cured her of following a will-o'-the-wisp. Her one idea was mirrored in her frown, in her gentle, stubborn voice.

"It's for the rent, you know."

Then her hands dropped in a gesture of finality.

Eugène slipped his cap on over his curls and studied his reflection in the little mirror over the buffet.

"You're not staying for supper?" she cried.

The youth looked abashed, his sensual mouth, with its soft feminine curves, pinched with chagrin. He hardly knew what to say or do.

"Well, you know, I—I've got to see someone . . . But tomorrow . . ."

And he beat a hasty retreat, slinking away from his mother's hurt expression.

"I've got to see someone. But after this . . ."

He reached the door, and had placed his hand on the knob when the children rushed in with wild outcries.

"Ah, Gène!" they shouted.

And they hung on his arms and legs. Lucille and Albert searched his pockets while little Gisèle pulled him by the sleeve, lisping :

"Did you bwing me a pwesent, Gène?"

Philippe stood haughtily just outside the door, giving his brother an envious look.

"If you have enough cigarettes, you might slip me a couple."

Eugène burst out laughing, flattered by this reception. Admiration from any source, even the most artless, delighted him.

"Here you are, you little bum!"

And he tossed Philippe a package of cigarettes he had just opened. Then he pulled a handful of pennies out of his pocket and threw them into the air, disregarding his mother, who stood looking on with compressed lips. Lucille and Albert caught a few in flight, then crawled under the table and chairs to quarrel over the rest.

Gisèle, less nimble than the others, began to whimper.

"None for me?"

And she stamped on the floor, commanding him in her shrill little voice :

"Gimme! Gimme!"

Eugène lifted her in his arms, wiped her nose with his big khaki handkerchief, and put a bright new penny in her round little hand, which began to tremble with delight.

"Here's one just for you," he said.

And the house was suddenly filled with intense gaiety and excitement. Albert and Lucille were counting their pennies, butting their heads in the process and almost ready to fall to blows. Dumbfounded, Rose-Anna watched them run off to the store on the corner. Eugène slipped out with them.

Alone with the little girl, who had taken refuge under a chair, singing to herself, Rose-Anna sank down at the table and let herself go in a moment of poignant grief. It had cut her to the heart to see that money flying through the air.

CHAPTER XX

EUGÈNE WAS no sooner out of the house than he raised his head and set off for Notre-Dame Street, whistling between his teeth. As he turned the corner of Beaudoin Street he took a deep breath, while his lips relaxed in a conceited smirk. First he rummaged feverishly in his pocket to make sure that he still had the new bill, then he unfolded a slip of paper he had been carrying in his hand and reread the name and telephone number on it. This called forth the image of a face with bright red lips, a pair of bold roguish eyes, and a mass of long wavy hair crowned with a small beret.

His cheeks burned. Sitting off in a corner as the soldiers crowded into the station waiting-room, the girl had swept up her long dark lashes and given him a faint smile when he passed. A moment later he was seated beside her, daring to ask her name. She crossed her long thin legs under his scrutiny and laughed softly: "Does your mother let you go out all by yourself?"

He'd show her that he was no kid. In his agitation he crumpled the piece of paper that he had torn from his notebook. If only she hadn't put him on the wrong tack, if only this telephone number were really hers!

Hurrying along, he made for the nearest cigar store and flung himself into a telephone booth. As he dialed the number he found himself panting. After a moment a strange voice answered. Whom did he want to speak to? "Yvette," he stammered. He was so afraid that the voice would ask him more questions that he began to tremble and drops of sweat stood out on his forehead. There was a pause, then the shrill soprano he remembered burst in his ear. He wiped his face on his sleeve, so relieved that he shook with nervous laughter.

He gave his name and took the plunge:

"How about a date tonight?"

Silence. A giggle. And then:

"Okay."

"Where?" he asked, choking.

She named a place and a time. Eugène's voice sank to a murmur. He hung up, and stood there a moment with his elbow on the box before leaving the booth. His face was very red, and he looked around with a furtive glance as he left the store.

Out in the street again, he realized that he had two hours on his hands before meeting Yvette. With a frown of displeasure he came to a halt on the sidewalk, wondering how to kill the time. His mother's sad and weary face came to his mind. He gritted his teeth and walked on aimlessly to rid himself of the obsession. Finding himself presently in front of the Two Records, he entered and asked for a package of cigarettes.

Sam Latour was listening raptly to a news commentator, his head bent over a tiny radio that he had installed on a shelf between some cardboard placards. He came up to the counter mumbling:

"By George, things are going badly in Norway!"

His voice trembled with excitement.

"When are they going to stop those Boche devils?" he asked, as if he had lost his bearings.

"Just wait till we get there!" cried Eugène.

Then with an air of nonchalance he drew out his ten-dollar bill and tossed it on the counter.

"By jove, you're in the money!" said Sam. "Ten-dollar bills don't stick to your fingers, do they?"

"There's more where that came from," replied Eugène, a cigarette dangling from his lip.

He scooped up the change carelessly, and slipped the bills into various pockets.

"Yeah," continued Latour, "you certainly are putting on side, Lacasse, my boy."

"It's about time," said Eugène, laying his arm on the counter, his legs crossed, his face turned toward the room in a pose unmistakably like his father's.

His thick curly hair grew low over his forehead, beneath which his eyes glistened with self-importance, eyes of a blue similar to Azarius's, but set much closer to his short straight nose, giving his face an altogether different expression, less frank, less direct.

While his father's glance was open and full of ardor, Eugène's was inclined to be stealthy and evasive.

"Yeah," Sam Latour repeated.

A passerby entered, then two workmen stopped in front of the shop, and hearing the radio commentator, came in also. From time to time Sam nodded his head and punctuated his own reflections with a shrug of his broad shoulders, or snapped his belt with a bellicose gesture. He had changed greatly since the period when he used to engage in so many futile discussions with Azarius Lacasse. His indifference had given way to a sense of outrage. Chewing at a cigar, he leaned over again to listen to a description of the invasion of Oslo. Normally of a happy and tranquil disposition, he went into childish transports of anger when he felt deeply moved. Incapable of subterfuge himself, he reacted more violently to fraud than to injustice.

The end of the broadcast was greeted by a long silence. Sam turned off the radio. And immediately the little restaurant was filled with a babble of voices.

"The sneaks!" Latour exploded.

He moved up to serve the customers, his head sticking out like an angry bull's.

"To go skulking into a country, dressed like the folks who live there, and grab everything before you know where you're at! What skunks! What traitors!"

He passed out packages of cigarettes and gum, bottles of coke, banged the cash register with his powerful fist and poured out a flood of abuse at the same time.

His customers were in no haste to depart. Several of them stood at the door reading the evening paper for further information. Others were studying a map of Europe that Sam had pinned up on the wall.

"The Norwegians are good people," said one. "They never wanted war."

"No more did we," said one of the workmen, his lunch box under his arm.

"They were fairly progressive and up to date," said another, who seemed rather well informed.

"They had their traitors all the same," roared Sam Latour.

"Oh, you find traitors everywhere," added the man who had been the first to speak. "But still it's a mystery to me how a man can sell his country——"

Sam Latour interrupted. "Some men would sell their mothers for money or a promotion, by Jove!"

He chewed viciously at his cigar, pulling at his collar in his characteristic gesture.

"I wonder if anyone can stop them," put in a thin little man, taking his nose out of his newspaper.

Eugène stood erect, his hands stiff at his sides, his face bristling with defiance. It had not escaped him that these cautious and temperate workingmen gave him an occasional glance of approval. Seeing himself through their eyes, he was intoxicated with pride. He represented valiant youth, fighting youth, in whom people of ripe age, the old, the weak, the irresolute, placed their trust. A defender of the oppressed, of women and children, that's what he was. The avenging angel of outraged society. His eyes flamed.

"You bet," he cracked. "You bet we'll stop them. Like this . . ."

And he sprang forward in the gesture of thrusting a bayonet through the wall, scowling as if he were meeting stubborn resistance. Then he made a dry, clucking sound, let his arms drop, and eyed the group with a look of intense self-satisfaction.

"Yeah," said Sam Latour.

"Yeah," said Eugène.

The door opened. Léon Boisvert entered, dressed in new clothes, a newspaper folded neatly under his arm, a wary look on his face. He stood wiping his shoes on the mat, cocking his ear before advancing farther.

Eugène gave him a mocking glance.

"You're still in civvies, eh?"

Léon Boisvert was disconcerted. Five weeks earlier he had succeeded in getting a job as bookkeeper in a nearby office. The fear of being drafted haunted him constantly, sleeping and waking. The war itself had suggested nightmares of bodies run through with bayonets, of men pursuing him and putting weapons in his hands by main force, but added to all this now was the terror of losing his first bit of good luck, the little job he had sought manfully for so many years. A sickly pallor spread over his face.

"When a man can't find a job, he can always go into the army, of course," he replied with an attempt at a sneer.

Eugène slouched against the counter, smiling arrogantly.

"We'll have conscription soon," said he. "I'm in a position to know. There's only one way out for you. Run away to the woods. Or else get married," he added, snickering.

He crushed his cigarette against the counter.

"Besides," said he, "the guys who volunteer are going to get the best jobs after the war."

Then he swaggered through the door out into the street.

The air outside seemed light. He felt as if he were floating on a cloud, the master of his fate. Goodbye to uncertainty and scruples. Yes, he thought, the world owes me something, I guess, considering the risks I'm taking. With long easy strides he reached the streetcar stop and elbowed his way through the crowd to get on board. It seemed to him that even the sluggish passengers looked at him with special interest. His joy knew no bounds. And his demands on life grew more and more unreasonable. We shouldn't have to pay for anything, he was thinking. It's a damned shame. It's because of us that they can take it easy.

The wait at the base of the Maisonneuve Monument, the trysting-place Yvette had proposed, seemed unbearable. In a highly nervous state, he smoked one cigarette after another. Yvette was late. Consulting the clock on the Aldred Building, he noticed that the girl had already kept him waiting ten minutes. But youth and jollity and entertainment were all due him, without delay. He paced up and down, and suddenly he saw a sharp image of his mother's face when she had given him the ten dollars.

He put his hand in his pocket, and counted over what was left of it. A feeble impulse urged him to return home, made up partly of pity for his mother, and partly of resentment at the girl who was keeping him waiting, who was perhaps laughing at him.

"Ma," he whispered, overcome by a vague feeling of compassion, and so vexed at Yvette that he yearned to console his mother, and restore himself in her good graces. He pictured himself returning what was left of the ten dollars, while she, proud and reassured, tucked it away immediately in her secret hiding place. And what delighted him most was not his mother's gratification, but his own part in the little drama, his generosity, and Rose-Anna's regret at having doubted him. Ma was afraid I would spend it all, he thought. He turned the project over in his mind until he felt that it was as good as carried out: it warmed the cockles of his heart, and raised him even higher in his own esteem. At this moment he saw a streetcar coming from the east side. The doors opened and Yvette stepped out, clad in a full coat that hung wide to show her long legs, and a red dress that molded her figure. The picture of Rose-Anna faded from his mind as that bright color caught his eye. He threw away his cigarette, and crossed the square, whistling, to meet the girl in the flamboyant dress.

CHAPTER XXI

FLORENTINE HAD grown insensible to the emotional appeal of spring. April had gone by, May was coming in shyly; undismayed by the encroaching cement, the old trees in the streets had turned green without her observing the slightest change in her walk between the store and the house.

This evening, however, as she left the five-and-ten, she was pulled up short by the surprising softness of the air; she was shocked in a way, as if the transformation had taken place while she was absent, and every stage of it had escaped her. Despite the late hour the sun still lay warm on Notre-Dame Street. Over the shoemakers' shops and fruit stalls and bars the windows of apartments were flung open, the sounds of family life mingling with the hubbub of the street, and after a train, a truck, or a streetcar had passed by, one could hear the distant ringing of bells.

In front of the tower at the Saint-Henri station a few flowers stuck their heads up out of the famished earth. And high up, beyond the belfries that surmounted the layers of soot, the verdant flank of the mountain spread out, its swaying branches weaving a lacy pattern of pale green leaves. Spring was all about her, Florentine realized, perhaps even a little past its prime here in Saint-Henri, with a suggestion of dust and sultry weather to come. The passage of time thus was forced on her; she could no longer deceive herself, she must accept it. At this her stark fear emerged from the depths where she had kept it hidden, ringing like a wild bell that would never stop, ringing louder than all the bells in the city—the fear that had stalked her for days, for a long time, perhaps ever since that Sunday in March.

Was there any way of quieting her fear? It seemed as impossible as trying to stop the great bells ringing out in chorus over the roof tops. She could no longer use reason against that constant cry of alarm. She must act, today. But what could she do? Should she let Jean know? This had been in the back of her mind for some time, but she had rejected the idea in order not to admit the inevitable. But now it came back to her. Instinctively she had been walking in the direction of St. Ambroise Street.

No definite plan of action sustained her. She did not reflect that all her efforts to find Jean might be in vain. Her fear and unhappiness were so overwhelming that she imagined luck would be with her this very day, a miracle would come about, and she would meet him. But even without this hope she would have made her way toward the part of town she associated with him, so complete was her surrender to some secret intuition.

At Atwater Street, she turned to go down toward the canal. The taverns along the way blew their rank smell in her face through open doors, and the snack bars that served haggard little newspaper vendors exhaled a nauseating reek of fish and chips. Suddenly, as she rounded the corner of St. Emile Street, she caught sight of the familiar pushcart of the tobacco huckster, an old rustic from whom Azarius was in the habit of buying a strong, bitter pipe tobacco; in a moment the whole market place came into view. Hundreds of flowers and plants were displayed in the sunlight on ramshackle stands; feathery masses of ferns swayed in the soot-filled air; pale jonquils bowed to the least breath of wind; bright-red tulips burst on the eye. And behind the parade of flowers Florentine saw the even ranks of smooth-skinned apples, of blue-veined onions, of heads of lettuce in which drops of water still sparkled. She turned her head away, hurt by this festival of colours, this wealth of earthy smells, in which she could never again take pleasure! Spring gave no quarter to those who hoped to ignore it! All its riches were spread out before her eyes, while the living effluvia of hothouses, sugar trees and barnyards pricked at her nostrils. The thick golden syrup, the bricks of maple-sugar candy, the hares hanging by their tails, their fur drenched with blood, the cackle of hens poking their heads through the slats of crates, and the round uneasy eyes of those who were thrown alive into the scales—everything there seemed to be telling her that life was easy on some people and hard on others, and that there was no way of escaping this pitiless law.

She walked faster, tempted to turn her back on the lively scene from which she felt excluded. But now, behind this spring of terror and self-revelation, all the springtimes she had ever known surged up in her memory, especially those farthest away in time. It was like a glimpse of Heaven, a drop of water for her thirst, but in the end the recollection of the simple pleasures of her childhood only added to her present anguish. In the old days she had often come here with her father to shop of a Saturday evening. As a little girl she used to love to carry the market bag. Her father would stop for a chat with that stout country woman who to this very day, Florentine suspected, wore the same old sweater, brown from the sun. She sold them little green pickles of which Azarius was particularly fond. Sometimes they would go to the fish market to pick out a fish for supper. Her father taught her to distinguish between catfish and carp, and if she grew restless, would playfully push her little fingers into a basin of water where live eels swam about.

Oh, how far away all that seemed! How foolish of her to be thinking back on Saturday evening at the market! And yet it was true that as a child she had been petted and happy. There are wealthy children who never have known the feeling of being loved that she possessed in her childhood. She remembered Rose-Anna's grave warnings as she left the house with her father, her trusting little hand in his. "Take good care of the little one," her mother would say over and over again, for she had been called "the little one" until she was twelve years old. And the things her father talked about as they walked along! And the feeling of complicity between them when he would grip her hand in his large soft palm and whisper: "Your mother said she didn't want any cream, but suppose we buy some all the same, just to see how pleased she'll be tomorrow when she eats her porridge!" On the stony streets they traveled together there had been little round pebbles all along the way, shining pebbles, oddly tinted, that had made them cry out with delight. Could she have continued to be happy if she had followed the same path? No, that was a foolish notion. She had made her choice, knowing full well that she could no more have done anything different than stop breathing. Even now, if she had it to do all over again ...

Having made full circle, Florentine pursed her lips and gritted her teeth with such force that she looked quite ugly. None of these reflections helped solve her problem. What good were all these memories of the past, her childhood and her family? What good, what good? She almost cried out in rancor against the weakness that had come over her.

She was walking very quickly now, her eyes set, wracking her brains for a practical solution, seeking some hope, some refuge from her terror. The rest made no difference. It was from her terror that she wanted to be saved.

Continuing down toward the canal, she was soon besieged by the clatter of chains and the hoarse blasts of the siren. At the lower end of the market place, near the pavilion with its yellowish tower and its jagged coping, the drawbridge was moving away from the sidewalk, and Florentine could see the smokestack of a freight boat advance between two long lines of waiting cars and trucks.

She stiffened—not with interest, for the sight was familiar enough to be commonplace—but because suddenly she saw life under a new guise, one that paralyzed her with fear. Hundreds of other boats had steamed through the canal at this point without making the slightest impression on her, but this one held her eye in spite of herself, as if it were the first she had ever really noticed.

It was a tramp steamer, with a gray keel, dented sides befouled with offal, and a mainmast that conjured up the mists of the estuary. She had already completed a long voyage from distant ports, and as she made her way through the city, through the passage, so absurdly narrow in contrast with her power, from barrier to barrier, from obstruction to obstruction, she seemed to be aiming straight for the open channel of the St. Lawrence, and later on, the rolling waves of the inland sea. With her crew on deck, some holding the hawsers roped around their hands like lassos, other hanging their laundry in front of the bridge, the ship glided by with a smooth, indolent motion. It was as if she had come to parade her indifference to the dangers confronting lands-men at the very crossroads of toiling humanity. As if she were trumpeting the poignant appeal of far horizons that finds an echo in every heart.

She passed on between the walls of the factories bordering the canal, and the rumble of her propeller faded away. But other smokestacks rode up from the port, belching great clouds of soot over the shining thread of water. A tanker led the way, flattened out like a raft; behind it came a barge heavily loaded with lumber, its decks awash, stirring up the smooth surface of the water with its strenuous exertions. And still more masts, more weather-beaten flags, more mist-laden keels moved on between the roofs and the signboards! And every prow that took shape, every puff of smoke that appeared in the distance, instead of filling the horizon, seemed to purify and broaden it, until the mind in torment perceived the vast lonely spaces in which each life must be spent. On the bank, grimy with smoke from the passing ships, stood the watchman's box, a gloomy, neglected shack, like all control booths set up in barren places to serve the needs of highways, bridges, and canals. Beside it was a flat-roofed lunchroom sunk beneath the level of the sidewalk.

As she took in this scene Florentine realized that she was alone in the world with her fear. Certain experiences, she sensed, brought you face to face with yourself, entirely alone. She had a glimpse not only of her own loneliness, but of the solitude that lies in wait for every one of us, that walks beside us always, ready to fall on us at any time like a shadow, like a cloud. And to her mind this horrible state, this loneliness was an offshoot of poverty, for it was inconceivable to her that people of wealth or easy cir-cumstances might make a similar discovery.

But such thoughts were leading her nowhere. Closing her eyes, she tried to find within herself her wilful, imperious desire for Jean—the only thing that seemed comprehensible after her mental wanderings—yet she could summon up nothing but a meaningless vision of barges in movement. But deep within her, something else was growing too, a sense of bitterness so sharp, so frightful, so ugly that it poisoned her whole spirit.

No, Jean would never know the fear she walked with this spring evening, an evening made for laughter, for holding hands. Such an evening made her fear even less acceptable, even more unjust. A man's life, she realized, involved no backward looks, no regrets, and this thought was infinitely more tormenting than the burden of her own fault. In a little while he would have forgotten what she looked like. He would love other women. To recall some picture of her to his mind would require an effort. And that she could not bear. Since he was lost to her, she wanted him to be doomed to suffer as much as she. Or rather let him die. This thought gave her some satisfaction. Yes, if he were dead the old scores might be wiped off. But as long as he lived and breathed she would suffer the humiliation of not having known how to hold him.

Or else if she could strike a blow at his liberty while he lived, if she could be a burden to him, a constant reproach, thwarting his ambitions daily, then perhaps she herself might find life worth living. Her nostrils quivered. She fancied meeting him and planned what she would say, the bold, passionate words that would pour from her lips, such words as haunted her in the evenings when she sat with her mother, her secret buried within her, unnerved by the silence and hating each thought that grew out of the silence.

Then from her heart came a low moan, a cry of misery, pleading for Jean to love her still, in spite of the hatred she felt for him. To be freed of that hatred, to be freed of her fear, he must love her. And she searched her memory for some word or phrase as proof of his affection. She seized on these words, like a beggar turning a coin he has just received over and over, hoping to see it become transformed and magnified through the magic of his desire. But no, the gift was small, trifling. Why, oh why had she given herself to him in exchange for such niggardly alms? Her thoughts went round and round in the same groove, ending up always at the dubious revelation brought by her surrender to the demands of the flesh. It was for this then that the earth turned on its axis, that men and women, deadly enemies, called a truce to their enmity, it was for this that nights were soft and a path seemed marked out solely for one pair of lovers! It was for this that her heart gave her no peace! O misery! She forgot her moments of delirium, her moments of happiness, she could only see the trap that had been laid for her weakness, and as this trap seemed brutal and coarse, she felt unutterable scorn, stronger even than her fear, for her womanhood.

She reached the house where Jean had been living. With its gutters leaking water like the scuppers of a ship, its peeling paint and the drone of propellers all about, the house had the air of an old freighter in drydock. Florentine passed and repassed it, still uncertain what to do. She had already been here twice before, but had not had the courage to go in. Instead she had sent her brother Philippe with a letter for Jean. The boy maintained that he had lost the letter; but the next day he had asked for twenty-five cents as the price of his silence. At the end of the week he returned to the charge and demanded double the money.

Florentine repressed a fierce temptation to run away, anywhere, and thereby hold on to some shreds of pride. But where could she go? To whom could she turn if Jean continued to fail her? Since the trip to Saint-Denis her mother had grown more and more despondent. Her father? What help, what support had he ever given them? It was all very well to recall the delights of her childhood, but later on his contribution to the household had been limited to fine talk, an occasional surprise—and bad news. And whenever she thought of Eugène, after learning that he had never returned the money he had borrowed from her mother, she wanted to box his ears or scratch his eyes out. On his last leave she had passed him in St. Catherine Street, with a flashy-looking girl on her arm. That evening their mother had served them bread and scraps of cold meat for supper, saying that she had not had time to go shopping. The wretched taste of that meal came back to her now; it was food that never could be digested. By yielding to Eugène's demands, Rose-Anna had forfeited Florentine's good will. The girl had lost all interest in helping her family. And this increased her resentment toward her brother, because he had made her lose the best part of herself.

Indications of their rapid disintegration as a family multiplied in her mind. But even before this they had begun to break away from one another. All the run-down houses they had ever occupied appeared before her eyes, a whole series of homes where the same sacred pictures, the same family portraits hung on the walls, and the walls always closed in on her. Even the smell was the same. And because of this it seemed to her that she had been looking for Jean all her life, ever since she was born.

She took out her compact, ran the powder puff over her cheeks, and looked at her reflection in the mirror attached to the lining of her bag, torn between pride and self-pity. And she regretted not having bought a silly little hat, a tiny piece of straw covered with flowers that she must have noticed, in spite of her troubled spirits, in a shopwindow on her way, perhaps today, perhaps a long time ago. Oh, if only she had been prettier or better dressed on such and such a day when he saw her, Jean might not have spurned her!

She went up two steps and pressed the door bell. And while she stood there waiting, she saw in a flash what a picture she made, how poor and forsaken she must look in last spring's outfit, furbished up to be sure, but no longer in the latest style.

The door opened a crack. Florentine heard herself asking for Jean in a low, expressionless voice. While she was speaking she could hear a step ring out on the sidewalk and the gay, impudent whistle of a passerby. She was sure that if she turned to look she would see Jean's square shoulders disappearing around the corner. It seemed as if all her life she would see him vanishing around a corner. The past, the present, the future, all became mingled in that moment, filling her with a sense of irreparable loss.

As through a fog she caught: "He went away without leaving his address." And it seemed to her that she had already heard these words before, night and morning, every time she woke up with the dread that she would be cornered into making a confession.

Her head bowed, she walked on toward the foundry in St. Jacques Street. A bunch of glass cherries, tinkling at the brim of her hat, beat a soft tattoo in her ears. She was numb, unable to think clearly. When she reached the foundry she stood still for a moment, and as the tinkling stopped her mind started working again. She remembered how, not quite two months ago, Jean had greeted her at this very spot with the utmost coldness. Her cheeks flushed as she remembered her humiliation. What had made her come here, when all she could remember was his contemptuous smile? How could she have brought herself to walk where he had walked? Suddenly she despised herself more for her maneuvers to snare him than for her lost dream.

She retraced her steps. In the face of her inability to bring Jean back to her—only in defiance she called her impotence unwillingness—she began to question her own fears. And now she entered a new phase, aware that her terror was waning, and reveling in the luxury of feeling no pain for the moment. Perhaps she had been mistaken all along. Perhaps she had been too quick to believe that the consequences of her act were inevitable. And this state of half-doubt was so comforting that she quickened her steps as if speed alone would put an end to all her uneasiness. The farther she went from the quarter where Jean used to live, the more of her dread she left behind her. Oh, if it only were true that she had been wrong, how she would make up for these silly, baseless fears, for these chimeras that had haunted her this evening! She must have been mistaken. Now she remembered that her mother had once . . . The pulsations of fear became more sporadic. The bell that had been ringing in her ears for hours chimed more and more faintly, at moments was quite still, and Florentine succeeded in picturing her downfall as a stupid accident—a piece of folly she would be careful not to think of as an ineradicable stain by dwelling on it too much.

At Notre-Dame Street, which she reached a bit above the Cartier Theater, she found solace in the neon lights and the millinery shops; for the first time in her life she found the milling crowd friendly and pleasant.

A flood of jazz poured out of a small restaurant as she passed. Tottering with exhaustion, she dragged herself toward the cheerful sound. She entered, ordered a hot dog and a coke, and as soon as she was alone in the booth, lit a cigarette. Almost with the first puff, a feeling of relaxation came over her. She sank gladly into the deafening, overheated twilight atmosphere of the place, which had been the climate of her soul for so many years, and outside of which she felt lost. It seemed to her now that she would even be happy to be at the five-and-ten-cent store, where the clatter and bustle never ceased. The silence everywhere about her this evening had been horrible, the deserted streets full of terror. If she ever survived this abominable night, as she had no doubt she would, the only memory she would retain would be the sense of loneliness, of desperate loneliness she had known as she watched other couples walking hand in hand, in step with the hot jazz being blared out of every café juke box.

The music stopped, and with it the impression that she had found a shelter from loneliness. She dropped a nickel in the slot, and to the accompaniment of an ear-splitting jitterbug tune, she took out her comb, rouge and powder, and began to apply her make-up with care. She would take a puff of her cigarette and then put it down, apply a dab of rouge to her lips, a little more powder to her forehead, her feet beating time to the music under the table.

Studying the final result, she was satisfied. Under the rouge, her cheeks were pale, but she was pretty, prettier than ever with her hair loose on her shoulders and her eyes still wide with terror. She looked down at her trim figure as if she were seeing it for the first time. She noticed how her hair shimmered under the sconce in the mirror of the booth, she held out her hands and examined her delicate fingers, her lacquered nails, and as her eyes moved up her rounded white arms she began to love life again. On the spot she resolved to buy the little hat she coveted, recalling now the very shop on Notre-Dame Street where she had seen it. That was how she would take revenge on Jean. Her lips parted in a smile of incredible naïveté. She planned to be so smartly dressed that if by chance he should meet her some day, he would be sorry he had dropped her. But then it would be her turn to show no pity.

The jazz pounded in her ears and the cigarette smoke made her not unpleasantly giddy. She reviewed all the trinkets she had been yearning to buy, and visualizing herself adorned with them, she decided in favor of one and against the other. By acquiring all the outward appurtenances of happiness she would make happiness come to her—not a vague sort of happiness, but something clear-cut, cold, metallic, like a silver coin.

The thought of money brought her back to her mother. And in the tender mood that swept over her—induced by the lull in her torments—she grew conscious of her own magnanimity. This feeling of virtue was so delightful that she let it take complete possession of her. Yes, from now on she would be a tower of strength for her mother. What if Azarius and Eugène did not do their part? She would never abandon her mother to their wanton indifference.

As she tapped her feet in rhythm with the music all the sacrifices she intended to make seemed easy for her. From time to time, however, the passionate wail of a siren hung over the quarter, and for a moment she was back in spirit along the canal, with a premonition of gray, dreary days ahead; then she tipped her head back and gulped down her drink, puffed at her cigarette, and shook herself out of it. At last she fixed on a symbol to signify her break with the past: if on returning home she found nothing changed, she could infer that her anguish had had no basis. Charmed by this thought, as if it settled everything, she rose, took a last glance at the mirror, and went out.

As she walked down Beaudoin Street she could see the dining-room light shining between the curtains. Its modest beam suddenly penetrated to some other vein of goodness than the defiant, calculating feelings she had entertained earlier, by which her virtue existed only as a medium of exchange. All unsuspected, a deep sense of comradeship sprang up in her heart. Their life together no longer seemed cramped and disordered, but a thing embellished by Rose-Anna's courage. Rose-Anna's courage suddenly shone before her like a beacon. Florentine approached the door slowly, lest too great haste break the spell, and it seemed to her that if she waited there for two or three minutes she would see the pattern of their lives drawn in a few bold lines, and everything would have its meaning and its truth. But this was gone in a flash; her desire to be healed was greater than her desire for the truth. Only her cure mattered. In her yearning for Rose-Anna, whom she saw in this moment of heightened sensibility as all shining perfection, there had really been only a childish longing to be comforted and protected. The home would take her in again, it would heal her.

She put her hand on the doorknob, but before turning it, stood there in suspense a moment longer, her heart swelling. Then she pushed open the door. And it was as if an icy blast of wind had come to strike down all her new-found hopes.

CHAPTER XXII

T HE DINING-ROOM was crowded with unfamiliar furniture; strange faces looked up from open packing cases and tubs crammed with linens; chairs were stacked ceiling high.

For a moment Florentine hoped that she had entered the wrong house in her haste, for although her pause on the doorstep had seemed long, it had in reality taken only a second. But there was no mistake; along with the mattresses piled on the floor and the decrepit wardrobes that belonged to some other family there were many objects she knew only too well: the old clock, the children's hats, the oilcloth cover on the table. And then too, there was her mother sitting on the edge of a chair, pulling absent-mindedly at her apron. Florentine trembled as she approached her. Rose-Anna gave her a distraught smile, and then rose to shut the kitchen door. This gave them a little privacy in a corner crowded with their own possessions. Once more the flight of time was driven home to Florentine; in a sort of stupor she remembered that it was May first, moving day.

"Sit down," said her mother, as if she had reached a point of frustration where any other remark would have been superfluous.

She herself sank back into a chair. Her term was approaching, and after the slightest exertion she had to look about for some support.

They looked at each other. The scene required no explanation, but Rose-Anna felt constrained to say something.

"As you see, we have the new tenants on our backs." Then her voice grew plaintive; she continued as if she were speaking through thick layers of misunderstanding and worry and loneliness: "I thought we'd have a few days' grace, but these people paid in advance. So it's their house more than ours. I couldn't keep them out."

What a ghastly mess, Florentine was thinking. She was of course used to their moving bag and baggage once a year—sometimes they had been obliged to move at the end of six months—but never before had their home been invaded by strangers before they themselves had left. Then as she heard children whimpering in the next room, she fell into a cold fury. Was this what she had hoped for when she came home yearning to find everything in its place? Was this the good omen she had counted on? Why hadn't her mother and father seen to it before this that they had a place to live? She herself had spent the last few days blind to everything but her own torments, to be sure, but she could not forgive the negligence in others that brought them to such a pass. Would those strange children never stop their whining?

"You shouldn't have let them in," she snapped.

"What could I do?" answered Rose-Anna. And then in a gentler tone she went on to tell how she had provided for their most immediate need: "Our sleeping arrangements for tonight will be hard on everyone. But I've spoken to the woman next door; she'll lend us a room. I also kept Philippe's room for the children . . . my children," she added, as if a distinction should be made. "I put them to bed as early as possible. The noise they made playing with the other children—the other woman's children, I don't know her name yet—the noise was enough to drive you crazy!"

She broke off and looked up at Florentine, who sat there rigidly, not seeming to hear a word.

"Where have you been all this time? It's late," she said. But she expected no reply.

Rose-Anna stared fixedly at a worn spot in the linoleum. And suddenly, on a weary, droning note, she began to enumerate their misfortunes, as if at last she could not be satisfied to leave any of them out, the old and the new, the little ones and the big ones, trials of long standing and trials of recent date, those whose pangs were dulled with time and those that still throbbed in the open wound.

"Your father," she said, "your father was supposed to find us a house! You know your father! He keeps us on tenterhooks up to the last minute with his false hopes. Always false hopes! He was going to find us a good house, to hear him talk. A good house! It's up to me to look after everything. But how could I? I had to spend all my time at the hospital . . . with Daniel at the hospital," she felt obliged to recall, as if in unwinding the skein her fingers were caught in a knot. "Daniel, and Eugène on my mind too! What business had we to go to the sugaring! Daniel has been sick ever since. We were born unlucky. It's practically impossible to find a place now, at the beginning of May. Where in the world are we going to live?"

But beyond these misfortunes, beyond the grievances brought out into the open, she saw others, a whole legion of them starting up at every turn of the maze she was following. And she fell silent.

Can one ever describe the night, the fire dead on the hearth, the glacial darkness? Who can give words to what is in a heart bereft of hope? And then, even though she was fairly sure that Florentine was not listening, there are things one dares not even breathe in the presence of another human being. The burden of so many secret troubles awakened Rose-Anna's compassion for others.

"Have you eaten?" she asked, her heart melting suddenly. "I can make you an omelet."

But Florentine did not open her mouth. The tears rose to her eyes, not tears of resignation, but scalding, rebellious tears. This was what she found when she came to her mother for help: a darkness so impenetrable that it stifled all hope in her breast.

For the first time in her life she saw Rose-Anna in a soiled dress and with her hair unkempt. And the present dejection of her mother, who through all their troubles had remained stouthearted, seemed to her a sure sign that the family had gone to pieces, and she at the bottom of the heap. It seemed as if she had risen above her despair of a moment only to plunge deeper into the pit that opened at her feet.

Rose-Anna fingered the edge of her chair with a tired, futile gesture that was new to her—just like her grandmother, thought Florentine. Her shoulders swayed from side to side as if she were cradling a child, or quieting some chronic ache. Or perhaps she was trying to deaden her fatigue, and forget all her unhappy thoughts. But the hollow in her dress between her knees, the curve of her arms, the swing of her body and her bent head reminded Florentine of how Rose-Anna used to hold little Daniel and soothe him when he was feverish.

Daniel! He was so little for his age. His face had always been so pale, almost transparent. But before he had fallen so ill, his precocity had astonished them all. In the quarter there was an old saying that children who were too bright did not live long. He was so frail, so serious, little Daniel! What torments he had suffered already! May he live! thought Florentine, and I will take his recovery as a sign of my own deliverance!

And her mind slid back into the old groove. She returned to her terror like an invalid to the grim portents of heightened pain. As she fought off a rising nausea she knew that she could no longer pretend to ignore her suspicions. She must speak to her mother. But what should she say? She must do it now! Through a humming in her ears she heard Rose-Anna speaking:

"What can your father be up to? It's late and he's been gone since two in the afternoon. What is he looking for at this hour? What can he be doing?"

This trite exclamation, one she had heard repeated a hundred times, aroused no pity in Florentine. She was sinking into stifling darkness where no help or advice could reach her from any quarter. Everything spun around her. A spasm caught her at the pit of her stomach.

When she sat up again, pale and shamefaced, her mother was staring at her. She was staring as if she had never seen her before, speechless with horror. There was no pity in her regard, no sympathy, only horror. Her voice rising with hysteria, she cried:

"What's wrong with you! Yesterday morning, and now tonight . . . You act as if you were——"

She was silent, and the two women glared at each other like two enemies. The only sound in the room came from behind the thin partition where the new tenants were settling into their new home, into what had been the Lacasse home.

Florentine was the first to lower her eyes.

Once again she looked up at Rose-Anna, her lids heavy, her lips quivering, her whole body wracked with pain. For the first and probably the last time in her life she was prepared to appeal for help, like an animal at bay. But Rose-Anna had turned her head away. Her chin had sunk to her chest. She seemed inert, indifferent, half-asleep.

Then Florentine, as if she were standing off at an infinite remove, saw herself as a gay young thing, all aglow under Jean's glance. And since that far-off joy was not to be endured, since it was more terrible, more galling than any spoken reproach, she turned on her heel, opened the door wide, and fled in a gust of wind.

CHAPTER XXIII

SHE RAN BLINDLY down the deserted street, the tap of her heels pounding in her ears, fleeing from her terror, fleeing from herself, when suddenly in the midst of her headlong career she remembered that Marguerite had often invited her to spend the night with her. She had never cared to cultivate the acquaintance of girls of her own age, suspecting that they were envious or malicious, or simply boring; and among those who had been friendly to her at the store, none had irritated her as much as Marguerite, whose persistent sympathy always gave her an excuse to be sarcastic. But she knew how warmhearted Marguerite was, and she was so disconsolate that all she wanted was to be near someone—however silly—who would show her some consideration, and who above all knew nothing of her mishap. She picked her way through the streets, terrified by the dark and even more by the feeling that she could no longer delude herself, that she would always reproach herself for her own downfall.

The walls of the big cotton mill on St. Ambroise Street enveloped her in shadow, behind which the machines panted and wailed. Everything conspired to increase her melancholy; the factory that seemed to spring up out of the bowels of the earth, the passersby who eyed her curiously, the clouds lowering in the sky, and the trees in the depths of the courtyards tossing their branches in a plaintive murmur.

She came out into an open space between high mill walls and recognized the house where Marguerite lived by its green gables, facing St. Zoé Alley. It was one of those venerable dwellings of the small-town type, of which a few are still to be found in Saint-Henri. Little islands in the advancing flood of warehouses and factories, seeming to make a greater display of stiff lace curtains, immaculate doors and fresh paint the more they are challenged by soot and grime.

A light was shining on the first floor, in Marguerite's room. Florentine dared not knock at the door lest Marguerite's aunt, a stiff-necked, stern old woman, come to open it; instead she stood under the lighted window and began to call, at first barely above a whisper, then louder. At last a shadow appeared behind the curtains. Florentine gasped:

"It's me, Marguerite. Come down and open the door. Don't make any noise."

Only when she found herself in Marguerite's little room, and felt assured that the rest of the house was undisturbed, did she perceive the necessity of explaining such a late call. What time was it anyway? She had no idea. Had she been wandering around this way only one evening or all her life? The fear of betraying herself made her tense. Her throat was so dry she could only stammer:

"My family is moving tomorrow. There's no place for me to sleep."

But in a frenzy that belied her words she seized Marguerite's hand, pressed it fiercely, and begged:

"Let me stay here, let me stay here!"

Marguerite wrapped herself in a striped dressing gown and ran her fingers through her short fluffy hair, by way of sprucing up for her friend.

"Of course," she said cheerily, "We'll have a nice long gossip."

But as she beheld her friend's pallor and wild eyes, she grew uneasy.

"What's wrong with you? Are you sick?"

"No, no," cried Florentine.

She had collapsed in an armchair, and her trembling hands fluttered between her hair and her handbag, which she was struggling unsuccessfully to open. The sight of her reflection in the wardrobe mirror made her shudder. To cover up her confusion, she resorted to her usual practice and made a pitiful effort to smooth her hair, then pulled herself to her feet and rummaged among Marguerite's belongings for a lipstick, which she applied to her dry, chapped lips. But before she had finished she turned away, unable to look at herself, her shoulders sagging. And the laugh with which she tried to hide her agony was heartbreaking.

"Goodness knows what I look like," she sighed. "I'm growing ugly, eh, Marguerite?"

"Of course not," said Marguerite. "You always look well, even when you're tired."

"Yes," Florentine agreed weakly. "That's it. I'm tired." Then she confessed her defeat: "I want to go to bed, Marguerite. I want to go to sleep, Marguerite."

It was more of a wail than a wish, a wail she could not smother a moment longer.

"I want to go to sleep!"

The narrow bed against the wall was unmade.

"I'll change the sheets," said Marguerite. "It won't take me a minute."

And she left the room to look for clean linen. As soon as she was alone, Florentine rushed to the mirror to study this new face of hers in the absence of a witness. The sight of those strange features filled her with aversion, their drawn look terrified her, and she only barely managed to restrain the tears that rose to her eyes. Then hearing the doorknob turning, she fled back to her chair and assumed the pose of a moment before.

Before long the covers were turned back invitingly over the white sheets. Florentine ripped off her shoes and stockings, her sweater and skirt, and threw herself into bed. And as her weary body touched the cool sheets she suddenly lost control of herself and burst into tears. She wept with exasperation rather than release, concealing her face from Marguerite. At times she turned and struck her head against the wall, groaning through her sobs at the self-inflicted punishment.

Marguerite let her cry for a while. Then she moved over, put her arms around the girl, and began to talk to her as if she were a child.

"Tell me what's the matter. It might help you to tell."

She felt Florentine grow tense, but she persisted:

"Tell me what's hurting you." And as if she were extracting a confession from a child, she went on: "Is it something your mother said to you? No? Is it because your boy-friend walked out on you? There are other boys, you know. There are plenty of fish in the sea, as they say. It's not that?" And then her voice became grave: "Is it because people are talking about you?"

"Who?" said Florentine sharply through her tears. "Who's been talking about me?"

"Oh, no one. I was just wondering," said Marguerite, who nevertheless remembered a few slanderous remarks. "You mustn't cry about such things. That's just gossip. You mustn't worry about that. I know you've done nothing wrong."

This uncalled-for expression of confidence, added to a certain reticence that she felt on Marguerite's part, infuriated Florentine. She shrank back on her side of the bed and declared:

"Well if you won't tell me who's talking about me, that's your affair. Don't tell." Then she cried out defiantly: "Anyway there's nothing wrong with me, nothing at all!"

But no sooner had she said this than she burst out crying again, appalled at the gulf that lay between her and the girls she knew. She dug her nails into Marguerite's shoulders as if she wanted to shift her torments to her friend.

"Put out the light," she begged.

But in the darkness she felt even more at the mercy of something inhuman and terrifying that was to be her lot and hers alone, something she could neither reject nor share. She clung desperately to Marguerite, biting her lips to keep from admitting everything.

Marguerite, guessing the truth instinctively, said nothing. It had not escaped her that her friend had altered greatly in the last few weeks, nor that the other waitresses had been extremely curious about her somber mood. They had scrutinized her every movement on the sly, and often exchanged knowing glances or malicious comments when Florentine was particularly irritable.

My goodness, can it be true? she wondered. And she was surprised to discover that she did not despise Florentine. Yet up to then she had held very strict views about love outside of marriage. At the store she had even joked about the matter herself, rather enjoying the slander the other girls whispered. But now that she saw the ruin facing Florentine, her first desire was to cover her up and protect her.

What would become of poor Florentine? She was so young, in reality no younger than Marguerite herself, but weaker, more frivolous, and therefore more to be pitied. The girl was prettier too, and therefore more subject to temptation. What could the poor child do? Would she lose her job? To what lengths might she not go in her despair?

Aching with pity, Marguerite felt bound to obey the dictates of her own heart, whatever others might think.

She was not sure that she had enough courage to go through with it, but hoping to force herself into an act of disinterested justice, she let herself be carried away by her own words.

"Listen, Florentine," she said. "Maybe you're caught. If that's it, I'll help you. I'll help you, do you hear?"

But that was not enough, and she knew that she must commit herself further to overcome the instinctive selfishness that urges us all to limit our share in another's pain.

Marguerite grasped all this and whispered:

"Listen, Florentine, I'll see you through. We'll be together, Florentine. I promise you. I'll stand by you. If they say a word against you at the store they'll hear from me! It'll be a secret between you and me."

And foreseeing all the difficulties ahead in spite of her good will, she went into ways and means, while Florentine, too dazed and angry to utter a word, let her maunder on:

"I have a little money laid aside," she said. "That will come in handy. I'll lend it to you, if you're too proud to take it otherwise."

Florentine lay there dumb. She too was thinking. But far from being moved by Marguerite's offer, she was petrified to learn that her secret had been discovered and especially that Marguerite dared to speak of—of—what was to come later on, of something so dreadful that she herself was unable to envisage it. What a fool Marguerite was! Florentine could not stop reviling her friend in her imagination, yet she was careful not to offend her openly. Her practical nature, yearning for prompt relief, warned her not to spurn a helping hand from any quarter. But she found the girl's suggestion contemptible. Her pride kept her from giving Marguerite any hold over her by admitting her suspicions. Had she sunk so low as to grovel for help? Marguerite was the kind who let out a howl before she was hurt. What could you expect of a fool like that? She, Florentine, had not lost her head yet. No, she must be calm at all costs and not hasten things. But in the first place she must throw Marguerite off the track, the big booby.

"You're out of your mind," she said, hesitating between anger and mockery. "Where'd you get such an idea? I tell you there's nothing wrong with me. It's my nerves, my nerves, I say."

She repeated this over and over, raging, defiant, as if to persuade herself that it was true. And when she saw Marguerite half-convinced, she felt so relieved, so positive that she would yet be saved, that she piled on more reproaches:

"It's lucky for you that you said that in fun, because otherwise I'd be very angry. I'd leave this house right away if I knew you thought that of me. Take it back, or I'll be angry at you. How dare you? Must you be so silly?"

Then she pretended to yawn and stretch, and in a dry voice, harsh in the quiet room, spoke her last word.

"Now let's go to sleep, or we'll look like the devil tomorrow morning. Let's go to sleep."

And she pretended to drop off immediately, in order to escape any further solicitude. When at last she heard Marguerite's regular breathing, then only dared she stir. Propping herself up against the pillow, she peered into the darkness as if there were eyes everywhere to read her shame in her slightest move, before abandoning herself to her thoughts.

At first she was surprised by the terrifying calm that had come over her. Faced with the evidence, as shown by what Marguerite had said, by her pity even more than by the symptoms in her own body, she decided that it was too late for regret or shame. Holding her cold hands to her throat, she asked herself quite simply : What am I going to do? Her eyes darted in perplexity from one dark corner of the strange room to another, as if she had forgotten where she was. And always that question beating at her brain : What am I going to do?

She sat up in bed, rubbed her eyes, and pressed her hands to her temples, hoping to squeeze out some plan, some ray of hope. And as she forced herself to examine the possibilities, she remembered a working girl who had once made a horrible confession to her as they walked down the street. And she remembered too that that day life had seemed morbid and cruel beyond belief. Suppose she had to resign herself to that solution! She played with the idea, her flesh crawling with dread of the physical pain involved, and knowing full well that she would never submit to it. Besides, whenever she thought of such things, of this secret that had stuck in her memory like a poisoned dart, it always brought to her mind a totally different vision, in which the church, the saints in their niches, and the burning tapers at mass that morning with Emmanuel were curiously mingled. Days of pure, artless joy came back to her memory, and the contrast made her feel cut off from the sun, from light and life, like a dead thing. She was tempted to do herself some violence, but since she could not persuade herself that there was no other way out, she was not very sincere about it. In the end she gave up the idea, admitting that she could never bring herself to go through with it.

And again the maddening question beat at her temples : But what am I going to do? Should she confess? Confess to her mother? No, never! But what then? Confess to Marguerite perhaps? A lump came to her throat. No, she couldn't do that either. Marguerite with her promises to help her and keep her mouth shut! She could afford to be generous, that one! No one had ever loved her, no one ever took her out but Alphonse, a fellow on the dole, a fellow she supported, no doubt! Marguerite was a girl who knew nothing about life. She had probably offered her services to see what she could find out. And to be able to run her down later. Oh, women! she thought with disgust. And besides, can one woman really help another woman? And if not, who, who in the world could help her?

She cudgeled her brains for another solution. She was still young and pretty. Other young men besides Jean Lévesque had noticed her. Such and such a one had paid her compliments at the restaurant. She lingered a while over his thought, which flattered her cruelly wounded self-esteem, but the very next moment the memory of her recent experience stabbed her. Her lips moved to say Jean's name, as one stammers the cause of one's misery, then rolling over on the pillow, she mumbled hysterically: "I hate him, I hate him, I hate him."

Until daybreak she lay there shaking and sobbing. At last a thin ray of sunlight threaded its way into the room under the lowered blind. Then Florentine stopped tossing. She lay prostrate, motionless, drained of tears. Her love for Jean was dead. Her dreams were dead. Her youth was dead. And at the thought that her youth was dead, she had one last shudder of pain, light as a ripple in the water of a pool, barely troubling the surface as it spreads in a widening circle.

Calm had come to her, a dull stupefying calm, layers on layers of calm. Nothing could pierce her apathy. Neither memories, nor happiness, nor regret. Against her reason, against her own nature, she would wait passively, and this decision simply to wait gave her the feeling of something lasting and permanent.

Her mind was made up. Whatever happened, she would never open her lips to tell anyone her secret. She would go on living, she would let come what might, she would wait, not without hope, but beyond hope. She did not know what she was waiting for, but she would wait. A faint flicker of pride that she had not betrayed herself sustained her, and she recalled too that there was still time in which to reflect further.

The quarter began to wake up; she could hear a milk wagon rumbling over the pavement, then the clink of bottles, and a jolly whistle accompanying quick footsteps, and in her heart the desire to live rose despite everything and took the form of defiance. All was not lost. None of the choices that had occurred to her would do; only a miracle could save her now, and perhaps she deserved a miracle for holding her tongue and being so brave. Her eyes, drooping with fatigue, fastened themselves on the beam of sunlight that was gradually invading the room. Exhausted, but with her mind made up, she was ready to face the future in what seemed to her the proper spirit, calmly and warily, keeping her troubles to herself. There was to be no turning back.

CHAPTER XXIV

O N THE SAME EVENING that Florentine fled from her parents' house, Azarius returned home at about ten o'clock.

"I've found the place for us," he said, as he came in the door. "Five rooms and bath and a bit of a porch. And besides that, a small yard in the rear to hang out your clothes, Rose-Anna. I've settled the deal. If you wish, we can move in early tomorrow morning."

Since Florentine had left, Rose-Anna had not stirred from her chair, and it took some time for Azarius's announcement to penetrate to her brain. At first she heard only the sound of his voice, then gradually she seized the meaning of the words. Her hands beat the air as if she were trying to overcome her own inertia. And then suddenly she was on her feet, looking for something to lean on, a gleam of relief in her lusterless eyes.

"You mean it? You've found us a house?"

For the moment that was all she wanted to know. Where it might be and what it was like were questions she never dreamed of asking. He had found them a shelter, a nook of their own, a private refuge for the joys and miseries of her family. She roused herself up quickly, for only now did she realize how much the idea of living under the same roof with strangers had upset her. Their troubles exposed to the curiosity of intruders! No, a hovel, a stable, a cellar of any kind was preferable to the torture she had been undergoing for the last few hours. She could not bear the ordeal of knowing that her family was breaking up while she stood by helpless, she could not bear to see the thin walls about their private lives crumble away and leave them adrift among the sad wreckage of people just like themselves, good God no!

Her eyes met Azarius with renewed courage; her energy poured back into her veins in waves. A typical working-class woman, she seemed to have an inexhaustible reserve of strength. It was just when she seemed most overburdened that from some mysterious source, from some deep, dark, ever-running spring, a fresh flow of vitality came to her, at first in a weak stream, but growing steadily until she was cleansed of all her weariness. She seized the edge of the table firmly and leaned far over it toward Azarius.

"Look here," she said on the spur of the moment, "why don't we move right away? It's not too late yet."

Azarius looked at her first in surprise, then approvingly, and at last in full agreement. Ever since the idea of running away had first come to him, he had been unusually gentle to Rose-Anna, as if he hoped thereby to acquit himself of a heavy debt. His recent run of bad luck seemed to have made him especially willing to yield to Rose-Anna in everything. Forlorn and humiliated as he had never been before, he was learning at last to conceal his passion for freedom and novelty, and tried to please her with almost pathetic submissiveness.

"I've arranged for a truck tomorrow morning," he said, "but I don't see why I can't get it tonight. If you insist, I'll go and see about it right away. It'll only take me about fifteen minutes."

"Go then," she bade him. "If we hurry we'll have time to set up a few beds there and we can go to sleep by ourselves tonight. It's well worth the trouble. You can always fetch the rest of the things tomorrow morning."

And then her voice grew gentler:

"Besides, with two families in the house, it would be so awkward tomorrow morning, when we both had to use the stove and the bathroom at the same time. And then——"

She raised her arms in a gesture of infinite lassitude:

"—And then, Azarius, it would be such a relief to be in our own home!"

Whereupon he left, and she set to work gathering up pots and kettles and frying pans without delay. There were always several large paper cartons kept in the storeroom behind the kitchen for just such occasions. Having fetched them one by one, Rose-Anna got down on her knees and packed first a layer of household linen, then a layer of dishes, a layer of linen and a layer of dishes, until she had one large box filled. From time to time she cast a glance at the kitchen clock. Mercy, she would never be done at this rate! Her short wind and rapid pulse forced her to stop and rest frequently.

After a time she admitted that she could never finish in time without help. Reluctantly she decided to wake the children. She opened the door of the dining-room very softly and tiptoed into the bedroom. Other people's privacy was inviolable to her. She respected it as stubbornly as she did her own. As she trod on the creaking floor-boards, she was all pity for the strange children asleep on chairs set end to end. Rose-Anna's heart was not insensible to the universality of misfortune, but she had formed the habit of not thinking too much about other people, of being sparing with her sympathy, of putting a check on her own generous impulses. The idea that charity begins at home was deeply ingrained in her. But at this moment her habitual reserve and prudence deserted her; she gave way to a spontaneous gesture of good will toward the strange woman in her house.

"Don't mind me," she breathed. "Use anything you need. We won't be in your way much longer."

And as she spoke she felt relieved of a vague burden of rancor that had been weighing on her.

She went on through into Philippe's little room and whispered in the darkness to her children.

"Get up," she said, "and don't make any noise."

As they opened their eyes wide and sat up in fright, she quickly helped them slip their clothes on.

"We're going home to our house," she repeated over and over.

Her voice was so firm and composed in the darkness that the children's fears were quieted.

She dressed them all, except little Gisèle, whom she left sleeping, picked up the pillows and the blankets, and led them away on tiptoe.

When they reached the kitchen, she returned to her own work without loss of time, and calmly assigned each child a task.

"Yvonne, you're not clumsy. Take my best dishes and wrap every piece separately in newspaper. Every piece," she repeated.

To Albert she said:

"You, my little man, go and get Mamma's tub from behind the door. Don't make any noise now, and be careful not to bump into anything."

Little Lucille also asked for something to do, and Rose-Anna consented:

"All right, you may help Yvonne, but don't break anything, child!"

They were surprised by their mother's even, almost grave tone. Not understanding what a terrible effort it cost Rose-Anna to be patient and gentle at that hour, they soon began to find it all rather fun. When Philippe returned home presently, his mother did not ask him where he had been, with her usual frown. Instead she told him quietly to fetch other packing boxes from the cellar.

At first the children obeyed her commands in silence, then, emboldened by her forbearance, they grew boisterous. The idea of moving in the middle of the night filled them with delight. Their voices rose, and little disputes sprang up as they all tried to do the same task. Rose-Anna, however, would not lose her temper. It seemed as if she would never be cross again. Out of her great weariness she merely asked them to be a little quieter.

"Now children," she said, "don't make such a racket. This isn't our house any more."

And with a ghost of a smile she promised them :

"We'll be home soon. Try to restrain yourselves. It won't be long now. We'll be home in a little while now."

Home!

With what variety of expression Rose-Anna knew how to use the word, and how different it sounded if she used it to refer to the place they were leaving or the place where they were to begin all over again! She could put a thousand shades of meaning into it. Sometimes it had a banal sound, like any other word; but sometimes it left her lips fresh, rejuvenated, with an indescribable power of magic and repose, carrying undertones of stability and permanence, or perhaps a sudden illumination, a quickened hope.

It was an old word for them, one of the first the children had learned. It came to their lips unconsciously, at all times of day. It had served over and over again. It was the word that had been used to designate a damp cellar in St. Jacques Street several years before. It had been used to refer to three sweltering little rooms under the eaves of a filthy tenement in St. Antoine Street. "Home" was an elastic word, at times hard to understand because it evoked not one place but a dozen, scattered through the quarter. For the children it implied a certain amount of nostalgia and sorrow, and always a trifle of uncertainty. It was related to the annual migration. It had the color of the seasons. It echoed in their hearts like a quick farewell; and when they heard that sound they seemed to hear, 'way back in their memory, the sharp cry of migrating birds.

Winged word! Just what did it mean? A fixed spot? Not for them. What did it mean then? What new, fresh, happy thing that made their lips tremble? Did it imply some security—perhaps in the past—that had strengthened them for this new trial flight?

Strange, infinitely strange word! Every spring it had taken on a new meaning for them. It had traveled with them from street to street, from hope to hope, from hunger to hunger. It should have been worn out, used up, weighted down with disappointment. And yet this was not so; it was still intact and full of promise.

Marvelous word! A word that had no exact definition, and yet contained boundless hidden riches. A word that belonged above all to Rose-Anna.

Flushed and happy, the children's bright little faces were lifted to hers, their feelings so deeply stirred that at times they all fell silent together.

But after she had set them all a-dreaming, how well Rose-Anna knew how to arm them against illusions!

"Let's not count on finding a millionaire's apartment," she said. "There will be plenty of corners to scrub. You remember how dirty it was here when we arrived. We can't expect the new place to be all cleaned up." And returning to tangibles again, she gave sharp orders: "Has anyone thought of the broom? It's very important. We'll want to have it handy when we reach the new house. With water and a broom, you can always get the dirtiest place shipshape. I always say, give me a broom, first thing."

Ordinarily she was not very talkative with the youngest children. Communication between her and the little ones was generally limited to amicable scolding, her love being understood. But tonight she reproached herself for the departure of Florentine, and strove to redeem herself by bringing the little ones closer to her.

She was speaking volubly now, addressing them as equals, not placing herself at their level but raising them to hers. They were deeply impressed by this. Their mother had never spoken to them before in such a loving, serious tone. At one moment she looked them straight in the eye to speak of some important matter, at the next she would say something in passing, mention some trifle, or sigh in a way that emphasized her reliance on them. It was as if she guessed, with that sure, profound intuition of life she had, that the time had come to draw them to her to look for new horizons, to work for new purposes. It was as if, on the threshold of this new adventure, she must assess their combined strength, rally their spirits, and make sure that each child assumed his share of the common burden.

"We have our troubles, to be sure," she said. "It's not pleasant to move like this in the middle of the night. And yet I don't know. Look at other people. We're no worse off than others. Right now, in the countries at war, there are people much more unfortunate than we are. Over there the poor people must be having a hard time."

Then she held her tongue, wondering whether she should speak to Azarius about Florentine tonight or wait until the next morning. And suddenly it came to her that she had done well not to breathe a word about it, and that the incident—now so much like a dream—ought to remain a secret for ever.

Several packing boxes were filled. They all joined forces to pack up another, kneeling in a circle in the middle of the kitchen floor. And Rose-Anna felt a wild desire to stretch her arms out and gather them all together in one reassuring embrace.

"At any rate the new place can't be worse than this," she said. "We were all on top of one another here. At least there will be more room there. Your father spoke of five rooms. You might have a room to yourself, Yvonne. You mustn't build any castles in Spain, naturally, until we see the house, but I have a feeling we'll be more comfortable. From what your father says, there's a porch; we can have a few pots of flowers. The yard will be a help; we might plant some vegetables if it's large enough. Then as I said before, if it's dirty that's nothing; I can always clean it."

All this time the children's busy little hands were emptying closets and stripping walls. The atmosphere of home was disintegrating, until the last remaining links were the old clock on the shelf, trimmed with crêpe paper, and a few caps hanging on the door. The atmosphere of home was dead, but there was no regret in their faces. It was as if it were already being rebuilt in their shining eyes, and how much better!

Their happiest moments had always been those just before moving to a new house, but this they did not remember. There were ever so many ugly, portentous things that clung to them like leprosy, but happily they had lost even the memory of them.

The kitchen was piled high with utensils and packing boxes, all tied up, when Azarius returned. They knew all the tricks of moving quickly. Experience had given them extraordinary ingenuity in devising ways of saving space, and the speed almost of gypsies who can break camp within an hour.

With tacit understanding, they all set to work to load the truck. Philippe and his father carried the heavier articles between them. Rose-Anna gathered up the more fragile objects herself and put them in the back of the truck under the tarpaulin, making careful note of where she placed them. The children ran after her, one carrying the precious kitchen clock, another with a battered doll she had just located under a heap of soiled linen. Albert, a provident and sensible child, brought up the rear, tripping over himself with a great armful of wood piled up to his chin.

What a sorry look all the bizarre equipment of a home takes on when bit by bit it is exposed to view, torn from its normal setting!

Around the lighted doorway a group of children and idlers was beginning to gather.

"What do you think of that! The Lacasses are moving! They seem to be in a hurry!"

Rose-Anna heard these remarks, and blessed the darkness that cloaked their departure. The night was more charitable to their shabby furnishings.

Too often they had moved in the pitiless glare of the sun. Too often their faded mattresses and rusted bedsprings, their dilapidated chairs, scratched tables, and discolored mirrors—the visible signs of their poverty—had joined the parade in the full light of day, a part of the motley caravan that filled the streets on May first, rags flying in the wind, grease spots exhibited for all to see.

At last the things they needed most in the new house were loaded on the truck according to a traditional arrangement: a large basket of provisions, of which Rose-Anna took charge personally, the nightclothes in an old valise, the table, chairs, and even the kitchen stove in their usual places. Rose-Anna had said firmly: "You must take the stove down right away, Azarius. I don't care how late it is. Tonight or tomorrow morning we might require hot water for something or other."

After the kitchen was cleared, it seemed quite large and strangely quiet as Rose-Anna ventured into it to take one last look around. She thought she had come back to be sure she had forgotten nothing, for she could not otherwise explain the feeling that drew her once more to the bare room.

To be frank, she felt no wrench in leaving. They had been much too cramped here, packed so tight that they constantly irritated each other. Living in such close quarters made them hate their home. They had suffered a great deal here. And yet how many memories rose up out of the dusty corners! Memories both glad and sad, all mingled together. Here Eugène had slept for the last time before he enlisted, under the roof that would never shelter them all again. Who knew whether they would ever sleep again in the same house, all of them? Here little Daniel had played his grave, innocent little games before his illness. Here, one cold gray October morning, she had discovered that she was going to have another baby, when she was over forty, and for the twelfth time. Here Florentine just a little while ago had turned a look of entreaty on her.

Florentine, her first baby! Rose-Anna's heart went out to the girl, full of doubt, anger, and disappointed love. But there was no sense in grieving. Florentine would come back. She would explain everything. And perhaps there was nothing to explain. Rose-Anna seized on that hope. Florentine, who had been a pious and gentle child, like Yvonne, was incapable of doing evil. Rose-Anna took herself to task. And thinking that her daughter might return that very night, she tore off a leaf from the calendar, picked up a pencil, and wrote a few lines in a cramped hand. "We have moved," she wrote, "You can sleep in Philippe's room tonight. Tomorrow at lunch time I will send Yvonne or Lucille to the store to show you the way home." She hesitated a few seconds, then signed herself: "Your mother."

With a lighter heart, she went to get her hat and coat from behind the door. Then very quietly she slipped through the dining-room door to the buffet, and without turning on the light, gathered up a few religious objects from which she could never bear to be separated even for a day.

The new tenant stirred in the darkness. Rose-Anna bade her goodnight with feeling.

"There will be no one here but my daughter, who may come in later tonight," she said. "The rest of us are leaving now. You can make yourself at home."

At this moment Azarius came in. He went through to Philippe's room and picked up the sleeping Gisèle in his arms, lifting her gently and wrapping her in a woolen blanket. And side by side they left the house.

Only once did Rose-Anna turn around to look at the gray walls that rose silent and void of light under the starry sky.

When Azarius took the wheel, she relieved him of the sleeping baby. The motor roared in her ears and reverberated through her weary brain. She peered through the glass behind her to make sure that all the other children were in the truck. They were standing up or had perched themselves on top of piles of furniture, the figures plainly visible in the light of the street lamp. She was aware that everything she had been able to save from disaster was around her, and furthermore, that a large part of her wealth was still intact. From the depths of her subconscious a feeling of repentance came to the surface: she had doubted divine godness; for some time she had refused to hope; that was wrong, very wrong. But slight as it was, this repentant mood had already drawn her closer to Him who had been the source of her courage. She put her hand on her husband's arm and murmured:

"Let's go!"

Azarius started off with a jerk, scarcely seeing the street before him. Though blind as a rule to his family's misery, and loath to accept his responsibilities, he was nevertheless touched to the quick by this flight in the dark. Grief of a kind he had rarely felt was clutching him by the throat.

He put the truck in high, the tires screaming at the first sharp turn.

Much later in the night, when the children lay asleep on mattresses placed around her on the floor, Rose-Anna raised herself cautiously on one elbow and peered into the shadows. She was listening to the silence, trying to fathom the mystery of this strange house where they had found shelter.

A new house always fanned her hopes. It cowed her too, inspiring the same vague terror she felt at making a new acquaintance.

A strange house in her eyes always held some secret associated with the lives of other people. And for some time they would have a sense of never being alone, of eyes spying on them, of phantoms in every room.

Rose-Anna leaned on her elbow and wondered: Is this a house where people have been happy? She had a notion that certain houses predispose people to be happy while others are fated to shelter the unfortunate.

As yet she had not really seen it. Having forgotten to bring electric light bulbs, they had installed themselves as best they could by striking innumerable matches.

She had not seen the house, but she had taken her bearings by her sense of smell, of touch, and especially of hearing. A little after midnight she had felt it quake violently at the approach of a train. Then she had understood, and with the moral courage that sustained her, she had resigned herself to it at the same time. There must be some disadvantage. There was always some disadvantage. Sometimes the house was dark; sometimes there was a factory close by; at other times the house was much too small for them; in this case it was the proximity of the railroad.

The house had revealed its painful secret in its muffled thunder, in the frantic rattle of its loose windowpanes, in all its panic-stricken framework.

No wonder the rent is low, thought Rose-Anna. So near the tracks, it's scarcely habitable. I'll never get used to the noise. And yet she refused to admit defeat. Not yet. She never gave up so quickly. There must be some advantages with the disadvantages, she was thinking. I'll see it better in the morning. I mustn't be in such a hurry to look on the dark side.

Azarius stirred beside her. She leaned over and put her hand gently on his arm to see if he were asleep. He trembled.

"Can't you sleep?" she asked sadly.

"No."

A long silence. Then she spoke again:

"Can't you stop fretting?"

He mumbled vaguely and buried his face in the pillow.

Nowadays he could measure the extent of his failure at every moment of the day or night. Even the hapless plight of his family, which he had refused to see for years, was beginning to be familiar to him, but it had become familiar in the manner of an old fellow-traveler who had one day fallen behind him on the road. It had grown as familiar as something that had happened long ago. Rose-Anna . . . she had once been young, then she had grown weary, and now worn out. And in the end she lay beside him on a wretched pallet. There had been low moans in the night from the sleeping forms around him. . .

He tossed again on the mattress. And the sudden jerk made Rose-Anna conscious of him again.

"Don't wrack your brains too much," she said. "It does no good. You'll only tire yourself for nothing."

And sitting up, she began to talk to him as if he were one of the children, unable to fall asleep.

"We're still together, Azarius. We still have our health and our strength. Nothing much worse can happen to us. Believe me, we'll pull through if we're willing to work hard. It doesn't help to wrack your brains!"

She stopped abruptly. For some time her baby had been stirring. It was kicking now as if in protest against her weariness.

She tried to find a more comfortable position, and feeling drowsy in spite of herself, she enjoined him heavily.

"Sleep, my poor man. Try to sleep. Sleep will give you a fresh outlook. Sometimes sleep is what we need most, you know."

A little later, at dawn, when he had at last dropped off, she roused herself bravely and explored the house, going from room to room in bare feet. Then she dressed and put on her shoes.

And by six o'clock in the morning, as the first ray of sunlight filtered through the grimy windowpanes, she had already been at work a long time, scrubbing the floor, with a bucket of dirty water beside her, and her hair plastered to her forehead.

CHAPTER XXV

EMMANUEL LEFT the train at the Saint-Henri station toward nine o'clock one Saturday evening. The night was fresh and soft, with distant stars shining through the lacy clouds.

It was a warm languorous evening, punctuated with the incessant cry of the siren, and bathed in the fumes that rose from the biscuit factories. But in the background of this cloying smell, a bouquet of spices was borne on the south wind from the lower regions along the canal and reached the slight elevation near the station in pungent gusts.

There are rarely two such evenings a year in Saint-Henri, and none like it in those parts of the city unvisited by these spicy aromas, these whiffs of illusion. An evening composed of prosaic and exotic elements so thoroughly mingled that one cannot tell where reality begins and where the mirage. And yet an evening the like of which Emmanuel seemed to remember all through his childhood. One of those evenings when all the working people,

spinners, rollers, puddlers, with one accord desert their ⌐
and set out in search of adventure on Notre-Dame Street. H
had often wandered about on nights like these, seeking he k⌐
not what rapture in harmony with the magic of the sky overhea⌐

He walked to the end of the platform. And from there in the midst of familiar scenes and smells, he surveyed the quarter. His village in the great city! For no part of Montreal had kept its limits so sharply defined, had preserved its village life, its particular, narrow character as much as Saint-Henri.

Children were playing hopscotch all around the station, and their shouts could be heard through the whistle of the locomotive as the train gathered speed and ran along between the yards, the starved trees, the clotheslines heavy with washing, past those dismal interiors of which train travelers always catch a glimpse as they pass through a city. From where he stood, Emmanuel could see the parish steeples above the clouds of smoke. The quarter was continuing its ordinary life, a life constantly interrupted by arrivals and departures, but always indifferent to any arrivals or departures. On Notre-Dame Street, the owner of the fruit-stand was putting away her vegetables for the night. Her busy figure kept moving back and forth in front of the windows. The chips vendor drove up in his cart, pulled by a jaded horse with a long, sad neck. In front of the Two Records, passersby slowed up to listen to the radio barking into the street. Next door the bookseller was selling greeting cards. Housewives were hurrying by with huge packages in their arms. And in his box high over the roof tops, the railroad signalman leaned out of his sooty window now and then, as though he were watching a colony of ants beneath him. All the windows of the houses were open, and domestic noises, the clatter of dishes, the sound of voices, floated through the air as if men and women no longer dwelt behind walls but shared their lives and secrets with the whole world.

It was a quarter of contrasts, like no other, thought Emmanuel. Here the eye fell on a thick cluster of roofs under a rain of soot; there a tree grew out of the cement sidewalk like a miracle. Farther off a fountain rippled in a sleepy square. On one side it was pretentious and middleclass, with its three-storey buildings and spiral staircases, but over there a small house in the native style gallantly clung to its rustic airs and graces, with a barrel hoop over the gate in the guise of a trellis.

Over yonder freighters, tankers, tugboats, flatboats, and Great Lakes barges went sailing by, carrying wares from the four corners of the earth: huge Norwegian pines, Ceylon tea, the spices of India and nuts from Brazil. But on Convent Street, when the church bells rang for vespers and the nuns passed two by two be-

hind a grille, Saint-Henri might have been any small provincial
town.

During the day it knew a life of relentless toil. In the evening it
had its village life, when folks gathered on their doorsteps or
brought their chairs out to the sidewalk and exchanged gossip
from door to door.

Saint-Henri: an antheap with the soul of a village!

Emmanuel, matured by a few months' travel, was returning
home clear-eyed and observant. He saw Saint-Henri as he had
never seen it before, yet despite its infinite variety, it had no
secrets for him. In a way he was more deeply attached to it than
ever, the way a man loves his birthplace on returning from adventure in foreign lands, delighted to find everything as before, and
people greeting him on every hand.

With a lighthearted gesture he flung his duffle bag over his
shoulder and set off on his way.

"A beautiful evening," he repeated to himself as he walked
along, grateful for the fine weather and his own happy mood.

Then he stopped in perplexity, feeling the impossibility of sus-
taining such a mood. Pasted on all the shopwindows, and at every
street corner, news bulletins carried Gamelin's last pathetic order
of the day to the French troops:

DEFEND YOUR POSITIONS TO THE DEATH!

Emmanuel was shocked by the incongruity of his earlier reflections. A scene of blood and suffering came to his mind, replacing
the one before him. He seemed unable to draw air into his lungs.
And at last an indefinable malaise that hung over the quarter took
on visible form before his eyes. He noticed how careworn the
workmen looked as they strode by with their lunch boxes under
their arms and their caps pulled down as if saddened by a catas-
trophe beyond their ken, even though they themselves went un-
scathed for the moment. And in the same breath, Emmanuel noted
how few young men were abroad in the main thoroughfare, and
of these how many, like him, were in uniform.

He went on his way with overcast brow. Then he found himself in front of the five-and-ten-cent-store, and the thought of
Florentine came to him. Stopping at the door a moment, he
glanced toward the restaurant, but the crowd around the counter
was so thick he could not see the girl. He was tempted to go in and
speak to her. But in that crush, he thought, what chance would I
have to say a word? Then he played with the idea of waiting for
her outside, since it was almost closing time. But it occurred to
him that he was covered with the dust of traveling, and that he
would be more presentable after shaving and washing up. His

cheeks turned scarlet as he went on his way again, whistling the popular air "Ama Pola" that was being blasted forth from all the juke boxes along the street. His whistling was deliberate rather than carefree, more like whistling in the dark.

Ten minutes later he was kissing his mother and his sister Marie, and pulling photographs of his regiment out of his bag, which lay open in the middle of the parlor. Then, while his family exchanged the snapshots and puzzled their brains to find him in the group, he went up to his own room. It gave on the square, and the trees outside his window were alive with birds. The fountain purled its fluent song. Emmanuel put his head out of the window and basked in the warm air, enjoying a feeling of peace that washed away all memory of the army, all threat of danger. After filling his lungs with the scent of lilacs, he turned about and began to wash up. As he was shaving, he looked about his room with approval, and tried to define the satisfaction he felt in being there. Formerly he had found it tedious to stay at home; he used to execrate the dull life of a civilian and resent even his mother's solicitude. Now his room seemed very pleasant, as a young man's room should be. His neckties hung neatly from a bar, bright-colored neckties his sister had given him. A few months ago he had considered them outlandish, but tonight he was sorry he could not wear either the blue one with the white polka dots or the one with red and black stripes. He ran his hand over the pipes in a rack on the chest of drawers, smiling as he remembered that he used to smoke a pipe—when he was very, very young, about eighteen. . . . So many incidents, so many memories came rushing back to his mind at the mere touch of a pipe, at the musty odor of old tobacco in an ashtray, at the sight of a little snapshot stuck in the frame of the mirror . . . He almost laughed at the picture of himself there in the country, looking so wistful and wretched! What a sullen, boring youth he must have been! He returned to the window, still whistling "Ama Pola," which he could not drive out of his head, and then wheeled around suddenly to study his face in the wardrobe mirror. Florentine! Would she love him? Would she discover something agreeable in the face he was examining so fearfully? Would she see that he was very sincere, very much in love, and above all very unhappy without her?

He scanned his features as if they belonged to a stranger. The mouth was delicate and serious; a certain timidity gave his face a look of more youthfulness than he would have wished. But in the gray-blue eyes there were shades of thoughtfulness, courage, melancholy. A man's face is so ineffectual, he was thinking, to express what's in his heart . . . so inadequate . . . especially when it persists in remaining boyish like mine! A lock of ash-blond hair fell over his forehead; he tossed it back and tried various ways of parting his hair to make him appear older.

Then he went once more to the window and leaned out. Florentine! He was torn between the desire to run to her and the pleasure of daydreaming about her here with his head thrust out into the soft night air. When had he begun to love her? Was it the first time he had seen her at the restaurant? Or was it when he had danced with her till he lost his breath? Or was it in camp, when she had appeared to him in clouds of cigarette smoke at the canteen? Little by little she had become a familiar apparition, bringing repose when he stretched his weary body out on his narrow cot and lay there for hours with his eyes closed. Oh, Florentine! Had he been deluded, all those nights in camp, when he had imagined himself dancing with her, talking with her, exploring the city with her, eating with her, laughing with her? Was she the girl he had dreamed about, was she the strange figure that had relieved his hours of boredom, or was she quite different, and must she learn to love him? The Florentine of his dreams loved him, she was like him, sometimes wildly gay, sometimes sad for no perceptible reason; she followed all the twists and turns of his thought. But what of the real Florentine?

Downstairs, in the parlor, Marie Létourneau was laughing softly. Emmanuel began to listen for his sister's fresh, delicious laughter. She almost never laughed. For his homecoming she had assumed another character, trying to hold him by pretending to be gay. Little sister Marie! he thought warmly. And yet he realized that although he had just returned home and loved his mother and sister dearly, he was already burning to be gone. It was as if he had only one night in which to be happy, although he had enough emotion to draw on for a whole lifetime.

Finishing his toilet, he ran down the steps two by two. With a quick, embarrassed "Goodnight" to his family, he shot out of the door as if he were escaping from prison. It was a pleasant jail, not too Spartan, and his chains were those of love, but sometimes it got on his nerves. Disburdened of his bag, disburdened of the time that had passed and that was drawing him closer to Florentine, he marched down the street on the double-quick. For a moment the thought crossed his mind that his mother might learn the object of his haste, and he felt very uncomfortable. Then realizing that she was bound to find out some day or other, he promised himself to speak to her about it at the first opportunity, but at heart he was amused by the idea of surrounding his love with some mystery, at least for a time.

He stepped out with long, graceful strides. Military training had improved his carriage. His head was held more erect, although it still tended to droop slightly toward his right shoulder as soon as he escaped from the strict army discipline.

By the time he reached Beaudoin Street, his eyes were glowing with anticipation. He decided that he had done well, after all, not to stop at the store. For his first visit, the one that would mark the beginning of their new relationship, it seemed better to present himself at Florentine's house in the role of a serious suitor. And he smiled at the implication of the words "serious suitor," which up to now had terrified him.

He recognized the house immediately, although he had only been there once before, in the morning—how well he remembered?—when he had brought Florentine home after mass. He recognized it, but now he realized that it had seen better days, and his heart ached with the injustice of it. How could she live in such a hovel when she herself was so fastidious, so trim!

Not finding the bell, he grew impatient and knocked at the door; then he ran his hand over his chin and tugged at the collar of his tunic. His forehead broke out into sweat. He wiped it off and screwed his mouth up in a smile as though deriding his own nervousness.

At last a strange woman, her face drawn with care, came to the door.

No, the Lacasses didn't live there any more. They had moved. She didn't know where. Her husband might know. She would ask him.

After a moment that seemed interminable she returned with an address scribbled on a scrap of brown paper. Emmanuel seized it and went off stammering his thanks. He had some trouble finding the new house, and was obliged to ask directions of several passersby. It was at the end of a blind alley opening out of Convent Street. No sidewalk led up to it. It was pinned right up against the railroad tracks, a few hundred feet from the station.

Emmanuel was moved to think that earlier in the evening, when he had ventured out to the end of the station platform, he had been quite near Florentine's house without being aware of it.

He did not know whether he ought to try the front entrance. In order to reach it he was forced to skirt the tracks, and the door was so thick with soot that it looked as if it hadn't been opened for months. Deciding to chance it, Emmanuel rapped his knuckles against the door jamb. In a matter of seconds Rose-Anna came running to answer his knock.

She recognized him instantly, although she had not seen him since the days when she had worked for the Létourneaus. Her face lit up with pleasure.

"Ah, you must be Monsieur Emmanuel!" she said.

She was clad in a loose housedress, and seemed to be in the midst of cleaning, for her face was streaked with dust.

Pressing him to come in and sit down, she led the way into the only room that had some semblance of order, and where the portraits of her parents and the scared images re-established the atmosphere of countless other lodgings.

He was not adroit enough to refuse this mark of esteem, but sat there on tenterhooks, waiting for her to reassure him. At last she broached the subject, for he was too embarrassed to give the reason for his call, hoping that Rose-Anna would guess it herself.

"You came to see Florentine?" she asked, meeting his glance.

The young man nodded and smiled.

"She hasn't come home yet," she said, and looked away.

They were both silent. Poor Rose-Anna was trying to find some way of explaining Florentine's strange behavior recently without hurting the young man, especially without shocking him. But how could she tell him that Florentine only returned home to eat and sleep, and that at such times she locked herself in terrifying silence? How could she tell him that Florentine was no longer the gay carefree girl he had once met? And yet she read such frankness, such strength of character in Emmanuel's glance that she was on the point of confessing many things she would never dream of admitting to Azarius. Besides, perhaps Emmanuel might revive Florentine's lost gaiety and vivacity. For all she knew, Forentine might be breaking her heart over Emmanuel. The girl had not tried to clear herself since her flight. Returning the next day, she had never breathed a word about her escapade, except for dropping a hint to the effect that she had been too worn-out to know what she was doing.

Rose-Anna looked up with a gleam of hope.

"Have you tried the store?" she asked. "Maybe she's working late tonight. It's Saturday . . ."

He smiled lamely, knowing quite well that the girl could hardly be working at this hour. Rose-Anna went on :

"Sometimes she spends the night with her girl-friend, Marguerite L'Estienne. She might have gone there tonight. Sometimes they go to the movies together, or go for a walk if the weather is good."

She stopped in confusion. Emmanuel must find it very strange that she should not know exactly where her daughter was. Then, perhaps to change the subject, or simply to thank him for his visit, and show her high regard for the Létourneau family, she thought of inquiring about each member. She queried him with some reserve, feeling that she could not presume on their acquaintance, even though the young man's visit put the relations between the two families on another plane.

"How is your sister Marie? Is your mother well?" she asked. "Tell them I've not forgotten them."

"They haven't forgotten you either," replied Emmanuel quickly, hardly aware of what he was saying, for of all Rose-Anna had said, only one thing stood out in his mind: Florentine must be with her girl-friend, Marguerite.

He stood up, trying not to seem in too great a hurry, but showing his impatience so clearly that Rose-Anna could not miss the point and try to keep him. She accompanied him to the door and awkwardly repeated her kind wishes for the health of his parents. Then she stood for a moment in the open door, as one does in the country, watching him go, and calling to him:

"Come again, now that you know the way. You might be luckier next time."

And at this she recalled her farewells to Azarius long ago, when she would stand in the door as now, shouting to him through the wind that leveled the grass in front of the house: "Now that you know the way, come again. . ." The memory was so bitter-sweet that she rushed blindly back into the house, overcome by some inexplicable sorrow, by a poignant renewal of youthful feeling.

Emmanuel, however, was almost out of sight already, his thick-soled shoes digging into the gravel. At the intersection of Convent Street and the railroad he halted to plan his next step. The best thing to do was to set off in pursuit of Florentine at Marguerite's house. He started out in the direction of St. Zoé Alley, for he remembered a Marguerite L'Estienne who lived there and he was fairly certain that it was she who was Florentine's friend. His pace was still brisk, but a feeling of anguish began to weigh on his heart. He was not, however, altogether discouraged. All he foresaw was that he might spend all of this beautiful evening without Florentine, without Florentine walking beside him as she ought to be. But it was enough to make the night seem overcast and disagreeable. He had so little time. A two-weeks' furlough slips by so quickly. Every moment must count double. This was what he told himself, for he dared not admit that the girl might have forgotten him completely, although that was what he feared most, and what made him hurry to find her without heeding the proprieties or the ridicule to which he might be exposed.

Marguerite was not at home. Her aunt had no idea where she had gone.

Beneath his hope, Emmanuel had dreaded this moment all evening long, knowing that when it came, cold sense would get the better of him, and that he would find himself confronting a host of doubts. Could Florentine really care about him after so brief a friendship? Had she not made other friends during his absence? Had she not come to his party out of curiosity or the desire to be amused? And had she not danced with him as she might have danced with any other man who made a good partner?

He began to wander along Notre-Dame Street, his mind now closed to thoughts unfavorable to his suit, now open to doubt from every quarter, like a cleared field to the wind. But he abandoned no hope without returning to it immediately, even more desperately. Every once in a while he felt certain of seeing Florentine again this very night. At such times he would observe carefully all the girls who went by, beginning with purely feminine groups, and ending up with eyes only for girls who were accompanied by young men. Sifting over what Rose-Anna had told him, he thought he could discern a slight reticence, indicating that Florentine might have gone out with a boy-friend. This reminded him of Jean Lévesque, and he frowned. Jean and Florentine! How could they be friends when they spent all their time gibing at each other? That had been known to happen, of course. Some people were always at swords' points, always wounding each other, and yet were helpless to overcome a mutual physical attraction. . . . But as he thought it over, a friendship between Florentine, who was proud, and Jean, who was biting and sarcastic, seemed altogether impossible. Besides, Jean had written him a note to say that he was leaving Saint-Henri for good to take a position at Saint-Paul l'Ermite. A postscript in English had added: "Out for the big things."

Emmanuel reached the top of the hill. His walk had made him thirsty. He hurried toward the Two Records.

CHAPTER XXVI

SEVERAL MEN were standing motionless in the middle of the restaurant; others were leaning against the counter, their teeth clamped over their pipes; all were listening to the war news. At that period the broadcasting stations often interrupted their regular programs for late news bulletins. Some light music had just stopped, the announcer's voice broke in with a few facts, and then the music came on again. The men relaxed and several began to speak at once.

One voice rose distinctly above the others, like a moan:

"Poor France!"

Emmanuel, sucked into the current of ideas he had hoped to

banish from his mind at least during his furlough, lit a cigarette with trembling fingers.

The man who had just spoken stood near him, his elbows on the counter and his face in his clenched fists. He pulled himself erect slowly, with an effort, as if he were lifting a terrific weight of care on his shoulders, and Emmanuel, seeing his face, recognized Azarius Lacasse, who had formerly done odd jobs of carpentry for his parents. He immediately held out his hand with the warmth and simplicity that always made people trust him.

"Monsieur Lacasse, I'm Emmanuel Létourneau," he said. "I know your daughter Florentine."

Azarius looked up, startled to hear his daughter's name.

"Things are going badly," was all he could answer. "Poor France, poor France!"

He seemed deeply moved. This queer man, who had witnessed the disasters of his family without admitting failure, this loafer, as he was called in the neighbourhood, this dreamer seemed on the brink of despair because in a far-off country that he knew only by hearsay, the fate of armies was being decided in bloody battle.

"France!" he murmured again.

And the word on his lips had both a familiar and a magical sound, evocative of certainty in common things and wonder at something rare and strange.

"Such a beautiful country."

"How do you know it's so beautiful?" interposed the usher from the Cartier Theater. "Were you ever there?"

This young man never passed up a chance to quarrel with Azarius, who had once reproached him for not being in the army.

"How do I know France is beautiful?" answered Azarius, in a rich low voice, not at all angry. "How do you know that the sun does you good? Because from 'way far away, from millions of miles away, by what the astrologers tell us, you can feel its warmth and see its light, isn't that so?

"How do you know anything about the stars? Those tiny holes in the sky? Because you see them shine at night across miles and miles and miles of space, when it's dark."

As he warmed up gradually, a note of lyricism, natural, unpolished, crept into his voice.

"France," he said, "is like the sun or the stars. We may be far away, we may never have seen it, we Frenchmen, Frenchmen of France but gone from France, we don't know just what France means, we Canadians. No more than we know what the sun is or the stars, except that they give us light by night and day. Night and day," he repeated.

He looked at his idle hands, turning them over and over, as if he would always be surprised to find them so white and useless, and then raised them suddenly in a dramatic gesture.

"If France should perish," he declared, "it would be just as bad for the world as if the sun dropped out of the sky."

No one answered. All these men, even the toughest and the most uncommunicative among them, loved France. Across the centuries they had retained a singular attachment for the country of their origin, a glow in their hearts, a vague nostalgia, rarely expressed, but which clung to them along with their stubborn faith and their beautiful language. But to hear this simple truth stated by one of their number made them somewhat uncomfortable, as if they had suddenly bared their hearts to one another. Emmanuel, who had followed the speech of Azarius at first with surprise, then with leaping heart, now stood apart with a meditative air. Knowing that such flights of patriotism resolved none of his torments or his need for justice, he listened to Azarius's final words with some reserve. A few of the older men gathered around Azarius, and one of them clapped him on the shoulder, exclaiming:

"Well said, Lacasse!"

Behind the counter, Sam Latour was scratching his neck, more moved than he liked to admit, and quite unaware that he was swelling with the same inexpressible pride he felt once a year, when listening to the speeches on Saint-Jean-Baptiste Day.*

"Yes, but all that doesn't help much," he said, trying to bring the conversation down to a less exalted level. "You mustn't forget that instead of preparing for war in France they acted like that bird—what do you call him, the ostrich?—that buries his head in the sand when he sees danger coming. I told you, Lacasse, that their Imaginot Line wasn't worth much. Imaginot! Imaginot! It's like imagination. They imagined things, that's what they did."

"First of all, it's not Imaginot, but Maginot, that's all," retorted Azarius. "Named after the engineer who made the plans, a man named Maginot."

"It's their imagination all the same."

"May be. But that's neither here nor there," snapped Azarius. "A fortress is only a fortress. It's not a country. A country is something else. A country isn't necessarily beaten when a fortress is captured."

The oratorical urge was upon him again, roused by the pleasant

* Saint-Jean-Baptiste is the patron saint of French Canada. His feast day, on the twenty-fourth of June, is a provincial holiday in Quebec, celebrated with a historical pageant, parades, singing, and a great many patriotic speeches.

sensation of having a receptive audience. He turned around as if to address not these few impressionable onlookers, but a great crowd whose applause thundered in his ears.

"France is not beaten," he said.

"I told you their Imaginot Line wasn't worth a damn," Latour began again. "I told you so. Look here, it was like me behind my counter. All you had to do was to come up on my flank . . ."

And delighted with his own facetiousness, he invited the spectators to witness his demonstration. But Azarius interrupted him almost rudely :

"France is not yet done for. Every time France has come to grief, she has risen more radiant than before. We have seen France more than once in the hour of danger. We have seen that in history. But we have seen too, that in the hour of danger France has always had someone to lead her to victory. In the old days she had Joan of Arc. She had Napoleon Bonaparte. And in the last war, don't forget, she had Marshal Foch. Who will it be this time? No one knows yet, but she will find a savior. In the hour of peril, France has always found a liberator."

He stopped to moisten his lips, and looked about him for signs of approval. But reacting against the emotion that had stirred them before, the men seemed inclined to make fun of him now.

"By God, Lacasse," trumpeted Latour, "you have your history at your fingertips! Are you going to night school?"

The others laughed heartily at this quip, and some carried the joke even further. "He has plenty of time to study, all right!" cried one. "He certainly remembers his lessons," said another.

"I read, I try to find out about things," retorted Azarius.

His face had clouded over. Then he spied Emmanuel, whose bowed head seemed so young and thoughtful that he placed his hand on the soldier's arm with a fraternal gesture.

"You're a lucky fellow, soldier!" he said.

His eyes traveled around the room from one person to another with a look of disappointment, then returned to Emmanuel.

"You're young," he said, "you're in uniform and you have the arms to go and fight."

"By Jove, you talk as if you were as old as Adam," bellowed Latour. "You're not a damn bit older than me."

"I'm no longer in my first youth," returned Azarius.

And there was a sudden quaver in his voice.

He pulled himself together almost immediately, however; he stood up to Emmanuel as if to measure himself against the youth, his blue eyes flashing.

"I salute you!" he cried, and went out.

A few minutes later, Emmanuel also left the restaurant.

He had been deeply affected by Azarius's outburst, and especially intrigued by the complex personality of the man, who, according to rumor, had never succeeded in earning a decent living for his family, however noble the convictions he expressed in public. Emmanuel suspected that his own emotional reaction had been due in part to his interest in the man. And since thinking about Florentine's father was one way of drawing closer to her, he tried to clarify the impression that Azarius Lacasse had left on him. There was a certain nobility in the man's conception of France, but it had some dangerous implications that made him hesitate to accept it entirely. To be sure, he too loved France. Like all young French-Canadians who had been educated in the Traditionalist schools, he had formerly entertained many conservative ideas—such as racial survival, faithful observance of ancestral traditions, the cult of the national holiday—stuffy notions that had no power to nourish the imagination of the young, nor even to fire their courage, he thought. Thus his father, fervent nationalist though he was, had done everything to dissuade him from taking up arms and flying to the aid of France, which he claimed nevertheless to love so dearly. Emmanuel remembered that at one time he too had been a French-Canadian nationalist, subscribing to a cult that seemed living and youthful when he had made it his own. Like Azarius, he had perhaps accepted, without knowing it, more than this single loyalty to the past. Even in his extreme youth, perhaps he had perceived the glory and the beauty of living France. But he knew that that was not the only spring of his action. He loved France, he loved humanity, he felt compassion for the people of the conquered countries, but he knew that there had been plenty of suffering in the world before the war and that it could not be relieved by force of arms. And in spite of his great sensitivity, the idea of justice had a stronger hold on him than pity, and he wondered whether the slow martyrdom of China, for example, or the deep unrest in India did not revolt him as much as the invasion of France. And as he reviewed all these considerations, he asked himself what had driven him to volunteer. What was he fighting for? At length he wearied of this constant, irritating self-examination. The time would come, he knew, when he must go into these questions deeply in order to discover what incontrovertible truth they had for him, but he did not want it to be this evening. He wanted to allow himself a few days of complete relaxation first. And that brought to his mind the charming face of Florentine.

Several times, as he strolled about aimlessly, he found himself in Convent Street, a few steps from the Lacasse house, but he dared not go back there for fear of troubling Rose-Anna.

Toward eleven o'clock, he was struck by a new idea, and went over to the Cartier Theater. Posting himself at the exit, he scrutinized a score of people as they left the place. One girl, viewed from the back, seemed so like Florentine that he rushed over to her, his hands outstretched. The girl turned around and, at the sight of Emmanuel's discomfiture, burst out laughing.

Retiring in embarrassment, he berated himself for mistaking the girl for Florentine. On second thought she seemed very different, not at all pretty, and he wished he could confess his error to Florentine right away, so that they could laugh over it together. Then a disquieting thought came to him. How well did he know Florentine? What was she really like? Was she fundamentally sad or gay? Stormy or gentle? Probably a bit stormy, he decided, remembering the scene at the restaurant when she had been furious with him and Jean. But with all those rough men hanging around, what would you expect. Such a disagreeable job. It must be so tiring, he said to himself. He began to go over her features one by one, closing his eyes to refresh his memory, for he had kept her picture in his mind ever since that day at the store. Their later meeting had added nothing to his first view. He could see her straight little nose, her glowing eyes, the fine, almost transparent texture of her skin, and even the vein in her neck that throbbed at the least excitement. He remembered how slender her waist had seemed when he danced with her, and a remark of Jean's came back to him. "Too skinny," Jean had said. No, not skinny, thought Emmanuel, but delicate, very delicate. And he loved this word, which, for him, defined Florentine completely. He imagined that this would be the first word he would use, for example, to describe her to a friend. Delicate, quite delicate . . . he said to himself as he walked along. He felt a clutch at his heart as he recalled the wretched lodgings of the Lacasse family, and Rose-Anna sitting there, so resigned, so gentle. She too, he thought, must have been delicate and pretty once upon a time.

Returning to the thought of Florentine, he said aloud : "That's not where she belongs. . ." He was referring both to the cheap glitter and clatter of the emporium in Notre-Dame Street, and to the house buried in soot beside the railroad tracks. "That's not where she ought to be," he repeated stubbornly, as if by declaring himself opposed to Florentine's lot he could mitigate its wretchedness.

A loud, metallic voice blared out at him from the open doors of every shop. A sentence begun, was left hanging in the air until at the next shop the same voice began another unfinished sentence. A hundred radios, to the right, to the left, in front of him, behind him, poured out bits of news, doing their best to remind him of the world's agony. He would not listen to them, or if he happened to hear a phrase, he closed his mind to the onslaught of darkness and terror. The words that slipped through to his consciousness seemed void of sense. At moments he felt so far away from what the radios were trying to pound into his head that he seemed to have wandered into another era and another world. He recalled the impetuous move he had made toward the strange girl at the theater, and this gave him the measure of his passion, the only thing left to him that seemed normal and simple.

Gradually he was beginning to recover from his disappointment and look forward to the next day. I'll see her tomorrow, he said to himself. Tomorrow . . . And the word filled him with delightful confusion. He wished that the night were over already, reflecting that perhaps it was just as well not to have seen Florentine as soon as he arrived. In this way, all his joy was yet to come, his store of happiness was untouched.

Tomorrow . . . he said to himself, urging himself to be patient, like a walker determined to cover a great distance, who puts his destination further and further off. Tomorrow . . . the day after tomorrow . . . if necessary. But he knew very well that he could not bear the waiting without some human companionship. Returning home was out of the question, however. His mother would ask: "How did you spend the evening, Manuel?" and that would revive all his disappointment. If he were to confess that he had spent the whole time on a wild-goose chase she would scold him affectionately, saying (he was so very sure of what she would say!), "But Manuel, my dear, you could have your pick of the most refined girls in Saint-Henri!"

"Refined" was a word she often used, mused the young man. It made him smile. Refined! Was Florentine refined? No. She was more like a street urchin, with crude turns of speech and vulgar manners. She was better than refined, she was life itself, with her knowledge of poverty and her revolt against poverty, with her long flowing hair and her determined little nose, with her odd sayings, her sharp comments, and her truthfulness.

No, the more he thought about it, the less he was inclined to believe that his mother would approve his choice. This grieved him but did not weaken his resolution. And yet he felt unprepared to challenge his family's opposition. Tonight he was not in the mood for a tug of war.

What should he do then? Should he go in search of one of his old cronies? He could think of no one whose companionship at this time would offer him anything in the way of pleasure or profit. None of them seemed to be living on the same planet as he any more. Young men who went on existing during the war, aware of nothing but the controversies within their own small circle, annoyed him profoundly. It seemed to him that he would get more out of exchanging a few words with the first stranger he met in the street than out of a long discussion with the men he associated with ordinarily. He and the workingmen of the town, he felt, were wandering about tonight with the same doubts gnawing at them. He had left too many things unresolved in his own mind. Perhaps a chance meeting with someone of humble origin would bring him light. This desire to understand the soul of the great mass of men was long familiar to him, but he had never felt it so intensely as now. In projecting himself toward the common people he seemed to be continuing his search for Florentine, a search that would lead him to understand her far better and remove all the obstacles between them. Somewhere, somehow he must find a voice that spoke to him in Florentine's language, in the language of the people.

And then he bethought himself of his old comrades in St. Ambroise Street, the gang that used to meet at Ma Philibert's. Their disgruntled faces, already scarred by life, rose before his eyes. How could he have forgotten them so completely, his first friends, the little ragamuffins who had prevented him from growing spineless and self-satisfied? He was eager to learn what had become of them, but there was also a melancholy cast to his thoughts as he realized the diverse paths they had been following for some time, paths that had led them far apart. It's easy to forecast Jean's future, he reflected. If you're not troubled by too many scruples, you make your way in the world. But Alphonse, Pitou, Boisvert? What would become of them?

He turned sharply on his heel and walked toward St. Ambroise Street.

CHAPTER XXVII

THE DOOR of the restaurant stood wide open, exposing its smoke-blackened walls and pendant cobwebs to the street. The place seemed empty to Emmanuel, empty and sad. It was only after he entered that he saw Alphonse in his usual spot near the stove, even though the fire was out. The young man lay stretched out on two chairs, his head flung back, his hands clasped behind his neck. His eyes seemed to have been fixed for hours on the same inperceptible point above him. A shadow lay across his face.

"Hello there!" said Emmanuel, reaching over the back of the chair and tapping Alphonse's shoulder lightly.

He ran his eyes around the shop. Behind the curtain that screened off the back room, Ma Philibert could be heard dragging her slippers across the floor. Toward eleven o'clock she began preparing a meal for her husband, who came back from the factory at midnight. The restaurant was filled with the smell of boiling cabbage.

Emmanuel swung a chair around and straddled it in front of Alphonse. He was conscious of making a great effort to be gay.

"You're warming yourself at a dead fire!" he began jokingly.

Alphonse raised his heavy lids, then dropped them as if the light caused him unbearable pain.

"Dead or burning away, it's always company for a man!" he growled.

He held out his hand for a cigarette, waited with a look of patient suffering until Emmanuel passed his lighter, then shifted the weight of his body from one buttock to the other.

"Haven't you noticed that winter is over?" asked Emmanuel, laughing.

"You mean it?" said Alphonse.

And he shut up again like a clam.

"Where are the others?" inquired Emmanuel. "What's become of them?"

Alphonse yawned.

"Don't know."

Then he began to laugh maliciously.

"Haven't you seen Boisvert?" he asked.

"No, I just arrived tonight."

"You'd have seen something really funny . . ."

His falling inflection implied further revelations, and was meant to convey the impression that he would have much to tell if only he felt like it—a trick that almost always aroused the immediate attention of his listeners. But since Emmanuel did not press him to go on, he scowled and assumed an air of silent hostility. In the long run he broke down, however, and threw out another piece of bait.

"There's a guy who's made a good thing out of the war."

"Yes?" asked Emmanuel.

"Yes," said Alphonse. "He's got everything: a job, new shoes, a new hat, a watch guaranteed for six months, and Mlle Eveline into the bargain. Tomorrow or the day after, you'll hear the wedding bells ring. Monsieur Boisvert will walk down the aisle with the charming Miss Rochon of the five-and-ten tied to his neck for the rest of his life: a damn good guarantee against being drafted.

He's guaranteed from head to foot, that guy. He's even taken out accident insurance; in case he hurts his little tootsies crossing the street. A little wonder. He'll be the same all his life. At eighty he'll be just the way he was at seventeen. You remember him. A young squirt who bummed cigarettes from everybody, and then when he had some of his own he'd say : 'These belong to me. If you want cigarettes, buy some for yourself. Why don't you earn them like me?' A regular monopolist. 'What's yours is mine, and what's mine is mine.' You know a guy can go far with ideas like that."

"So he's working at last?" asked Emmanuel, amused.

"Yes, and you'd think he was the first guy to invent a job. It's my office here, my office there. My office, my pen, my business affairs! He's deep in figures from morning to night—a bookkeeper, you know. Then to rest from his work, he figures out to the cent what his marriage is going to cost him, in a nice little red note-book. He's buying his furniture on the instalment plan. Fifty cents a month for the frigidaire, fifty cents for the electric iron, fifty cents for the washline, fifty cents for the engagement ring. He even knows what it'll cost him to have his new pin-striped suit cleaned three years from now. If you want a course in three lessons on how to succeed in life and get married on eighteen bucks a week, go find Boisvert. He has it all written down in his little red note-book. He's a wonder, I tell you! A two-bit Rockefeller."

Emmanuel laughed heartily, suspecting that Alphonse had approached Boisvert for a loan and been brushed off.

"And the others? Pitou?"

"Don't know. That crowd's too fast for me, the lot of them."

"And you?"

"Me? You see me. The last of the unemployed. The last of my kind. A curiosity!"

And he repeated with clownish delight :

"The last of my kind."

"See here," said Emmanuel, "you're crazy. A fellow never had a better chance to find a job than nowadays."

"Listen to him talk!" grumbled Alphonse. "Another wise guy!" He drew his knees to his chin, and sat up with a grimace of pain, rubbing his haunches and wagging his head like an old man. A blast of the siren rocked the quiet shop. He rose to his feet.

"You might buy me a coke at least," he said tearfully.

Then he seemed to think better of it.

"No, let's beat it out of here. The old woman might bob up and chuck me out. She's insufferable now that her darling little Pitou doesn't come round to sing to her. Besides, she's got some curious notions. She wants to know when I mean to pay up. I ask you!

Come along now," he growled, as Emmanuel lifted the curtain and said a few words to Ma Philibert. "You want me to talk, eh?" he said, alone in the middle of the room. "All right, you'll hear me talk."

But once they were outside, he seemed to have forgotten that Emmanuel was there. His legs were still numb and stiff and his knees gave way under him as if he were drunk. As they neared St. Zoé Alley, he revived somewhat and exclaimed:

"Hey, don't let's go that way. I don't want to meet Guitte!"

"Guitte?"

"Yes, Guiguitte. Guiguitte L'Estienne. I get around to the five-and-ten myself once in a while. That's where I met Guitte. You must have noticed her when you hung around her girl-friend, the beautiful Florentine."

"Let Florentine alone," said Emmanuel sternly.

"All right, all right, I didn't say a word!" protested Alphonse. And he added, arrogantly: "I was supposed to treat Guitte to the movies tonight." He burst out laughing, and confessed: "I just didn't have the cash. She's waiting for me still."

"I've an idea she won't give you a second chance," said Emmanuel.

"But you know, it's a funny thing," Alphonse went on. "There are women who don't like to be so sure of their game. And she's a good wench, my Guitte. If she hadn't lent me so much money, I wouldn't be so embarrassed. Look here, she bought me this hat. And these shoes, too, if I remember rightly."

"Oh, drop it!" said Emmanuel.

They walked on for some time in silence. Alphonse pointed to a garret in St. Jacques Street where a light was shining.

"Well, well," he said, "my father's come to town."

"Your father? Oh, yes. He's all the family you have left. I don't think I know him."

"You missed something," sighed Alphonse. "My father is quite a character."

He asked for another cigarette.

"I'll return them all at the same time," he said, "with the money and the drinks I owe you for." As Emmanuel's lighter flared up, he stopped and stared at his shaking hands. "Have you ever been at the city dump?" he asked.

"At the dump?"

"Yes, the dump down at Saint-Charles Point?"

"No."

"You haven't, eh?"

He smiled in a strange way, and then poured out a morbid tale, so shocking that Emmanuel wondered at first if it weren't made of whole cloth.

"I once knew a fellow," began Alphonse, "who built up a nice little business at the dump. He collected all the tin pots and pans that were left there; he cleaned and straightened them, and then he sold them to an old junk man. It was a small business, you understand. There were weeks when the scrap didn't amount to much, but at other times, truckloads full of lard buckets were dumped by the river bank, and this guy hit the jackpot.

"He had a room in town. But there are thieves at the dump just as there are thieves everywhere. So he built himself a little country house at the dump to keep an eye on his affairs. At one time there was quite a village there, a group of shanties not much larger than dog kennels. You didn't have to ask permission to build, and you didn't have to go far for your lumber. Boy, the building material on that dump was a real windfall. There were bed posts, and pieces of sheet iron and big cardboard boxes you could use if you weren't particular. You took what you wanted, a section of stove pipe, four pieces of sheet iron for the roof, and you picked out your building lot right on the river, where the stink wasn't too bad. Some folks boast about laying out a thousand bucks for a week-end cottage near the river. The chaps at the dump had all that for nothing, except the weekends. And it was so peaceful there. You'd have to go far out in the country to find such a quiet place. The quiet of the grave, of something that's been dead a long time. At night the only sound you could hear was the rats in the garbage. The town was behind you, the town with its dole, the town with its bums on the bread line, and all its senseless noise! No more streetcars clanking in your ears, no limousines honking at you as if you had the pest, no trains roaring by, nothing. You were at home.

"But to come back to my foxy friend, I must say that he managed pretty well. He owed no one a cent, and he didn't cost the city a cent. And he brought up a little boy into the bargain. But one day the health officers came to visit the dump, because a poor devil had been found dead in his shack, half eaten by the rats. And do you know what they did, Létourneau, those fine gentlemen of the health department, when they came to the dump, holding their noses for dear life?"

Alphonse wiped the sweat from his forehead.

"They set fire to the whole damned village. They burnt it up, Manuel. Everything, the dog kennels, the old mattresses, the vermin and all." He was breathing rapidly, as if the tale had worn him out. "And the next day," he added, "my friend was back on relief."

After a long pause, he laughed and went on :

"But once you've had a taste of country air, you come back to it, you come back for more. The damned village rose up again. Not one shack less, not one shack more. Just as before. Just as many chimney pots on the roofs. Just as many pots cooking inside. And just as many starving cats, gangs of cats, coming from wherever there wasn't enough for them to eat! And you may not believe it, but flowers began to grow in front of the shacks in the sunshine; the seeds were blown there by the wind, I guess. And whatever you may think," he said defiantly, "in that country they have as good a life as other people. Because it is another country; it's not the same country as this at all. You go about your business quietly, without anybody bothering you, then, on Saturday night, if you happen to want to see someone in the city, you shave, you come to town, and you go the rounds. You pay a visit to those in the other country . . ."

Emmanuel held his tongue; he could no longer doubt the truth of the story. It made him sick at heart to penetrate so deeply into Alphonse's life without being able to help him in any way.

"Alphonse," he said at last, "why don't you enlist? A man forgets his little troubles when he's in the army."

"His little troubles!" gasped Alphonse.

They had reached the entrance to the tunnel on St. Jacques Street. Suddenly Alphonse threw away his cigarette. He stopped near a niche in the wall, where a green light burned behind a wire netting, casting a glaucous sheen over the dripping cement. The draft from the subway disheveled his black hair, and his face was scarred with black bands of shadow, as if he stood behind bars.

"Listen, Manuel Létourneau," he said. "I'll tell you another story. See what you can make of this one." He choked off a laugh, and then confessed : "One day, after I heard your fine speech at Ma Philibert's, I made up my mind to enlist. The very next day, I think it was. Anyway, there I was with a bunch of recruits marching through Saint-Henri, the drums rolling, the best-looking soldiers up front, and the down-and-outers in the back. You must have noticed that too, eh? They put the husky guys in the front rank; then the poor old wrecks at the end of the line don't attract too much attention. It's a good trick when you think of it!"

"But I didn't know. You never told me——" began Emmanuel.

Alphonse shrugged his shoulders. He continued :

'Anyway, I happened to be standing at the curb that day, like the class dunce, looking pretty spry, believe you me. I was shifting from one foot to the other, trying to thaw out somewhere, when what should I see but the whole gang coming down the street. The drums were beating, the big fellows up front were stepping out as if they were heading for a gold mine, the Klondike or something like that. 'Dammit!' I said to myself, 'dammit, Alphonse, it's been a long time since you've seen men so well dressed and so well fed. Fall in line,' I said to myself. 'Fall in line!' And that's how I found myself in the gang with the other bums.

"There was one little chap in my rank who gave me a wink. I winked back. I'm not inclined to be familiar with strangers, but in a case like this, when you start off on a walk that may take you to the end of the world, you might as well exchange a word or two with the fellows crawling along beside you, because it'd be a hell of a long walk if you had to do it all alone. That wink between us meant: 'If I fall, you pick me up, and if you fall, I'll pick you up.' A bargain of a sort. It always makes me laugh to think how fast bargains are struck between bums."

"Go on," said Emmanuel sharply.

"Okay, I'm coming to the best part of the story," chortled Alphonse. "I was no sooner all rigged out with a partner than someone ahead began bawling left, right, and we began to move—forward march, left, right, left, right. We did the best we could, imitating him—you catch on quick as the devil—left, right, and so it went until we reached the barracks, a fine bunch of fools! We collected more and more fellows as we went along. At the corner of Atwater Street alone we caught three or four more, I think. The funniest thing of all, you know, is that as soon as you're caught yourself, you're not satisfied until you catch some others. That day nothing would have suited me but a line stretching from here to the coast, enough to go around the town a hundred times! I turned around now and then, and saw that the gang was growing, but still it was not enough for me. It shocked me to see chaps standing on the sidewalk to watch us go by. 'Come along,' I wanted to say to them, 'we're in a damn lonely business unless everybody's in it with us!' But the little chap marching beside me, the one who winked and made the bargain, he was not the least bit lonely. He was a fine kid, too, hale and hearty, with curly hair and round cheeks. No down on his lip yet. He sang the whole way. 'Hey there, take it easy,' I said, 'you'll run out of songs before we find a place to sit down.' But if ever you saw a cocky little runt, it was that kid. We made a turn at a windy corner; the wind grabbed at us and tried to tear the rags from our backs. And then the little fellow yelled in my ear: 'There's a future in the army, eh, bud?'

"On the other side of me there was an old man marching along, bucking the wind like an old rag bag. An old man . . . well anyway, past forty, and pretty short of breath, you can take my word for it. But he too told me as we were pushing up a hill: 'There's a future in the army.' It was a joke to hear that old grandpa talking about the future. You hear the funniest things, you know, when you march along with a gang of men who're going to enlist. The future! I guess every one of them had the same idea. Well it got me too. There I was, marching along between the two of them, the kid of eighteen and the old man with the stooped back, and I too could see the future."

"What then?" asked Emmanuel.

"What's your hurry?" said Alphonse. "I'm telling you a story that people will listen to ten years from now, and in twenty years they'll understand it, maybe, and you say : 'What then?' Well, I'll tell you anyway. We reached the barracks, and there they began asking every one of us questions, like for first communion, only instead of first communion we were preparing for the last sacrament. But we were supposed to know quite a lot even for the last sacrament. I suppose you went through all that too. I don't know whether you had to deal with a blockhead like the officer who questioned me; probably not. There can't be many like him. He pulls out a fancy pen, settles back in his throne, blows his nose, scratches himself, stretches his legs, and then starts asking me questions in arithmetic. With a pencil and paper and no one around to interfere, I might have worked it out, but he shoots it straight at me. He gives me no time to think the business over, and the first thing I know, there he is hopping mad. 'Where have you been all your life to be such a dunce?' he says. 'Where have you been all *your* life?' I ask him. 'Did you grow up alongside the canal?' 'Good God, no,' he answers. 'So I see, no offense intended, I'm sure,' I snap back at him.

"After that, they made me strip and took me to the doctor. 'Open your mouth!' he said to me. 'By jingo, I never saw so many rotten teeth in all my life. I can tell you've never gone to see a dentist!' After that another one bawled me out because instead of buying eyeglasses when I was ten years old I bought myself an all-day sucker. The funniest guy of the lot was the one who gave me hell because I'd been brought up on canned beans instead of good pasteurized milk. But you know, I refused to give up. There's a future in the army, I told myself. As long as the kid and the old man and all the newspapers in town said so, it must be so. They'll give me a going-over, and I'll be all set for the future they're talking about."

There was a silence then, broken by the ringing of the railroad signal bell. A deep rumble filled the street. Under the heavy tread of the locomotive the earth shook.

"Didn't they accept you?" asked Emmanuel, unable to bear the suspense any longer.

Alphonse broke into a wild fit of laughter, shaking like a tree in a storm.

"You're always in such a hurry," he said. "You're always in a hurry to get back to the gang. You'll always be in a hurry. But wait a minute, because what I'm going to tell you now is the funniest of all. They patched up the old chap like new; they made another man of him, gave him glasses, pulled out his tonsils, vaccinated him from head to foot, stuffed him full of vitamins; they even straightened out his nose, which was a bit lopsided. He certainly will make a fine-looking corpse, with his false teeth and his straight nose. As for the kid, they did a quick job on him! He had all his teeth, all his hair, all his limbs, and all his gay spirits into the bargain . . ."

He took Emmanuel's arm, and pressed it roughly as for a final farewell.

"And all his gay spirits too," he repeated, "the kid who winked at me and made the bargain . . . All his gay spirits still!"

Then his face resumed its usual expression, gloomy, bored, indifferent.

"That's right, that's right, I must leave you here," he said. "You're in a hurry, I see. Well, goodbye, goodbye, Létourneau," he added. "I'll be seeing you at the next armistice day, Létourneau!"

And he took himself off immediately, his coat ballooning in the wind. His long thin figure was blotted out in the tunnel.

Emmanuel's eyes followed him until he was out of sight. Alphonse seemed more dead to him than all the future dead of the battlefields. And he went on his way, disconsolate, repeating to himself as in a dream a thought that had begun to be an obsession, a refrain he could not drive out of his mind: "The peace was as bad as the war. The peace killed as many men as the war. The peace is as bad . . . as bad . . ."

CHAPTER XXVIII

NOTWITHSTANDING the late hour, Emmanuel kept tramping the streets, wrestling with his problems. He could not shake off the thought of either Azarius Lacasse or Alphonse Poirier, two men whose utter loneliness had been revealed to him by chance this evening. Why should they trouble me so much? he wondered. They're strangers to me. I mean nothing to them; they mean nothing to me. Suddenly he understood that their failure shook the foundations of his own fine ardor, his own faith and will.

"You're a lucky fellow, soldier!" Azarius had said to him. And the other chap too, poor devil, had implied the same thing in his bitter way. Lucky! Must life be so dreadful to some men for him to be an object of envy, for his regular pay and even more perhaps for his uniform and gun, his bayonet, and other instruments of death! Those who envied him hardly understood against whom these instruments were to be used; Alphonse, for example, was incapable of hating the enemy any more than he hated his own country. Was Alphonse the only one of his kind? No, for Emmanuel could have named twenty, fifty, a hundred others like him. Perhaps less venomous, but with the same tendency. What could you offer them, what could you offer men who remained unconvinced, what could you find to lead men to war singing, singing as the drums rolled? Emmanuel shuddered, for he felt that he had put his finger on something terrifying and irrational, something that staggered the imagination and yet seemed to answer some need in mankind. In order to go to war, one must be filled with love, with some violent passion, one must be exalted, intoxicated, else war was absurd and inhuman. How strange it was that war should demand such a pure flame! Emmanuel was even more surprised to discover that war was possible and plausible only when some sort of superhuman sacrifice was required, some stupendous offering of oneself. In order not to blush for shame or tremble before the responsibility involved, man must go to war with a burning heart, armed with a powerful attachment for something, ready to die, but with an infinite love of life. What passion was strong enough to uplift and carry men to that point? Was it an ideal of justice, of beauty, of fraternity? Did he himself have that ideal as yet? That was the crux of the matter. Alphonse did not have it, neither did Azarius. Could he, Emmanuel, hold fast to that ideal, the passion of his youth, or would he go into battle without knowing where it was leading?

The suburb held him fast in a prison of doubt and solitude. He decided to climb the mountain, where in the old days he had found some release for his troubled spirits. Reaching Greene Street, he ascended the steep hill to Dorchester Street with long strides.

He was now in Westmount. On the way he had left behind the smells of flour and oil and tobacco; high above Saint-Henri the pure air was filled with the fragrance of new leaves and fresh-cut grass. Westmount, city of trees and parks and quiet homes, welcomed him.

Turning to the west, he soon reached the barracks on St. Catherine Street. At the gate a young soldier stood on guard duty, with fixed bayonet. Emmanuel was about to pass on, after greeting this comrade-in-arms, when he caught sight of the boy's face.

It was Pitou.

Pitou it was who patrolled the barracks, clicking his heels as he turned to retrace his steps, alone in the night with his gun on his shoulder.

Army rules would not permit him to stop when he recognized Emmanuel, but his face lit up with pleasure.

"Hullo there, Manuel!" he mumbled, continuing his rhythmic march.

"Hullo, Pitou," said the other man, falling in step.

They marched along this way for some time, as if the little sentry had acquired a tangible shadow to accompany him on his monotonous rounds. Then Pitou turned about smartly and clicked his heels, his eyes lighting up with the old mischief.

"Thumbs up!" he said in English.

"Thumbs up!" repeated Emmanuel.

And for the first time he said the words hesitantly, as if his mind were not quite made up.

"D'you like this?" he asked.

"You bet," said Pitou.

An intense excitement appeared on the little redhead's freckled face; his smile almost cracked his round, apple cheeks.

"We'll be seeing each other," promised Emmanuel.

"You bet . . . in England!"

"Goodbye, Pitou."

"Goodbye, Manuel."

They parted.

Emmanuel continued on his way, more slowly now, his head drooping more heavily toward his right shoulder, and abandoned himself completely to his thoughts. Recalling the discussion at Ma Philibert's, he wondered if he had not had some influence on Pitou's decision to enlist. It was almost frightening to possess such great powers of persuasion. Was he reaching the point where he could convince others without being able to convince himself? Would he go on arousing enthusiasm among his friends without being able to keep any of it for himself?

Pitou in the army! It seemed incredible, impossible! Pitou, the Benjamin of their little band. The boy they used to protect from the big fellows—only yesterday, it seemed—the boy they called "Chubby Cheeks," or "Baby." He remembered how, when they used to race madly along an old towpath, Pitou's voice would rise above the sound of their running feet, crying: "Wait for me, wait for me, I'm coming!" Sometimes they tried to leave him behind, just to tease him, or simply because he was too young for their games.

Yes, that was it, Pitou was too young for their games.

But Pitou would always turn up somewhere behind them, a comical little figure in outgrown pants that ended above his round calves, a windbreaker too large for his slight shoulders, and an enormous man's hat shadowing his face. From a distance you saw only the hat in motion; it seemed to climb the slopes and roll over the banks, animated by some strange magic. Always behind them, but never discouraged, he would squeal: "I'm coming too."

Those were the days when they would trudge along in single file for hours, sometimes going as far as the old canal to bathe. At one wild spot only lazy clouds were mirrored in the abandoned canal, the water flowing between still banks where people were rarely to be seen. A clump of trees here and there seemed like deep forests to them; a field in which a solitary cow stood grazing seemed like the open prairie. This was the countryside of their childhood. Alphonse, who always preferred the shadiest and most rugged paths, would talk of going on until they reached the river, there to put off in a boat for some great adventure. It was he who used to yell at Pitou when the boy persisted in following them, delaying them by falling into puddles of water or getting caught on barbed-wire fences: "Beat it, you little leech! You stick like glue!" But he was always the first to notice that Pitou had disappeared, the first to turn back to help him, the first to give him a cuff as he pulled him out of blackberry brambles or mud holes. One day he declared in a violent passion: "I'm damned glad I don't have a little brother like you, you infernal nuisance!" But everybody knew he meant the opposite. And Pitou, under his large hat, stood there sucking a blade of grass, smiling enigmatically, very sure of himself.

Later on Pitou learned how to make them wait for him. One evening they had been surprised by the sound of music coming from behind a pile of lumber on the edge of the canal. And there was little Pitou, a pied piper with a harmonica. The child kept them enthralled the whole evening. Even Alphonse had succumbed, and demanded peremptorily: "Play us 'Home On the Range,' Pitou."

After that they had roamed all over the quarter, giving circuses and concerts on street corners, Pitou at the head of the procession with his harmonica. The guitar came next. Hot nights, without the least breath of air, and Pitou seated on the canal wall, his legs dangling over the edge, making them go or stay as he wished now, he who so often had been left behind.

"I caught up with you. Ha, ha! I caught up with you."

Someone would ask: "Where'd you get the thingamajig?" And Pitou, beaming, would reply: "From an old Jew. He said: 'If you can play a tune on it, I'll give it to you for nothing.' And that's how I got the thingamajig."

But as the years passed, Pitou drew sadder and sadder songs from his guitar. If someone asked for a lively tune he sometimes said: "Oh, let me alone!" And then, perched on Ma Philibert's counter, he would suddenly ask: "Is there a single solitary job to be had in this town? Is there a single job to be had?" And you could see his run-down heels and his ragged soles swinging in the air.

Emmanuel walked more slowly as these memories came back to him. He could see as if it were yesterday those thin, worn-out, rain-soaked shoes swinging over his head at Ma Philibert's, with the two great holes in them growing larger and larger.

Pitou in the army! Alphonse must have known, and probably was heartsick about it, since he had refused to speak of Pitou. And then Emmanuel remembered suddenly: The cute little kid with the curly hair, the kid who winked and made a bargain, the kid who still had all his gay spirits ... It was Pitou who had paraded through the streets with Alphonse!

Pitou was a child, only a child! Yesterday he was playing with his harmonica or his guitar; today he was carrying a bayonet. And then Emmanuel thought with horror that Pitou need mourn no longer because he was unemployed. Pitou was earning his living now—he lived like a bird anyway and asked for so little— Pitou could be happy, and it was not surprising that he clicked his heels so smartly. Pitou was happy because he held in his hands his first working tools.

Emmanuel bowed his head.

The stars were very bright. Only on the mountain can you see them rise up out of the infinite depths of the sky. Here no film of dust obscured their steady twinkle, like a message flashed to humanity since the beginning of time. Emmanuel recalled what Azarius Lacasse had said: "France is like the sun or the stars ... they give us light by night and day."

This had seemed very fine when he had heard it from the lips of Azarius. He remembered the extraordinary lift he had felt at the time. But now he asked himself if a night without stars were not descending on the earth, without light of any kind. He wondered if this night had not begun to encircle the earth with its shadows long before the war.

Whence was the light to come to guide the world?

He found himself on a street where the stone houses with their Georgian windows, neat lawns, and climbing honeysuckle convey the very essence of gracious living; and the contrast between his thoughts and the mellow, deep, seemingly invulnerable calm of the place was so great that he sank into even greater melancholy than before. Emmanuel had never resented the rich. Of old, when he had climbed the mountain with his noisy comrades on a night when no breeze stirred, to shouts of: "Let's go see how the millionaires live up there!" it was not to commit acts of vandalism, but to fill his lungs with fresh air, and since he was secretly starved for beauty, to fill his eyes with it in passing.

Emmanuel had never hated the rich, perhaps because he had never been poor enough to turn morbid and envious, like Alphonse.

But as he walked past the stately private houses, he felt a growing disquiet. It was not bitterness, it was not loathing, it was not even the embarrassment he used to feel when he came to Westmount as a boy. It was something indefinable. All the restlessness and the anguish of the lower quarter of the town seemed to have clung to him when he left Saint-Henri, and the higher he had climbed, the closer he felt to those down below. And now it was as if he had no right to enter this citadel of calm and order bearing the rank smell of poverty. Up here too they wanted him to sacrifice himself, but they would have none of his doubts, his indecision or his tormenting problems. While accepting the offering of the poor, the rich could not see their agonized faces. The wealthy town stood silent in the night, refusing to ally itself with this representative of the poor.

Emmanuel grew hot with resentment. Like so many others, he put the problem to himself in this way: *Those of us who enlist from down there give all we have to give; maybe our arms, maybe our legs.* Looking up toward the high fences, the winding gravel walks, the sumptuous façades of the houses, he wondered: *Do they give all they have to give?*

The rich, polished stone glittered like steel, hard, indecipherable. And suddenly he felt the enormity of his presumption and of his innocence.

The stone, the wrought-iron fences, the oaken doors, the heavy brass knockers, iron, wood, stone, brass, silver—all seemed to come to life and croak in a hollow voice, with an undertone of mockery that communicated itself to the shrubs and clipped hedges, echoing through the night:

"How dare you think such thoughts, poor man! Do you by any chance pretend to put yourself on our level? Nothing on earth is to be had cheaper than your life. We others, stone, iron, steel, silver and gold, we're the things that cost dear, we're the things that last."

"But life, a man's life," insisted Emmanuel.

"A man's life! No one has ever reckoned its value. A man's life is so unimportant, so ephemeral."

Overborne by the weight of his thoughts, Emmanuel reached the observatory on top of the mountain. He leaned over the parapet and saw the myriad lights of the city spread out below him.

He seemed to be alone in the universe, on the edge of the abyss, holding in his hands the most tenuous, the most fragile thread of the eternal human enigma. Which ought to be sacrificed, wealth or spirit? Which contained the true power of redemption? And who was he to be grappling with such a problem? A young man who up to now had led a comparatively easy, pleasant life, a young man without any special discontent or great ambition, a simple young man like so many others, moderately educated, middle class, a young man who, if events had not precipitated him into a conflict too vast and too fierce for him to understand, might never in his life have concerned himself with anything more serious than his job and his humdrum existence. This whole question of justice and the world's salvation was beyond him; it was imponderable, it was immense. How could he expect to clarify it?

His feeling of ignorance increased his sense of loneliness. His solitude was the only thing he could measure rightly. He could judge its depth by the freedom of the scented breezes that blew about the heights. He could estimate its duration by the distance that separated Saint-Henri from the mountain.

Leaning far over the parapet, he searched among the lights to the southwest that sparkled like fireflies in a lake of darkness, and picked out one that might be that of Florentine's house.

And suddenly the girl's image came to him again, blotting everything else out, and replacing the doubts, the indecisions, the violent conflicts of the whole evening with a tumultuous desire for love.

CHAPTER XXIX

THE WAYSIDE STAND on the bank of the river struck Florentine as charming—a place where she might forget her sorrows, and where, by considering her past afresh, she might find some thoughts that gave her no pain. In front of the door Chinese lanterns hung from a tree whose swaying branches shuffled and blended all the bright colors together; a festoon of gaudy bulbs was looped over the low doorway. Having obtained this picturesque touch, the owner seemingly had relied for the rest of his decorative scheme on advertisements of every product he had for sale, as well as many others that could not possibly have been found in his establishment. The narrow front and the decrepit walls of the little building literally disappeared under vast quantities of signs; bathing girls stretched out on miniature beaches by some strange thought association glorified the mildness of a special brand of cigarettes, while others, even more scantily dressed, endorsed the properties of some soft drink. The number of advertisements was incredible; there were tin plates of every size, display cards, billposters of all descriptions. The effect was bewildering to the eye, but Florentine found it very pleasant. It was not the sort of place to nourish gloomy thoughts.

Under a pretense of an arbor there stood a weather-beaten garden table bearing a faded brewery trade mark. As she glimpsed this rustic touch, Florentine had murmured:

"Isn't it jolly?"

And hoping to please her, Emmanuel had suggested that they have dinner there.

But she had refused to take anything but a hot dog and a soft drink. Inside the restaurant Chinese lanterns hung from the ceiling; the breeze from the river kept them in constant motion. The tables were painted bright red; the smudged walls were covered with crude designs of Hindu temples, Japanese pagodas, triremes on a quiet crayon sea. There was a juke box in the corner, and Florentine kept asking Emmanuel to play the same hot jazz tune over and over again.

The proprietor himself served them. Emmanuel, seeing that Florentine had no appetite, ordered the same light snack for himself. They were alone for the most part. From time to time a couple would enter, buy some cigarettes or sandwiches, and leave, laughing boisterously and teasing each other as they went off down the road along the river.

So far the day had not come up to his expectations, and yet it had a certain flavor of suspense that fell in with his mood. Waiting patiently for a word or a gesture that would change the direction of both their lives beyond recall, he was willing to let things take their natural course. He was all alive to Florentine's presence across the table, but wondered whether it was the fear of losing her or the certainty of winning her that made her seem so vivid. Every movement she made, every pose she took was etched on his mind, and he realized that the day would leave him with a multitude of memories. Sometimes he felt as if the day had already gone by, as if it were in the past, so great was his eagerness to live over every moment of it.

In the morning he had gone to high mass at Saint-Henri church, hoping to find Florentine there, for with a sudden access of shyness he had preferred to meet her as if by chance rather than risk another fruitless visit to her home. He would never forget the air of mingled joy and hostility with which she had greeted him. As if she were trying to overcome her desire to see him again . . . yes, that was it, as if she were struggling against her own inclination, uncertain whether to run away or remain with him.

Everything else still seemed strange and confused in his memory. Florentine in the church portico, all dressed up for Easter! Deeply moved, not knowing how to begin, he had squeezed her arm gently and murmured: "A new outfit, eh?" And she had accorded him a twisted little smile, which turned into a frown, as if he had said something displeasing. But quickly she had answered: "You notice everything, don't you? Some men never look to see how a woman is dressed!" As if he could ever forget her little black silk dress, the one she had worn to his party, or her green uniform at the store, and the paper rose she stuck in her hair!

They went down the steps of the church together. And he thought to himself with delight: We're leaving church together like sweethearts. But he could make nothing of her fretful manner. She bit her lip as she walked, looking at him out of the corner of her eye with a perplexed, hesitant, almost stern expression. He went over the things they had said to each other in the crowd, the stiff, self-conscious words, every nuance, every inflection of which came back to him again and again: "You haven't changed a bit, Manuel!"—"Neither have you, Florentine." "You're going overseas?"—"Yes, pretty soon now. I have two weeks furlough, and then . . ." "Your last furlough! That's not much time . . ."

She had said: "That's not much time," in such an odd, reflective tone, that he had peered down at her to find the explanation in her face rather than in her words. But she had turned away, swinging her handbag and tapping her foot nervously.

Why had she said: "That's not much time"?

He stretched his hand across the table and seized her fingers in a tight grip.

Florentine spoke in a tone of slight mockery, and yet she must have been rather uneasy too, for she frowned and a tremor passed over her lips as she asked:

"You have something on your mind, I bet. What's on your mind?"

"You," he said unaffectedly.

With a satisfied smile, she released her hand from his and took out her compact. Since they had been together he had seen her make herself beautiful three or four times. The game amused him. She reminded him of a kitten washing its face. He had observed that first she compressed her lips and made her face rigid while she powdered her nose. Then she wet her fingers on her tongue and ran them over her eyelashes, curling them over her nails. All this diverted him, but what was most interesting was to find her staring into her mirror with a doubtful look, absorbed, questioning. What could she see there that upset her so?

A few moments went by while they looked at each other covertly. Then as she was about to apply her lipstick, she said:

"Put a nickel in the machine, Manuel."

Her need for noise and bustle did not surprise him. Since the night before, he too had been in a state of agitation that demanded constant movement. He went to the juke box and picked out one of his favorites, a tune from *Bitter Sweet*. The title and the melody expressed his mingled feelings at their reunion. Not recognizing the song from the first bars, Florentine asked.

"What record are you playing, Manuel?"

Then she stiffened. *"I'll see you again. . ."* The sentimental phrase stabbed her to the heart. Her lipstick slipped and smeared her cheek. She could see herself again at the entrance to the theater, the night her downfall had begun, the night when she was already lost.

Emmanuel took her in his arms gently.

"Let's dance," he said.

All day long he had been hoping to dance with her and feel the warmth of her graceful body against his.

She made several turns without seeing where she was going, without knowing what she was doing. All she could remember was how cold she had been there in the lobby. How icy the wind had been that night! And all the dark streets from which Jean might have come were silent and deserted, silent and empty! *"I'll see you again. . ."* The mournful refrain crushed her spirits. Her thoughts were ugly, ugly. No hope, no joy. And cold! A wintry wind, a tornado was blowing through her. No one had come to meet her that night through the storm. No one had ever come to meet her.

"You're not following me," said Emmanuel reproachfully.

And he began to hum in her ear: *"I'll see you again. . ."*

Her body rigid, she stumbled around, trying to get at the meaning of these fantastic words out of the past, these false words that Emmanuel was repeating to her. She could see someone who must have been herself sitting inside the theater, trying to delude herself into believing that Jean had been prevented from coming. How could she possibly have been so innocent, so stupid, so childish! And suddenly she was tempted to take revenge on Emmanuel for Jean's perfidy. She wanted to say something nasty, a single word to hurt him so that she could watch the suffering in his eyes.

"But we danced so well together the last time," said Emmanuel. Noticing that her cheek was smeared with lipstick, he pulled out his handkerchief and held it out to her, but as she paid no attention to his outstretched hand, he wiped off the smudge himself, with great care.

Florentine laughed harshly.

"Watch what you're doing! You're awfully clumsy! Why, we look like a doting couple."

She saw that she had gone too far, that she had offended him. No, that was not what she really wanted. It was all right to hurt him, yes, but not to offend him and make him turn from her. She must remain on good terms with Emmanuel, she must control herself. Tossing her head fretfully, she gave him a saucy, flirtatious smile.

For a moment, the cherished image that he had of her faded. In its place he saw a fidgety, unstable, loud, over-rouged girl. And he thought: This is not my Florentine; I'm mistaken, I'm lost . . . But his terror was dissipated immediately. A simpler and more touching explanation occurred to him: she was restless and tired, just as he was. She hardly knew her own mind, no doubt.

"Let's go," she said. "It's dull here, don't you think?"

Wherever they stopped, it was she who proposed moving on. She kept saying to herself: It's harder than I thought—to make believe I love him . . . to make him fall in love with me. . . But whatever her torments she knew very well that she would never give up until she had achieved this end.

He helped her on with her new coat. Earlier in the day she had boasted: "Yes, it's new this spring. It cost me plenty of money. Isn't it pretty?" It was a coat of light wool material, full in the hips and with a large plastic belt buckle, a coat the duplicate of which was to be found in all the shopwindows of the quarter. His heart contracted as she flared up and snapped: "Well, say something, don't you think it's pretty?" "Yes," he had answered, "it's pretty, Florentine." And he had dreamed of all the clothes he would like to buy for her, since she loved to deck herself out. He had pictured himself accompanying her to the shops to help her with her purchases. And suddenly he had grown bold. "Florentine, this may seem odd to you, but for a going-away present, won't you let me buy you a dress, a really pretty dress? We could pick it out together. . ." He stopped, fairly sure that she would refuse him. But to his great surprise, she had pressed his hand with real delight. "Yes, Manuel, nothing would give me more pleasure."

She made him hold her gloves and bag while she put on her hat, a tiny toque all covered with leaves and flowers.

"And my hat?" she had asked. "D'you like it? You'd better . . ." she added threateningly, ready to flare up again.

She took her handkerchief out of her pocketbook, gave him a smile to wheedle him into being patient, and began to powder her face once more. It made him feel awkward to stand there holding all those feminine things in his hand, her gloves, her scarf, the open bag from which she fished out her toilet articles, but he was sure that later he would enjoy the memory of this very moment more than the experience itself. He waited patiently for her to turn round and tell him that she was ready to leave.

At length they resumed their stroll along the river. They had left town without any definite plans for the day. Florentine had said vaguely : "Let's go to the mountain." But on the way she had changed her mind. "Let's go to Lachine," was her next proposal. At first he had thought she had the same desire he used to feel toward the end of the summer holidays, to be everywhere at once. But now he understood, from certain remarks she dropped, that she was totally uninterested in the landscape and that everything escaped her notice—the extraordinary clarity of the air, the rowboats and sailboats moving on the river, even the charm of the islands in the offing. These deserted or sparsely inhabited islands had always attracted him, and he tried to arouse her curiosity by telling her their names and something of their history. Earlier in the afternoon, when they were walking along the boardwalk at Verdun, among the noisy pleasure-seekers, she had spent all her time looking for faces she could recognize. "There's no one I know here," she had said with some heat. And unable to tolerate his interest in the picturesque scene, she had hurried him on fretfully. "There's nothing to see here; let's go, Manuel!"

Whenever she put her bare hand on his arm, he saw in the gesture a secret desire to cling to him. This made him so happy that he forgot how often he tended to make allowances for the girl, or felt the need to condone her ignorance and lack of tact. If at times he had some qualms about her, they were soon suppressed.

When she spoke now, she seemed very weary.

"Where shall we go, Manuel?"

He suggested that they cross over to the south bank and visit Caughnawaga, the Indian reservation.

She seemed surprised by the description he gave her. From her childish questions he judged that she knew almost nothing about the environs of Montreal.

"If I had a month, I'd show you around the country," he said.

"Well, you've only got two weeks. It's not worth wasting your time on savages," she replied.

He offered to take her out in a launch. She hesitated, not daring to admit that she had a mortal terror of the water. He ended by asking regretfully :

"Would you like to go to the movies?"

That might have suited her another time. But no, nothing tempted her today. Even making up her mind was too fatiguing. She wished that night would fall right away—nowadays she preferred the darkness to the most beautiful sunny day—that night would fall and that Emmanuel would take her in his arms and say he could not live without her. That was what he felt in his heart, she was sure. Then why didn't he say so? If he admitted it, she could have some peace of mind at last.

From time to time she turned her head a little toward him and studied him from under her lashes. She recalled how he had held her bag at the restaurant. He loves me, she thought, he's madly in love with me. In fact the glance he gave her that moment expressed so much sweetness that she felt abashed. Then she said to herself : Too bad about him, if he loves me so much. . . It's too silly. And because her own self-esteem demanded it, she tried to persuade herself that she loved Emmanuel too, after her fashion.

She succeeded in this as long as she refrained from comparing Emmanuel's character with some of Jean's more outstanding traits. Then she would stick out her lips with disdain, giving the young man beside her a sharp look. Jean wouldn't give in to all my whims like this, she thought. And again she decided to be ruthless.

She tottered along on her high heels, so weary that Emmanuel began to be worried about her. "You can't walk any farther, can't you see?" he said, trying to support her by putting his arm around her waist. "You'll wear out your pretty new shoes," he said in jest. But he was really concerned. Dark rings encircled her eyes; her nose was pinched with fatigue, and she had turned dreadfully pale. Emmanuel at last laid down the law, and forced her to take a bus that was returning to the city.

But a little before Verdun, where they could hear the rapids, she stifled a sigh.

"Let's get off here," she said.

The motion of the bus nauseated her, and as her body weakened, so did her will. She was afraid of falling into a stupor, a state of complete indifference, and therefore she whipped herself up to appear gay and even to show an interest in the sort of thing that Emmanuel liked.

"It's so pretty here," she said, "the water and everything," but her eyes strayed no farther than her fingers. "Let's get off here," she added, "and watch the people fishing."

She had just remembered that when she was a little girl Azarius used to bring hers here of a Sunday when he went fishing. Sometimes she longed to make Emmanuel understand what her childhood had been like, to make him love her for what she had been in the old days. And she said, leaning on his shoulder :

"My father and I used to come here long ago. I would take off my shoes and stockings and play in the water. I must have been five or six then . . ."

It was the first time she had made the slightest allusion to her family in his presence, as if up to then she had been restrained by pride or embarrassment. This meager little confession moved Emmanuel. He took her fingers in his and pressed them warmly. And she, vaguely troubled by this recollection of her childhood, went on speaking with an inward look, her eyes fixed on the past:

"My father was good to us when we were little. My father . . . Some people say bad things about him, they say he doesn't like to work, they say he doesn't know how to keep a job. But my father was always good to us. Only he never had much luck, my father."

She repeated "my father, my father" like a refrain, like a prayer, or an apology, like an appeal to the jury, by which she might exonerate Azarius and justify herself at the same time. Emmanuel gave her an encouraging look.

Florentine caught the unconcealed look of pity in Emmanuel's eyes.

"Let's get off here," she repeated irritably.

They left the bus near the power plant and strolled along, Emmanuel doing his best to check her nervous pace. It seemed to him that she had exposed a corner of her soul so pitiful, so unhappy that his life would not be long enough to console her, and if need be pardon her for the disillusionment she might bring to him. When she said : "He never had much luck," he felt that she had described a whole lifetime. A whole lifetime of bad luck, of humble self-effacement. "He never had much luck."

He tried to soothe her by pressing her arm. She seemed more secretive than he had believed, and this discovery increased his uneasiness and his tenderness.

Florentine walked faster, compressing her lips. She felt she had been stupid to reveal the tiniest particle of her private life, to give him the slightest inkling of the gentler feelings still left in her heart. Sweetness and gentleness led you nowhere. It was gentleness that had blighted all their lives. No gentleness for her, thank you. Never. Furious with herself, she tried to get ahead of Emmanuel. The path they were following grew narrower as it rounded boulders along the way. He stood aside to let her pass, and fell behind even farther to watch her tripping gait and the way she tossed her mass of light-brown hair over her shoulders.

He wished she were bareheaded; she had such pretty hair. But she had started off on the walk dressed exactly as she had been at church, even to her gloves, which she was extremely careful not to soil. She would take them off, fold them up and entrust them to Emmanuel lest she lose them; a few minutes later she would take them back, pull them on again and look at them with the greatest complacence.

The late afternoon sun lay over the surface of the water like a golden mist. When they tried to distinguish the other bank of the river their eyes were blinded by the radiance. The air was turning cooler, however, and at times a stiff wind came up. Soon the mildness of the day would be gone; so every word they had said, every gesture they had made, would be swallowed up in the hidden craters of the memory. And this thought was so painful to the young man that he hurried to catch up with Florentine, took her by the shoulders, and turned her around to face him. But as she stood there in surprise, he had nothing to offer her but a touching smile.

Her attitude was one of waiting, but her glance was determined, almost commanding. He seemed on the point of speaking. By the lines on his forehead she understood that he was searching for the right words, that he was trying to describe a feeling he had never expressed before. He was struggling both to contain himself and to discover how far he might go in baring his heart. His mouth quivered; with a nervous gesture he wiped the sweat from his forehead. Then he regained his self-control. He spoke quietly, pretending to take it all lightly, but with something definitive in his voice, as if he had made up his mind beyond the shadow of a doubt:

"We should have met long ago, Florentine."

This was not what she had expected to hear. She was consternated, she was petrified with fear, more maddening than anything she had ever experienced. If she lost Emmanuel now, she would never see him again. Never. This time she would be lost for good. And strangely enough, she felt that losing him would be hard in more ways than one. Something more than her security and her peace of mind was at stake.

It seemed to her that Emmanuel might restore her desire to live, give her a new pride and joy in being well dressed, attractive, irresistible. Through him she had begun once more to think of herself as a girl of spirit. Was all this to be torn from her now? She stood plucking at the strap of her bag, her head bowed to hide the expression on her face.

"You'll tear your handbag," he said playfully. "Is it new too?" he asked, pretending not to see that she was sulking.

"It's all new," she burst out stormily. "I bought everything new this spring, to . . ."

"To make a guy crazy about you," he finished for her, half smiling.

But Florentine caught the tone of anxiety in his voice. That same feeling had been hers so often when Jean spoke to her and she could not understand his turn of speech. Emmanuel was looking at her searchingly; she saw his jaws working and guessed that his hands were clasped tightly behind his back. She was surprised to find him less enterprising than he had been at their first meeting; it alarmed her.

"Are you in love with someone, Florentine?" he asked.

She hesitated. What was the best way of bringing him to her feet? Making him jealous? Maybe yes, maybe no. She wasn't quite sure. She mustn't make a mistake. Above all, she mustn't make a mistake. At the tavern near Lachine, two couples had come in for a drink; one of the young men wore a naval uniform. She had given him a glance or two, perhaps even a smile, finding him young and pleasant looking. And she remembered how restless Emmanuel had become, how without a word he had made her change places with him so that she could not catch the young man's eye in the mirror. It would be silly, it would be a terrible blunder, she thought, to admit that she had once loved Jean.

She stood digging her toe into the ground, while she mapped out her next move.

"Oh, you know, at the store, lots of men make up to me . . ." she murmured.

"Yes, I know," he said.

His voice shook. Swinging his weight from one leg to the other, he affected a certain indifference, seemingly in no hurry for an answer. Florentine began to suspect that he had more strength of will than she had given him credit for. Unless she played the game simply, she might never be able to bridge the chasm between them. She burst out laughing, brushed her cheek against his, and laid her finger on his lips, crying:

"You fool! You fool! Before you left you asked me if I wanted to be your girl-friend. You know very well I was waiting for you, for no one but you."

Then all the unnatural resistance that Emmanuel had put up

crumbled. He took a deep breath, as if he had just come safely through a storm. Now he was aware that all day long he had been tormented by suspicion. At certain moments Florentine's little wiles, her petulant airs had driven him frantic. She tolerates me out of spite, he had thought.

But now all his fears were swept away by that simple, affectionate gesture of her finger on his lips. He took her hand and led her down toward the river bank, between crackling branches that brushed against Florentine's coat and whipped at her straight thin legs, and it seemed as if he were entering a world where there was no war or horror or doubt or suffering, where every sound was hushed save the rustle of the leaves and the silky swish of a girl's dress.

As twilight came on, they found a place to sit down in sight of a little cove, where the rumble of the city could be heard only in a faint murmur. The high bank sheltered their retreat. They were alone with the timeless roar of the river and the kingfishers darting through the sparse grass of the bank. A crane rose from the silvery water, its wings flaming; all that remained of the waning light seemed to follow the bird as it circled, now low over the reeds, now high among the elm branches. On the horizon purple clouds merged with the river.

They had chosen this spot because a large boulder, flat on top and lapped at the base by a small eddy, offered a comfortable resting place. Emmanuel had spread out his khaki handkerchief for Florentine to sit on without soiling her new coat. She had perched herself there, with her legs hanging over the side, while Emmanuel cradled her in his arms. He was still a bit timid and amazed at the familiarities she permitted him. To her the night was welcome; from now on it held no terrors for her, since it could never find her alone again. Night was merciful; it blurred their faces and veiled their features, fusing time past and present, bringing forgetfulness.

With a bold and yet caressing gesture she rested her heavy head against Emmanuel's shoulder. And this was not quite playacting. The oncoming night dulled her memories of the past and the stupid mistakes she had made. She felt almost innocent again, hungry for tokens of love. And this was not quite a lie. If the man beside her insisted on loving her, loving her desperately, perhaps she might still be capable of responding to the appeal of love. It might be better for her never to become so deeply involved as to suffer from love. Hereafter love would come to her in a milder form. The darkness calmed her spirits like a powerful drug.

Nestling against Emmanuel, she breathed in the odor of his hair and his uniform, she abandoned herself to the outward signs of love. In spite of all that had happened the only way to her heart was through kisses.

She felt Emmanuel's heart beating through his tunic. One part of her softened and yielding, the other part watchful and resolved, she studied him out of the corner of her eye.

But he disengaged himself slightly, caught again in his torments of the night before, unable to reconcile his vision of a world in agony with happiness, however transient. There was no help for it; he must appeal to Florentine to save both of them.

"Will you wait for me?" he asked abruptly, his voice low and harsh. "It's hard and it's not fair, but will you wait for me, Florentine? Will you wait for me till the world is cured of this dreadful sickness? It may be a year, two years, even longer. Till the war is over? Will you wait for me all that time, Florentine?"

She sat up, awake to the danger. What did he mean, "till the world is cured"? What language was he speaking? She feared this thing she could not understand, and yet she was certain that she held her own fate and Emmanuel's in her hands. Careful now! This at least she knew, that one feeling spoke louder than any grief, more imperiously than any language of the mind or spirit! She gathered up all her strength, her strength as a weak woman, her irresistible strength, against which the mind was powerless.

Turning her head on his shoulder, she gave him a woebegone look.

"Oh, Manuel, you're going away, and I'll never see you again! I don't want to wait all that time. I'd die if I had to wait for you all that time. I'd be afraid you'd find other girl-friends."

At that moment she was so intoxicated with the sound of her own voice and the warmth of her own words that she almost believed what they implied: that life would become unbearable when Emmanuel left her. Tears that were not entirely forced rolled down her cheeks. In a way she was weeping for her past folly and unhappiness. She threw her arms about Emmanuel. There was a great fear in her, and yet she had the feeling that she would get what she wanted through the force of her will. She saw herself reborn, beloved, prettier than ever, saved. As it grew darker around them, the night like a heavy wine, she gave him her lips, she gave him her mouth coldly, resolutely. But as she did so a wave of passion came over her. She could not tell whether it was the memory of Jean's caresses or Emmanuel's kisses now that made her heart leap. For a moment everything else was forgotten as her thin little face clung to Emmanuel's mouth.

This was joy he had not anticipated. From the very beginning of his furlough, from the moment he had stepped on the train with the image of Florentine constantly in his mind, he had feared that he might be carried away by his own ardent nature. To marry Florentine on the eve of his departure seemed unjust. He had only wanted to look forward to a fortnight of happy, easy comradeship. Other considerations he had cast aside, not foreseeing any need for going into them for the present, but they had nevertheless occurred to him. His family would frown on such a union, his father particularly. The grief he would cause his mother if this girl became his wife seemed all the more cruel in that he was leaving so soon; and lastly, Florentine's future relations with his family raised all sorts of problems. If he had had time to examine these questions, he might have decided to wait. But he had reached such a degree of fever and of exaltation that marrying Florentine in all haste seemed the most natural thing in the world. Most of the men married just before leaving. Why shouldn't those who were going to be separated, perhaps forever, have a little happiness? Could happiness wait on their return, on the chance of their return? Wasn't this a rare opportunity, to be seized upon the moment it was presented? He was so shaken by his sudden decision, so dazzled, that he forgot how Florentine had led him to it. It seemed to him now that he had had this idea himself for a long time, and that it was just as futile to struggle against it as to combat the disorder and madness that ruled the world.

Choking with emotion, he was unable to speak coherently, and yet his mind seemed more lucid than for months past.

"Time . . ." he said, "we haven't much time. A little less than two weeks."

The only obstacle left, he thought, was time, inexorable time.

But she gave him almost no encouragement. His impatience had swept her off her feet, and now that she saw where it might lead she began to have certain qualms. She sat motionless, peering through the darkness with wide-open eyes.

"Florentine," he stammered, "do you think we have time enough?"

He lit a cigarette and puffed at it rapidly.

"About two weeks." He turned to her suddenly. "We'll make it do," he cried feverishly. "I can go to see your parish priest early tomorrow morning. Everything can be arranged for Wednesday or Thursday. We'll reserve a room at a hotel. And we'll write on the register : Monsieur and Madame Létourneau."

He laughed aloud, but stopped short as he heard the laughter coming from his own throat; it was the first time in a long while that he had laughed.

And now Florentine too joined in the fun, dazzled by the prospect of spending several days at a hotel, with Emmanuel spoiling her and buying her all sorts of presents.

Neither of them gave a thought to anything beyond the next few days. What Emmanuel had in mind was a jealously guarded intimacy, a kind of flight into the land of dreams, an exquisite indolence, while Florentine was thinking of the bright lights of the theaters, and the department stores she would visit as a radiant bride. And they were both so pleased with their respective plans that after a moment's silence they kissed each other impulsively, with abandon.

The night fell completely on their embrace.

Emmanuel began talking, talking:

"You'll have an allowance, Florentine. And with what I can give you besides out of my pay, you won't have to work any more. You can even have your own house."

And he added to himself: her own house, that she can furnish just as she likes and where she'll be waiting for me.

"It won't be long," he went on. "I mean it won't be long till the war is over. We're still young, both of us. How old are you, Florentine?"

"Nineteen."

And she turned to him as if to say: I can begin all over again at my age. You can forgive me many things.

"I'm only twenty-two." he answered. "We'll still be young when I come back. We'll have all our lives before us . . ."

He hesitated, marveling at all the contradictions in his thoughts during these last few minutes. At first his ambitions had been modest, then they had grown bolder with the possibility of realization, and at last they had flown off into the future, trying to wrest from time the promise, the assurance of a happy life. Like a gambler who, after voluntarily sacrificing his future chances of making a fortune, wins the sweepstakes but refuses to pay the price of his ticket, Emmanuel now put a lower value on the joys he had hardly dared hope for an hour ago than on the capacity for happiness.

Suddenly he foresaw all the risks of a long separation for him and Florentine. He foresaw the loneliness they might know for years. And he murmured hoarsely:

"Only, Florentine, to do what we're doing, we must be sure that we love each other. That we love each other for all our lives."

This was a very serious question he was putting to her, as he returned from his disturbing journey into time. It was almost a prayer. It was a bold appeal to the future, whose dangers neither of them could foresee. It was a challenge to the slow dark passage of time that lay before them.

A faint milky glow hung over the river, but it did not reach them. Everything was still. They sat silent in the darkness.

Emmanuel tried to search her face, the face he had loved for so short a time; he struggled to recall the few words and gestures that comprised his knowledge of her. But it was very, very dark, and close as their faces were, he could not see her eyes. At this he clasped her tightly in his arms, dreading to be alone again. She knew that he could not see her eyes, and this was almost a comfort to her, for she felt that she herself could not have borne her own regard. Quickly she said :

"That's true. We must love each other for all our lives."

And for once she had spoken from the bottom of her heart. The storm was over. There would be no more heights of ecstasy or depths of horror in her life, only a smooth, quiet road ahead of her. She was saved.

CHAPTER XXX

ROSE-ANNA ENTERED Florentine's room without making a sound. She laid the green velvet dress that was to be her daughter's wedding dress over the foot of the iron bedstead, set the slippers on the floor and spread a pink rayon slip carefully over a chair. Seeing that Florentine still slept, her face hidden under her upflung forearm, she stepped forward and touched the girl's bare shoulder.

Ever since the night when she had guessed her daughter's disgrace, she had felt extremely embarrassed in her relations with the girl, as if she herself shared that disgrace. She hardly dared look at Florentine, much less speak to her.

Her uneasiness had died away, to be sure, in the last few days. As she saw the color come back into Florentine's cheeks, as she saw the girl apparently happy with Emmanuel, she had felt reassured. A weight had been lifted from her heart. She had permitted herself in all innocence to rejoice that Florentine was making such a good match; she had indulged in a few moments of pride, untroubled by her daughter's lack of enthusiasm. But this morning, as she was pressing Philippe's suit, she had found a note addressed to Jean Lévesque, in Florentine's handwriting, in a pocket stuffed with papers.

Her former misgivings returned in force.

It was growing late. Leaning over the bed, Rose-Anna hesitated a moment and then began to shake Florentine.

"This is your wedding-day. Wake up!"

She could not keep the impatience out of her voice. On her own wedding day she had waked at dawn without anyone's help, she had dressed at her sunny window with a song on her lips.

Florentine meanwhile had sat up with a start, looking about her wildly, squinting in her perplexity. The moment of waking still unnerved her, crippled her will and subjected her to the old torments. She bowed her head and sat dreaming for a moment. Why had she waked up this morning? Why should she ever wake up? But this morning, this morning especially, what new torment was in store for her? Sinking back against the pillows, she floundered a moment longer in a state of semi-consciousness, and then she remembered. Ah yes, this was her wedding day . . . the day of her marriage to Emmanuel. And the word "marriage," which had formerly been associated in her mind with a feeling of joy and triumph, now seemed austere and gloomy, full of pitfalls and dire revelations. She saw her mother's heavy figure moving about the room, and a vision of herself deformed in the same way became rooted in her mind. A shudder ran through her limbs; the thought of the ordeal she must go through filled her with indignation. How she hated the trap into which she had fallen! And now she was heading for it again, this time of her own free will. An expression of protest, almost of hatred, appeared on her face. Then as she caught sight of her mother's reproachful look, she leaped out of bed and began to dress.

Rose-Anna and Azarius had wanted to do the right thing for the marriage of their eldest child. Azarius especially had run around raising money in advance for a few days' work. "This is no time to count the pennies," he said. And Rose-Anna for once agreed with him. "You're right, Azarius. She must have everything of the best." They had left nothing undone to make Florentine's wedding outfit elegant, even if it was beyond their means. The Létourneaus must not say she was beneath them, Rose-Anna had thought with a sudden flare of pride. Emmanuel would not take her to the altar in rags.

She had been up all night putting the finishing touches to Florentine's silk underthings. And now with an aching heart she was waiting for a word of appreciation or at least a reassuring glance.

Before she slipped on her dress, the girl stood up to brush her hair. The room contained few articles of furniture, but it was still crowded with packing cases and boxes left over from the moving. Florentine looked so puny and frail that all Rose-Anna's resentment drained out of her.

What was it the child was holding back so grimly, so fiercely? Why wouldn't she unbosom herself? Some day or other, once Emmanuel went overseas and Florentine was living with them again, they would probably come to an understanding, as between women. But wouldn't that be too late? Ought she not act now if Florentine really needed help?

She held the dress out, and yet she hesitated to hand it over. Her rough fingers caught in the material and she crumpled it a bit, her eyes big with uncertainty.

"You know, Florentine, if you think you've made a mistake," she said quickly, "if you're marrying Manuel against your will, if you love someone else, it's not too late yet. You must say so . . ."

Florentine's only answer was to tear the dress from her mother's hands.

"Let me do it," she said, "I can dress myself without any help."

No, she would not change her mind. Her plans were settled once and for all. It wouldn't be quite the kind of life she had expected, but still it was a thousand times better than what it might have been. And she hurried through her toilette—she hurried fearfully as if to make herself over, to create a Florentine for a new way of life, a girl who might forget what she had been in earlier days.

She drew in her chin and studied herself from under lowered lids. How relieved she was, after her panic on waking, to see how slender her waist was still, and how young and small her breasts! She was so comforted that if only Rose-Anna had not been so stern, she would have tried to propitiate her mother. For a moment there she had been in terror of becoming misshapen overnight. Perhaps she had had a nightmare. Now she felt much calmer. She was going to be pretty, very pretty for her wedding. Emmanuel would carry a charming picture of her away with him. He would be far away when she lost her slender figure and turned ugly. He need suspect nothing. And she would keep her secret up to the last minute. No one would ever learn it from her. Never! She would never change her mind on the subject. No one, not even her mother, would ever drag a confession from her.

Rose-Anna saw her daughter's face in a little mirror hanging over the table. The mouth was hard, the eyes wilful, almost arrogant.

She was stupefied. That rigid mask, that furrowed brow belonged to some stranger. There was none of the old Florentine in those set features, not the least trace even of the hotheaded girl who at heart had always yearned to be forgiven. Rose-Anna felt so baffled that she gave up all idea of putting a direct question. It was rather for herself, rather to satisfy the demands of her own conscience that she said in a low voice :

"Marriage is a serious thing, my Florentine."

"You're always preaching," said Florentine savagely, goaded as much by her own qualms as by her mother's grief, for with all other difficulties removed, she could at last see clearly the lying and deception to which she was committed.

"I'm always preaching?" cried Rose-Anna.

She dropped her eyes. A picture of her cold, strait-laced mother obtruded itself on her mind; perhaps there was a resemblance. She tried to think of something to say that would not sound like sermonizing, but it did not come easily to her, because all her life she had heard nothing but pious old bromides. Then too Florentine's hostile attitude checked any natural outpouring of tenderness on her part. More and more, however, she felt that she herself was to blame for having discouraged Florentine's first attempt to confide in her.

"I don't want to preach, Florentine. But I want you to know that marriage isn't one long lark. There are lots of troubles in marriage too."

Her lips set in a hard line, the girl was powdering her face. She closed her mind to the gloomy scenes her mother had conjured up, scenes she herself had envisaged on waking, in favor of others more to her liking. The aisle of the church down which she would walk on her father's arm, the altar decorated with flowers, the wedding breakfast at Emmanuel's house, the compliments she would receive, and then their departure in a whirl of confetti, the visit to the photographer; all that would be so much fun. And afterwards . . . well, she refused to think about anything afterwards.

After all, Emmanuel was a good man. Only yesterday, when they were drawing up their plans together, she had been struck by his gentleness. Not touched by it, but reassured nevertheless. Suddenly she felt completely avenged for Jean's desertion, rehabilitated in her own eyes and in the eyes of her family. Thanks to her marriage, of course, she was now worthy of their esteem. At the thought that she had been clever enough to get her own way, she smiled, a slow, reflective smile, in which there was a spark of her old determination, as well as a longing to start afresh. She was on the point of throwing herself into her mother's arms, but Rose-Anna had turned away. After a moment's hesitation she went back to the kitchen.

Azarius was waiting there, dressed in his best suit, with a rose in his buttonhole, and talcum powder over his freshly shaven cheeks. His white shirt was too tight at the wrists and neck, making him look rather puffy and ill at ease. He was moved at the thought of leading his daughter to the altar. Florentine . . . He had always pictured her as a very little girl with her long tresses flying, and this image seemed so little in keeping with wedding preparations that he wallowed about in a sort of happy daze. Imagine Florentine getting married . . . and he, her father, so young still!

"Will she be ready soon?" he asked.

Going to the window, he peered out at the fragment of sky visible through the grimy panes, and shouted above the roar of a passing train:

"What a beautiful day! Sunny as can be!"

Even when they lived in Beaudoin Street, below the embankment, they had been surrounded by the hot breath of the trains, though their house was up the block from the railroad. But now they were almost on top of the tracks. The Transcontinental, the Toronto and Ottawa trains as well as the suburban lines passed their door. There were long freight trains, endless processions of refrigerator and coal cars. Sometimes the freight trains would come to a halt outside the door, then move backward and forward as individual cars were switched to another track, and while this went on the house was beset by the sound of bells ringing, couplings banging, hissing steam and clouds of soot. At other times expresses ran past with a long-drawn-out whistle, shaking the house to its very foundations. The windowpanes vibrated, the pictures swayed on the walls, even the contents of the drawers were tossed about. To be heard above the uproar you had to raise your voice to a quarrelsome pitch, and because of this constant shouting the members of the family tended to transfer their irritation to one another. Then when the howling train fled down the line and the house began to settle down, it seemed to them that the sun had set and a new day, as dreary as the last, was upon them.

This morning, however, Rose-Anna was thinking of other things. She remembered her own wedding day, a bright, clear morning, with the sound of the bells floating across the fields from the village. She remembered the smells of the earth on the way to church—how often she had thought of them since!—she remembered her joy in the hearty tang of earthy things, and she wondered why they seemed so far away from her now. Then as her eyes fell once more on the disorder around her, she almost hated the memories that had risen to her mind. Weren't those few poor days of grace at the outset of life a mockery? And weren't these wedding festivities today a mockery, in the midst of their settling into a new house, a house that was dirty and impersonal and had no associations for them?

The wind was driving swarms of sparks and particles of soot against the windows. It seemed as if the whole sky had emptied itself of soot and found no other place to deposit it than these ill-fitting panes. Azarius stood there, in the shadow made by the cloud of dust, tapping at the window frame, and yet Rose-Anna knew that his mind was elsewhere, as hers had been a moment ago.

She watched him out of the corner of her eye. He had not noticed how nervous Florentine had been for the last few weeks, she was certain; he had no suspicion of any drama being played under his very nose. But although he had seen nothing, and sensed nothing in the air, she had never been so loath to blame him or hold him responsible. During the last few days, he seemed to have unburdened himself of some great weight. His step was firmer, livelier. At moments his face grew somber, but he had learned to shift his glance and look impassive whenever he felt that he was being observed. Rose-Anna thought he must be nursing some secret hope. And sometimes the poor woman was more irritated at the idea that he still dared to hope, at his age, and despite their bad luck, than at the thought that she was excluded from her husband's confidence. Once or twice she had come upon him talking to himself, saying: "There's nothing else to be done; I must make up my mind." And when she had asked him to explain himself, he had leaped to his feet, and without a trace of embarrassment, had made a joke of it: "Let me be, Rose-Anna. You won't have hard times much longer. The money will come rolling in soon; we'll be able to take it easy."

She dreaded seeing him discouraged, but even more she had learned to fear his immature optimism.

A newspaper lay on the table. Nowadays Azarius bought one or two every day. Her eye fell on the front page without interest, but catching sight of the headline, *Refugees on the roads*, she murmured: "Like us . . . on the road . . . always on the road." The problems of her own family absorbed her to such a degree that she could no longer see the misery of others except in terms of her own predicament, as confirmation of all the torments she herself had undergone. Her glance slipped down the page, to another headline: *A new contingent of Canadian troops arrives in England.* Mechanically she looked for the date of the newspaper. It was yesterday's, the twenty-second of May.

"I wonder if Eugène's turn will come soon," she said.

And her mind ran on: Eugène, Florentine, gone already! Who will be next? Will we ever be together again? She took in the room with a weary, aggrieved look. No, they would never be happy here! She had known it the moment they had entered the house. What new threat hovered over her? A sense of foreboding clutched at her heart. Eugène, probably! She had reached the point where as soon as the barb of one affliction was blunted, she began watching out for the next, almost eagerly, as if by anticipating it she might deaden the sting.

"Poor child!" she sighed.

Azarius trembled visibly. For a moment he thought that she was talking to him. In the old days, in order to cure him of his illusions and console him for his defeats, she had sometimes taken him in her arms like a child and whispered these words to him. A longing for affection surged over him, and he realized that he would gladly give his life to see her happy, at least once. He glanced at his wife's care-worn face, her forehead lined with wrinkles, her poor hands bleached with washing. In him, too, Florentine's wedding began to stir long-forgotten memories, and they in turn stirred a kind of dead weight that must have been there all the time, that had dragged at his feet and trammeled all his efforts. And it was only now that he saw it plainly! Once he had recovered from the shock of admitting that Florentine was grown up and ready to take her first flight, he was horrified at what he saw behind him: days and days laid end to end, a few deeds, and a great many omissions. And that was the worst of it. He could forgive himself for having taken action, however ill-conceived it might have been, but he would always remember and resent the things he had left undone. Rose-Anna, for example! Nothing was more certain than that he had never loved anyone but Rose-Anna. And yet at no time had he been able to prove it to her. Well, the time had come to prove it. The time had come to stop making her suffer. He closed his eyes. It was for this that he was straining every nerve. To go away . . . not to see her suffer any more . . . it was only right . . .

He would have spoken—perhaps he had never before been so well prepared to explain himself and justify himself in her eyes— but at that very moment Rose-Anna rose from her chair and stepped forward with a constrained smile. Florentine had come into the kitchen.

Later she was to remember that there was barely time for her to see her daughter in her wedding dress, and that they had not even kissed.

Florentine asked:

"Does my dress hang right, Mamma?"

And Rose-Anna had made her turn around slowly while she examined the dress and bent over to pull out a few basting stitches. Then Azarius carried the girl off.

"Come now, my chick, we must hurry. We'll take a taxi down the street."

They lived only a stone's throw from the taxi-stand where Azarius used to work a few months previously. Rose-Anna posted herself at the window, and watched them crossing the railroad tracks. A few minutes later she recognized them as they drove by in a dark sleek car. Azarius had ordered the driver to make a detour by way of Convent Street to give Rose-Anna one last look.

She rubbed the grimy windowpane and peered out, but all she could see was a flash of pale green and a little hat tilted over a mass of shining brown hair. She waved her hand, a futile gesture, for the car had sped past, and besides, Florentine never looked back. When she left the house she had not faltered for an instant nor betrayed any feeling by so much as a glance. She had left as if nothing held her here any longer, as if nothing touched her heart, thought Rose-Anna. "Almost like a stranger!" murmured the poor woman, on the verge of tears. And catching herself with her arm uplifted for a tender farewell salute, she felt so heart-broken that she wanted to run away and hide.

She turned away from the window and sat down at the table, weary unto death. There were plenty of things to be done, many other worries to take her mind off Florentine. The little ones would be up soon. They must be dressed and washed and prepared for school. She must show great patience with Philippe and handle him with great care in order to induce him to do a few simple chores. There was no end to her anxieties. But she preferred to dwell on the one that grieved her most. Perhaps the only thing she wished for now was to be alone with her grief.

Her dressing gown fell open, revealing her swollen legs and vari-cose veins. And suddenly her head slipped down to the table. It had been a long, long time since she had wept.

But just at that moment, in the silent room, a light step was heard. Yvonne appeared in the doorway. She stood there appre-hensively, watching her mother without moving. Then in one bound she threw herself at Rose-Anna's feet.

Rose-Anna began to wind the little girl's curls around her finger mechanically. After a few moments, as if at last she realized who was there, she pushed Yvonne away, and embarrassed by the child's artless gaze, she gathered her dressing gown about her.

"What is it, Vonette?" she asked.

For a long time she had not called the girl by her old pet name. At an unusually early age, Yvonne had grown reticent, almost repulsively serious, with an inclination toward penitence and prayer that was bewildering to Rose-Anna. At times the mother had taken offense at such excessive piety. It often happened that she charged the little girl with domestic duties just as Yvonne was trying to slip away to church. "Don't you know that you serve the good Lord best by helping your parents?" she would say, to smooth away the girl's stubborn frown. And she would speak of the parable of Martha and Mary. But since the story was not fresh in her mind, she sometimes mixed the roles, saying: "Jesus said that Martha took the better part." To which Yvonne answered nothing.

The little girl began to cry softly on her mother's knees. And Rose-Anna wondered whether she had not misjudged and neglected the child. She put her hand under Yvonne's chin, lifted her head and looked into her eyes. The expression she read there troubled her deeply. It was no longer reproachful, as before; it was full of compassion.

The little girl bore Rose-Anna's regard steadily. Wrapping her arms around her mother's broad waist, she whispered:

"Poor Mamma, poor Mamma!"

Under the nightdress, Rose-Anna could feel the budding breasts of her daughter. Already! she said to herself. And at the moment she could not tell whether the thought gave her pleasure or pain. Playing with the girl's hair, she asked:

"Do you know you'll soon be as big as Florentine?" And her voice trembling, she whispered: "Will you be married too, some day?"

"No," said the little girl quietly.

She had dropped back on her heels at her mother's feet. Filled with exaltation, her eyes fastened themselves on the dirty wall as if she saw it all aglow with sunlight.

"I'm going to be a nun," she said.

Her voice sang.

"So you're going to be a nun," Rose-Anna repeated.

"Unless," Yvonne went on, "unless God takes my life. I have offered my life if Daniel recovers."

Rose-Anna said nothing. She could not see very well; a mist had risen before her eyes. Daniel! She had almost forgotten him in her concern for Florentine. They had all been so busy, each with his own affairs, that no one seemed to have thought about the sick child, as if he had ceased to exist already. Yvonne was the only one who had not forsaken him.

She knew that her voice would not be very steady. Half rising in her chair, she stared at Yvonne fixedly, and spoke quickly.

"I feel too tired to go to the hospital today. And you know the streetcar makes me ill. Do you think you could find your way all by yourself?"

The little girl jumped to her feet, her eyes shining.

"Oh yes, I'll ask the way. I'll go. I'll bring Daniel the orange I have left. And the chocolates Emmanuel gave us. Maybe Jenny will let him eat them. His good Jenny, his pretty Jenny!"

Rose-Anna had told her how much the little boy loved his nurse, and since then Yvonne had carried the thought of Jenny in her heart, offering up her childish prayers for Daniel's nurse. Having at last obtained permission to go to the hospital, she began to dress quickly, hurrying as if she feared her mother might change her mind.

Rose-Anna heard her singing snatches of songs, in which the beauty of the month of May seemed to figure largely. At last she appeared in her little convent dress, which was long enough to cover her legs but too tight across the bust.

At the door, before she flew off, she suddenly said with great seriousness:

"I haven't decided yet what kind of nun I'm going to be. I might be a Little Sister of the Poor, and then again I might be a nurse. They're both just as good in the sight of God, don't you think, Mamma?"

"Yes," said Rose-Anna absent-mindedly, "but don't cross the street without looking both ways. And take a few cents from my pocketbook in case you find yourself too tired to walk."

"I won't need it," said Yvonne.

And then she darted away, her graceful little body stiffly encased in her shabby dress, her arms weighted down with packages. Rose-Anna suspected that the brown paper bag hugged to her bosom contained other things besides sweets. There were probably sacred pictures, religious tracts, all the girl's most treasured possessions.

Stooping to peer through the window, Rose-Anna watched another member of her family depart. The trip to the mountain seemed a hazardous undertaking for a little girl who had never gone farther than to church alone. Then, too, because of what had just passed between them, Yvonne's departure seemed to have a peculiarly final character. When the child vanished around the corner of Convent Street, Rose-Anna found it difficult to remember what she looked like. Yvonne had withdrawn from the world to a point far beyond her reach. Of all the separations in her family, this one seemed the hardest to bear, the most mysterious, the most hopeless.

Yvonne had been torn from her. But Yvonne had never belonged to her.

Daniel had been crying a great deal. His eyelids were swollen, his eyes bloodshot. Over a week ago Jenny had been transferred to another ward, and he rarely saw her now. Whenever she happened to pass by she would tuck his covers in and bend her bright head over his pillow. But this was not enough for him.

He had called for her at the top of his voice, in fits of anger that threw him into a sweat and left him weak and numb. Then he had called for his mother, but she had not come to see him either for a long time. At last he gave up calling for anyone.

His transparent little face, with the skin drawn tight over the bones, took on a curious expression of old age. He was terrifyingly thin. The blankets lay flat on his wasted body; he hardly moved. In spite of the blood transfusions and injections of raw meat he had received ever since he entered the hospital, his disease had made rapid progress. Painlessly, gently, he was entering the last phase.

With the uncanny comprehension of a child, Yvonne knew the moment she saw him that he was going to die very soon. All the strength and will that remained to him was concentrated in the little boy's sharp glance.

Yet he pulled at the big package she had brought, tearing the bag in his impatience. All sorts of things spilled out over the bed. There were colored pictures that fascinated him at first, but then his eye fell on a little cardboard chick that stood up all by itself. Yvonne explained that she had drawn the pictures and made the cutouts at school before the Easter vacation, expressly for him.

At the word "school" he pricked up his ears. After a moment of reverie he dropped his eyes again and continued exploring the contents of the miraculous brown bag. His hand reached out for a series of little men cut out of white paper, all holding one another by the arm. This brought a faint smile to his pinched face. Then he pushed aside everything he had picked up at first to grab an orange that was rolling away in the folds of the bed covers.

Cupping it in his hands, he lifted it up toward the light, staring at it with a slight frown. At the hospital he had often received a liquid that had the flavor of orange. But an orange was not a juice. How could you drink it from a glass? It was a fruit that made you think of Christmas. It was a fruit you found in your stocking on Christmas morning, something you ate section by section, making it last as long as possible. An orange was like a new coat or a shiny tin flute, it was a thing you longed for and asked for again and again, and then when you had it in your hand, it didn't seem so important.

How strange it felt to receive an orange now! It wasn't Christmas, it wasn't even winter. His mother wasn't coming home with bulky packages, stowing them away in places known only to herself, before taking off her hat and coat. It wasn't winter, it wasn't Christmas, but still there he was, holding a round, soft, juicy orange in his fingers.

But he had no appetite. The orange fell from his hands. And turning his head toward Yvonne, he began to study her face. He had once loved her dearly, in a world that seemed quite different and far away. She used to help him with his lessons in the evening, during the short time when he went to school, and he had loved that earnest face beside his over the open book, he had loved to hear their voices spelling out the letters in unison, chanting them over and over again. Now he wondered what Yvonne's presence at his bedside could mean.

After a moment he gave her a timid smile. And then, although he had never been demonstrative before, he stretched out his hand to touch her face.

He ran his little hand over his sister's cheek with a baby's curious possessiveness.

Choking back her tears, Yvonne asked:

"Do you still remember your prayers, Nini?"

He nodded feebly, but then his face clouded over. He whispered:

"No, I can't remember . . . Only Our Father . . ."

"Our Father, that's enough," she said. "Our Father is the prayer that Jesus himself taught us. Say it with me, Nini."

This mystified him, but he began the prayer falteringly, reciting it alone, without any help, until he reached the words: "Thy will be done on earth as it is in Heaven." Then something seemed to be troubling him.

"Yvonne, will Jenny go to Heaven?"

"Oh yes, your darling Jenny will go to Heaven one day," answered Yvonne gravely.

"Jenny!" he said, his voice almost defiant, yet full of affection. Then he sighed. "She never makes the sign of the cross," he murmured sadly.

Yvonne hesitated, wet her lips, then forced herself to speak:

"Even so, I think she'll go to Heaven."

"And Mamma?"

"Oh Mamma surely," said Yvonne, this time with great conviction.

He seemed to be thinking for a long time before he whispered again:

"And you too?"

She was all that was left to him, and suddenly he loved her with all his heart, his poor little heart that had known so many cruel disappointments.

"Yes," said Yvonne, bending over to kiss him.

She too was beside herself with love, almost in a frenzy. To set Daniel's mind at rest at this moment she was willing to make any compromise with her own conscience, scrupulous though she was in matters of religion.

"There will be everything you love best in Heaven," she chanted. "That's what Heaven is: everything we love. The Holy

Virgin will be there to hold you in her arms. You'll be like the infant Jesus in her arms."

"But won't I have my new coat too?" he interrupted fretfully.

"If you like, you'll have your new coat, but you'll have other things that are much nicer. You won't ever be hungry in Heaven, Nini. You'll never be cold. Nothing will ever hurt you. You'll sing with the angels."

He closed his eyes, wearied by the visions she had summoned up. Then, before she burst into tears in his presence, Yvonne rose quickly. She placed the orange in his hands and fled, her skimpy dress flapping at her legs.

Daniel opened his eyes to see her running away. He called to her to come back, but his cry never reached her.

From then on he was listless; he said nothing and asked for nothing. One morning, a few days later, the attendant who came to relieve the night nurse found him cold and still. He had died quietly, without uttering a moan, without pain.

CHAPTER XXXI

ROSE-ANNA DRESSED the children as soon as they had finished their midday meal. Surprised by her haste to be rid of them, they would not hurry as she wished; they dawdled over their food and kept her waiting while they looked for their outdoor clothes. Rose-Anna hustled them out as fast as she could, herding them to the door, and charging Yvonne with the care of little Gisèle.

Yvonne dimly recalled other occasions when they had been bundled out of the house the same way. The look of pain on her mother's face also made her reluctant to leave.

"Let me stay home," she pleaded.

But Rose-Anna was very firm.

"No, no. I won't need you today. Go now; amuse yourselves until the school bell rings. And stay out to play after school too."

She watched them leave, hand in hand, with Gisèle in the middle. Hearing their voices diminish, she was tempted to call them back and kiss them once more, holding them close to her. Several times during her pregnancy she had had a foreboding of death, and now and then the prospect of resting seemed very welcome. But as she saw the children stop at the grade crossing, then scoot across all together, more cautious no doubt because they felt responsible for little Gisèle who was in their care for the first time, she pictured to herself all the dangers that threatened them today, tomorrow, and in days to come, and she thrust aside her longing for rest and death as if it were a sin.

She went back into the house, and the sound of the door closing behind her echoed a long time in her heart. Now she was alone, as women always are at such moments, she told herself, trying to pluck up courage . . . But no, she had never been so alone before, no one in the world could be more alone.

The house was forbidding in its ugliness and indifference. There was no solace to be found among all these signs of disorder and confusion. Like so many other houses they had come to live in, it was primarily a place where they could lay their heads when they were forced to move. She had not had time to fix things up properly. And yet without her regular routine, without the superficial appearances of stability, she felt lost. She had a sense of being imprisoned within these four walls only to suffer, and for nothing else.

She stumbled across the kitchen and knocked at the party wall in a prearranged signal to her neighbor that her time had come. All morning long the spasms had been recurring intermittently. At moments she prayed for longer intervals between pains, at others she was willing to forego even that short respite to end it all sooner. The first attacks she bore without telling anyone in her family, going about her work as usual. It was a matter of pride with her to hold out as long as possible, partly because she felt a kind of physical shame at the idea of asking for sympathy, and partly because of some childish belief that by being hard on herself she was helping nature.

Once the pain had passed, she denied its existence, and yet all her life she had been secretly terrified of it, as terrified as a child. But at last the moment had come when it could no longer be denied.

She went into her bedroom, a large, bare room, and lay down on the bed. Staring at the gray ceiling, she began to call Azarius, speaking his name in a whisper. Even when alone, she was ashamed to admit her pain. Azarius . . . where was he? Why had he failed her at this time? Only after a desperate effort, as if the most recent events had already grown as indistinct in her mind as her earliest memories, did she recall that Azarius had rushed over to the hospital this morning, after they learned that Daniel was dead. Later on, when she realized that Azarius was not coming back, she had made an arrangement with her neighbor, who was to go for the midwife in case of need. Daniel . . . Azarius . . . Her mind went round in circles. Which one was dead? Daniel? the little baby? But it seemed to her that it was he who was causing her all this suffering. It was he who was tearing her body apart. Poor little child! ... She saw Azarius carrying a little white coffin, very short and narrow, a tiny coffin. But no, she must not dwell on such thoughts. They were supposed to be bad for a woman in childbirth. But what could she think of but that tiny coffin, hardly bigger than a cradle? ... Funerals, christenings, all the important events of life took on the same bitter, unfathomable character in her mind. Sometimes she perceived a freshly dug grave, all ready to receive the tiny coffin, and sometimes a sleeping infant in its long christening dress ... Was the christening dress ready? Yes, it was, the same one that Florentine had worn ... Florentine! where was she now? Mercy, Florentine was married! Some day her body too would be given over to pain and humiliation ... Florentine ... She had been so happy when Florentine was born ... she had always wanted daughters. And yet at the last moment, each time, she had prayed that she might give birth to a male child, one who would suffer less than she. Always, in those last, dark, lonely moments, while her body was wracked with pain, she had been terror-stricken at the thought of giving birth to a girl.

She returned to the present with a start. The clock ticked slowly, so slowly that with every swing of the pendulum Rose-Anna felt as if she were sinking into a bottomless pit, then rising again and sinking once more ... She had heard many women claim that only the first confinement was hard. But she knew the contrary. She knew that each time her body dreaded the pain a little more, each time her soul shrank from the edge of the abyss with greater dread as she looked back after years of repeated pregnancy to her carefree youth, so far away, retreating further into the distance each time, further and further away.

Raising herself on one arm, she wiped the sweat from her forehead. She was sure now that her knock against the party wall had not been heard. Perhaps her neighbor had been out when she signaled. Should she get up and go for help? Sometimes she thought she had already dragged herself out of bed to do this, and then she realized that it was still to be done. At length she managed to slip off the bed, and by holding on to the wall and chairs as she passed, crossed the vast space between her room and the kitchen. A few steps more and her outstretched hands touched the wall. Then gathering all her strength, she began to knock.

Was that a voice answering through the wall? Were those footsteps at the door? A train went by. The locomotive whistle burst on her ears. With a superhuman effort she straightened up and went back to her room. As she fell on the bed she saw herself lying in a coffin in her turn, a rosary wound around her hands, now grown smooth and still. To die, to escape from all her suffer-ing seemed so inviting that she folded her hands on her breast in imitation of that vision. Gradually she began to feel as if she were watching each succeeding phase of her own death-struggle from a distance, while fully conscious that later, when it was all over, she would have all the preparations for the funeral ahead of her. What would she wear? And suddenly the horror of not owning one garment in which she could be decently buried brought her back to herself. She foresaw the disorder in her home; the children would have no one to dress or feed them; Azarius, a child himself, would not know where to find his Sunday clothes or his collar buttons. A thousand little cares ran through her mind. She ought to have mended the tear in Philippe's trousers. She ought to have asked him where he spent his time these days, why he left so early in the morning and what he did all day.

She whispered: "Jesus, Mary, let me die later, when my chil-dren are grown up . . ." And then she came to a decision: "I must go to the hospital." She pulled on her stockings, looked for her shoes under the bed, crawled over to the dresser and found her hat. But she could not remember where she had put her coat. Des-perately she racked her brain, looking around the room for a hint of where it might be. Her clothes were so threadbare . . . she was ashamed to appear before strangers in such guise. And yet as she fought off the grip of the pain, something urged her to leave just as she was, half dressed . . . At last she found her coat. Putting it on anyhow she staggered toward the door, without the faintest idea of how to reach the hospital and half hoping she would never arrive there. On the threshold she collided with her neighbor, just arriving with the midwife.

A few moments later, finding herself in bed again, she thought sadly: That did it; I must be in the hospital. She had always been afraid of hospitals, imagining the lights, the attendants, the treat-ment as harsh and cruel. Even on the advice of a doctor she had been unable to bring herself to go to a hospital at Philippe's birth, which had been very difficult. But this time she supposed that it was unavoidable.

Little by little, however, the smells and sounds of her own home penetrated her consciousness. A sigh of satisfaction escaped her. She opened her eyes warily, trying to find out what was going on. Two women were bustling about the room. Strangers, after all, she said to herself bitterly.

That had always been the most painful thing for her to bear. To be obliged to take aid from others, to lie exposed to their gaze. To need help so dreadfully. She tried to pull up the sheet and blanket.

A stranger? No, for now she recognized a face bending over her. It was the same face she had seen at the birth of Daniel and Gisèle.

Strong hands worked over her, humiliating her deeply. But at moments her thoughts detached themselves from the present and floated off into times long past. She was in a drifting boat, looking at the swiftly moving landscape. Now her eye was caught by a great curve in the river, now by a single clear point on the bank. The current of her life, up which she had fought her way so slowly, and at the cost of so many hardships, now carried the boat back at vertiginous speed, and things she had scarcely noticed on her first voyage now came into focus. But everything flashed by in such haste and disorder that she lost her bearings. Thus her life, now seen whole in this fragment of time, seemed strange and without much meaning. And the more her memories piled up, the less she could make of them all. There she was, an eager, glowing maiden, engaged to Azarius. And as she saw that girl, in a light summer dress, sitting on the bank of the Richelieu, she was inclined to smile at her, as at a stranger with whom a chance meeting might be pleasant but without importance. And then immediately afterwards she saw herself suddenly grown old, and accepting the sacrifice of Eugène . . . But no, there she was struggling with Eugène, struggling for the possession of a little money. He was snatching the money from her, money she needed to buy food and clothing. And again she found herself on the bank of the Richelieu, her muslin dress ballooning in the wind, her hair whipping against her cheek, smelling of hay and flowers . . . But now she was pounding the streets of the quarter, seeking a house where she could deliver her child . . . And then she was hurrying to finish a wedding dress. Was it for Florentine's marriage to Emmanuel? . . . No, it was before Florentine went away, it was when they were on relief . . . She was sewing to contribute her share to the expenses of the household . . . She must not be sick long . . . she would lose all her customers . . . Mademoiselle Elise wanted her dress without delay . . . She must get out of bed and finish the dress . . . Her sudden effort to rise sent a wave of pain through her. Now she was bending over a hospital bed. Who lay dying there? Who was suffering so terribly? Where was she? Was it Daniel? Was there nothing she could do to relieve the child's pain? Or her own? Their torments seemed to grow together and become fused with her own flesh . . . And then a feeble cry reached her. She fell back on the pillow. A voice spoke through thick waves of darkness:

"Did you see that, Madame Lavallée? Not one moan out of her. Not one little complaint. There are mighty few women as brave as Madame Lacasse."

"Not one moan," thought Rose-Anna. Where had she heard that before? And then she remembered: it was the midwife who had tended her mother. "Not one moan . . ." Rose-Anna felt closer to her mother than she had ever been before. Her heart beat high, as if in some strange way the memory of old Madame Laplante had brought her new strength.

Her mind reeled between a longing to sleep and a hundred petty concerns that were already beginning to prey on her. The time had come to return to them. With pointed finger she indicated the dresser drawer where the midwife would find garments for the newborn babe. She had always prepared everything in advance. Even this time she had everything ready: a complete layette of clean, warm baby clothes.

In a sudden panic she asked to see the child. She had never lost her terror of giving birth to a deformed baby.

"A fine boy," said the midwife. "A small fellow, but lively enough. Six pounds, I should say," she remarked, dandling him in her arms.

And with a sudden rush of joy, Rose-Anna yearned to hold him. When he was washed and wrapped in a quilt, he was brought to her. His tight little fists stuck out of the covers, and long blond lashes, as fine as down, lay on his satiny cheeks. The fragility of a newborn baby had always moved Rose-Anna deeply. She relaxed completely at last, one arm cradling the tiny bundle. All pain, all sorrow had been drained out of her. After each confinement, she felt this same tenderness and courage welling up in her heart, as if she had drawn once more on the mysterious, inexhaustible springs of her youth. It seemed as if this were not her twelfth, but her first and only child. And yet this excess of love did not exclude the other children. She heard Yvonne bringing them in a little later, after their afternoon walk. Stimulated by the fresh air and a sense of unusual freedom, they were clamoring for their supper. To her surprise, Rose-Anna found herself giving orders to the midwife, who, according to the custom of the quarter, performed the functions of a maid as well as a nurse.

"There's some cold meat and bread in the kitchen," she whispered. "Give the children something to eat. And see that their clothes are ready for school tomorrow morning. There are often holes that need mending."

And she tried to remember other things that might come up. Already her thoughts were back in the usual groove. The daily grind of household tasks was always the same, whether she was sick or not. Struggling against sleep, she inquired several times in succession:

"Has my husband come home yet?"

He had left early in the morning, grief-stricken at Daniel's death. But something else was rankling in his heart, she suspected: a deep horror at their way of life, a deep horror of his own inability to help them. Where could he have gone when he left the hospital? What torments was he suffering? And to what lengths could he have been driven by his despair? Poor man! She had held him responsible for their poverty, yet now it seemed to her that he had done what he could. A man cannot bear as much as a woman, she thought. I should have been more patient with him. He had his troubles too.

For a long time she had been careless of her appearance in the eyes of Azarius. Now she asked to be dressed in a lace bedjacket her husband had given her soon after their marriage. She also asked the women to spread a white cover over the bed, a precious cover always kept clean and starched, in readiness for important occasions. For a moment, as she watched the two women holding the corners of the bedcover, walking apart to stretch it out between them, Rose-Anna thought she caught a whiff of danger, some threat emanating from the stiff folds of the material. Her mother always used to say that it was bad luck to use the best linen in the house except in times of great need. And the phrase *great need* cloaked words one dared not say aloud: words that were nevertheless clearly understood, like accidents or death.

Then Rose-Anna smiled at her own absurd fears. Why shouldn't she indulge herself and appear all in white before Azarius, as she had liked to do when she was a young mother? Her tension eased. She dozed off quietly. Her great ordeal had relieved her of none of her problems; it had left her burdens intact. It had left her weak and tired, with the same anxieties as before, and yet for some strange reason more lighthearted. She was ready to start anew, buoyed up by all the urgent claims on her love.

CHAPTER XXXII

WHEN SHE AWOKE, night had fallen. The curtains had been pulled apart to let the air in. The railroad signal lights glowed red through the windows, and the room was filled with the fretful ring of the warning bell. Rose-Anna woke up with a start. Someone needed her. Someone was calling her desperately in her sleep. She sat up, and coming to herself quickly, she spoke her husband's name. Azarius . . . Where could he be, that she heard him calling her so distinctly? Was it only a bad dream? . . . No, she was sure that at a certain moment while she slept, Azarius had reached out for her in his mind to warn her of some impending trouble. Her quick move to sit up made her aware of her bruised body. She called her husband again, putting all her strength into her voice, as if it had to go far, very far now, to reach Azarius.

This time she heard someone walking in the next room. It was a man's heavy tread. The sound calmed her, and brought a slow, shy smile to her lips. An unexpected feeling of delight came over her, the sweet joy of returning to life after suffering, returning to her duties and affections, and even to her sorrows and torments.

The step came nearer. It was his step and yet not his usual step. She could feel the floor-boards shaking under thick hobnailed boots. He must have bought himself some new shoes, thick work-boots. And again she was projected back into the past. It was a May morning. The laundry she had washed the day before, wet with dew, flapped on the line in the sunlight, while chattering birds wheeled through the air. Azarius was leaving to go to work on the outskirts of town. Returning to bed after serving him his breakfast, she lay listening to his heavy footsteps on the sidewalk. Azarius went off singing that May morning. She was confident. She was full of hope for the child to be born, her first. She feared nothing. No misfortune could come to her. She followed her husband's footsteps as long as she could. Gravely, tenderly, she spoke aloud, addressing her timid love, addressing the present and the future : "He has gone to earn a living for us."

How happy she had been in those days! There was no gainsaying it; she had been very happy. She wished she could pluck one moment of joy from her youth, only one, any one, for there were several such mornings in May, and present it to Azarius as a mark of her affection.

The door opened a crack, then wider. Her husband's figure stood outlined against the yellow light. Rose-Anna sat up, a nervous smile on her drawn face, holding the sleeping baby out to him. For there were too many memories from which to choose, and perhaps even the happiest of them all was tarnished by some secret unhappiness. But the child represented the future, he was their refound youth, he was the great challenge to their fortitude.

"Put on the light so you can see him," she said. "He's just like Daniel when he was born, you remember, all pink and gold."

"Daniel!" he said.

He choked. Then he buried his head on the edge of the bed and began to sob convulsively

"He's not in pain any more," said Rose-Anna simply.

But she reproached herself for not remembering the child who had just died. Unlike her, Azarius had not gone to the limits of physical endurance in order to learn that death and birth have almost the same tragic significance. She knew that she would mourn for Daniel all the days of her life, she knew that her grief would become more and more intense after she resumed her normal life. She knew that her grief was there, benumbed in her mind, but for the moment Daniel seemed to have escaped the fate of mankind, escaped that share of unhappiness which she had bequeathed to him. And she felt as if a balance had been struck. No, Azarius had never gone down to those shadowy depths where life and death express the same indomitable pull of eternity.

She seized his hand.

"I can't see you, Azarius," she said. "Put on the light."

He did not answer immediately. Instead he dried his eyes clumsily. Then he sighed:

"In a minute, Mother. I have something to tell you first."

A heavy silence lay over them again. Then in a faltering voice, still broken with sobs, but overlaid with some secret resolution, he began:

"Prepare yourself for a great surprise, Rose-Anna."

She was not yet disturbed by this preamble, which in the old days would have been enough to make her blood run cold. Her hand merely gripped his more tightly.

"What have you done now, Azarius?"

A minute went by. The silence stretched out inexplicably. At any other time her heart would have warned her of some blow about to fall.

"Why don't you say something, Azarius? Have you been up to something again?"

He sniffed noisily, wiping off a last tear with his hand. Then he rose and pushed his chair back.

"Rose-Anna," he said, "you've been putting up with me a long time without saying a word. No use your denying it!" he exclaimed, overruling her objections. "You've had a hard time of it ever since we were married. It began with little disappointments, not enough to bother about, and then went on to big ones. They began to pile up until in the end you had no tears left, even when you hid your face from me at night. Yes, you reached the point where you couldn't even cry. And yet you were eating your heart out! Do you think I didn't know?" he cried. "Do you think I didn't see it all? And the worst of all was when you began to go out to work by the day, and I was too much of a coward to work at anything. I should have found work as a street cleaner, in the sewers . . ."

He seemed to enjoy humbling himself, admitting his defeat like a drunk at a revival meeting, as if that might win her forgiveness.

His voice broke. He must have shed a few tears, and made an effort to control himself, for he went on in a lower tone, his voice trembling:

"But Rose-Anna, that was because I couldn't believe that we had come to such a pass. I couldn't see it. Instead I saw the time when we had been young together and full of ambition. That's what I was thinking of all the time. I couldn't see how wretched we were. Once in a while, perhaps, for a moment or two, when my head was clear, I could see how unhappy you were, but still I couldn't believe it. I never noticed that you, who were once such a laughing girl, never laughed any more. Because I could still hear your laughter ringing in my ears. And I didn't want to listen to anything else; I closed my eyes and ears to the rest. I was that way for a long time . . . Try to understand, Rose-Anna," he ended with a groan, "that for ten years I never realized that we were really down and out."

"Azarius!" she cried, to make him stop, for she could not lie there and see their sufferings laid bare this way when she herself had always refused to admit them to anyone but herself. "Azarius, don't say that!"

He came and leaned over her.

"I'm speaking this way today," he said, "because your troubles are over, Rose-Anna. Listen to me now, Rose-Anna: we're going to start all over again. First of all, when you're strong enough to stand up you must look for the kind of house you like . . . a cheerful place, Rose-Anna, the kind you always wanted . . . not a house like this, where I've seen you lie awake all night thinking and planning!"

An accent of pride, of self-justification crept into his voice.

"Ah, you always thought I was incapable of planning our affairs, didn't you? Well, I've done it. Everything's settled. You can live as you always wanted to. I'll have given you that at least, Rose-Anna. I'm starting out late, I know, but anyway I'll have given you a few years of peace and comfort . . ."

"Peace!" she echoed incredulously. "Comfort!" Then she grew stern. "Don't talk nonsense, Azarius. Don't tempt Heaven!"

He took a deep breath and went on almost gaily:

"Nonsense! That's what you always say: nonsense. But just you wait and see if it's nonsense . . . No, no, Rose-Anna, I mean peace and comfort such as we've never had. Listen. Beginning with July, you're to get a large check from the government in the mail on the first of every month. What do you say to that, eh?"

He was speaking with the same glee, with the same deep satisfaction he had felt in the old days, when he used to give her all his wages. "Here, this is for you," he would say, slipping the roll of bills into Rose-Anna's hand and enclosing it in his own. "It's all for you." He seemed then to be making her a gift of all his industry and skill and physical strength, and of the future too, the future they both looked forward to so serenely. But to Rose-Anna that money was a distant memory. When there was enough money for their needs, the ties between them had been strong, but once the money was lacking, what a strain was put on their love!

"No, no," said Rose-Anna mistrustfully. "Don't make me long for comforts, you poor man. That's more than we can expect. It's better not to aim too high . . ."

"Too high!" he replied. "But listen to me. I tell you you're to get a big check every month. You'll have your comforts all right; they will come in the mail. Fifty-five bucks a month, Rose-Anna! Right in your hand! Every month! But wait a minute. That's just for you. You'll also draw something for the children. Altogether, you'll draw something like ninety-seven dollars. Won't that be enough for comfort?"

She smiled weakly, so far from suspecting anything ominous that after a few moments she began to chaff him, without malice:

"You'll never change! You remember you were going to make two thousand a year with your furniture business. Then you were going to make three thousand in the junk business. And with your sweepstake winnings you were going to buy a house at Notre-Dame de Grâce."

Then she softened:

"Never mind. We'll manage the way we've always managed. With our two hands, both of us. Believe me. It's better this way. It's better to depend on our own efforts than to be taken in by fancy schemes. Ninety-seven dollars a month in the mail! Can't you see that it's just another fine scheme? We never had that much money, and you know it. Not in a long time anyway. That's a lot of money, do you know? Where do you think it'll come from? Where'll we get it, my poor man? Where?"

"We have it, I tell you!"

And he went on quickly:

"You'll have it, you! Ninety-seven dollars every month! And that's not the best of it . . ."

He paced up and down, his hands behind his back, and then suddenly brought his arm up in a decisive, bitter gesture.

"The best thing of all . . ."

He approached the bed, breathing hard, and burst out:

". . . the best of all is that you'll be rid of me."

He became aware of a terrifying stillness as soon as the words escaped him. He had tried to speak lightly, in a tone of affectionate banter, but he had no sooner stopped than the silence struck him like a blow.

A fit of melancholy came over him. He went to the window, rested his elbow on the dusty curtain rod and stared out at the railroad lights. It was obvious that he had used that crude expression unconsciously because it was the guarantee of his own freedom. He stood at the window a long time, staring out at the shining rails. They had always fascinated him. By narrowing his eyes he could see them stretching out into infinity, carrying him to his new-found youth. He was free, free, incredibly free; he was going to begin life all over again. On his tongue there was a taste not of soot and coal but of open spaces and driving winds. He thought of the freighters he used to see passing through the Lachine Canal, and he yearned to be on his way. He thought of the old countries whose names in his schoolbooks had set him a-dreaming; he thought of "France," a word buried deep in his mind, a word that made him homesick. He visualized battlefields drenched with human blood, where a man could show himself in all his strength. He felt eager for adventure, for danger, for great risks. What if he had failed so miserably in little things, what if he had been incapable of relieving the want in his own home? He was burning with impatience to fight the great evils ravaging the world.

His forehead was damp. He stood there panting, not knowing whether he had acted for his own salvation or to save his poor family. But still he had a feeling of accomplishment, of resurrection.

A feeble voice, uncertain and yet touched with fear, reached him.

"Azarius, have you found work in the country? Are you going away?"

He made no answer.

The voice became raucous:

"Azarius, turn on the light! Let me look at you!"

Azarius went to the middle of the room and turned on a light that hung from the ceiling.

Blinded by the glare, Rose-Anna at first saw only his hands in the air, then his pale, set face, so youthful that her heart failed her. Her eyes fell to his shoulders, then to his waist, and down to his legs, clad in garments she did not recognize. She stared at him frantically. Her mouth trembled. And suddenly she gave a great cry, a single cry that was lost in the shriek of a passing locomotive.

Azarius stood motionless before her, dressed in the uniform of an army private.

CHAPTER XXXIII

KHAKI-CLAD FIGURES were rolling toward the Bonaventure Station in waves, carrying with them the bright colors of women's dresses, the sound of laughter and singing, of sobbing and sighing, the strong smell of rum, all the hubbub of an excited crowd.

Arriving early, Emmanuel and Florentine had found seats in the waiting-room. They sat talking, their hands clasped over the duffle bag that lay across their knees. Sentences were begun and never finished, last-minute instructions were exchanged between them, but their words were drowned in the tread of heavy boots and their private grief merged in the thousands of sighs that floated up to the vaulted ceiling.

Emmanuel stared with astonishment as his regiment appeared. Almost every face was lit up with joy. One of his comrades staggered in, held upright by two other soldiers who were laughing uproariously. Behind them came another, shouting drunkenly: "We're going to see the world! We're going to see the world!" Everyone was pretending to be hilarious, but the merriment had unhealthy overtones. Emmanuel turned his eyes away and embraced Florentine.

He had expected that it would be easier to leave her once they were married, that this bid for future happiness would bring him more confidence. But he realized now that happiness weakens a man's will. In this short interval certain ties had been forged, certain habits had been formed, not to be broken without a wrench. He saw Florentine trying on the dresses and hats he had bought for her twenty times a day; or else always impatient to go out and parade through the streets, stopping at every shop-window! At times so full of coquetry, and at times so sad and bitter! And then there were rare moments of tenderness when she would take his hand and say: "Oh dear, I'll be so lonely and bored when you're gone!" The days had slipped by like minutes, like a dream, like a flash of lightning, he thought. Men who go away to war ought not to form attachments.

The crowd was singing and laughing all around them. Why were they singing? Why were they laughing? What was so joyous about their departure?

They rose in silence. Florentine helped him lift his duffle bag to his shoulder, then they walked out toward the train platform, their arms around each other's waists, like a hundred other couples. As the milling crowd threatened to tear them apart, they clasped each other more closely.

At the main gate giving on the tracks they spied a large group of people from Saint-Henri. Emmanuel and Florentine went over to join them.

Sam Latour was there, shaking hands all around, with a paternal and comical air. His placid ruddy face, with its broad smile, was completely out of harmony with the flood of invective that poured from his mouth: "That dog Hitler!" he was saying. "One of you be sure to bring me back three hairs from his mustache. Or I'll tell you what I'd like even better. Bring me the whole damn thatch and I'll make a little scrubbing brush of it."

But stronger and more persuasive than all the others, rose the voice of Azarius Lacasse. As brassy as a sergeant, he went among the soldiers and harangued them. "Tell them to hold fast in France till we get there." He pulled out a newspaper and opened it wide, to show the headline: *The Allies Fall Back on Dunkirk*. Azarius smashed his fist into the sheet.

"Tell them not to give up till we come!" he cried. "That's all I ask! Tell them the Canadians are coming! And maybe the Americans too before long." He caught sight of a boy in uniform, a little fellow who seemed quite bewildered, and tapped him on the shoulder: "You there," he said, "you're good for thirty Germans, aren't you?" Then he added, laughing: "But don't kill them all, leave a couple for me. Don't end the war too fast!"

Behind him shone the face of Pitou. And behind Pitou there were other faces with the same look of exaltation. Emmanuel felt as if he were dreaming. Were these the unemployed of yesterday? Were these the fellows he had known when they were forlorn and browbeaten, down in the mouth? Could that be Pitou, the musician, who had beguiled his years of idleness with songs from his guitar?

His eyes returned to Azarius, and he was even more troubled. Was this the man he had seen so crushed, only a week ago? Was this Rose-Anna's husband?

Azarius seemed no older than Emmanuel today. Strength seemed to flow from him in an irresistible stream. His desire for action, so long repressed, had found an outlet at last. He felt himself a man again.

And so the men of Saint-Henri had found their salvation!

Salvation through war!

Emmanuel looked at Florentine questioningly. There was a hollow feeling in his chest at first, and then he felt a storm seething within him. He was torn and shaken with uncertainty. The torments he had suffered that night alone on the mountain seized him again. The problem had changed from "Why am I going to war?" to "Why are we all going to war? We're going together . . . we ought to be going for the same reason."

It was not enough for him to know his own personal reasons; he also must know the fundamental truth that was guiding them all, the prime impulse that had urged on the soldiers in the last world war too. Without some such guiding light their departure made no sense, it was only a monstrous repetition of the same mistake.

He leaned toward Florentine and put the question to her.

"Why do you suppose we are going off to war, your father, your brother and I?" he asked.

She looked at him in surprise.

"You mean why did you enlist?"

"Yes."

"Well, I can see only one reason," she said soberly. "It's because there's something in it for all of you in the army."

He studied her for a long time. Yes, he should have thought of that sooner. She was much closer to the people than he; she knew them better. Her answers were the right ones. He looked around at the crowd. And he seemed to hear the same answer that Florentine had just given him on thousands of lips. Behind the crowd's deep breath of liberation he thought he could hear the sound of money clinking.

They, too, he mused. They too have been bought, as much as anybody, more than anybody!

And it seemed to him that with his own eyes he was witnessing the final bankruptcy of humanity. Wealth had spoken the truth on the mountain.

But after a moment he took himself to task. He went on to think: But no, that's not the whole truth. Those who fight profit least from the war. There are ever so many Léon Boisverts and Jean Lévesques who will rise in the world and perhaps make a fortune, thanks to the war, without taking any risks.

But then why were armies on the march? There must be some underlying truth that few were able to grasp, even those who had fought in the last war. Perhaps under a thick layer of human ignorance there was some obscure purpose that man could not express in words.

Suddenly Emmanuel heard rising above the uproar a metallic, arrogant voice in English:

"We'll fight to the last man for the British Empire!"

The Empire! thought Emmanuel. Are we fighting to hold on to

territory? To keep the world's wealth for ourselves and bar the others out?

Now a whole group was singing: "There'll always be an England."

Yes, but how about me and Pitou and Azarius? wondered Emmanuel. Are we to fight for Merry England and the Empire? At this moment soldiers in other lands are singing their national anthem with the same enthusiasm. They're singing everywhere, in Germany, in Italy, in France. We French-Canadians ought to be singing "O Canada!" I suppose. No, no, he said to himself sternly, I refuse to be limited by a narrow patriotism... But am I the only one?

He tried to squirm away from the only explanation that was left. And yet it took a firm hold on his mind: none of them were going off to war for the same purpose. Some were going to the ends of the earth to preserve their empire. Others were going to the ends of the earth to shoot off a gun and receive a bullet, and that was all they knew. There were still others who were going away to earn bread for their families. But what would they find at the ends of the earth, aside from death, that could enlighten men on their common destiny?

At this point the gates opened wide and the crowd spilled over on the platform. All the rest was a nightmare to Emmanuel. He kissed his mother, his sister and his father. Then he embraced Florentine. In their brief life together he had discovered that she was vain, nervous, and sometimes irritable. He knew now that she was frivolous and weak, but he only loved her the more for it. He loved her like a child who needs protection.

As he put his arms around her he saw the tears streaming down her face. In the course of the last few days he had been mystified by her changing moods. Her coldness had often repelled him; her sudden outbursts of tenderness and her moments of reticence had perplexed him. Her tears now troubled him.

She stood there weeping on his shoulder. He could not know that she was crying with relief. But underneath her vanity there was also a vague feeling of sorrow. She was extremely impressionable. The whole scene of leave-taking, the tears and hand-waving, affected her superficial nature even more than the drama they symbolized. But Emmanuel, believing that at last she was deeply moved, almost broke down when he saw her tears.

He leaped on the moving train. For a moment he hung there on the step, clutching the hand-bar, his head bent forward in a pose that made him look as if he were faring forth on some heroic expedition. But still his internal torment, his burning question found no answer. He was leaving and still he knew not why.

And then, suddenly, the answer came to him in a flash. . . It came to him unexpectedly, not from Florentine, who stood there waving her hand, not from his mother, hardly visible now in the crowd, not from Azarius, who was swinging along beside the train. It came to him, like a miracle, from a stranger.

She was a tiny, shrunken, fragile old woman with a look of gentle resignation on her face, alone among strangers.

For one moment their glances crossed. And at that moment Emmanuel understood. The humble little woman was moving her lips as if to give him one last message. The words did not reach Emmanuel, but he could see by the movement of her lips that she was saying something that only he understood : "This will end. One day it will end. One day it will all come to an end."

And Emmanuel saw the light. This was the hope, so ill understood by most men, that was uplifting mankind once again : to do away with war.

Florentine was only a bright spot now. He saw her take out her powder puff and remove the traces of tears from her cheeks. Closing his eyes, he clung to the image of Florentine powdering her face as if he were already far, far away. Then he searched the crowd again for her thin little face, her burning eyes. But even before the train disappeared, she had turned her back and moved away.

She felt tired and nervous. Without waiting for her father she pushed her way through the crowd, and walked quickly to the station entrance.

The heat and the excitement had disturbed her, but she felt sad and oppressed too. It was not that Emmanuel's departure caused her any great pain, but she had a vague sense of loss, the extent of which she was only beginning to judge.

When she reached the lobby she stopped a moment to regain control of herself. What was troubling her? She had taken Emmanuel's sweetness and kindness for granted. These qualities had not surprised her. But his generosity had affected her deeply. Before he left, Emmanuel had turned over to her almost all of his last pay, in addition to his savings, which he had deposited in the bank to her account.

Florentine opened her handbag and fingered her checkbook and a roll of bills with a quiver of pleasure. Then she felt ashamed, and darted off into the street.

At the curb she just missed colliding with some young men who were getting out of a car. A woman had put out her hand to protect her. She was a tiny old woman, very frail and thin, all dressed in black.

"You've been seeing someone in your family off?" she asked. "Your father or your boy-friend?"

"My husband," said Florentine.

But she said the word with a feeling of dignity of which she became conscious only after she had spoken.

"You may be proud of him," said the old lady before she slipped away.

Florentine stood there dreamily for a moment. Then a timid smile, a new kind of smile came to her weary face. She had just remembered how people had looked at her in the last few days whenever she had appeared in public on Emmanuel's arm. And yet despite this pleasant memory there was a strange ache in her heart.

She did not love Emmanuel. At least she did not love him as she had once expected to love someone. But she was grateful to him, as if his love for her had evened the balance of her wrongs; and she had a sincere desire to return his affection.

She looked up. And suddenly she stood stock still, staring across the street at Jean Lévesque, who had stopped near a lamppost to open up a newspaper. He was wearing a dapper new suit, not a detail of which escaped her. She even noticed that his cravat was the same shade as his sport shoes. A picture of Emmanuel came to her mind, Emmanuel in a crumpled uniform and clumsy boots. And she was filled with rage because Jean cut a better figure than Emmanuel. And then other baser impulses came to her. For a moment she was on the point of walking up to him, to show him her wedding ring, and to let him see the pretty dress and slippers Emmanuel had purchased for her on the eve of his departure. And her suede handbag! He had selected everything for her. She had never been so well dressed. It was a shame to be so elegant without anyone to admire her, not even Jean . . . just for a moment. Just for a moment, she thought. Only to show him that I can get along without him now. It was so vexing to go away without having a laugh at his expense, without seeing his eyes light up with interest, with curiosity, and perhaps even with desire. . . To see his eyes flame, and then laugh at him and go on her way, avenged and happy, yes, really happy! The blood pounded in her ears. She kept her eye on him and yet she trembled lest he catch sight of her. . .

He lifted his head, folded his newspaper, and began to cross the street. Holding her breath, her hands damp, her temples throbbing, she turned her back and sidled up to a parked car. Without moving she waited for him to pass on. He did not recognize her, though his coat brushed her arm. It cost her a great effort to restrain a cry. After he had gone by she ran across the street and tore off in the direction of Saint-Henri.

For a long time she continued her headlong flight, barely conscious of where she was going. At last she slowed down and stopped, completely winded. And then to her amazement, she discovered that she was pleased with herself. Never before had she enjoyed the comfort of knowing that what she had done was wise and right. This was indeed the beginning of a new life.

Emmanuel's return, which she had heretofore anticipated with terror, now struck her as quite natural. Her path was clear. She was embarking on the future, without any rapture, to be sure, but without regrets. The calm that enveloped her after the turmoil of the last few months was welcome to her bruised spirit. So many things have happened in so short a time, she was thinking, and I have no doubt they'll be forgotten before long. . . It came as a surprise to her to recognize that there was almost no rancor left in her heart. And gradually she began to think of her child without resentment. It seemed to her that it was no longer Jean's child, but hers and Emmanuel's. She was not prepared to love it yet, this child that would make her suffer, and perhaps she would never love it. Even now she dreaded its coming, but little by little she would learn to dissociate the child from her own fall, from her own blunder. Emmanuel would take care of them. . . She must confess that she was better off married to him than to Jean. Emmanuel was the kind of man who gave himself away in a look or a word. You knew just what to expect of him. Of course she could no longer expect to be stirred by violent emotions, but she foresaw that affection, comfort and security would make up for everything else. And a proud need to redeem herself completely urged her to share this financial security and comfort with her mother and her sisters and brothers. For a moment, as she thought of Emmanuel's lofty character, which might turn violent if he were provoked, she felt a stab of fear. Perhaps it would have been best to confess everything to him. But she allowed herself to smile at the thought. And for the hundredth time, she congratulated herself on having managed so well. Besides, she had not been ruined, she had not blundered. All that was over. There was no past, nothing but the future to be considered.

She walked up St. Jacques Street as night began to fall, and her practical little brain busied itself with the only thing she enjoyed thinking about: the future. All sorts of plans suggested themselves, all sorts of charming perspectives opened up. With the allowance that she and her mother received, they could live very well from now on. Emmanuel had begged her to stop working, but she was greedy for the money. I'll continue as long as I can, she thought. We'll have that much more. She was growing ambitious, and secretly felt closer to her kin. By her kin she meant Emmanuel and the Lacasse family, but not the Létourneaus. Their cool attitude had wounded her; she intended to maintain relations with them on a strictly formal basis.

Giddy with pride and envy, she thought of a house for rent on the Boulevard La Salle, almost as nice as the Létourneau place. Why not? she said to herself. We have the money now. We're not obliged to live in Saint-Henri any more. She dared not admit that she longed to break with everything that reminded her of her stupid love affair with Jean Lévesque. We're going to live well at last, she kept repeating to herself. Papa did the right thing, he did the right thing to enlist. It's the finest thing he ever did in his life. And Mamma, oh well, Mamma has to be miserable about something. I wonder why she takes it so hard. She never had so much money before!

She walked rapidly, calculating the sum of their combined incomes. And she was delighted to see how well everything had worked out. To plan their life in a sensible way required some presence of mind, and the responsibility was quite new to her. Their troubles were over, they were far away now. Yes, a new life was beginning for them all.

And yet at times she felt a pang as she thought of all the money that would be given to them, the women, while their men risked their lives. But not relishing such thoughts, she returned to her calculations. Good gracious, she was rich! There were so many things she could buy for her mother and the children as well as for herself. At heart she rejoiced at the course of events, for without the war where would they all be?

The troop train meanwhile was running through Saint-Henri, and Emmanuel leaned out of the window for a last look at the Lacasse house. A light was burning on the first floor, probably in Rose-Anna's room, he thought, his heart swelling with pity for her lonely battle. Until it passed out of his line of vision his eyes were held fast by that receding gleam.

The railroad barriers, the bronze Sacred Heart, the church and the signal tower slipped past one by one. His final picture of the quarter was of a tree deep in a courtyard, its foliage drooping with fatigue before it had come into full leaf, its twisted branches pushing bravely up through a network of electric wires and clotheslines towards the sky.

Low on the horizon, a bank of heavy clouds foretold a storm.

THE NEW CANADIAN LIBRARY LIST

n 1. OVER PRAIRIE TRAILS / Frederick Philip Grove
n 2. SUCH IS MY BELOVED / Morley Callaghan
n 3. LITERARY LAPSES / Stephen Leacock
n 4. AS FOR ME AND MY HOUSE / Sinclair Ross
n 5. THE TIN FLUTE / Gabrielle Roy
n 6. THE CLOCKMAKER / Thomas Chandler Haliburton
n 7. THE LAST BARRIER AND OTHER STORIES / Charles G. D. Roberts
n 8. BAROMETER RISING / Hugh MacLennan
n 9. AT THE TIDE'S TURN AND OTHER STORIES / Thomas H. Raddall
n10. ARCADIAN ADVENTURES WITH THE IDLE RICH / Stephen Leacock
n11. HABITANT POEMS / William Henry Drummond
n12. THIRTY ACRES / Ringuet
n13. EARTH AND HIGH HEAVEN / Gwethalyn Graham
n14. THE MAN FROM GLENGARRY / Ralph Connor
n15. SUNSHINE SKETCHES OF A LITTLE TOWN / Stephen Leacock
n16. THE STEPSURE LETTERS / Thomas McCulloch
n17. MORE JOY IN HEAVEN / Morley Callaghan
n18. WILD GEESE / Martha Ostenso
n19. THE MASTER OF THE MILL / Frederick Philip Grove
n20. THE IMPERIALIST / Sara Jeannette Duncan
n21. DELIGHT / Mazo de la Roche
n22. THE SECOND SCROLL / A. M. Klein
n23. THE MOUNTAIN AND THE VALLEY / Ernest Buckler
n24. THE RICH MAN / Henry Kreisel
n25. WHERE NESTS THE WATER HEN / Gabrielle Roy
n26. THE TOWN BELOW / Roger Lemelin
n27. THE HISTORY OF EMILY MONTAGUE / Frances Brooke
n28. MY DISCOVERY OF ENGLAND / Stephen Leacock
n29. SWAMP ANGEL / Ethel Wilson
n30. EACH MAN'S SON / Hugh MacLennan
n31. ROUGHING IT IN THE BUSH / Susanna Moodie
n32. WHITE NARCISSUS / Raymond Knister
n33. THEY SHALL INHERIT THE EARTH / Morley Callaghan
n34. TURVEY / Earle Birney
n35. NONSENSE NOVELS / Stephen Leacock
n36. GRAIN / R. J. C. Stead
n37. LAST OF THE CURLEWS / Fred Bodsworth
n38. THE NYMPH AND THE LAMP / Thomas H. Raddall
n39. JUDITH HEARNE / Brian Moore
n40. THE CASHIER / Gabrielle Roy
n41. UNDER THE RIBS OF DEATH / John Marlyn
n42. WOODSMEN OF THE WEST / M. Allerdale Grainger
n43. MOONBEAMS FROM THE LARGER LUNACY / Stephen Leacock
n44. SARAH BINKS / Paul Hiebert
n45. SON OF A SMALLER HERO / Mordecai Richler
n46. WINTER STUDIES AND SUMMER RAMBLES IN CANADA / Anna Brownell Jameson
n47. REMEMBER ME / Edward Meade
n48. FRENZIED FICTION / Stephen Leacock
n49. FRUITS OF THE EARTH / Frederick Philip Grove
n50. SETTLERS OF THE MARSH / Frederick Philip Grove
n51. THE BACKWOODS OF CANADA / Catharine Parr Traill
n52. MUSIC AT THE CLOSE / Edward McCourt
n53. MY REMARKABLE UNCLE / Stephen Leacock

n54. THE DOUBLE HOOK / Sheila Watson
n55. TIGER DUNLOP'S UPPER CANADA / William Dunlop
n56. STREET OF RICHES / Gabrielle Roy
n57. SHORT CIRCUITS / Stephen Leacock
n58. WACOUSTA / John Richardson
n59. THE STONE ANGEL / Margaret Laurence
n60. FURTHER FOOLISHNESS / Stephen Leacock
n61. MARCHBANKS' ALMANACK / Robertson Davies
n62. THE LAMP AT NOON AND OTHER STORIES / Sinclair Ross
n63. THE HARBOR MASTER / Theodore Goodridge Roberts
n64. THE CANADIAN SETTLER'S GUIDE / Catharine Parr Traill
n65. THE GOLDEN DOG / William Kirby
n66. THE APPRENTICESHIP OF DUDDY KRAVITZ / Mordecai Richler
n67. BEHIND THE BEYOND / Stephen Leacock
n68. A STRANGE MANUSCRIPT FOUND IN A COPPER CYLINDER / James De Mille
n69. LAST LEAVES / Stephen Leacock
n70. THE TOMORROW-TAMER / Margaret Laurence
n71. ODYSSEUS EVER RETURNING / George Woodcock
n72. THE CURE OF ST. PHILIPPE / Francis William Grey
n73. THE FAVOURITE GAME / Leonard Cohen
n74. WINNOWED WISDOM / Stephen Leacock
n75. THE SEATS OF THE MIGHTY / Gilbert Parker
n76. A SEARCH FOR AMERICA / Frederick Philip Grove
n77. THE BETRAYAL / Henry Kreisel
n78. MAD SHADOWS / Marie-Claire Blais
n79. THE INCOMPARABLE ATUK / Mordecai Richler
n80. THE LUCK OF GINGER COFFEY / Brian Moore
n81. JOHN SUTHERLAND: ESSAYS, CONTROVERSIES AND POEMS / Miriam Waddington
n82. PEACE SHALL DESTROY MANY / Rudy Henry Wiebe
n83. A VOICE FROM THE ATTIC / Robertson Davies
n84. PROCHAIN EPISODE / Hubert Aquin
n85. ROGER SUDDEN / Thomas H. Raddall
n86. MIST ON THE RIVER / Hubert Evans
n87. THE FIRE-DWELLERS / Margaret Laurence
n88. THE DESERTER / Douglas LePan
n89. ANTOINETTE DE MIRECOURT / Rosanna Leprohon
n90. ALLEGRO / Felix Leclerc
n91. THE END OF THE WORLD AND OTHER STORIES / Mavis Gallant
n92. IN THE VILLAGE OF VIGER AND OTHER STORIES / Duncan Campbell Scott
n93. THE EDIBLE WOMAN / Margaret Atwood
n94. IN SEARCH OF MYSELF / Frederick Philip Grove
n95. FEAST OF STEPHEN / Robertson Davies
n96. A BIRD IN THE HOUSE / Margaret Laurence
n97. THE WOODEN SWORD / Edward McCourt
n98. PRIDE'S FANCY / Thomas Raddall
n99. OX BELLS AND FIREFLIES / Ernest Buckler
n100. ABOVE GROUND / Jack Ludwig
n101. NEW PRIEST IN CONCEPTION BAY / Robert Traill Spence Lowell
n102. THE FLYING YEARS / Frederick Niven
n103. WIND WITHOUT RAIN / Selwyn Dewdney
n104. TETE BLANCHE / Marie-Claire Blais
n105. TAY JOHN / Howard O'Hagan
n106. CANADIANS OF OLD / Philippe Aubert de Gaspé. Translated by Sir Charles G. D. Roberts
n107. HEADWATERS OF CANADIAN LITERATURE / Archibald MacMechan